Always Proper,
Suddenly Scandalous

Always Proper, Suddenly Scandalous

Scandalous Seasons Series

Christi Caldwell

ISBN: 1944240101
ISBN 13: 9781944240103

DEDICATIONS

To my amazing niece, Emilia.

With your gentle heart, intelligence, and strength, you are a perfect
heroine.

ONE

A gentleman should devote his energy and efforts to the
fruitful management of his landholdings.
4ᵗʰ Viscount Redbrooke

1818
London, England

A young lord in possession of vast holdings and wealth had to
be very particular in all matters. It served such a gentleman to
have his life well-ordered, without scandal, and properly plotted out.

When he'd been a young man, Geoffrey Winters, Viscount
Redbrooke's' now departed father, had advised Geoffrey of his familial
obligations.

Geoffrey had failed abominably in his responsibilities.

Until he'd assumed the title of Viscount Redbrooke, four years
past.

Seated at the mahogany desk in his office, Geoffrey stared blankly
down at the ivory parchment in front of him. His mind drifted back to
a dark night, muddied roads, a sky streaked with lightening. He'd not
always been above reproach…

The words upon the page blurred together.

Geoffrey gave his head a hard shake, and pushed aside his distracted musings before they took him down the path of old hurts and
still-strong guilt.

Just a week shy of his thirtieth year, Geoffrey was minutes shy of
selecting a young lady to make the Viscountess Redbrooke.

1

He picked up his pen and dipped it into the crystal inkwell.

The young lady must be of exceptional breeding.

He again dipped the tip into the ink.

The lady must _not_ have seen more than two Seasons.

After all, the most marriageable young ladies would be successfully identified by those gentlemen in the market for a wife within the first Season. Anything beyond two Seasons was not to be countenanced.

The lady must possess delicate sensibilities, a polite laugh, and not be given to great displays of emotion.

Yes, his ideal match would not be a woman given to flights of fancy or possessed of any naïve visions of love. There had been a time when he'd believed the nonsensical emotion of love was more powerful than responsibility.

His lip pulled back in a sneer. That mistake had been a costly one.

Geoffrey tossed his pen down and pulled open the top drawer of his desk. He rustled through several sheets of parchment, and then pulled out another familiar list. His gaze quickly surveyed the names upon the sheet of young ladies who might admirably fill the role of viscountess.

Lady Diana Shorington. An Incomparable of the Season, she would make him an excellent match. With her fair skin and golden hair, she well fit with Society's standards of beauty. Given her status as the well-dowried daughter of the Marquess of Castlebury, Geoffrey expected she'd make a match relatively quickly that Season.

He drummed his fingertips along the top of his desk.

There was Miss Anna Adams, daughter to the Viscount Wethersfield, always very stoic and composed at Society events.

Or Lady Beatrice Dennington, the only daughter of the Duke of Somerset. She, too, possessed a delicate golden beauty.

Geoffrey's gaze fixed on Lady Beatrice's name, as he further contemplated her suitability. Demure, proper, and exceedingly polite, she would make an exceptional Viscountess Redbrooke.

All the prospective young ladies had one unremarkable trait in common—they were exceedingly dull...which was his first and foremost consideration of all the prospective ladies.

Geoffrey blew lightly on the fresh ink, drying the parchment.

He'd not be so foolish as to make the tragic mistake of being lured by a passionate, unconventional young lady. Not again. He'd sooner turn his fortune over to a stranger than turn his deadened heart over to a feckless creature.

Yes, Lady Beatrice would do very well as his viscountess.

He opened his top desk drawer and pulled out yet another, earlier compiled list that detailed essential components for wooing a respectable young lady.

Ices at Gunter's.
A walk in Hyde Park.
Several waltzes.
A trip to the theatre.

"If we do not leave this instant, dear, we'll be late."

His head whipped up as his mother sailed into the room, a frown wreathing her plump, unwrinkled cheeks. She held her gloves in her hand.

Geoffrey neatly stacked the three lists and placed them back in his desk. "My apologies." He closed the drawer with a firm click and, then rose.

Even if many members of the *ton* preferred arriving fashionably late to events, Geoffrey valued punctuality. The matrons of Almack's had the right of it, barring those more than twenty minutes late from attendance. He mentally ticked punctuality onto his list of attributes for his future wife.

"Geoffrey," his mother began as they started their walk toward the foyer and their waiting carriage outside. "You do know I've been patient. You are going to be one and thirty in three days."

"Thirty." He gave his head a rueful shake. Hardly endearing to have one's own mother forget how many years he'd spent on this Earth.

She blinked. "Truly?"

He nodded. "Truly."

Mother wrinkled her nose. "I was so very sure—"

"You're wrong," he interjected with a curt impatience.

"Regardless," she began again, this time her tone less convincing. "It is time you take a wife."

"I know."

They walked down the long corridor; their quickened steps muffled by the long red carpet that lined the hall.

"You've not been to any events in nearly a fortnight. A fortnight." She spoke as though Geoffrey hadn't attended a single *ton* function all Season. "All the most marriageable misses have already received offers. Why, I heard from Lady Tisdale, who learned from one of her maid's, that Miss Anna Adams is to receive an offer from the Marquess of Edgebury any day."

Well, it was a good thing he'd not settled on Miss Anna Adams as his future viscountess. He silently inked her name permanently off his list. "I visit my clubs," he groused under his breath.

Her eyes widened. "Your clubs? You will not find a marriageable lady at your clubs, Geoffrey," she bemoaned. "It is time you fulfill your responsibilities as viscount."

Geoffrey's gut tightened as the familiar guilt licked at him, more painful than the biting sting of a lash. He knew well what his obligations were…to wed and propagate the Redbrooke line with male issues. His father, and his father's father, and his father's father's father had done a rather deplorable job of producing sufficient spares to the heir.

Mother let out a little huff. "Do you know what will happen if you fail to marry and produce an heir?"

"I've not an inkling what should happen if I fail to wed."

She continued on, ignoring the sardonic twist to his words. "The line will pass to a distant Scottish relation," she said, as though he hadn't spoken. She wrinkled her nose as though nauseated by the mere prospect of a Scott inheriting the title.

Yes, in the event Geoffrey failed to produce an heir, his solicitor had informed Geoffrey that he'd traced the next in line to great-great grandfather's second cousin, once removed.

Mother paused, forcing Geoffrey to stop and look back at her. "Scottish." The one word came out as slowly as if she were speaking to a simpleton.

Geoffrey widened his eyes. "Egads, never tell me a Scot?"

His mother narrowed her gaze on him. "This is not a matter to be taken lightly, Geoffrey. Can you imagine a man with the name of…?" She wrinkled her brow. "McTavish assuming the title?"

"McMorris," he corrected, automatically.

She continued marching forward with a beat to rival a drum; as she walked she slashed the air with her hand. "McTavish. McMorris. It is all the same. The gentleman possesses Scottish roots. You must wed. Immediately."

"I concur." He forced the words out past gritted teeth.

His mother froze in her steps, and looked to Geoffrey. Her blue eyes wide like saucers. "You concur?"

A muscle at the corner of his eye twitched. "I do." He'd spent nearly five years trying to atone for his past sins, and yet, it would appear his mother still didn't trust that he'd reformed. "I know well my responsibilities, Mother." He resumed walking.

She hurried along, and fell into step beside him. "I never imagined…" Her words trailed off.

Geoffrey waited. All the while, knowing she dangled that unfinished sentence before him in a paltry attempt at intrigue.

She tapped him on the arm with one of the white gloves she carried. "You are supposed to ask me what I'd never imagined." A frown marred her lips.

The steady tick-tock-tick-tock of the long-case clock at the center of the hallway filled the stretch of silence until his mother glowered up at him.

He sighed. "As you wish. What have you never imagined?"

"That you would acquiesce and find a suitable bride without my prodding. After all, most gentlemen are forced kicking and screaming to the proverbial altar. Your father and I despaired of you doing right by the Redbrooke line. Especially after that…that…Emma Marsh woman."

Geoffrey's gut clenched in pained remembrance of that great mistake she could never forgive. How could she forgive him, when he would never be able to forgive himself?

His mother seemed oblivious to the inner turmoil raging through Geoffrey. She tugged on her gloves as they reached the expansive marble foyer, and dusted them against one another. "I should have known better to question your intentions. Not when you've become so very committed, so very dedicated to the title of Viscount Redbrooke."

Mother prattled on with her high-praise even as the butler, Ralston, hurried to open the door.

As Geoffrey and his mother exited the house and entered the carriage, he ruminated over his selection in Lady Beatrice. Modest, demure, and lovely with flaxen curls, she would make him a lovely wife. He had it upon good authority that the young lady would be in attendance at Lord and Lady Hughes's ball this evening.

The groom closed the carriage door, and a few moments later, the conveyance rocked to motion. Geoffrey consulted his timepiece. Tonight would mark the perfect time to launch his courtship. If he were to maintain his very rigid timeline and wed, three Sundays past his thirtieth birthday, he couldn't afford to tarry.

"Have you settled on a young lady?" His mother interrupted his ponderings. "Oh, surely with your rigid expectations and insistence on propriety, you must have."

He frowned, not particularly caring for that unflattering description from the woman who'd given him life—even if it was a fair assessment of his character.

"Do tell?" his mother pressed.

It mattered not that she'd discover soon enough, his mother was as tenacious as a dog with a bone.

"I do not require any assistance on your part."

Mother pressed a hand to her breast. "My goodness," she said, with hurt flashing in her eyes. "Do you imagine I would be unable to assist you?"

"I don't imagine I'll need anyone's help securing the young lady's hand," he said, dryly.

She leaned over and patted him on the knee. "Why, every gentleman requires the help of one's mother, dear boy…" Her words cut off abruptly. A glimmer flicked to life in her eyes. "Ahh, so there is a *particular* young lady."

Geoffrey bit back a curse. With his mother's ability to ferret out secrets, she'd be better served working for the Home Office.

The carriage drew to a blessed stop.

Mother sat back in the red velvet squabs with a huff. "Very well," she groused.

A servant rapped on the door.

"Just a moment, Geoffrey. Won't you tell…?"

"No."

Her lips turned down at the corners. "I shouldn't have to gather it from gossips and newspapers."

He jumped out of the carriage and made his way up the steps of the townhouse awash in the soft glow of candlelight. As his mother fell into step alongside him, she grumbled under her breath.

They sailed through the doors, into a wall of heat from the crush of bodies that filled Lord and Lady Hughes's ballroom. From his place in the receiving line, he scanned the room in search of the woman he'd decided to make his wife.

As he sought her out, he contemplated his very deliberate courtship. If he were to secure a waltz and a quadrille this evening, and a waltz and some country reel at the next event they attended, it would send a very clear message that…

He froze.

That…

Geoffrey's body went taut, and the breath left him. His stare fixed on a tall, lithe young woman, a veritable Spartan warrior princess

7

amidst a room of lesser English ladies. With midnight black locks arranged in an artful design, and elegantly high-cheekbones, she possessed the kind of beauty that made a man do foolish things, like forget to breathe, or what was worse, caused a man to forget responsibility.

Remembrances of past transgressions teased his mind, but the woman, a stranger to him, was like a siren, silently calling, beckoning him. Two loose strands hung down her creamy white shoulders. Another toppled from the butterfly comb that held back those magnificent tresses, ending all such illusion that the flyaway locks were at all deliberate. He ached to capture one between his fingers and ascertain whether the strands were as silken as they appeared in the glow emitted by the chandelier's gentle flame.

As if being mocked by the gods, Lady Beatrice Dennington's brother, the Marquess of Westfield, walked up to the young woman, a glass of ratafia in his hands. He held it out to the unfamiliar young lady, and whispered something close to her ear. Even from across the ballroom, the husky quality of her full laugh reached Geoffrey's ears. Nearby lords and ladies looked on, their lips pulled back in a sneer at her unladylike expression of mirth.

And god help him, for the first time in nearly five years, he wanted to send propriety to the devil with a bow and a parting wave, and forever hear that fulsome sound.

The lady must possess delicate sensibilities, a polite laugh, and not be given to great displays of emotion.

Westfield's presence, combined with the words Geoffrey had dashed upon his list served as a taunting reminder of his intentions for Lady Beatrice.

"Geoffrey," his mother murmured, giving him a sharp look. "Are you well?"

"Oh-uh, yes, very well." Geoffrey stroked his palms along the front of his waistcoat and awaited their introduction.

"The Viscount Redbrooke and the Viscountess Redbrooke," the servant called.

From his vantage point, Geoffrey sought the tall beauty who'd so captivated him. He frowned. Gone. She'd disappeared from her spot alongside the pillar like an apparition he'd only conjured in his great imaginings.

His chest tightened with inexplicable disappointment.

"I see Lady Tisdale," his mother said, calling him back to the moment.

Geoffrey managed a faint nod as his mother took her leave, and he returned his search for the temptress. For four years, he'd managed to convince himself that he craved a placid, calm, poised young lady for a wife. Great beauties roused grand passions and wrought all manner of heartache. In the span of a heartbeat, the winsome creature in the crowd made mockery of his efforts at atonement.

Christ, what in hell is wrong with me?

The sole purpose of his being at Lord and Lady Hughes's ball was to partner Lady Beatrice in two sets; a waltz and a quadrille, and indicate his interest in the young lady. It would not do to be observed standing like a foppish gent just out of university with his mouth agape over an altogether different young lady.

Except...his mind was filled with images of too red lips, and a tall, lean frame, and...he gave his head a shake. Standing here, lusting after some unknown lady would not help him accomplish his goal of marriage to Lady Beatrice.

In desperate need of a drink, Geoffrey took a step toward a liveried servant bearing a tray full of champagne when his black Hessian boot suddenly snagged the hem of a young lady's skirt.

The tear of fabric ripping blended with the din of conversation around them.

The lady gasped, and pitched forward. Even as the glass of ratafia in her hand fell to the floor, her hip collided with the passing servant who teetered on his feet. The young man's serving tray tilted precariously, and for an infinitesimal moment Geoffrey believed the servant had steadied his burden.

But the servant's tray slipped from his fingers. Champagne flutes careened to the floor, and sprayed the bubbling liquid onto the gown of several matrons standing nearby, who cried out in shock and scurried off.

9

"Pardon me," Geoffrey murmured to the servant, and then returned his attention to the woman he'd inadvertently sent reeling. A mere five or so inches smaller than his six foot frame, she stood taller than most of the ladies present. "Forgive me. Are you all...?"

She smiled up at him.

His question died upon his lips as he gazed down at the woman who'd unwittingly beckoned from across the ballroom mere moments ago. His eyes traveled the high planes of her cheekbones, the gray irises of her eyes, her full, red lips.

...and then her slipper met the moisture upon the marble floor. Like one of the skaters at the Frost Fair on the River Thames, she slid forward, into a nearby pillar. "Ouch."

Geoffrey's arm shot out and he sought to steady her.

"Thank you," she said. She shook out her sea foam green skirts and unlike the horror that wreathed the faces of the surrounding ladies, wry amusement fairly glittered in her gray-blue eyes. "I am uninjured," she assured him.

His eyes widened and with alacrity, he released her.

She cocked her head to the side. "Are *you* injured?"

Her flat accent did not possess the clipped proper tones of a proper English lady. He blinked. "Injured?"

"You appear unwell, sir."

By God...

"You are an American," he blurted.

A mischievous smile played about her lips. "I am." She looked around and then back to him. "Never tell me you're scandalized by me being an American?"

He was scandalized by the wicked direction his mind had wandered that *involved* an American woman. If his mother was outraged at the prospect of a Scott assuming the Redbrooke title, what would she say to an American lady having garnered Geoffrey's attention?

"Ahh, you do smile," the young woman said.

Geoffrey frowned. "I beg your pardon?"

"Alas, it is gone," she said with a long, exaggerated sigh.

Geoffrey became aware of the appalled stares of Polite Society's most respectable peers, trained upon him. From across the room, his mother, who stood alongside Lady Tisdale, glared with blatant disapproval. It was the much needed reminder of past failings and inner weaknesses that had wrought much agony upon his family. By standing here engaging this...this...stranger, in the midst of Lord and Lady Hughes's ballroom, he opened himself up to public censure. His intentions were marriage to Lady Beatrice, and any hint of untoward interest in another would not be countenanced by the Duke of Somerset or his daughter.

Geoffrey folded his arms across his chest. This American upstart might have a face and body to rival Helen of Troy, but possessed the uncouth manners one would expect of an American. "Miss," he said from the corner of his mouth. "We've not been properly introduced, therefore, any discourse between us is highly improper."

Her lips twitched, with, he suspected, mirth. "I would say toppling over the host's servant and spraying his guests with champagne and glass is also improper, but you've done that, sir."

Geoffrey felt heat climb up his neck, and resisted the urge to tug at his suddenly tight cravat, shamed by the accuracy of her charge. He did not create scandals. Not anymore. He was proper. And poised. And...

She arched a brow.

Well, in this instance he'd created a small scandal. Still, he needn't raise further eyebrows by talking to the vexing miss.

Even if he wanted to.

He needed to go. Immediately. Anywhere but within mere inches of the lady who smelled like lilacs and lavender and now champagne. "Again, forgive me for causing you distress." He bowed deeply and beat a hasty retreat.

Geoffrey had made a fool of himself once over a young lady. He'd not be so foolish again.

TWO

A gentleman's responsibility is first and foremost to his
family's material comforts and well-being.
4th Viscount Redbrooke

From where she stood near the other partner-less young ladies, Miss Abigail Stone stared after the gentleman who'd gone and thoroughly shredded the delicate lace trim of her satin gown. She ignored the sideways glances directed her way by the row of ladies and slid into an empty seat. For the first time in a month since she'd taken up residence with her uncle, the Duke of Somerset, interest stirred through her.

The serious looking gentleman had fled faster than the God Hermes in his winged sandals, but not before Abigail had detected a flash of discomfit in the greenish-blue irises of his eyes. It hadn't been mere guilt from someone who'd ruined her gown, but something more, something far deeper. In that, she'd felt a kindred connection to the stranger.

It had taken Abigail's entire twenty years and a handful of days to learn that guilt drove a person to desperate measures. A sense of guilt could force a person to give up their family, home, and everything they held dear.

It could drive one to brave the perils of turbulent storms and unpredictable sea voyages.

She sighed. Guilt was a rather nasty thing.

Just then, from across the ballroom floor, a young lady raised her fingers to her lips and with a direct look at Abigail, pointedly whispered something to the lady at her side. A case of tittering ensued.

Abigail glanced away. After her brief time in London, she'd come to appreciate that an unknown ocean crossing was far preferable to having to live amidst the cold censure and disdain of people who'd judged her and found her wanting.

Abigail redirected her attention to the commanding, stern-faced man who'd fled her side. He stood, conversing with a young lady and a tall, handsome gentleman—a gentleman who seemed unable to remove his stare from the blonde woman on his arm.

An odd pang tugged at Abigail's heart. There had been a time when a gentleman had studied her with that very look. She'd not realized until after his betrayal that eyes could lie.

Her gaze slid away from the trio, out to the sea of twirling dancers and wondered how her life might have been different if she'd come to London as merely the niece of the Duke of Somerset and not a relative fleeing scandal.

Abigail's mouth tightened. The sooner her mother and father came to accept that she would never again be their sought-after, much respected daughter, the sooner her world could resume a semblance of normalcy.

Her heart twisted with the bitterness of truth. There would never again be anything normal about her life.

The young lady whose hemline he'd destroyed sat along the wall, studying him. Geoffrey frowned. Respectable young ladies didn't stare. It wasn't proper. Or polite.

Then, there was a boldness to this American woman so different than anything he'd ever witnessed amongst English women. He should be more appalled by such indiscretion. And yet, he couldn't dredge up the appropriate level of shock.

"Are you looking for someone, Geoffrey?"

Geoffrey stiffened, and turned to face his sister, Sophie, now the Countess of Waxham, and her husband, Christopher, Earl of Waxham. The couple had wed just a few short weeks ago after quite a scandal, which had only fueled Geoffrey's determination to avoid any hint of impropriety.

Of course his observant sister should have noted his interest. Geoffrey strove for bored indignation. "I don't know what you're speaking about."

His sister snorted. And he knew he'd failed.

"It appears as though you're searching for someone." His sister looked to her husband. "Doesn't it, Christopher?"

"It…"

Geoffrey turned a frown on his brother-in-law.

Waxham offered a sympathetic grin, holding his palms up sheepishly.

Sophie's timely appearance however reminded him of his purpose that evening, and it wasn't to act like a foolish swain over a mysterious American lady. Geoffrey inclined his head. "I'd like you to perform a certain introduction for me."

Sophie opened and closed her mouth several times. "Introduction? To a young lady?" Disbelief underscored her question.

"Is that so very hard to believe?" Geoffrey rescued a flute of champagne from the tray of a passing servant, who eyed him with a wariness that said the servants had already discussed the Viscount Redbrooke's remarkable lack of grace.

Sophie and Waxham exchanged a look.

Geoffrey frowned over the rim of his glass. When he'd been a young boy, his father, the former viscount, had schooled Geoffrey in his roles and responsibilities as a noble. The line would continue with him. His jaw set. He was determined of it. Geoffrey would never be absolved of his guilty actions on that night nearly five years past, but continuing on the male line would be a final act of penance for those sins.

Sophie caught her lower lip between her teeth. "You are not at all yourself this evening, Geoffrey." She made to press the back of her hand against his forehead but he shifted out of her reach.

Geoffrey closed his eyes a moment and prayed for patience. "I don't know what you mean." He knew exactly what she meant; he didn't *feel* much like himself this evening.

Sophie waved her hand. "There was that whole incident with your knocking over Lord Hughes's servant."

For an instance, Geoffrey felt a kindred connection to Sophie, who'd battled such gossip over the years. His sister had wrought much havoc upon Geoffrey's household and in public, only it hadn't occurred to him, until now, that the attention may have been unwarranted. "I did not knock over Lord Hughes's servant." He looked to Waxham one more time, in an unspoken male plea for support.

"Ah, yes. I believe it was a young lady your brother knocked over," Waxham offered.

A growl escaped Geoffrey. It had been the young lady's blasted hem he'd stepped upon.

His sister's eyes went wide in her face. "Did you just growl, Geoffrey? How very," she wrinkled her nose. "Primitive of you."

He'd had enough of Sophie's needling. "Will you or will you not perform the necessary introductions?" Geoffrey bit out.

"Oh, dear," Sophie muttered to her husband. "I do not like that look."

"And I don't care for your public discussion on a matter of delicacy," Geoffrey bit out on a hushed whisper.

Waxham said something close to Sophie's ear.

Sophie sighed. "Very well." She turned her focus to Geoffrey. "I shall help. And I shan't ask any questions." She made that final statement with a scowl for her husband.

Perhaps Geoffrey had unfairly judged the other man after all. Any man who could elicit Sophie's cooperation deserved some modicum of respect.

Sophie folded her arms across her chest. "Introductions, however, will require you to impart the identity of the lady who had caught your attention earlier."

Geoffrey couldn't very well admit that the woman who had ensnared his notice was not in fact the woman he'd selected as his future viscountess.

He did a cursory search of the crowd and caught sight of Lady Beatrice Dennington. The only female born to the Duke of Somerset, she stood alongside her brother the Marquess of Westfield, heir to the dukedom, known by Society as something of a rogue. Westfield was not unlike the man Geoffrey once had been…the man he'd resolved to never be again.

Sophie tilted her head. "Geoffrey?"

"Lady Beatrice Dennington," Geoffrey said quietly.

Sophie blinked. "I beg your pardon?"

"I'd like you to introduce me to Lady Beatrice."

She wrinkled her nose. "Hmph."

Pause.

"Aren't you going to ask why I said, 'Hmph'?" she said after a moment.

"No."

Sophie shook her head. "You are utterly exasperating. You weren't always this stodgy, rude fellow. Mother said at one time you were quite the rogue." He shot her a black look, quelling the rest of her words. She sighed. "Very well. I shall perform the necessary introductions."

Whether I approve or not. Geoffrey would have placed a significant wager, if he was still the wagering type of gentleman, that his sister muttered those words under her breath…or some other variant.

"Come along," Sophie encouraged and set out, forcing Geoffrey to hasten his step like he was one of the Queen's terriers.

"You do know she is enjoying this immensely," his brother-in-law said, with far too much humor in his pronouncement.

Geoffrey spoke through clenched teeth. "Yes, yes she is." His sister Sophie had courted scandal since she'd made her come out. For all his efforts and pleading, she'd not changed at all in her more than two London Seasons. He imagined his relying on her assistance caused her a good deal of amusement.

The trio weaved in between lords and ladies. Sophie, however, moved through the throng with purpose better suited to a woman following the drum. She didn't bother to occasionally pause for politeness sake, but continued onward until they reached Lady Beatrice Dennington, who stood amidst a cluster of young swains—swains who would only serve to complicate Geoffrey's intentions.

He favored the group of gentlemen with a black glare that sent them scurrying.

Sophie shot him a sideways glance, and shifted her attention to Lady Beatrice. A wide smile filled his sister's plump cheeks. "Hello, Lady Beatrice," Sophie greeted.

Lady Beatrice returned Sophie's smile and dipped a curtsy. "Hello, my lady."

Sophie waved her hand. "Please, no need for such formality. Allow me to introduce you to my brother, the Viscount Redbrooke."

Lady Beatrice looked at Geoffrey, before directing her demure gaze to the floor. "My lord." He strained to hear her faintly spoken words.

He battled down disappointment at the young lady's meekness; his response made little sense. Such reserved politeness befitted the young lady who would be his viscountess. Such a woman wouldn't be capable of deceit and trickery. Nor would such a woman need to trap an unsuspecting, gentleman into marriage.

His father would have approved of this match.

That should be enough. It had to be.

Waxham discreetly nudged Geoffrey.

Geoffrey offered a hasty bow, and claimed Lady Beatrice's hand. "My lady, it is a pleasure."

She sank into an elegant curtsy.

The orchestra concluded a lively country reel. A smattering of applause filled the crowded hall. If memory served him, a waltz was the next set. A waltz and a quadrille. A waltz and a quadrille. That was his intended plan for an unspoken declaration of his courtship.

"Lady Beatrice, will you to do me the honor of partnering me in the next set?"

The young lady blushed. "It would be my pleasure, my lord."

With the exception of the earlier stir Geoffrey had caused involving a teasing, American temptress, everything appeared to be going exactly as he'd planned.

THREE

A gentleman must remain free of scandal. Always.
4th Viscount Redbrooke

Wist the tip of her slipper, Abigail tapped a steady beat upon the Italian marble floor.

There were four mythical centaurs. She chewed her lip. Or were there five? Of course, it would really depend on whether one included the centaurs and centaurides as one.

After the scandal she'd created at Mr. and Mrs. Van Buren's ball, Abigail had developed the oddest nervous tendency of cataloguing mythical Greek figures. It served as a welcome distraction from the gossips.

Asbolus. Chariclo. Chiron. And Nessus. Yes. Yes. "There are four."

"I beg your pardon?"

Abigail started, realizing she'd been counting aloud, and looked over at the plump young lady who occupied the seat next to her. The woman shoved her wire-rimmed spectacles back upon her nose and studied Abigail like she'd sprouted a second head.

"Forgive me." Abigail opened her mouth to engage the brown-haired, brown-eyed lady in conversation, but the woman directed her attention elsewhere.

Abigail sighed. After her fall from respectable society, she'd learned rather quickly that aloof condescension was not reserved for a single continent. Since her uncle had introduced her to London's Polite Society, Abigail had braved soirees and dinner parties and visits to the theatre, amongst lords and ladies who peered down their long noses at her—the curl of their lips indicating that, without even knowing her, they'd found her wanting, simply because of her birthright.

"Where did you take yourself off to?"

Abigail jumped at the sudden appearance of her cousin, Robert Dennington, the Marquess of Westfield. She climbed to her feet. "I merely desired a rest from dancing."

Robert folded his arms across his broad chest, and arched a golden brow. He looked down the row of young ladies behind her. "A rest? You've not danced once this entire evening."

Abigail frowned. Nor did she intend to. She was trying to spare herself that humiliation as long as possible. She'd not expected her roguish young cousin to note as much. She sighed. "Yes. That is true. I wanted to sit."

He glanced down at her ripped hem. "Ahh, yes...Redbrooke and your hem."

She furrowed her brow. "Redbrooke?"

Robert reached for a champagne flute from a passing servant and took a sip. "The gentleman who nearly toppled you into Lady Hughes's servant.

Redbrooke. It was a strong name that bespoke power and seemed to perfectly suit the square-jawed, thickly muscled gentleman.

Robert spoke in a quiet whisper. "You do not have to sit here, Abby."

Her back went up. "I want to, Robert." After her scandal in America she'd found she rather preferred obscurity to notoriety. She had received enough attention to last the remainder of her life and then well into the hereafter. No, wallflowers were most times spared from undue notice and dancing and Abigail was quite content to join their ranks. "You needn't feel like you must watch over me, Robert," she hurried to assure him. He'd already spent the better part of the evening at her side. "Your sister—"

"Is still otherwise engaged with Lord Redbrooke," Robert interrupted. He tipped his chin across the ballroom, and Abigail followed the gesture.

Her heart's rhythm did the oddest little sputter.

Lord Redbrooke stood alongside Beatrice and a trio of other unfamiliar individuals.

Even with the length of the ballroom between them, Abigail detected the pink blush on Beatrice's cheeks.

They struck quite a pair; Lord Redbrooke's tall, lean, muscle-hewn frame and olive coloring, next to Beatrice's petite frame and flawless cream-white skin and golden ringlets.

Something the gentleman said raised a dimpled smile in Beatrice's cheeks and Abigail would wager her father's entire line of ships he'd said something perfectly gentlemanly, perfectly charming to her cousin.

"I do not see you as a burden, Abby."

Abigail wrenched her gaze away from Lord Redbrooke and returned her attention to her cousin.

His brotherly concern warmed her through. With his more than six-foot-tall frame and fair coloring, he so reminded her of her elder brothers, Nathaniel and George. "I'm all right. Truly. I'm sure there is a game of cards somewhere you'd rather see to."

His frown deepened. "Are you trying to be rid of me?"

She winked at him. "Yes."

A chuckle rumbled up from his chest, and he shook his head. "If you're certain…"

"I'm *very* certain."

"I'll return in a short while and partner you in a set."

A little shudder wracked her frame. "Only if you're determined to punish both me and your feet." Her papa had always used to say Abigail could accomplish anything and everything…with the exception of dancing and embroidering. With Abigail's lack of ladylike talents, Mother had despaired of Abigail ever making a match. In the end, Mother had been all too right.

Robert ran his eyes over her face, and must have seen something written there. "What is it?"

She waved her hand. "It is nothing."

"Would you rather I stay and dance?"

Abigail laughed and swatted at his arm. "You're insufferable."

With a wink, he excused himself.

Abigail embraced the momentary solitude.

For the better part of the evening she'd battled tedium, which had lifted the moment Lord Redbrooke had shredded her hem with the heel of his boot. Something in his sea-green eyes had reflected the haunted look of one who knew pain and heartache.

Abigail knew. Because she, too, had known both those wrenching emotions.

Loud, yet muffled whispers interrupted her musings.

From the corner of her eye Abigail noted the nearby lords and ladies who eyed her, an American oddity in their glittering, perfectly ordered world. Her toes curled inside her ivory slippers and yet, she jutted her chin out, and boldly met the stares of the nobles around her with a frankness her mother would have deplored. It had the desired effect and the nosy peers directed their attention on some poor other unfortunate miss.

Abigail's gaze collided with Lord Carmichael. Old and rotund, the gentleman had requested one of her later sets. The lecherous reprobate ogled her exposed décolletage a moment, and winked at her.

Shivers of distaste ran down her spine. She yanked her stare away from Lord Carmichael's and instead directed her attention toward the crowd of shifting figures, who performed the intricate steps of a quadrille. A wistful smile played about Abigail's lips at the sight of her cousin moving so gracefully, so elegantly, through the movements of the dance. Not like Abigail, who bumbled through every set and whose own dance tutors had deemed her unteachable.

Beatrice glanced up at her dance partner—Lord Redbrooke. The angular lines of his harshly beautiful face were set in a stoic mask. Every so often his thin, firm lips would move, and that pretty pink hue of Beatrice's skin deepened.

Beatrice had been nothing but good and kind to Abigail…so this hideous envy that dug away at Abigail's insides was petty and wrong. But God help her, how she longed for the restoration of her own innocence. Unlike Abigail, who had given away everything dear to a young lady, Beatrice remained unsullied, and pure, and therefore perfectly suitable for marriage to an honorable, worthy man.

The pain of past transgressions stabbed at Abigail with all the intensity of a dull knife being twisted inside her.

Suddenly, a longing for home filled her. At home she'd be outside on the cool, dew-kissed grass, inhaling the fragrant scent of sea air, gazing up at the constellations revealed in the stars.

She looked toward the long row of floor-length windows at the central part of Lord and Lady Hughes's ballroom and imagined herself far away. Through a slight slit in the gold brocade curtains, a distant glint flickered, beckoning, calling, as it so often did.

The London sky, thick with fog and dirt kept hidden the jewels of the sky she enjoyed in her seaport home. But sometimes, on the rarest of nights, rarer than a star shooting through the sky, the fog and dirt lifted and presented the stories contained within the stars.

Abigail took advantage of her position along the wall to plot her escape from the ballroom. With purpose to her steps, she skirted the perimeter of the spacious room, and then stole down a long corridor, needing to put distance between herself and the hot crush of guests. Abigail came to a long row of floor-length crystal windows with double doors that overlooked a grand terrace. She glanced over her shoulder to ascertain that she was in fact alone, and then opened the doors.

Abigail slipped outside. She picked her way around the stone patio, and wandered over to the balustrade. Gripping the edge, she leaned out much the way she had from the hull of her father's ship and surveyed the magnificent sight of the star-studded sky. The full moon hung high above, casting a white glow upon the walled in garden of thick green shrubbery and cascading flowers.

Abigail closed an eye and pointed her finger out at the darkened horizon, fixing on the bright tip of the Corona Borealis. She studied the crown-shaped constellation not feeling remarkably different than Ariadne abandoned by Theseus.

She inhaled deep in hopes of a familiar scent of the sea, but the slightly stale, stagnant air drove back memories of home.

Mama had grand aspirations of Abigail making a proper English match with some wealthy, young lord. Her mouth twisted bitterly. As though one of the proper English gentlemen could dismiss the scandal Abigail had created back in America and forgive a lack of virtue in his lady wife. Abigail stood a greater chance of the mythical Dionysus coming down with the crown of stars from the heavens and placing it atop her head.

No proper English lord would be willing to take to wife a young woman who'd given her virtue to a scoundrel. No, what was left of Abigail's heart belonged to the seaport home she'd been born to. Soon she'd return.

Her heart twisted. It would never be the same. She could not regain what had been lost; her virtue, her pride, her good name. When she returned, which she would, the same derision she'd fled would still await her there.

Abigail opened her eyes. Mama had asked the Duke of Somerset to give Abigail a proper London Season…and when the Season was done, Abigail prayed she would be welcomed back into her family's fold.

"I suspected you'd be looking for me, lovie."

Abigail jumped at the nasally voice that slashed into her private musings. She spun around.

The heavily wrinkled Lord Carmichael, stared at her through watery, brown eyes that bulged in a way that put her in mind of a great bluefish she'd once caught fishing with her brother.

She cleared her throat, and spoke with hesitancy. "Lord Carmichael. If you'll excuse me, I was just returning to the ballroom." She made to step around his corpulent frame, but he placed himself directly in her path, cutting off escape.

Her stomach roiled with unease.

"What is the rush, lovie?" His paw-like fingers reached out and caught a strand of her hair. "I saw you direct your pretty little chin toward the outside window."

He'd misconstrued her focus on the starry night outside Lord Hughes's long windows as an invitation. She shook her head. "No. You were mistaken, my lord. I merely desired fresh air."

Lord Carmichael rolled the lock of hair between his fingers.

"Remember yourself, sir," she bit out.

He gave the curl a sharp tug that caused tingling pain to radiate along the sensitive flesh of her scalp. Tears sprung to her eyes.

"My lord," she said in the same tone she reserved for her youngest brother and sister. "Remember yourself. My family, the *duke*, will be missing me." She hoped the reminder of her uncle's status would force Lord Carmichael to relinquish her.

Her efforts were met with his cackling laugh. "I'll release you." He leaned close so his breath fanned her cheeks. "Just as soon as we have a bit of fun out here."

She recoiled from the scent of heavy liquor, sweat, and garlic that clung to his podgy frame.

"Come, don't pretend you aren't interested. I saw you talking to Redbrooke and without proper introductions. An American piece such as yourself, you've probably had all manner of men between your legs. Savage men."

An indignant gasp escaped her. She slapped him so hard his head whipped back. The sound of her hand connecting with his flesh reverberated around the still of the night. Momentary satisfaction filled her at the stark, white imprint her palm had left upon his fleshy cheeks.

Abigail took advantage of his distraction and hurried around him but her satisfaction was short lived. The tip of her slipper caught upon the blasted torn hem, and she stumbled to her knees. She bit the inside of her cheek. Why hadn't she tended the ripped garment instead of seeking out a moment's solitude?

She stifled a cry as Lord Carmichael's fleshy fingers closed around the delicate flesh of her forearm. He jerked her upright and pulled her against his frame. "I've heard stories about you," he rasped.

"Stories?" Her voice sounded hollow to her own ears. She struggled against him and managed to free herself from his hold. Panic hummed in her ears. Good God, had word of her scandal already reached English soil?

Carmichael used her distraction to tug her close with a strength better suited to a man thirty years his junior. "So you like it rough, do you?" He chuckled. "Very well."

Abigail jammed the heel of her slipper down upon his booted foot. Her ineffectual efforts only raised the old letch's amusement.

She wrestled against him. "Release me." She detested the quiver of her high-pitched command.

"I will." His lips caressed her neck. "Just as soon as I get a sample of your charms, lovie."

Terror surged through her. She struggled against him but he pawed and grabbed at her like a determined animal. She'd come to London in desperate hope of setting aside the shame of her scandal. Instead, it would seem she'd merely traded one scandal for another.

Lord Carmichael tugged the décolletage of her satin ball gown lower, and fury gave strength to her fight.

By God, she would not allow him to further ruin her already tattered reputation. She jabbed him in the side with her elbow.

He grunted, but only shifted his attention to her breast.

God help her.

FOUR

*With the exception of rigorous practice in Gentleman Jackson's
ring, a gentleman should never engage in fisticuffs.*
4ᵗʰ Viscount Redbrooke

Geoffrey drained the contents of his champagne flute and passed
the empty glass onto the tray of a nearby, liveried servant.

He'd had his quadrille with Lady Beatrice. If his memory served,
there were two country reels and a waltz in between their next set.

The evening had been productive in terms of advancing his
courtship.

Except...

His gaze scanned the bodies, searching for a too-tall young lady,
with fire in her eyes. Guilt had filled him the moment the young lady
had taken her leave of the ballroom, surely hurrying off to see to her
torn gown.

It had been nearly a quarter of an hour and the young lady had not
returned. Geoffrey tapped his finger along the side of his thigh considering her absence. He didn't expect a young lady, an *American* should
understand the possible scandal of disappearing, unchaperoned in
her host's home. Or worse, the bold creature was meeting with some
young swain.

Rage clutched at him. He squared his jaw. It was merely his strict
appreciation for propriety that accounted for the need to find the
young lady and redirect her to the ball. After all, considering his
actions had resulted in her departure from the soiree, it would only
be the gentlemanly thing to do to make sure she'd not come to any

further trouble because of his actions. Geoffrey set out in search of the American lady.

His quickened step had nothing to do with a desire to see the alluring beauty.

Nothing at all.

Geoffrey strode down Lord Hughes's halls and followed it to the old earl's balcony and gardens.

He stared down the corridor. The bright glint of moonlight cast shadows through the crystal windows and reflected off the walls.

Geoffrey froze. The lady wouldn't have gone outside to repair her torn skirt. He turned around when a soft cry split the quiet.

Disregarding the fact that gentleman did not run, amidst their host's home, no less, Geoffrey sprinted toward the double doors. He threw them open, and froze.

The young lady hissed and clawed like a cat cornered in Cook's kitchens. She raked her nails over the side of Lord Carmichael's cheek, leaving a streak of bloody tracks down his fleshy cheeks.

"You bitch," Lord Carmichael spat, and shook her hard.

Some kind of savage beast stirred to life within Geoffrey's chest. A primitive growl worked its way up his throat and spilled past his lips. He raced forward and ripped Carmichael off the woman's struggling form.

She clawed at Geoffrey's arms, a wild, haunted look in her eyes. Her chest heaved from the exertions of her struggles.

Geoffrey knew the moment logic replaced the horrified panic inside her. She blinked several times, and then sank to her knees, inching backwards, until her back borrowed support from the stone wall that overlooked the grounds.

"Redbrooke," Carmichael wheedled. "What are you about? I'm just having a good time with the American girl. She invited me out here."

"I didn't," the young lady said, her voice flat.

"She did. She motioned to the windows and led me a merry little chase out here. Now she'd have you believe she's some innocent young miss. What proper lady would be out here unchaperoned, Redbrooke? Only a wh—"

Geoffrey punched Carmichael. The sharp jab to the older man's fleshy cheeks knocked him to his knees. The lecherous bastard pressed a hand to his nose to staunch the blood flow. From around his hand, Carmichael glared up at Geoffrey. "What did you do that for?" he whined. "She wanted it. Led me out here—"

Geoffrey punched him in the nose and this time, the old reprobate's eyes slid to the back of his head and he fell into a heap at Geoffrey's feet.

Geoffrey stared down at his clenched, bloodied fists, and counted to ten. Except the insidious, loathsome remembrance of Carmichael's sausage-like fingers upon the lady's skin, twisted around his mind. He took a step toward Carmichael.

"Don't," she murmured, as if she'd anticipated Geoffrey's intentions.

He looked back to the young woman. Several strands of her hair hung in long, wispy waves like a midnight waterfall about her shoulders and down her back. Geoffrey was certain he'd never seen a woman of greater beauty.

Also certain that in his twenty nine, three hundred and seventy-three, nearly seventy-four days, he'd never descended into this crazed, half-mad state.

"Are you hurt?" he asked, his voice gruff to his own ears. He closed the distance between them, and fell to a knee beside her.

A hand fluttered about the bodice of her gown, and he averted his gaze as she righted the material.

The air left Geoffrey on a hiss. "By God, I'll kill him."

"I'm all right," she said with a shocking steadiness to her voice.

Any other lady would have descended into hysterics following such an attack.

Geoffrey brushed the back of his knuckles along her cheek. "Are you certain?"

"He didn't..." She wet her lips. "That is, he didn't..." She colored. "I'm fine," was all she said.

Geoffrey reached inside the front of his evening coat and withdrew his monogrammed kerchief. "Here. Allow me." He touched the fabric to the corner of her lip.

She winced and his gut clenched at having caused her pain. "My apologies." He handed the cloth off to her, mourning the loss of contact between them.

"I know we've not been properly introduced but after your timely intervention, I imagine we've moved beyond rigid politeness. My name is Abigail. Abigail Stone."

It was an unfamiliar name. An American name.

Somehow wildly exotic in its simplicity.

He wondered what this American woman was doing in London.

Geoffrey sketched a short bow. "Geoffrey Winters, Viscount Redbrooke."

"Geoffrey," she said, the word rolled off her tongue as though she tasted the feel of it upon her lips.

"Lord Redbrooke," he corrected. "It's not proper for us to refer to one another by our Christian names." Even if there'd never been a sound more right than his name upon her lips.

His admonition must have roused whatever sense of misguided guilt she had over Lord Carmichael's attack. Her gaze shifted to the ground. "I cannot stay out here but," she spread her arms wide. "I cannot return like this."

Unbidden, his stare fell to her décolletage, previously exposed by Carmichael's assault. He balled his hands into fists to keep from bloodying the bastard all over again.

However, with the exception of her still-torn hem from their earlier encounter in Lord Hughes's ballroom and those glorious wisps of hair about her shoulders, she appeared largely un-mussed.

She shook her head back and forth. "My cousin will call him out. I'll have caused a scandal. My mother will again be disappointed."

Geoffrey resisted the urge to inquire as to what she'd done to have earned her mother's displeasure. It would be the height of impropriety to delve into the young lady's personal affairs. "Here," he said, gentling his tone. He worked to arrange her long, silken strands back into a semblance of something her maid had attempted with the glorious crown of wavy, black locks. He studied his efforts.

"Do I look presentable?" The question merged hopefulness with resignation.

Geoffrey's eyes traveled along the high lines of her cheek-bones, to the intriguing birthmark just at the corner of her lip. *Glorious. Magnificent.*

Instead, he said, "You'll do."

"I should go," she said quietly.

"Yes."

They both should.

And yet, they both remained rooted to the spot, gazes locked.

Something strong, and powerful, a masculine hunger brewed inside him, until he wanted to toss aside his proprietary responsibilities and his commitment to strict decorum and make her his. As if a man possessed, Geoffrey's hand came up of its own volition to stroke the silken curve of her cheek.

Geoffrey didn't recognize the savage beast who'd taken down Lord Carmichael with his bare fists, and now longed to carry off this American stranger, take her someplace far away, where they'd both be sheltered from Society's rigid expectations.

She leaned into his touch. "Dionysus," she whispered.

His breathing settled into a smooth, steady cadence.

She looked up at him, her face bathed in moonlight; the full orb reflected in the irises of her eyes and placed her palm in his. "You saved me," she breathed. Then, Abigail guided their joined hands upward, leveling them at the stars glinting above.

Geoffrey looked to their interlocked fingers, lit by the moon's glow.

Lord Carmichael groaned, and jolted Geoffrey from whatever spell the American enchantress had cast upon him. He glanced down at Carmichael's prone form.

A stark white scrap of fabric lay, partially obscured by the man's foot. Geoffrey bent down and tugged it free. The length of fine Italian lace must have been concealed somewhere within the bodice of the lady's gown. He cleared his throat. "I believe this must belong—"

Her gasp cut into his words. She reached for the lace with tremulous fingers. "Thank you." Abigail leaned up and placed her lips along his cheek. "I…just, thank you." The husky timbre of her voice washed over him.

Then, Abigail fled.

He swiped a hand across his eyes.

Christ. This was very bad, indeed.

Abigail hurried down the same corridor she'd walked only a short while ago, before Lord Carmichael's attack, before Geoffrey Winters, Viscount Redbrooke, had rescued her from certain ruin, before he'd done the oddest thing to her heart's rhythm.

"There you are!"

Abigail gasped, the soft pads of her white satin slippers slid along the marble floor.

Her cousin, Beatrice, reached out to steady her, a sparkle in her kind blue eyes. "Where have you been, Abby? My brother has been searching for you. I explained you had a tear in your gown. This isn't where one goes to have her hem r…" Her words died. Of a sudden, Beatrice seemed to take note of the out of place locks that had fallen around Abigail's shoulder. The warm, teasing light always found in Beatrice's eyes flickered out, replaced by a hard fury better suited to a ruthless warrior than her gentle-spirited cousin. "What happened to you? Who did this?" she hissed.

Abigail brushed a strand back into place with trembling fingers. "D…did w…what? It is merely my hem that is ruined. Truly." With her eyes, Abigail implored Beatrice not to ask any further questions. Now that Abigail was free of Lord Carmichael's clutches, the reality of his assault began to settle around her brain like a serpent sinking its venom into her and poisoning her with the hideous memories of Carmichael's touch.

Her cousin was good enough not to press Abigail for details. "We need to leave. You can't be seen like this." Beatrice glanced around. "Come," she murmured, and took Abigail by the hand.

"Where are we going?"

"Shh, we must be quiet," Beatrice whispered as she tugged Abigail along. "We'll find a place for you to wait while I have the carriage called for."

"Your father and brother—"

"I'll tell them your hem was ruined beyond repair, and must leave at once. Robert will see us home."

Oh, God. Her cousin would need only a glance to know that she'd nearly been ruined here this evening.

Beatrice held her gaze. "You look perfectly lovely." *You'll do,* he'd murmured in a silken baritone that had washed over her. Beatrice pointed her eyes to the towering ceiling. "Many witnessed what transpired, Abby."

The breath lodged in Abigail's chest. "What happened?" Her voice emerged as a hoarse croak.

Beatrice spoke in a gentle whisper. "The whole manner in which Lord Redbrooke knocked down that poor servant and ruined your gown." She wrinkled her nose. "He is a very severe, proud man. Lord Redbrooke, not the servant," she clarified.

"Beatrice," Abigail chided. Though serious, and driven by propriety, Lord Redbrooke had also been the man who'd intervened and saved her from certain ruin.

Beatrice shook her head. "Regardless, Robert will never assume anything else is to account for your appearance."

Abigail bit the inside of her cheek to keep from pointing out that Lord Redbrooke *had* in fact stepped on her hem, but it had been *Abigail* who'd knocked into the servant and sent his *tray* falling.

Her cousin ran her pale blue gaze over Abigail's face. "Are you certain you were unharmed because Robert will gladly call out the scoundrel who—"

"No! You mustn't say anything. It was merely my hem that was ruined. Just my hem." She'd not allow Robert to risk his life on a dueling field. Abigail's tattered reputation didn't deserve such a sacrifice. And for that matter, she'd already ruined enough lives with her scandalous ways.

Beatrice said nothing for a long moment, and then gave a slow nod. "Very well."

Abigail's eyes slid momentarily closed. "You are too good to me."

"Do hush. I'm just very glad for your company. I've had a remarkable lack of feminine companionship." Her mother, the duchess had died giving birth to Bea. Beatrice took Abigail's hands and gave them a slight squeeze. "And I've always wanted a sister."

Abigail managed her first smile that evening. She and Beatrice had fallen into a fast friendship from the moment Abigail had set her unsteady sea legs upon English soil. Beatrice had been waiting for her at the wharf side with her father and brother. Unlike Abigail with a gaggle of brothers and a sister, Beatrice remained the sole female in a male household.

Beatrice paused beside a closed door. She shoved it open and peeked inside. "No one is in here," she whispered over her shoulder. "Go and wait for me," she ordered, gently propelling Abigail into Lord Hughes's office. "Now, lock the door. Do not open it until you hear me."

Abigail managed a nod and shut the door behind Beatrice. She turned the lock.

The hum of silence filled the room, punctuated by the steady ticktock of the clock.

Abigail closed her eyes, and rested her back alongside the thick wood-panel of the door. Lord Carmichael's attack swirled through her mind. She hugged her arms close to her chest to ward off the chilled remembrance of his vile grasping. Tears filled her eyes, and the dimly lit library blurred before her. She blinked but the tears would not fall.

As abhorrent and reprehensible as Lord Carmichael was, there had been merits to the charges he'd hurled at her.

Abigail considered Geoffrey Winters, the Viscount Redbrooke's gallant rescue. He'd saved her from ruin, restored her hair to rights, and retrieved her lace memento…and what was more, not once had he looked upon her with the icy condescension she'd come to expect from respectable members of society. Lord Redbrooke might be a proper lord, but he possessed the kind of heroism the Greeks had made into legend.

Abigail dropped her head into her hands, and wondered whether he'd be so quick to rush to her defense if he learned she'd given away her virtue on an undeserving gentleman.

FIVE

A gentleman conducts himself with honor and integrity in all matters.
4th Viscount Redbrooke

The next morning Abigail kept company with Beatrice in the Yellow Parlor. Abigail sat at the window-seat that overlooked the walled-in garden at the back of the duke's townhouse, and sighed. She rested her forehead against the cool pane and gazed down at the stream of sunlight reflected off the armillary at the center of a collection of rose bushes.

He'd rescued her.

He'd rescued her as though she were the pure, innocent woman in desperate need of saving.

Well, the latter part of that had been true, anyway.

Since last evening, Geoffrey Winters, Lord Redbrooke had occupied every single corner of her mind.

She considered Beatrice's visage reflected back in the glass window pane. Head bent as she worked diligently on her very ladylike endeavor. Her cousin moved the needle in her hand with expert precision through the embroidery frame upon her lap. Beatrice represented everything Abigail was not—a flawless lady. Her skills upon the dance floor were only rivaled by her mastery of watercolors and embroidering.

As though she felt Abigail's stare upon her, Beatrice paused mid-stitch and looked up. She tipped her head at a slight angle and set the frame aside. "You have a sad look about you, Abby."

Abigail fixed her gaze on the fuchsia rose bush below. "Do I?" She'd felt mired down in sadness since the night of her great scandal—except, last evening when she'd nearly been knocked down by stiffly proper Lord Redbrooke. For a too-brief moment she'd remembered what it felt like to smile again, and laugh, and yearn for all manner of things she'd thought forever lost to her after Alexander.

"Did you love him?"

Abigail froze at the probing inquiry.

"I'm sorry," Beatrice said quickly. "I shouldn't have asked. I thought it might be helpful to speak of h…it. Please forgive me."

Abigail shook her head, and turned to face her cousin. She dropped her legs over the side of the window-seat, and her emerald green muslin skirts fluttered about her ankles as her slippers graced the floor. "No, it is fine," she assured her." Abigail considered Beatrice's question. "I believed I loved him." Now, she suspected she'd worshipped him with girlish eyes.

"Does it hurt to speak of him?" Beatrice asked tentatively.

"It doesn't." And oddly, Abigail meant it. The shock of Alexander's betrayal, she believed, would always sting. Only, since her flight from America, it seemed to have faded.

Beatrice eyed her expectantly.

Abigail folded her hands upon her lap and studied the interlocked digits. "His name was…is," she amended. "Alexander. He was my brother Nathaniel's closest friend. They went to school together. He would visit my family." A wistful smile played about her lips. "He would tease me when I was younger." He'd continued to tease her about her fascinated interest with the stars when she'd grown into a woman. Alexander had seemed perplexed by her unconventional knowledge.

"Oh," Beatrice said, with so much pity and so much sadness in that one, tiny little utterance, Abigail's smiled died. "What happened? You really needn't feel like you must answer. Truly, I—"

"I fell in love with him," Abigail cut into her cousin's words, feeling freed by the admission.

Something wistful stole across Beatrice's face. "How very fortunate you were."

Abigail balled her hands into fists, and clenched them so tight she suspected she raised blood on the sensitive skin of her palm. Abigail had been all manner of things where Alexander Powers' was concerned; foolish, impulsive, illogical. Fortunate had never been one of them.

She'd once carried a dream in her heart for more than the formal, rigid arrangements worked out by families.

And yet...she'd never taken Beatrice for a romantic. Something in the wistful, faraway look of Beatrice's eyes gave her pause. Had she ever been as blessedly innocent as Beatrice?

"Has a particular gentleman captured your attention, Beatrice?"

Color flooded Beatrice's cheeks, and she looked around as if to ascertain they were alone. "There is...a gentleman," she said, with far more seriousness than Abigail had come to expect from her.

Abigail's heart hitched. Lord Redbrooke and Beatrice had performed those intricate steps of the quadrille so elegantly. "Lord Redbrooke seems a kind," *gallant*, "good man."

Beatrice wrinkled her brow. "Lord Redbrooke? Surely you jest? He is a very serious, unpleasant kind of fellow."

Surely they spoke of two different gentlemen? Lord Redbrooke, though solemn and stringently proper, had exhibited both a strength and honor Abigail had never before encountered in a gentleman. "The gentleman you speak of, the one who had captured your attention is not, Lord Redbrooke, then?" The question emerged halting.

An inelegant snort escaped Beatrice. "Hardly." Why should her cousin's words rouse this relief within her breast? "I do not believe Lord Redbrooke capable of any grand passion."

Abigail opened her mouth to protest, and then promptly closed it. She'd not reveal the identity of her rescuer. She rather suspected Lord Redbrooke to be a private gentleman who'd not welcome or appreciate any fanfare.

Seeming unaware of Abigail's sudden quiet, Beatrice continued, "I'm certain Lord Redbrooke will enter into a union that is based on nothing more than wealth and who will make him the most advantageous match." She caught her lower lip between her teeth. "I suspect Father would like very much for me to encourage the viscount's suit."

37

The Duke of Somerset's daughter presented an ideal match for the Viscount Redbrooke. Until just then, however, Abigail had never considered that her cousin would aspire to anything beyond a strategic match in which mutual attraction was secondary.

"He would make you an excellent husband," Abigail said softly, hating the truth of her utterance.

Beatrice snorted. "I assure you, I'd never settle for the Viscount Redbrooke. With his stern looks and constant frown, he could hardly inspire any deep affection in a lady."

Oh, you are so very wrong, cousin. A man such as Lord Redbrooke could never be one a lady settled for, but rather a gentleman who ladies tossed their kerchiefs at.

"Do you desire a love match, Beatrice?"

Another inelegant snort escaped her usually always ladylike cousin. "I'm not a broodmare, Abby. I might be a proper English lady, but even I aspire to love." Her eyes sparkled. "But you mustn't tell Father. He'd be scandalized."

"I'd be scandalized by what?"

Abigail and Beatrice's gazes flew to the doorway. The duke stood in the threshold. Several inches greater than six feet, he possessed a wide, broad muscle-hewn frame better reserved for one of the men who worked upon her father's ships than a peer just a smidgeon shy of royalty. A smile creased the lines of his austere cheeks.

"Father," Beatrice murmured, and hurried across the room. She leaned up and placed a kiss upon his cheek.

An ugly frisson of envy spiraled through Abigail; a longing for the familiar presence of her bear-like father and his booming laugh. Only, the disappointment she'd seen reflected in her own father's eyes would forever haunt her.

The duke smiled fondly down at his only daughter, and then shifted his focus to Abigail. "I'd like to speak with you Abigail."

She wet her lips as sudden trepidation filled her. What if the duke had somehow learned of Lord Carmichael's attack? Abigail nodded. "Your Grace."

The duke looked to his daughter. "Please excuse us, Beatrice."

Clearly accustomed to his ducal orders, Beatrice nodded, with a final glance over at Abigail as she took her leave. She closed the door in her wake; the slight click resounding in the quiet of the room.

The duke motioned for Abigail to claim her seat and moved deeper into the room, sitting in the wide King Louis chair alongside the yellow velvet sofa. "You are well, Abigail?"

"Oh, very," Abigail replied as she took her seat. "Thank you for taking me in."

The duke folded his arms across his broad chest. "That is what family does, Abigail." He frowned. "My father was a foolish, pompous man. He sent your mother away because he disapproved of her wedding your father."

"My father was a footman." Abigail felt the need to remind him.

A snorting laugh escaped her uncle. "I didn't say she made an ideal match. But I'd not turn out my own child and force them across the ocean for anything."

Abigail's breath hitched, and she knew the moment her uncle realized what he'd said. He sat back in his chair with a sigh. "Your parents love you dearly, Abigail."

"Yes." Or they had. She suspected Mama and Papa would never truly forgive Abigail her great offense. For that matter, Abigail could not find fault with their decision. They still must consider dear Lizzie, who would one day wed. As a fallen woman, Abigail had greatly hindered her sister's future opportunities.

"Your parents want you to make a proper match."

She stiffened and smoothed her palms over her skirts. "I—"

"Need to, Abigail," he interrupted, his tone a blend of gentle concern and stiff resolve. "Eventually the reason for your visit to London will reach Polite Society."

Abigail glanced down at her feet. Some rumor or another about her scandalous past would eventually find its way into London drawing rooms. She'd allowed herself to hope, foolishly, that the distance would protect her.

Her uncle was relentless. "Do you aspire to a family?"

Abigail blinked, momentarily taken aback by the unexpectedness of the question. In spite of Alexander's treachery, she still longed for a family of her own.

"Your silence is your answer, Abigail."

Geoffrey's image flitted through her mind. "I'll not trap a gentleman into marriage."

Her uncle leaned back in his chair, folding his arms across his broad chest. "I'm not asking you to trap a gentleman. You come from noble origins. You are a strong, courageous woman. Not many would brave a long, ocean voyage alone, as you did."

She managed a smile. "I grew up on the water, Uncle."

A wistful smile tipped his lips up at the corner. "Yes. I do forget that. My sister lived a whole life without me knowing any part of it."

The former Duke of Somerset had cut Abigail's mother, Lady Margaret, out of the fabric of the family as neatly as snipping the thread off a garment. Abigail's parents had made a life for themselves in America, with Papa ultimately becoming a prosperous, and very successful shipping magnate. Her family had only been welcomed back into the folds of their English family after grandfather had died.

Her uncle spoke, interrupting her ponderings. "Your father asked that I give you this." He reached into the front pocket of his coat and withdrew a folded parchment emblazoned with her father's wax seal.

She'd expected it would take more than a month for her family to get word to her across the ocean.

"The ship's captain carried it over, and your father asked that I pass it to you when I felt you were ready to read the contents of the note."

Abigail accepted the thick parchment with tremulous fingers. Nearly every day in this foreign land, she'd longed for some word from home. At her most rational times, she realized that their disappointment in her had surely killed all affection. In her most optimistic times, she'd hoped they had forgiven her enough to at least write.

"Thank you, Uncle," she murmured.

She waited until he took his leave, and then shifted her focus to the letter. Abigail tore into the note with the same enthusiasm she had in tearing into Cook's confectionary treats.

Her eyes scanned the single sheet of parchment.

My dear daughter,
By this time, you are safely and comfortably settled in London. It is
mine and your mother's greatest wish that you at last find happiness.
As much as we'd wished for you to have a marriage based off love,
we realize your comfort and happiness requires you to find a suitable
gentleman who will properly care for you.
    Please understand, my wishes for you stem from the life I myself
knew. I hope you can someday understand that.
It was signed simply.
Your Father

Abigail frowned, turning the note over in her hands. Disappointment stabbed at her breast. After sending her away he'd penned a mere...she jabbed her finger at the paper, one, two, three, four, five sentences? She fisted the parchment into a ball, and tossed it on the table in front of her.

Her father, her uncle, and mother, everyone's greatest concern was her marital state. What she'd done, so very shameful and wrong of a lady, had resulted in her exile. Was that penance not enough that she should now turn her life over to the hands of a gentleman to save her reputation?

As Abigail sat there, she considered the urging of her father and uncle. They wanted her to make a speedy match, and she would honor their wishes in at least entertaining an honorable gentleman's suit.

Her uncle had been clear—Abigail needed to make a match before word of her scandal found its way to England.

However, Abigail rather feared the only man who'd stirred her interest since she'd arrived in London, was the highly proper Lord Redbrooke.

SIX

A gentleman is obligated to make the most advanta-
geous match with a proper, respectable young lady.
4th Viscount Redbrooke

eoffrey tugged back the curtains and peered out at the passing
London streets as his mother prattled on and on. Since the
carriage had departed his townhouse, bearing them to Lord and Lady
Essex's ball, his mother had filled the silence, it seemed, not taking a
moment to so much as breathe. One of the great travesties in honoring ones obligations as a nobleman was the constant barrage of inane
amusements a gentleman was forced to attend.

"Attending another ball," his mother said on a laugh.

After Lord Hughes's soirée last evening, Geoffrey would be glad to
never step foot in another crowded ballroom.

"Which of course can only indicate your interest in making a
respectable match..."

He sighed.

"...with a proper lady."

He'd consider it a very fine day when he was wed, and freed from
attending another blasted ball.

Only, a winsome American beauty flitted through his silent
musings.

"It *is* the Lady Beatrice!"

Geoffrey' flinched as his mother's high-pitched cry filled the confines of the black lacquer carriage.

He dropped the curtain back into place, and frowned. "Mother, remember yourself."

Her smile widened and she leaned across the carriage to swat him on the arm. "You sly, dear boy. You left me to wonder as to the identity of the woman you'd chosen for your viscountess. But Lady Beatrice Dennington, why there is no finer match," She frowned. "Well, perhaps Lady Diana." Mother tapped a finger against her lip. "Then, Lady Diana is a mere marquess' daughter, and you, dear boy, have landed a duke's daughter."

Geoffrey's jaw hardened. "I've not *landed* anyone, Mother." Not for the first time, he wondered about the American woman's identity.

"Are you listening to me, Geoffrey?"

She'd uttered the name, Dionysus.

He furrowed his brow. The name, of a Greek God. Something so very odd. Geoffrey went back to his university days and struggled to drag up the story of Dionysus.

"Geoffrey, I said, are you listening to me?"

"Yes." *No.*

Mother's frown said she knew he lied. "I was suggesting we host a dinner party." She clapped her hands together as though in doing so, the matter was settled. "Yes. We shall have a dinner party and invite the Duke and Lady Beatrice." Her eyes twinkled. "Why, we shall even invite Lady Diana. After all one can never be too confident in a lady's affections and Lady Diana would also make you a splendid match." She wrinkled her nose. "No unseemly relations there, as far as I'm aware, and I am aware of these things, you know."

"No, dinner parties," Geoffrey said harshly. He preferred to launch a swift courtship and avoid as much of Polite Society as possible.

His mother's face took on a pitched look. "No dinner parties? Hmph. Very well."

As his mother carried on, he pulled back the curtains and peered out into the dark London streets clogged with conveyances. Marriage to Lady Beatrice or Lady Diana had seemed the very best options for him when he'd drafted that bloody list.

They both fit with one of his additional requirements—they were *exceedingly dull.*

Lord and Lady Essex's townhouse pulled into focus. The front windows filled with candlelight, cast a warm, fiery glow out into the street. Normally one who loathed soirees, in this particular instance, Geoffrey rather found he preferred the mad crush of Lady Essex's ballroom to his mother's company.

He shoved the door open.

"Geoffrey!" His mother gasped as he stepped down without the benefit of a servant's help.

"I'll hardly come to harm opening my own door, Mother," he drawled.

She snapped her burgundy silk skirts, and glared at him. "There are appearances to maintain. Why, we do not need people wondering about your eagerness and attributing it to Lady Beatrice." She stepped over the muddied path with Geoffrey's assistance, and made her way to their host's entrance. "After all, ladies do not favor an eager gentleman." She nodded her head. "It is a certainty."

He bit the inside of his cheek to keep from pointing out that they also didn't favor a possible future mother-in-law who harped.

Geoffrey gave silent thanks when they reached the receiving line.

Laughter blended with the lively music being played by Lord Essex's proficient orchestra.

His mother scanned the sea of nobles. "I'm off to join Lady Ashford, and do remember, you mustn't appear too eager."

Geoffrey briefly closed his eyes and sent a prayer skyward for patience, grateful when his mother hurried off to greet one of Society's most notorious gossips.

"There you are, brother!"

His sister slipped by several couples deep in conversation, earning frowns of annoyance, which by her smile, she seemed wholly oblivious to.

She leaned up and kissed Geoffrey on the cheek.

He stiffened at her public showing of affection.

Sophie laughed and swatted at his arms. "Oh, you're ever so stodgy. Surely it is permissible to show affection for one's sister?"

"Surely it is not," he said in clipped tones.

Sophie waggled a brow. "Even if one's sister has some rather beneficial information?" She dangled that piece like the bait he used to fish his well-stocked lake in Kent.

He feigned a yawn. He'd had nearly twenty-two years of perfecting stoic control where his sister was concerned.

She let out an indignant huff. "Very well. If you'd rather I not point out exactly where Lady Beatrice is, and allow you to find her through this great crush of…" her eyes lit up as he surveyed the crowd. "Ahh, I see I have your notice now, brother."

She did.

He'd simply developed enough self-control not to say as much.

Sophie leaned close, and whispered, "She is at the central portion of the ballroom floor, conversing with her brother, the Marquess of Westfield."

Geoffrey gave a curt nod. "Thank you."

She pointed her eyes toward the ceiling. "There really is no need to thank me. After all, family helps one another, no?"

Before Geoffrey knew what she intended, Sophie leaned up once more and placed another kiss upon his cheek and then hurried off, her figure swallowed up by the crowd of people.

With a single-minded purpose, Geoffrey started toward Lady Beatrice and her brother, Lord Westfield, taking care to walk the perimeter of the floor and avoid the circle of couples performing the quick steps of La Boulanger. His eyes focused on the crop of golden curls and the lady's flushed cheeks. She really was quite lovely, possessing all the attributes of a flawless English beauty.

After a long night of battling improper yearnings for a tempting American, Geoffrey had managed to rise that morning and brush the memory of her aside. He didn't need an unconventional miss with a ready smile for unfamiliar gentlemen. No, Lady Beatrice would never do something as forward as to continue to engage a gentleman as Abigail Stone had when he'd stepped upon her gown last evening.

Geoffrey reached Lady Beatrice's side. The young lady stiffened and for a moment Geoffrey detected a flash of disappointment in her eyes.

He claimed her hand and bowed over it. "My lady, it is most agreeable seeing you this evening."

The young lady lowered her eyes to the floor, with what seemed to be a perpetual blush upon her fair cheeks.

Marquess of Westfield greeted him with a bow. "Redbrooke, a pleasure as usual." The dry edge of humor in Westfield's tone suggested the marquess' words were not wholly sincere. Westfield inclined his head. "Ahh, forgive my lack of manners. Allow me to introduce you to my cousin." He shifted, revealing a young lady clad in a sapphire blue satin creation fully engaged in conversation with the Earl of Sinclair.

There was something so very familiar about the elegant lines of her back, the graceful flare of her hips...

A loud humming filled Geoffrey's ears and he knew with a certainty he'd be willing to wager the Redbrooke line on, the identity of Lady Beatrice's cousin before the lady even fully revealed herself. "Lord Redbrooke may I present Miss Abigail Stone."

At that precise moment, Abigail said something to Lord Sinclair, who tossed his head back and laughed. She turned around.

And froze like the deer who'd caught sound of Geoffrey's hunting dogs.

Geoffrey sucked in a breath. His eyes traveled the high planes of her cheekbones, the charcoal gray irises of her eyes, the full lower lip, the...

Her eyes widened.

"You," she breathed.

Geoffrey's mind spun. This warrioress who'd battled Lord Carmichael, his American Helen of Troy, was in fact Lady Beatrice's cousin. He silently reviewed all the research his solicitor had done on Lady Beatrice. The information he'd uncovered about the young lady had indicated there were American relatives there. It had not, however, indicated she had a cousin with a fulsome laugh and silken tresses as black as sin.

Lady Beatrice's brow wrinkled, and she alternated her gaze between Abigail and Geoffrey. "You know Lord Redbrooke?"

Abigail and Geoffrey looked at one another and silence stretched out into an awkward pause.

The Marquess of Westfield settled a hard, narrow-eyed stare upon Geoffrey. "You two have met?" he asked, repeating his sister's earlier question.

Abigail and Geoffrey spoke in unison.

"Yes."

"No."

Christ.

Abigail discreetly coughed. "Uh, that is to say, no, we have not."

Westfield's brows lowered, and rogue that he was, surely recognized his cousin wasn't being altogether truthful.

Lord Sinclair used the opportunity to interject. "Perhaps, Miss Stone referred to her meeting at Lord Hughes's ball?" He looked to Geoffrey and grinned. "I believe you knocked down Miss Stone? Or was it a servant?"

Geoffrey clenched his teeth, resisting the urge to point out that he hadn't knocked down either Miss Stone or a servant. Considering the precariousness of the current exchange, he supposed he should be far more grateful for Sinclair's intervention. Except, presenting him as a bumbling, graceless lord would hardly help him in his quest for Lady Beatrice's hand.

Why did that possibility not alarm him as much as it should?

"Lord Redbrooke did not knock a servant down," Abigail murmured. She angled her head. "Nor did he knock me down. He *nearly* knocked me down."

Laughter moved throughout the group, but it served its purpose and Westfield dropped his questioning.

Geoffrey studied Abigail, so composed and seemingly unaffected by his presence. Geoffrey held her gaze. "Are you well, Miss Stone?"

Abigail appeared to understand his unspoken question. She inclined her head. The subtle movement only served to elongate the impossibly long neck. "I am, my lord. Thank you."

"I am trying to convince Miss Stone to dance with me," Sinclair said to the group. He held a hand to his chest. "Alas, it appears I've failed to appropriately charm the lady into partnering me."

Good. He'd rather send Sinclair to the devil than out onto the dance floor with Abigail. Something tight, and wholly uncomfortable gripped Geoffrey's chest. Something that felt very nearly like jealousy, which made very little sense considering Geoffrey's intentions for Lady Beatrice. It shouldn't matter to him if Abigail partnered with Lord Sinclair or the Prince Regent himself.

"I've told His Lordship that I'd hardly repay his kindness by trodding upon his toes," Abigail said with a laugh.

"You do not dance, Miss Stone?" Geoffrey's taciturn question killed the levity amongst the group.

She shook her head, and seemed the only person immune to his severity, for she smiled up at him. "To my mother's chagrin, I'm rather deplorable."

His attention should be reserved for the woman who would one day, if all went to plan, become his future viscountess. Instead, he fixed his gaze to Abigail. "Was it that you did not have suitable instructors in America?"

Lady Beatrice gasped, and it occurred to him, too late, the pomposity of such a question. Even before his most jaded days, he'd never been capable of the effortless charm as exhibited by rogues like Sinclair.

Geoffrey shook his head. "Forgive me. I..."

Abigail waved off his apology. "I assure you, Papa hired some of the most proficient instructors from Europe. I however, proved a remarkably poor study."

Lady Beatrice made a sound of protest and rushed to her cousin's defense. "That isn't true, Abby. Why you're a lovely dancer."

Abigail smiled. "I'm remarkably fortunate to have you as a champion, Beatrice. However, I hold no false modesty. I'm truly deplorable."

Geoffrey was hard pressed to believe such a graceful, elegant woman would be *deplorable* at anything.

Lord Sinclair sketched a deep bow. "Well, I insist that you allow me to at least make a determination for myself on your skill or," he arched a single brow, "lack thereof, during the next waltz, Miss Stone."

And now he wanted to plant his fist in Sinclair's far too-charming smile.

Color flooded Miss Stone's cheeks, and she fiddled with the card dangling from her wrist.

"I'll not take no for an answer, Miss Stone," Sinclair pressed.

The blush on Abigail's cheeks deepened to a dark red hue that put Geoffrey in mind of a ripened strawberry in the heart of summer. And God, if he didn't suddenly have a taste for the fruit.

Abigail met Sinclair's eyes with a direct boldness not suited for an innocent debutante. "Well, if you'll not accept a rejection on my part and you're willing to risk the well-being of your toes, than I'd be honored."

In that moment, Geoffrey who loathed dance as much as he loathed being an object of Society's scrutiny, wanted to take Abigail in his arms and waltz her throughout an empty ballroom floor. It wasn't practical. Or proper. Nor would dancing with her serve to advance his goal of marriage to Lady Beatrice, which, just then, didn't seem as important as it had before he'd arrived at Lord and Lady Essex's ball.

A waltz.

A waltz and a quadrille.

Geoffrey squared his shoulders and looked to Lady Beatrice. "My lady, will you do me the honor of partnering me in the next set?"

Lady Beatrice's gaze flitted over to Abigail and Lord Sinclair, and Geoffrey frowned at the wistful longing he saw in her innocent blue eyes.

When she looked back at Geoffrey, she smiled up at him and he assured himself that he'd merely imagined the brief flash of regret in Beatrice's eyes. "Of course, my lord."

From the corner of his eye he detected the manner in which Abigail continued to fiddle with her dance card. In the past years, he'd come to consider himself an excellent read of character...which was rather fortunate, because prior to that, he'd been quite dismal at it.

Miss Stone's distracted movements suggested the young lady was nervous. Or troubled. Perhaps both.

The tip of her nail inadvertently loosened the ivory ribbon and her dance card fell in a fluttery, spiral path toward the Italian marble floor.

She gasped, and made a desperate reach for it but the satin ribbon slipped through her fingers and landed ignominiously at her feet.

"Allow me," Geoffrey murmured, and stooped to retrieve the item.

"No. I have it!" she said far too quickly.

He ignored her protestations and picked it up. As he stood, his eyes happened upon the names penciled in on the sparse card. It was wholly accidental. Yes, it hardly mattered to him which gentlemen lined Miss Stone's dance card.

Lord Sinclair. Waltz. Rogue.
Lord Pemberly. Country reel. Reprobate.
Lord Ashfield. Quadrille. Profligate gambler.
Lord Masterson. Waltz. Six children. Far too many for a young lady...

Four partners in total. He frowned. Surely Westfield, as her chaperone, knew that none of the gentlemen would make an acceptable match for any lady, and surely not for his own relative...?

"Redbrooke?" The dry amusement in Lord Sinclair's tone cut into Geoffrey's musings.

As though burned, Geoffrey relinquished Abigail's dance card, and wordlessly handed it over to her. Heat flooded his neck at having been caught studying the names there. He stole a sideways glance at Lord Westfield, who had a black scowl trained on Geoffrey.

It had been unintentional, his reading the names and all. Why, it hardly mattered to him that four wholly unacceptable, entirely too-roguish gentlemen had claimed her sets.

Geoffrey extended his arm to Lady Beatrice. She placed her fingers upon his sleeve and allowed him to escort her onto the dance floor. Why did it feel like he lied to himself?

Abigail schooled her expression so that Lord and Lady Essex's guests didn't note her untoward interest in Beatrice and Geoffrey, who now took their places amongst the other dances.

Lord Redbrooke, she silently amended. *Lord Redbrooke.*

Her fascination with the stoic gentleman merely stemmed from his rescue at last evening's ball. There was nothing else for it. He was ever so serious, and seemed to wear a perpetual frown.

However…she had learned from Alexander the perils in trusting a gentleman with a too-ready grin.

"Miss Stone?"

Abigail jumped, and turned back to the tall, *grinning* gentleman forgotten at her side. With his unfashionably long black curls, and sapphire eyes, he was more beautiful than a gentleman had a right to be. Yet, she found herself preferring the understated beauty of Geoffrey Winters' tall, lean frame. Abigail made a show of retying the card around her wrist, all the while doing a quick inventory of names.

It was the height of rudeness to forget the name of the gentleman one had spoken to for nearly a quarter of an hour. The orchestra plucked the opening strands of a waltz. She scanned the four names. *Ah, yes, she had it!* "Lord Sinclair—waltz!"

She winced as the words echoed off the pillar and couples turned around to study her as though she were an insect that had crawled its way into Lord and Lady Essex's ballroom.

Lord Sinclair's grin widened, displaying two perfect rows of even white teeth. He sketched a bow. "I do believe I've been insulted."

Not for the first time, Abigail gave thanks that her mother and father were not present, lest they witness her rather dismal failings at a London Season. There were four gentlemen who'd requested a set. Four gentlemen…and she couldn't remember the name of the one man who'd been conversing with her for several minutes now? It was that blasted Geoffrey Winters.

The Earl of Sinclair cleared his throat, and she jumped. He nodded toward the card at her wrist. "It doesn't appear I've left much of an impression, Miss Stone, if you require the assistance of a card to remember my identity."

"I…" Abigail sighed. "Forgive me," she muttered. She'd never mastered the art of dissembling.

"Sinclair," Robert drawled from where he stood alongside her. "The dance has begun."

Eternally grateful to Robert for rescuing her from her plight, she placed her fingers on Lord Sinclair's arm and traded one embarrassment for another. Until this moment, she'd done a remarkably exceptional job of avoiding all dance at *ton* events. She'd feigned a turned ankle. That had allowed her a handful of dance-free evenings. Then they'd attended the theatre. The opera. A musicale. Oh, then there had been the dinner party at Lord and Lady Pembroke's. She furrowed her brow. Or was it Pemberly?

"Miss Stone, are you unwell?"

She supposed she could lie to Lord Sinclair or pretend to swoon. Abigail sighed. Alas, the ability to feign a swoon had eluded her just as the ladylike arts of embroidery…and dancing…and watercolor… and…

"I am merely warm, my lord," she lied.

After a fortnight of attending social functions, it would appear she would at last have to demonstrate for all English Society her shocking lack of grace.

She was renowned for her extreme lack of dancing skills all over the state of Connecticut and well into parts of New York. She supposed she could now add London, England, to the expanding list.

As Lord Sinclair led her onto the dance floor, she felt much like a thief being marched to the gallows. The last thing she desired was any more of Society's undue attention.

The dancers had already begun twirling in elegantly graceful circles about the ballroom floor. Mayhap no one would notice. Mayhap the crush of dancers about them would obscure Abigail just enough that they'd fail to realize...

She took a deep breath and...

Lord Sinclair winced.

"Forgive me," she rushed. The tip of her slippers came down hard upon the top of his boot.

He quickly righted her, sparing her from toppling over for all to see.

Lord Sinclair smiled. "This is the most fun I've had this evening."

"Which is not saying a good deal about Lady Hughes's festivities," Abigail muttered beneath her breath, stumbling again.

He tossed his head back and his laughter echoed throughout the crowd.

Abigail peeked around the ballroom to ascertain whether Lord Sinclair's bold laughter had earned the focus of nearby dancers. After all, her intentions in coming to London were to avoid any hint of untoward behavior.

She caught a glimpse of Lord Redbrooke and Beatrice.

Lord Redbrooke scowled at Abigail and Sinclair. Heat slapped her cheeks and she yanked her attention away from Geoffrey and stared at Lord Sinclair's immaculately folded cravat.

He winced as she stepped upon his toes yet again. "I'm sorry," she said, automatically.

"Think nothing of it, Miss Stone."

Abigail silently counted. One-Two-Three, One-Two-Three. If she focused on the rhythm of the orchestra then she'd not have to notice Geoffrey as he swept her graceful cousin about the floor while she, ungainly Abigail, tried not to destroy poor Lord Sinclair's fine Hessian boots.

"Ouch."

Tried and failed.

"Forgive me."

Lord Sinclair adjusted her in his arms, shifting Abigail ever so subtly toward him, so that he bore the weight of their off-center movements.

"Oh," she said, her mouth falling open with surprise. "That is vastly better."

"For the both of us," he drawled.

"For...oh." She clamped her lips tighter than a New England clam at the suggestiveness of his words; words that reminded her of Lord Carmichael's ill-opinion and recent attack. She'd fled America in the hopes of escaping those suggestive glances.

One-Two-Three, One-Two-Three.

"Tell me, Miss Stone? Are you enjoying your time in England?"

She faltered, and again he adjusted her in his arms. "Yes." *No.* She yearned for the day she could return to her family. A pang struck her heart. That is, if she were ever able to return. She wondered not for the first time how long the scandal of being discovered in a man's arms would be gossiped about by the prominent families of their Connecticut seaside town. Mother had said forever.

Which would mean she'd never be welcomed home.

"Are you counting?"

She nodded.

"I do believe I've never partnered with a young lady who counted."

Abigail glanced up. "Oh, I'm sure the young ladies you danced with can count, my lord. They most likely just do not do it aloud."

He blinked, and then again tossed his head back and laughed. "You're a delight, Miss Stone."

You're a delight.

Alexander Powers had whispered those very words into her ear many a-time. *Foolish. Foolish.*

Fortunately, the set concluded, and Lord Sinclair's boots seemed to have survived the heavy trampling under her slippers. Wordlessly, he escorted her back to her cousin, Robert.

"Miss Stone, it was a pleasure. May I be permitted to call upon you?"

Abigail cocked her head. "Call on me?" Lord Sinclair wanted to call on her, which implied he wanted to court her, which would be utter madness—on his part. She was the ungraceful, too loud American woman with a scandalous past. He did not know that latter part, but nonetheless...

Robert spoke for her. "That would be permissible."

Lord Sinclair bowed low at the waist, and with a last lingering look for Abigail, took his leave.

"Sinclair is a decent enough gentleman," Robert said in a hushed tone.

Abigail wet her lips, not pretending to misunderstand him. "Robert..." They couldn't have this discussion. Not here. Not with all English Society's leading lords and ladies present. Her cousin did not know the full extent of what had brought her to London.

Abigail had been sent to London in the hopes she would make a match. Yet, in spite of her family's rather low opinion of her, Abigail possessed enough integrity to not trap an unsuspecting gentleman into marriage. Gentlemen had stringent expectations for a wife, and a lady who'd tossed away her virtue on an undeserving scoundrel would never make anyone a suitable bride.

She'd come to reconcile that her mistake had merited her parents hastily packing her up and shipping her off to England.

Only now, for the first time since she'd been discovered with Alexander, Abigail wished she'd made altogether different decisions, wished she was still the pure, unsullied lady worthy of an honorable and honest courtship.

Unbidden, her gaze sought out Geoffrey. He and Beatrice cut an impressive figure as they took their leave of the dance floor and made their way back to Abigail and Robert.

It hadn't mattered that she was unfit for a gentleman—until now. Until Lord Redbrooke had tugged free her scrap of Italian lace from under Lord Carmichael's boot and held it out to her.

Now, it seemed to matter, too much.

Geoffrey bowed over Beatrice's hand, and then turned to Abigail. "May I have this dance?" Geoffrey asked curtly.

His harsh, angry tone hardly belonged to a man who desired her company. Abigail inclined her head. "I fear with your seriousness, my lord, you'd only be appalled by my shocking lack of talent and grace."

The firm, square line of his jaw hardened. "Are you denying my request?" He spoke with the conviction of a man whose status had clearly grown him accustomed to having his wishes met.

She tipped her chin up. "Is it a request, my lord?"

Beatrice and Robert's gazes moved from Abigail to Geoffrey.

"Is that a reply, Miss Stone?"

She felt the warm flush of color suffuse her cheeks. Goodness, with his directness, the man was unconscionable.

She glanced down and quickly looked over her card. Of course he'd gathered from before that her next set was available.

Why would the Lady Essex's orchestra play a second waltz? Still considered scandalous, the dance would require Geoffrey to take her in his arms. Her eyes flew to his, and he arched a brow in unspoken challenge.

Abigail tilted her chin back. She'd braved the cut direct from Connecticut's leading families, been shamed before her family; she'd not be cowed by this man's effrontery.

He held his arm out, and as they were attracting the notice of those around him, Abigail placed her fingertips along his sleeve and allowed him to guide her onto the dance floor. They took their position among the other dancers.

"I was not jesting when I said I am a deplorable dancer," she murmured as the orchestra began to play.

"No. I observed as much in your set with Lord Sinclair," Geoffrey's words dripped with a cool indifference. His gaze remained fixed upon the top of her head.

Oh, the wretch.

Abigail ground her heel atop his slipper. "Oh, pardon me."

With his veneer of icy coolness, Geoffrey made Abigail wonder whether she'd imagined the chivalrous gentleman who'd rescued her last evening.

Some emotion, volatile and hot, blazed to life in his eyes.

No. This was in fact, the same man.

His firm lips, which seemed sculpted in a perpetual frown, deepened, and his chestnut brown eyebrows knitted into a single line, indicating that he'd accurately gathered her misstep had been intentional. "I must admit, Miss Stone, I believed you would have provided one excuse or another to avoid dancing with me."

His words sent her back upright, and she angled her head. Did he suppose she was intimidated by his churlish behavior "Do you expect I should be embarrassed by my lack of skill?" She didn't allow him to respond. "I'm neither a coward, nor a liar, my lord." There was the matter of secrecy on her scandal with Alexander Powers, but that was entirely different. Her silence was no lie, but rather a desperate bid at survival. The world was not kind where fallen women were concerned. She didn't expect this proud, proper man would be at all different.

Geoffrey shifted her in his arms. "Tell me, Miss Stone, is dancing not an art perfected by American ladies?"

She blinked innocently up at him. "Oh, yes, my lord, by rule American ladies do not dance. Nor do they embroider or paint."

He leveled her closer, and lowered his head so that his breath, a blend of mint and brandy, fanned her cheek. "Are you making light of me, Miss Stone?"

Abigail suspected Geoffrey was not a man used to being insulted. "You are very serious."

"I am."

Her lips twitched at his succinct reply.

"You find fault in a gentleman who values respectability."

She stumbled, and he expertly righted her. "Miss Stone?" he prodded.

"I find fault in a gentleman incapable of humor," she countered. Abigail trailed her gaze over the angular planes of his face. A muscle at the corner of his mouth twitched, an indication that he'd been affected by her subtle insult.

His lip pulled back in a condescending sneer. "And are American gentlemen a humorous lot?"

She again faltered as his words ripped through her already ravaged heart; his unknowing reminder of one American *gentleman* who had been quick to smile and had teased her mercilessly. "They are," she said.

Fortunately she was saved from further questioning. The music drew to a close, and Abigail and Geoffrey stopped amidst the dance floor, studying one another. Never before had Abigail been more grateful for the end of a set. She dropped a curtsy. "Good evening, my lord. Thank you for the dance."

And before he could reply, she turned on her heel and fled.

Geoffrey Winters, Viscount Redbrooke posed a danger to her frayed emotions and she would be wise to avoid him.

Abigail grasped the sides of her skirts and crushed the smooth, satin fabric within her fingers.

Then, she'd never been wise were gentlemen were concerned.

SEVEN

A gentleman should rise at a respectable hour and be fruitful with his time.
4ᵗʰ Viscount Redbrooke

Geoffrey stepped out of his carriage, his gaze trained on the Duke of Somerset's townhouse. Following Lord and Lady Essex's ball, he'd taken his leave with a renewed sense of commitment to his plans of wedding Lady Beatrice Dennington. One sole dance with Abigail Stone had served to remind him of the perils of a headstrong miss with cheeky retorts.

So then, why did he relish the possibility of again seeing the winsome beauty? As he strode up the duke's steps, he gave his head a hard shake. His reaction to the lady was utter madness.

He'd been unable to rid himself of the memory of her; the pale glow of moonlight kissing the generous crest of her décolletage, or her laugh better suited to bedroom games and naughty deeds.

Geoffrey cursed, and climbed the handful of steps to the threshold of the Duke of Somerset's door. He shifted the bouquet of hothouse flowers he held, over to his other hand, and knocked on the front doors of the impressive smooth-finished, cream-colored stucco townhouse.

His back fairly prickled with the fascinated eyes of those lords and ladies out at this fashionable hour. The news of his courtship of Lady Beatrice had surely already found its way into the scandal sheets. Geoffrey frowned, detesting the scrutiny.

The door opened. A butler in fine red livery apparel and a powdered wig greeted him.

Geoffrey held out his card. "To see Lady Beatrice Dennington."

The butler looked down at the card, and inclined his head. "If you'll follow me, Lady Beatrice is receiving callers."

Geoffrey's frown grew as he followed the butler. He liked the idea of competing for Lady Beatrice's affection even less than he cared for the unwanted attention he'd received on the duke's front steps. Geoffrey would rather not compete for the lady's affections. After all, it would only serve to complicate his courtship and interfere with the strict timeline he'd set to have his marital affairs in order.

The butler paused beside a door. "The Viscount Redbrooke, my lady."

Seated upon a chintz sofa at the center of the room, Lady Beatrice looked up from her needlework, a perfectly acceptable ladylike talent. She stood so quickly her embroidery frame toppled to the floor. A flash of something akin to disappointment flared in her eyes.

"My lord," she murmured.

Geoffrey entered the room, and stopped beside her. He bowed, holding the artfully arranged flowers out to her. "My lady."

She accepted them with a quiet thanks and motioned for him to sit.

Geoffrey claimed the seat nearest her, and proceeded to study her.

His mind turned over all manner of appropriate discourse. He beat his hand along the side of his leg. "We've been enjoying lovely weather." He winced inwardly at his paltry attempt at discourse.

Lady Beatrice nodded. Her gaze flickered over to the window and then back to him. "Yes. Yes we have," she said softly.

Silence fell.

It stretched on, thick and unending, punctuated by the tick-tock-tick-tock of the ormolu clock atop the fireplace mantle. Lady Beatrice's fingers plucked at the upholstery of the velvet sofa she occupied, a telltale indication of her discomfort.

Well, surely most matches amongst the *ton* began with such discomfiture. Geoffrey supposed it should take several more visits before they were comfortable in one another's presence.

Her cousin, the lovely Abigail, danced through his mind. He imagined the bold-spirited young lady would fill such a void with lively chatter and unrestrained laughter.

A sound of impatience rumbled up from in his chest.

"My lord?" Lady Beatrice's halting question jerked him back to the moment.

"Uh-I beg your pardon?"

Silence.

His mind drifted back to his first meeting with Abigail Stone.

Dionysus.

What had she meant with that single utterance?

Perhaps he should revisit the Greek classics and reacquaint himself with the details of that particular myth. Not because it mattered per se, but because a gentleman should be versed in...

"My lord, are you all right?" Lady Beatrice asked, her head tilted at a small angle.

"Yes. Fine." He resisted the urge to pull out his watch fob and consult the time. Now that he'd launched his courtship of Lady Beatrice, he could see to his other matters for the day. There were the ledgers that needed going over. A trip to Gentleman Jackson's. Except a round with the legendary Jackson only put him in mind of Carmichael's attack on Abigail; the panicked light in her eyes, the exposed flesh of her full, cream-white breasts, the...He gripped the edges of the seat so tight he left crescent marks upon the gold velvet fabric of the King Louis chair he occupied.

Geoffrey took a deep breath filled with the sudden urge to hunt down Lord Carmichael and bloody the reprobate bastard senseless.

Lady Beatrice leaned down and retrieved her embroidery frame. She longingly studied the vibrant threaded floral arrangement upon the fabric and it occurred to him that the young lady would rather be seeing to her needlework than keeping company with him.

The realization should chafe. He frowned. Yet, oddly her indifference left him wholly unaffected.

"You embroider," he said, in a desperate bid to engage the woman he'd selected for his future Viscountess Redbrooke.

"I do."

Well, the young lady certainly wasn't making this visit any more comfortable.

A sharp burst of laughter followed by a deep chuckle from outside the parlor interrupted their stilted exchange.

Geoffrey's gaze shot to the doorway where Miss Stone stood alongside her cousin, the Marquess Westfield.

"I say, Abby. I find all that rather hard to…" The marquess registered Geoffrey's presence. His amusement died, only to be replaced by an inscrutable expression that conveyed neither approval nor disdain. "We have company. Or, Beatrice has company. Redbrooke," he greeted.

In a frantic attempt to keep from tracing each line of Abigail's face, Geoffrey rose, his gaze trained on Westfield.

When Geoffrey managed to convince himself that his interest in Miss Stone was that of the same curiosity reserved for an act at Piccadilly Square, and not of any real masculine interest, he allowed himself to look at her.

God punish him as a liar.

Abigail Stone smiled, as if she knew he lied to himself.

And to Lady Beatrice.

Lady Beatrice rose in a flurry of ivory skirts, and rushed over to Miss Stone. "Dearest, Abigail, you remember Lord Redbrooke from last evening, don't you?"

Abigail dipped a curtsy. "I do."

He expected her to drop her gaze as Lady Beatrice and any respectable young English miss might. Instead, she unflinchingly met his stare, a fiery glitter in her eyes; eyes that put him in mind of a summer storm.

"Miss Stone."

She curtsied. "My lord."

"You must regale Lord Redbrooke and me with your story," Lady Beatrice insisted. She took Abigail by the hands and guided her over to the sofa she'd occupied mere moments ago, all but dismissing Geoffrey.

"Abigail has the most brilliant stories," Westfield said, sinking into the seat across from Geoffrey. He waved over to Abigail. "You must finish, Abby."

"Oh, please do," Lady Beatrice said, scooting to the edge of her seat and with the light in her eyes, she was more animated than she'd been since Geoffrey had entered the Duke of Somerset's parlor.

Abigail looked to Geoffrey. "I'm sure Lord Redbrooke doesn't want to hear a story about a squirrel."

Yes, at any other time, told by any other person, he imagined that would be an accurate statement. Not here. Not now. Not with this woman. "I would care to hear your tale." Three pairs of eyes swung in his direction, all filled with varying degrees of shock. "I would," he said, a touch defensively. Not normally one for storytelling; especially potentially improper stories about foreign creatures, told by engaging young ladies, Geoffrey found this time, he cared to hear her particular tale.

She smiled at him and it transformed her from stunning goddess to ethereal creature memorialized in songs and sonnets by great poets.

"Well, you see, the summer months in Connecticut are quite unbearable. Mother insists we adhere to propriety and leave the doors and windows closed, even if it means we all nearly swelter to our deaths. Last year, Mama was visiting a neighbor one afternoon and Papa instructed the servants to open all the windows and doors."

Lord Westfield grinned. "And?"

"And," she continued. "A squirrel darted through the front door and ran the servants on a ragged chase through the house. Papa's dogs, two, more than slightly overweight sheepdogs, believed the squirrel to be some form of sheep or another and ran the poor little creature around the house." She gesticulated wildly. "He climbed up Mama's curtains and tore the lace beyond repair." Abigail caught Geoffrey's eye and bold as you please, winked. "Needless to say, that was the last time Papa had the doors and windows open."

Geoffrey frowned.

Abigail arched a brow. "Is there a problem, my lord?"

Boldness must be a character trait reserved for Americans.

"It would seem if your father had left the windows and doors closed, that your mother's lace curtains would be intact."

She waggled a brow at him. "I do believe that is what makes the story amusing, my lord." There was no mistaking the reproachful note threading her thinly veiled admonition. "You are rather serious, my lord."

Lady Beatrice gasped, the delicate sound drowned out by her brother's sharp bark of laughter.

"There is something unseemly in being proper and respectable, Miss Stone?" Geoffrey challenged.

She sat forward on the edge of her seat. "If you say so, my lord."

He blinked. "I beg your pardon?"

"There is no need to apologize. I agree."

Geoffrey folded his arms across his chest. "I meant my words as a question. Not a statement."

Abigail leaned back in her seat. "Ahh."

"Ahh?"

She smiled. "Is that another question? Or another statement, my lord?"

"Do behave, Abby," Lady Beatrice said, gently.

Abigail glanced over at Beatrice. "Even if it is very fun teasing Lord Redbrooke?"

Lady Beatrice's eyes went even rounder in her face.

It took a long moment for Geoffrey's head to cease spinning.

Westfield, who up to that point, seemed to entertain the possibility of tossing Geoffrey out on his arse, gave him a commiserative look.

Suddenly, filled with a desperate urgency to place much needed space between himself and Abigail Stone, Geoffrey turned to Lady Beatrice. "My lady, will you accompany me for a walk in Hyde Park?"

Silence met his terse request. Bloody hell, he must apply a bit more romanticism to his courtship. Ladies required romanticism. He silently added that to the list he'd compiled for courting a very marriageable miss.

"It is lovely out," she murmured, and damn if it didn't sound as though the young lady were trying to work up the resolve to join him. Her eyes lit up, suddenly. "Abby you must accompany us. And you, as well, Robert."

Hell. That most certainly hadn't been part of Geoffrey's plans for the afternoon. He expected in any moment she'd begin issuing invites to the chambermaids and footmen to spare her from his solitary company.

Geoffrey couldn't imagine anything more disastrous than the tempting Abigail Stone joining them on their outing.

"That would be lovely," Abigail said, with far greater conviction than her cousin, the distinguished Lady Beatrice had exhibited mere moments ago.

And damn if his blasted heart didn't lift at the prospect of her joining them.

EIGHT

A gentleman must demonstrate restraint and calm in all matters.
4th Viscount Redbrooke.

Abigail, Beatrice, her cousin Robert, and the Viscount Redbrooke strolled along a walking path in Hyde Park that overlooked the wide man-made lake filled with pink pelicans and elegant white swans.

With the tip of her finger, Abigail tapped her chin.

There were fourteen men. Seven women. She wrinkled her brow and mentally tabulated figures again. No, there were *eight* women. She'd forgotten Cassiopeia. Mustn't forget the vain beauty who'd been forced to sacrifice her only daughter to atone for that vanity. Sixteen, Seventeen, Eighteen land animals. "Nineteen," she amended.

"Nineteen what?" Robert asked, shooting her a sideways glance.

"Land animals," she murmured.

Robert glanced around, as if searching for the nineteen creatures she'd mentioned.

Abigail smiled, grateful he didn't ask further questions about her odd tendency of cataloguing the mythical creatures that made up part of the Greek constellations.

Robert leaned down the several inches separating them in height. "It appears Redbrooke would like to make a match with Beatrice."

Abigail stumbled a bit and her cousin steadied her.

"Beatrice won't have Lord Redbrooke, not if he were the last titled gentleman in all the kingdom," he whispered.

As though Lord Redbrooke sensed he were the subject of discussion, he glanced over his shoulder. That familiar, dark frown lined the harsh planes of his face before he redirected his attention on the path in front of them. With his somberness and stern demeanor, Geoffrey could not be more different than Alexander Powers. Alexander had possessed a light sense of humor, so vastly different than the often grave viscount.

"Are you very familiar with Lord Redbrooke?" she asked, unable to quell the urge to know more about the hardened young lord.

Robert lifted one shoulder in a shrug. "He's a stodgy fellow. But he wasn't always that way. We attended Oxford in the same years." He grinned. "Many considered him something of a rogue, then." He dropped his voice to a low whisper. "There were rumors of a young woman who'd captured his affection, but I'm not privy to the details. No one is."

Robert fell silent, and she bit the inside of her cheek to keep from pressing him for further details.

Just then, Beatrice let loose a startled shriek and stumbled. She pitched forward with a small cry but before she collapsed amid the rocks and gravel of the path, Geoffrey caught her.

Abigail breathed a small sigh of envy, and then remembered herself. Goodness, she was daft as a ninny. "Beatrice! Are you all right?" She rushed over to her cousin's side.

The viscount cradled Beatrice close to his chest.

Thick, ugly tendrils of guilt wrapped their cloying hooks about Abigail's heart, which she shoved aside, shamed at the petty sentiments.

Tears filled Beatrice's pretty blue eyes. "How silly I am. I believe I turned my ankle."

"Not silly at all," the viscount murmured. He seemed to waver, alternating his gaze between Beatrice and the marquess. It occurred to Abigail he wanted to inspect Beatrice for injury but hesitated to do so, probably out of fear of the impropriety of touching her cousin.

Again, Abigail's stomach tightened at the idea of Lord Redbrooke learning of her scandalous actions in America.

Robert scooped up his sister. "Rather careless of you, Bea," he muttered.

Ever the model of ladylike decorum, Beatrice dropped her gaze to her brother's cravat.

"Don't be silly," Abigail hurried to assure them. "I'm sure you stepped upon a rabbit hole or..." She glanced down at the untouched earth. Her gaze collided with Beatrice, who gave her a desperate look. Abigail's eyes widened as she realized her cousin had feigned an injury. "Or perhaps a large rock, or some such, that caused you to fall." Beatrice mouthed a silent *thank you.*

"Abigail, why don't you continue walking? It is ever so beautiful out and it would hardly be fair to require you to abandon your outing," Beatrice said.

Geoffrey blanched.

Abigail's eyes narrowed. "I'm sure the viscount has more important matters to see to than walking with me around Hyde Park."

She expected him to offer at least a haphazard protestation. When it became apparent he didn't intend to say anything on the matter, she wrinkled her brow. *Oh, the ninnyhammer.* He appeared incapable of even feigning polite interest in escorting her on the remainder of the stroll.

Not that she wanted him to pretend, per se.

She did, however, not care to be made to feel less than an afterthought.

"Now, you're being silly. The viscount would be glad to accompany you. Isn't that right, my lord?" Beatrice directed her question to Geoffrey, who stood, arms clasped behind his back, his face a stoic mask. Beatrice didn't wait for him to respond, but motioned to the servant who'd accompanied them. "Please remain with my cousin Miss Stone and Lord Redbrooke. My brother will see me home."

"That really isn't necessary." Abigail's words sounded a touch too-pleading to her own ears.

"Oh, I insist." Beatrice tapped her brother on the arm.

Abigail folded her arms across her chest, tapping her foot upon the ground as Beatrice and Robert took their leave.

In the distance, Beatrice peeked out from behind her brother's shoulder, and winked.

Abigail let out a beleaguered sigh.

It would appear she was to be alone with Lord Proper...whether either of them wished it or not.

A breeze tugged at her skirts, and freed a strand of her hair from the Italian lace woven through her hair by her maid. Abigail surveyed the swans and pelicans that flitted about the wide, man-made lake. Abigail touched her fingers to the delicate strip of fabric and forced herself to look at Lord Redbrooke.

He stood, his large frame immobile, as if he feared any movement would cause him to splinter into a thousand million pieces.

He glanced back toward the direction Beatrice and Robert had disappeared.

"Are you afraid of me, my lord?"

Geoffrey's gaze snapped back to her. Annoyance glittered in his eyes. "I beg your pardon?"

She smiled up at him, and then dipped her voice to a conspiratorial whisper. "I assure you, you need not fear being alone with me. I'll not bite." Abigail held out her arm.

Geoffrey stared at her like she was the mythical sea monster, Ketos. He stared so long she began to feel rather foolish standing there with her arm out to him, for all the passing English lords and ladies to see. She lowered her arm but met his gaze directly. She'd not be cowed or humiliated by an English lord. Not when she'd come here for an attempt at a fresh start for past transgressions.

"I didn't think you would," he said at last. And closed the small distance between them. This time, he extended his arm.

"Excuse me?"

"I didn't think you would bite," he clarified.

Her lips twitched. She hesitated a moment, and then placed her fingertips along the sleeves of his coat. "I was merely jesting," she murmured. "Are you always so serious, Geoffrey?" she asked, when they began strolling along the walking path.

"Yes."

She stole a peek up at him. "And laconic?"

"Yes." Pause. "And it wouldn't do for you to be overheard calling me by my Christian name."

The crunch of gravel beneath his booted feet and her slippers filled the quiet.

"That might be true." She winked up at him. "But I plan to do so, just the same." This man had saved her from Lord Carmichael's unwanted attention. He'd seen her shamed and humbled at his feet. It seemed odd to think of him by any name other than his Christian name.

Abigail stopped, and forced Lord Redbrooke to either halt, or drag her down to the ground. "I wanted to thank you for your intervention at Lord Hughes's ball."

The muscles under the fabric of his coat tightened, and for a long moment, it seemed he might not respond. Perhaps the decorous gentleman had been appalled at having come upon her as he had that night. She disentangled her arm from his and wandered several steps ahead, needing to place distance between them, uncomfortable with the idea of his scorn.

Except there was no scorn in Geoffrey's tone as he spoke. "There is no need to thank me, Miss Stone. I would have intervened for any young lady in your…circumstance."

Abigail walked to the edge of the lake. She studied the short flight of a swan as it glided upon the water's surface and dunked its head a long while before emerging with a fish in its mouth. She believed Geoffrey would have come to the aid of any woman who'd been in a like situation. And yet, it hadn't been just any woman he'd rescued.

He'd rescued her.

"You saved me from certain ruin," she said, softly. If he hadn't come upon Lord Carmichael…she shuddered, there was no doubt he would have violated her.

Gravel crunched under Geoffrey's feet, indicating he'd closed the space between them. "Do not make more of it then there was, Miss Stone. I'm no hero. I merely came to the aid of an innocent young woman, as any gentleman would."

The unknowing reminder of her sullied virtue burned like vinegar tossed onto an open wound,

She expected she should be deterred by his almost scathing tone. "I'm not a naïve young miss, my lord. I'm not so foolish as to believe in fairytales." And most certainly not in the silly dream of a hero. She peered at him from the corner of her eye.

He caught his chin between his thumb and forefinger and proceeded to study her like she were an oddity he couldn't identify. "I thought all young ladies believed in fairytales."

She snorted. "Only the silly young ladies do."

He fell silent.

Abigail stared pensively out at the fowl swimming about the lake. "They're beautiful, aren't they?"

Geoffrey looked around.

"The swans," she clarified.

"Hmm."

"I'm certain there is no more lovely sight than the swan etched in the night sky."

"I'm certain you are wrong," he said, with a softness she didn't expect of him. Then with his next sentence, cool haughtiness replaced all imagined warmth. "And, swans are not *etched* in the night sky."

"Do you know, they say Cygnus took on the body of a swan, giving up his immortality and all hope of a normal life, all to save his friend?"

Geoffrey snorted. "A foolhardy thing to do."

"He did it because he loved him."

"Mores the fool he."

At the cynical twist to his words, Abigail glanced up. There was something so very hard, so very unyielding in those four words. It confirmed her earlier suspicions that this man had known pain. "Do you not believe in love, Geoffrey?"

"I thought you didn't believe in fairytales, Miss Stone," he shot back.

She folded her arms across her chest. "I'd not considered the Greek myths a fairytale, Geoffrey."

"Lord Redbrooke," he automatically corrected. He peered down his aquiline nose at her. "And, you appear to be splitting hairs."

"You never answered my question as to whether you believed in love. Are you being deliberately evasive, *my lord?*" She detected the imperceptible tightening at the corners of his mouth and suspected there was merit in her charge.

"I believe emotions such as love only disrupt a well-ordered world."

Yes, her great folly with Alexander was proof of that…and yet, deep inside, part of her dreamed of that elusive, beautiful sentiment.

She looked out at the swan as it dunked its long neck under the water's surface once more. "A well-ordered world is a dull world, Geoffrey." Abigail felt his heated gaze upon her and she looked up at his stern countenance. "Do you know what I believe?" She didn't wait for him to respond. "I believe you are very different than the stern, too-proper figure you present to Polite Society. I believe under the veneer of propriety, you are a man of passion and humor…and…"

Something ruthless and unforgiving flashed in his eyes, and the remainder of her words died upon her lips.

"Considering you've known me but several days, you presume a great deal." His tone was harsh.

Abigail tipped her chin up a notch. "With your cool rigidity, you make it seem as though there is something wrong in finding joy in life."

He leaned close, so his lips were a mere hairsbreadth from hers. "Do not speak of what you don't know, Miss Stone."

She raised a single, black brow. "I know that for all the struggle and difficulty I've known, a life without joy is a life not worth living."

His jaw hardened. "So you've known struggles and difficulty, Miss Stone?" he asked, his words as satiny as the smooth edge of a blade. "Is that what has brought you to England?"

Her stomach clenched uncomfortably at how remarkably close to the mark his well-placed question had come. Still, she refused to be cowed by his questioning. "I did not say that."

"You needn't have to. It is written in those creased little lines at the corners of your eyes."

Abigail took a step away from him. Then another. And another. She pressed her palm to her breast, noting the way his gaze fell to the slight swell of bosom revealed by her modest sapphire blue muslin dress.

"Ahh, so that is it."

He was as relentless as a hunter stalking its prey.

"You're wrong." She'd braved the scorn of her American compatri-ots. She could not countenance having to weather the very same scan-dal. Abigail willed strength back into her spine. She tipped her chin up, and took a step toward him so the mere span of a hand separated their bodies. "I'm merely here visiting my uncle."

Geoffrey inclined his head. "Do you know, Miss Stone, I find I don't believe you. You seem to me a woman of many secrets."

Warning bells went off at the accuracy of his supposition.

Not many secrets. Rather one secret. One very shameful, damning, and damaging secret. She should be filled with terror at how very close Geoffrey had come to the truth. Abigail wet her lips. Instead, she was nothing more than a shameful creature unable to take her eyes from the broad width of his shoulders, the thick corded muscles of his arms, the sun-kissed, olive hue of his skin.

He lowered his head, his breath fanned her cheeks.

Another breeze wafted over them. It caught the strand of lace woven through her hair and the fabric danced to the ground, mocking her shameful wantonness.

The magical pull between them shattered, Abigail dashed ahead, reaching for the precious lace, but the wind caught it and carried it further down the walking path. She hurried after it, but Mother Nature seemed to be playing a cruel kind of game. The fabric slipped through Abigail's fingers. The wind continued to carry it along. She gasped as another breeze carried the precious gift from home out onto the lake.

"No," she cried, and took a step toward the edge of the water. Water touched the tips of her satin slippers.

Geoffrey came to stop alongside her. His gaze moved from her to the lace atop the smooth surface of the water. "It is just a piece of fabric, Miss Stone."

"It's not," she said. She'd not expect him to understand.

"It appears as though it is," he drawled.

"My sister gave it to me," she blurted. "She told me to touch it whenever I was lonely and missing my family. She…" Abigail took a deep breath, knowing how silly she must sound waxing on about the seemingly insignificant piece.

Geoffrey was indeed correct; it was nothing more than a small piece of fabric, but to Abigail it represented the fragile thread that connected her to the family she'd been forced to leave behind. "I know it seems utterly fool…"

Geoffrey cursed. He bent down and tugged at his black Hessian boot.

She gasped. "What are you doing?"

He tossed the boot aside, and reached for his other foot. "Retrieving the blasted thing," he muttered. "Can't have you crying in public. People will assume I've reduced you to tears. Gossip will spread," he mumbled, and waded into the water.

Abigail swallowed back the laughter that bubbled in her throat as Geoffrey picked his way through the water.

He glared over his shoulder, back at her. His foot slid out from under him and he flung his arms out in a futile attempt to stop his fall. "Bloody hell."

Abigail clamped her hands over lips, horrification and humor blended as one. Nearby lords and ladies gasped and halted to observe Lord Redbrooke's display.

He rose out of the shallow depths. Water ran in rivulets from his soaked chestnut locks, down his rugged cheeks. His coat, hopelessly beyond repair, hung open, displaying the translucent water-dampened fabric of his white cambric shirt.

He glowered at the voyeurs witnesses to this great spectacle and they had the good sense to scurry off.

Abigail rushed over. "My lord, I don't know what to say. I…"

He held out his dripping hand and displayed the slip of lace, clasped between his thumb and forefinger, more precious than the crown of diamonds Dionysus had given his Ariadne. "Here." Geoffrey waved it about.

Abigail grasped it with her fingers. Her throat moved up and down as she fought back a swell of emotion. Geoffrey had rescued her first from certain ruin and now, he'd sacrificed his fine attire and braved the censure of passing members of Society, all to save her piece of lace.

"Thank you."

She blinked. "I'm sorry?"

"You can simply say thank you."

A giggle burst past her lips. She tried desperately to quell the inappropriate expression of mirth. After all, considering his scandalous actions it hardly conveyed suitable appreciation.

Geoffrey's eyes narrowed, apparently of like mind.

"Th-th…thank you," she managed between deep gasping breaths of laughter. She clutched the Italian lace to her chest, all amusement dying at the hard-indecipherable expression he leveled upon her.

Her toes curled in the soles of her slippers. In America, she'd become accustomed to the gentleman's gentle smiles and the teasing light in their eyes. There was nothing soft, or teasing about Geoffrey. He was as different from Alexander as the day sky was from the night.

Perhaps that explained the tug of unwarranted and unwanted interest in Lord Redbrooke…the gentleman who'd been quite clear in his intentions for her cousin, Beatrice. Beatrice, however, had been equally clear that she'd little interest in making a match with the viscount.

Silent pity filled her with the knowledge that Beatrice would never welcome his intentions.

Abigail shifted back and forth upon her feet. "You should return home."

He arched a single, icy, *wet* brow. "Are you suggesting we not finish our walk?"

"Well, no. Not considering the state of…oh, you're making light of me."

Hmm. So it appeared, Geoffrey did have some degree of humor. Even if the firm set to his mouth and frown at the corners of his eyes suggested him incapable of cheerfulness.

Abigail studied the lace in her hands, and then looked up to find Geoffrey's heated gaze trained upon the distracted movement of her fingers.

"You should leave, Miss Stone."

She tilted her head back and leaned closed, whispering, "In light of last evening, and today, do you still believe we shouldn't call one another by our Christian names?"

"It..."

She held her fingers up, so close to his mouth they might as well have been touching, so close, that the hot, seductive scent of brandy upon his breath fanned her skin. "...wouldn't be proper," she finished for him.

If they hadn't been so close she might have failed to note the way his throat bobbed up and down, the first real indication that Lord Redbrooke, Geoffrey, was not as indifferent toward her, as he led her, and mayhap himself, to believe. But she was this close. And she saw it.

He yanked his stare to a point beyond her shoulder. "Madam, we are in public. And you are making a spectacle of you and me. If it hasn't been clear to you before this point, I have launched a formal courtship of your cousin, with the intention of marriage to Lady Beatrice. Therefore any of this improper closeness and attention you are demonstrating is to cease immediately. Is that clear?"

Her stomach clenched at the pained reminder of his interest in Beatrice, and more than that...the clear condemnation in his eyes, that indicated he'd judged her and found her wanting. In that moment, she forgot about his rescue at Lord and Lady Hughes's and his recovery of the scrap of lace given her by Lizzie. In that moment, she hated him for making her feel less than the gravel under his sopping boot. And more, she hated herself for having given away her virtue to Alexander Powers and proven this pompous lord correct.

"It is abundantly clear," she said, when she trusted herself to speak. "Thank you for the lace, my lord. I bid you good day."

Abigail remembered to dip a curtsy. The servant who'd been hovering discreetly in the distance rushed to keep up with Abigail. As she fled, Geoffrey's heated gaze fairly scorched a hole upon her retreating frame.

NINE

A gentleman does not engage in common activities. Ever.
4th Viscount Redbrooke

"**M**y goodness, Geoffrey! Whatever have you done?" his mother screeched as Geoffrey sailed through the front doors of his townhouse, leaving a trail of puddles in his wake.

He stomped past her indignant frame and started up the stairs.

"Geoffrey!" she called, from the bottom step. He paused, and spun about so quickly he sent bits of water spraying. His mother gasped as water landed upon her cheek. She brushed it back as though he'd tossed a dead trout at her person.

He didn't suspect Abigail Stone would be so shocked by the feel of water upon her skin. Quite the opposite, really. He imagined she'd embrace the cooling feel of it. All manner of wicked yearnings filled him, all of which involved Abigail Stone laid out upon satin sheets, her arms open, her…

"Did you hear what I said, Geoffrey?" His mother's harsh question jerked him back to the moment.

"No." He continued his climb.

"Geoffrey," his mother cried. The soft thread of her slippers upon the marble steps confirmed her pursuit.

He hurried his steps.

"A kitchen maid heard from Lord Carmichael's groom that you went swimming at Hyde Park, and were touching that, that American woman. Whatever were you thinking? It is unfortunate enough I had to expect such scandals from your sister, but…you…?"

Geoffrey stopped so suddenly, his mother stumbled against him. He wanted to toss his head back and snarl at the mere mention of Lord Carmichael, that reprobate bastard. To think he'd ever considered for even an infinitesimal moment, wedding his sister Sophie to that fiend. He held a finger up. "First, I did not go for a swim. I fell into the lake." A bloody lake he'd rushed into. That, however, was neither here nor there. "Second, that American woman is the cousin of the Duke of Somerset and some respect should be afforded the lady for the connection to that distinguished title."

Considering any further discussion on the matter officially ended, Geoffrey continued his march. He reached the main hall when his mother called out to him.

"You do know what they say about American women. Nothing proper. They are a scandalous lot, Geoffrey. Why, even her name, Abigail. What decent Englishman and woman name their daughter after a lady's maid?"

He fisted his hands, as a thin haze of rage descended over his vision. Geoffrey tamped down the immediate defense that sprung to his lips. To do so, however, would encourage Mother's argument. And he'd long tired of discussing the matter with his mother.

Unfortunately, she seemed quite eager to continue the rather one-sided discourse. "You are the last male in line for the Redbrooke title. You mustn't do something as...as foolhardy as to sully the title with American bloodlines. Why, her father is a footman."

"Was a footman."

Her eyes flew open with shocked outrage at his insolent response. "Are you making light of this situation?"

"I wouldn't dare."

Her eyes narrowed as if trying to determine the veracity of his words.

"Mother, I'm wet. And cold." He held a staying hand up when she made to speak. "I have no intention of wedding Miss Stone. I was retrieving something for the lady and I fell. There is nothing more to it than that. My interest lies with Lady Beatrice."

Mother's mouth formed a small moue of surprise. She blinked. "Truly? Because last evening the gossips reported your interest in that…Miss Stone, creature. I observed you myself, Geoffrey. You were staring."

He gritted his teeth. "I do not stare." Last evening he had. However, in the light of day he chose to blame such an uncharacteristic reaction on too much champagne. Only, he hadn't had any spirits that morning, so how did one account for actions at Hyde Park? Geoffrey continued on toward his chambers.

His mother quickened her pace in a very un-viscountess-like manner to meet his long strides. "You are absolutely brilliant then! Why, of course Lady Beatrice, who is a perfect match for you, would be so very grateful that you should have helped her cousin retrieve…" Her brow furrowed. "What is it you helped the young woman retrieve?"

"A piece of lace," he said, automatically, not thinking about how foolish his actions would appear until he'd spoken them aloud. Only, it hadn't been any mere scrap of fabric but rather a token given by her family before she'd journeyed to London. Surely such an item merited him wading into the lake with all of Polite Society staring on?

They reached the door to Geoffrey's chambers.

His mother wrinkled her nose. "Hmph. Regardless, it must have mattered to the young lady, and Lady Beatrice will surely know as much and be so grateful and…"

"Good day, Mother," he muttered, and turned the handle. He closed the door on his mother's indignant gasp, and locked it for good measure. The viscountess' tenacity would have driven Boney to defeat faster than the whole of the British infantry and navy together.

He dropped his forehead against the wood panel of the door and banged it ever so slightly.

For a brief, too brief, moment on the walking path alongside the lake, Geoffrey had wanted to dip his head, and lay claim to her full lips, explore the hot, wet, cavern of her mouth.

Instead, he'd gone and leveled reprehensible accusations about her public behavior and demeanor. Geoffrey could name just two other times he'd truly hated himself; following his father's death and Emma's betrayal…and now, he could add his haughty treatment of Abigail to that list.

Geoffrey dragged a hand through his hair, his mother's admonition blended with his own sense of responsibility. His interest in Abigail, though bothersome, could be explained by the obvious desirability of the winsome beauty. He valued respectability, but hell, he was still a flesh and blood man.

If he were to secure Lady Beatrice's hand and affections, it would serve him well not to be linked in the scandal sheets to Miss Stone's name...and it would also serve him to be free of scandal. The Duke of Somerset by the very nature of his title and status in Society could secure the most advantageous match...and, Geoffrey was already at a disadvantage with a mere viscounty.

A knock sounded at the door.

"Who the hell..." he took a deep breath, remembering himself. "Yes," he called through the wood panel.

"My lord, I've arranged a bath and..."

Geoffrey unlocked the door and pulled it open. His valet Williamson stumbled forward. The young servant's eyes widened at the sight of Geoffrey standing there in his ruined Hessians and soaked garments. He seemed to remember himself and motioned to the small army of servants bearing a tub and steaming buckets of water.

Geoffrey shrugged out of his soaked jacket and tossed it aside. Williamson caught it before it hit the velvet-like material of the burgundy Wilton carpet. His valet eyed the thoroughly ruined material as though he'd just been handed the body of his sole heir.

Moments later, the servants paraded out of the room until only Williamson remained. "Will you be remaining in, my lord or going out."

"I'll be visiting my clubs."

"Very well, my lord." Williamson rushed to select Geoffrey's attire.

Geoffrey hurried through his ablutions and a short while later assessed himself in the bevel glass. Properly attired in a brown coat, striped linen waistcoat, and fawn trousers there could be no mistaking this man as the fool who'd toppled over in Hyde Park. He gave a pleased nod, and accepted the top hat with its curled brim from Williamson. A trip to White's and several glasses of brandy were in order.

With that in mind he left, hurrying through his house before Mother could harangue him over his seeming interest in Miss Abigail Stone.

Williamson had clearly been so intuitive as to anticipate Geoffrey's intentions, for when he made his way to the foyer, the butler Ralston handed Geoffrey his black cloak. "Your horse has been readied," Ralston murmured, glancing pointedly around the foyer.

The viscountess must be near.

Geoffrey nodded and hurried out the door to the waiting groom, who extended the reins of Geoffrey's mount, Decorum. He climbed astride and nudged the horse forward.

As he rode, he considered his recent meeting with Abigail Stone. For whatever reason, the young woman had slipped into the recesses of his mind and would not relinquish her hold. He supposed a good deal of his interest in the young woman stemmed largely from her exotic beauty, but with the clean spring air filling his lungs, he realized his fascination was a product of more than mere physical lust. Abigail possessed a bold spirit and unabashed candidness that he didn't understand, and yet, oddly because he didn't understand it, found himself intrigued by it. Since Father's death, Geoffrey had taken great care to avoid passionate women such as Abigail.

Geoffrey guided Decorum down St. James Street, and drew on the reins, bringing his mount to a stop in front of the familiar white stone front of White's. He dismounted, and handed the reins over to a waiting servant.

Intent on putting aside the memory of Abigail's husky laugh and siren's voice, he strode up the steps and entered his club.

"Redbrooke!" A booming voice called in greeting.

Geoffrey looked around, until his stare alighted upon Lord Alvanley in his place of honor at the bow window, alongside the Earl of Seaton.

Geoffrey raised his hand in greeting and wound his way through the club, nodding as he passed acquaintances, until he reached his table in the far back corner. He slid into the comfortable folds of his seat and motioned for a bottle of brandy.

A servant hurried over and placed the bottle and glass atop the table.

Geoffrey reached for it and proceeded to splash several fingerfuls into the glass. Raucous laughter caught his notice. He frowned around the rim of his drink, and took a long swallow. Several foppish young dandies stood around the infamous White's betting book.

Lord Walsh, a reed-thin dandy in garish golden satin breeches, said something that made the three gentlemen around him howl with laughter.

"Bloody swains," a deep voice drawled, jerking Geoffrey's attention back from the indistinguishable words among the young dandies.

Geoffrey looked and frowned—Lord Sinclair. *Bloody fantastic.* He and Sinclair had moved in the same circles once upon a lifetime ago. Only, Sinclair still carried the reputation as something of a reckless rogue.

Sinclair had also secured one of Abigail's waltzes last evening.

Geoffrey detested him even more.

"Might I join you, chap?" Sinclair didn't wait for Geoffrey to confirm, but pulled out the chair across from Geoffrey and settled into the seat. "Mind if I help myself to a glass of brandy?" He glanced around and then held his hand up. A liveried servant came over with a glass, which he placed in front of Sinclair. The young man bowed and then took his leave.

Sinclair poured himself a glass and took a sip.

Geoffrey stared across the table at the other man. He and Lord Sinclair had attended Eton and Oxford in the same years, but beyond that, they tended to move in very different social circles.

Very different.

Which made Sinclair's intrusion so very odd.

And unappreciated.

Sinclair cradled his glass in one hand and drummed the fingertips of his other along the edge of the table. The rhythmic tapping grated, and Geoffrey gritted his teeth until Sinclair suddenly stopped. He leaned over, placing his elbows upon the table. "Lady Beatrice, is it?"

Geoffrey blinked. "I beg your pardon?" It would certainly help if the other man spoke in complete sentences.

"Or is it the lovely, ever-intriguing Miss Abigail Stone who has snared your attention."

Geoffrey's mind went blank at the other man's blunt questioning. He reached for his too-tight cravat, and then remembered himself. Clearing his throat, he clenched the edge of the table. "Of a sudden you are interested in my marital intentions?"

Sinclair's eyes lit. "Ah, so you do have, how did you phrase it, marital intentions?" He arched a brow. "Hardly the romantic, are you, Redbrooke?"

Geoffrey silently cursed and downed the remaining contents of his glass. That hadn't always been the case. Emma's visage flashed behind his eyes. He reached for the bottle and poured himself another. "You're worse than the bloody matrons at Almack's."

Sinclair grinned. "Who knew you had a sense of humor?"

Geoffrey sat back in his chair, and took another sip of brandy. He frowned. Geoffrey didn't know why, or how to explain it, but this unfavorable opinion carried by Abigail and Lord Sinclair rankled. He had a sense of humor. That is, when something happened to be funny. Not crudely amusing. Or inappropriately amusing. But, well, *amusing.*

Another round of laughter rent the quiet conversations of White's. Simultaneously Sinclair and Geoffrey stared off at the trio of dandies.

"You never answered my question, Redbrooke? Is it Lady Beatrice or Miss Stone you've set your marital cap at? If I was a wagering man," he glanced toward the men clustered around the betting book. "And I am, a wagering man, I would venture it is Lady Beatrice you are poised to make your viscountess. Hmm, no word?" Sinclair said, leaning close. He took another sip of his brandy.

Geoffrey had sought out his clubs to rid himself of his mother's barrage of questions. It would appear he'd merely traded one nuisance for another. "It's none of your damned business, Sinclair."

Sinclair arched a brow. "What if it is my business, Redbrooke? Or rather, what if I care to make it my business?"

Geoffrey's frown deepened. He crossed his ankles and leaned back, feigning nonchalance. "I don't see how my intentions should matter to you. That is, unless you have honorable intentions for…" His words trailed off. From around the rim of his glass, he studied Sinclair.

The earl took a long swallow of brandy.

Hell. "You intend to court Lady Beatrice," Geoffrey said. He remembered the fascinated manner in which Beatrice had studied Sinclair at Lord and Lady Essex's ball. This would certainly complicate Geoffrey's timeframe.

Sinclair choked on the contents of his glass. He waved off a passing servant and the expressions of concern. "Lady B…Beatrice?" he sputtered, on a hushed whisper solely for Geoffrey's ears. "Lady Beatrice." Another fit of choking ensued. When at last the fit had ceased, Sinclair gave his head a clearing shake. "I didn't come to ascertain your interest in Lady Beatrice, but rather her cousin."

Geoffrey cocked his head. Sinclair's words humming through his ears like he'd been submerged under water, and left there too long. "Her cousin?" he asked blankly.

"Yes," Sinclair said with a nod. "Miss Abigail Stone. The scandal sheets had written of your seeming interest in Lady Beatrice, however, there seems to be some uncertainty as to whether it is the Lady Beatrice or the lovely Miss Stone who has you so enthralled."

All manner of suitable responses escaped him. He should vehemently protest the charges, and yet his focus remained on why the too-roguish, too-charming Sinclair should concern himself with Abigail Stone.

"She's an American," Geoffrey said at last, choosing to keep his tone neutral.

"I suspected you would find her unsuitable," Sinclair said more to himself. "Told Drake and Emmaline," he said referring to the Marquess of Drake and his marchioness, Lady Emmaline, who happened to be Geoffrey's sister's dearest friend. "That there is no way you would be interested in an American." An entirely inappropriate half-grin turned the other man's lips. "I, on the other hand, well, I have very little problem with her being an American." Sinclair shoved back an unfashionably long strand of black hair that fell over his eye.

With their dark coloring, Sinclair and Abigail would make a striking match. Another growl worked its way up Geoffrey's throat.

"I say, are you all right?"

Geoffrey imagined the wicked Sinclair with the charming Miss Stone, and all Geoffrey's earlier imaginings of her spread upon satin sheets, her arms extended toward him, were replaced with her reaching for the bastard Sinclair. Something Geoffrey didn't recognize, something he'd never before felt, not even with Emma, something primal and dark reared its ugly head until he wanted to snarl and toss the table aside and bloody Sinclair the way he'd bloodied Carmichael.

He gave his head a shake. *What the hell is wrong with me?* He must be going mad. Geoffrey drew in a steadying breath and lied through his even, white teeth. "I have no interest in the lady."

Sinclair smiled. "Splendid, Redbrooke." Laughter from over at the betting book snagged his attention. "What the hell are they wagering on?"

Geoffrey shrugged and because frankly he'd had enough of the idea of Miss Stone and Lord Sinclair together, Geoffrey used that diversionary question to make his much needed escape. "If you'll excuse me," he said, and rose.

Alas, Sinclair seemed unable to identify a clear dismissal. He jumped up from his seat and fell into step beside Geoffrey. "Bloody dandies," he muttered to Geoffrey. "Were we ever that foolish?"

Geoffrey scowled at the other man. "I wasn't."

Sinclair blinked. "Did you just insult me, Redbrooke?"

They reached the rainbow menagerie of too-bright satin waist coats, sparing Geoffrey from responding to Sinclair. As one, the group of gentlemen fell silent, eying Geoffrey with a hesitancy, even as they parted to allow him access to the betting book.

He scanned the wagers.

Lord Ashville bets Lord Forbes 200 guineas to 10 that an event between them understood takes place before another which was named. May 17, 1818.

Lord Montgomery bets Lord Avondale 100 guineas to 20 that Lady Waxham will be enceinte before the Season is concluded.

Geoffrey frowned at seeing his sister's name in the betting books, and continued reading.

Sinclair's black curse sent three of the dandies hurrying off.

Geoffrey continued reading.

Lord Carmichael bets Lord Havensworth 50 guineas to 10 Miss Abigail Stone will...

His body went immobile, as the words inked in black upon the page blurred before his eyes.

Geoffrey's gaze narrowed.

...find herself compromised by an English gentleman, and shipped back to the Americas with a sullied reputation.

That dark, primordial urge reared its ugly head. Geoffrey spun around, and the remaining young gentleman who'd not possessed the sense to flee before, went wide-eyed. The brightly colored peacock gulped and fled for his respective table.

Geoffrey turned back to the damned page. He reached for the parchment.

"Don't," Sinclair said quietly, anticipating Geoffrey's hasty actions.

Geoffrey stared down at the page, unable to explain this unholy urge to defend the lady's honor.

Sinclair cleared his throat, looking pointedly at Geoffrey's hand.

As if burned, Geoffrey yanked his fingers back. He'd just tried to rip a page from the famed betting books. What in hell was wrong with him?

Abigail Stone.

The sooner the young lady returned to America, the better off he would be.

He looked to Sinclair. "You shall meet no resistance from me in your courtship of Miss Stone." With those words, he bowed, and took his leave; for the first time hating his dedication to propriety and his image amidst Society.

TEN

A gentleman must be diligent in his studies and have
an appreciation for matters of intellect.
4th Viscount Redbrooke

The following morning, Geoffrey rose and dressed, with his resolve to court and wed Lady Beatrice strengthened. He'd already focused enough of his too important time upon the unsuitable Miss Stone. Determination fueled his strides as he marched up the front steps of the Duke of Somerset's townhouse, and rapped on the door. As he waited for the butler, he turned out and studied the busy street and carriages with a direct intensity that caused the passing gentlemen and ladies to politely avert their attention.

He spun around as the door opened, and held out his calling card. "To see Lady Beatrice." Not her cousin. Not the delectable, troublesome American miss.

The expressionless servant bowed, and motioned for him to enter. Geoffrey handed his cloak and hat over to the butler and followed him as he led him to Lady Beatrice.

Each step that carried him closer to Lady Beatrice echoed with the words his father had tried to ingrain into him.

Duty.

Words Geoffrey had so foolishly ignored for the love of a woman.

Honor.

A woman who'd wanted nothing more than to foist her bastard off on him.

Responsibility.

…and enjoy the wealth marriage to him would have assured her. *Decorum.*

His father's lifeless face flashed in his mind, and he momentarily closed his eyes at the familiar ache of guilt and pain.

Atonement.

The butler stopped and opened a door. Laughter, clear, and honest as a summer's day filled the brightly lit parlor, and spilled from the room. The husky, delicious alto could only belong to one woman.

"The Viscount Redbrooke."

Upon his introduction, conversation in the bright, sunny parlor, died. His gaze alighted on Lady Beatrice, seated on a floral upholstered sofa, an embroidery frame in her hands. She set it down on the table in front of her and rose, amidst fluttering elegant pink satin skirts.

With her golden curls and the refined lines of her heart-shaped face, she epitomized genteel English beauty.

Then his eyes fell to Abigail, who occupied the seat next to Lady Beatrice.

He wanted to find the generous swell of her breasts and gently flared hips unbecoming on a proper lady. But by God, Abigail Stone possessed the kind of beauty man fought wars for.

She tipped her chin up a notch under his lengthy scrutiny. The slight tightening of her lips indicated she believed he'd evaluated her and found her wanting.

When in truth, he was the only one to be found wanting.

He bowed. "My lady. Miss Stone," he greeted. He loathed the pull she had over him; a pull that made a mockery of the vow he'd taken after his father's death.

Lady Beatrice nudged Abigail.

Abigail sprung to her feet, and curtsied. "My lord."

Geoffrey felt Abigail's stare on him and it occurred to him that she expected cool disdain from him. His mouth tightened. It appeared she possessed a rather ill-opinion of Geoffrey. "Hello, Miss Stone."

"Hello, my lord."

Beatrice motioned to the matching King Louis chair next to her seat. He hesitated a moment, eyeing the remaining spot alongside Abigail with a covetous longing he should be flogged for.

"Would you care for refreshments? Abigail was sharing her knowledge of the Greek myths," Beatrice explained, folding her hands upon her satin skirts.

"No, refreshments," he murmured. He quirked a brow in Abigail's direction. "Greek myths?"

She colored, quite prettily from the tip of her head, down her neck, until he wondered just how far the heat of embarrassment ran.

Beatrice continued. "And she's been teaching me of astrology and astronomy. She knows a good deal about the constellations. Abigail suggested that I might someday visit the Royal Astronomical Society." Beatrice blushed.

It would appear Miss Stone had turned Lady Beatrice into something of a blue-stocking, not something he'd dashed upon his list of acceptable traits for his future viscountess.

Geoffrey directed his attention to Abigail. "You study the constellations, Miss Stone. I find that rather interesting endeavor for a respectable young lady."

She squared her shoulders. "I take it you disapprove of a lady who is learned in such matters."

He hooked his ankle across his knee. "Quite the opposite. I value a woman who possesses a keen mind and sharp intellect."

He could tell by the slight widening of her eyes that he's startled her with his admission.

Her lips tilted up at the corner in the hint of a smile. "My father is a shipping magnate in America, my lord. An appreciation for the stars and all things having to do with the sky is something he instilled in his children from early on."

So the young lady's family owned a shipping venture. Yes, he'd known a powerful shipping magnate had been connected to the Duke of Somerset in some way or another. The research provided by his solicitor had confirmed as much. "What manner of goods does your father deal in, Miss Stone?"

Lady Beatrice looked at Abigail and shook her head once; the meaning quite clear. Young ladies did not to discuss matters of business with gentleman.

Geoffrey wondered for a moment if Abigail intended to shift the conversation to more mundane matters such as the weather, and the latest soirees.

She tipped her chin up. "My father's owns a line of clippers that run textiles down the Atlantic, to a chain of islands in the Caribbean waters." She met his gaze squarely, as though she expected him to be scandalized by the mere mention of a gentleman dealing in trade.

"Ah, textiles have proven quite lucrative for me as well. Though a good deal of my business ventures are with India and in this part of the world."

She stared at him, with wide, unblinking eyes. "You deal in trade?" she blurted.

He bit back a grin at having properly silenced the presumptuous, if endearing American miss.

"Abigail," Beatrice said chidingly.

His lips twitched with mirth. It would appear Abigail neither knew, nor perhaps cared, about what constituted proper discourse among ladies and gentlemen.

Abigail ignored her cousin, and held Geoffrey's gaze. "I shouldn't expect that a proper English gentleman would deal in matters of business."

"You would be wrong then, Miss Stone," he murmured.

Polite Society did not approve of nobles who dabbled in trade.

What they did, approve of, however, were nobles in possession of outrageous amounts of wealth. And in spite, of Abigail's rather low opinion and Society's stringent expectations, Geoffrey had only expanded upon the mercantile empire built by his father.

Abigail opened her mouth to again speak, but Beatrice coughed discreetly into her hand, and those words went unspoken.

Geoffrey returned his attention to the lady he'd selected for his future viscountess, and he steered the discourse back to those topics she'd expressed an earlier interest in. "You care for matters of astronomy then, my lady. Is that something you'd like? To visit the Royal Astronomical Society?"

Lady Beatrice shook her head emphatically. "Oh, that wouldn't be at all proper, my lord."

Alas, Abigail would not allow him to remain focused upon Lady Beatrice.

"Whyever not?" Abigail interjected. "What harm is there in your visiting the Society?"

Lady Beatrice's expression conveyed a blend of skepticism and horror.

Twin splotches of color filled Abigail's cheeks, a deep red hue putting him mind of a succulent apple plucked from the tree. "Well, you can," she said, a touch defensively, wholly unaware of Geoffrey's desire for the summer fruit. She waved her hand. "Why, my father was born a servant. He worked in some fine lord's household."

"And then he fell in love with Aunt Margaret." The whimsical quality to Lady Beatrice's quiet utterance gave Geoffrey pause. With those few words, and wistful glimmer in her eyes, Geoffrey had his first indication that Lady Beatrice aspired for more than a cold, calculated wager between two suitable members of noble blood.

He shifted, uncomfortable by the sudden realization. He'd sought a match with Lady Beatrice who represented the practical choice. She possessed impeccable bloodlines and conducted herself with poise and grace amidst Society.

Now, she'd revealed herself given to more fancy than he'd ever considered.

Beatrice continued, seemingly unaware of Geoffrey's turbulent thoughts. "Isn't that true, Abigail? They have a great love, don't they?"

"They do," Abigail said softly.

Geoffrey's jaw hardened. The love she spoke of had cost her mother the respectable place she'd held in Polite Society. She'd been forced to travel an ocean away to a foreign world and reestablish a life for herself...all because of love.

Lady Beatrice looked over at him and must have glimpsed something dark in his expression. "You disapprove of a marriage based on love, my lord?"

Again, Emma's regal face flashed to mind. Since Abigail Stone had entered his life, all the old, ugly remembrances had resurfaced.

He detected the intent glimmer in the eyes of both ladies and Geoffrey knew whatever he next spoke would matter a great deal... it would seem, to both Abigail and Beatrice. "I believe there are great risks in making decisions based on emotion."

Abigail's body froze, like a deer caught in a snare, her eyes wide, unblinking.

Beatrice touched Abigail's hand and the winsome American jumped. "Are you all right?"

"Fine," Abigail said hurriedly, so that Geoffrey wondered as to her reaction.

Suddenly uncomfortable with the discussion on the sentiments of love, Geoffrey returned his attention to Beatrice. "What other *lessons* have you learned from Miss Stone?" From the corner of his eye he detected the slight tightening around the corners of Abigail's lips.

Beatrice smiled. "Abigail has also begun teaching me about the stars."

Geoffrey looped one ankle over the other, and looked to Abigail. "The stars?" he asked Beatrice, all the while directing his attention to Abigail Stone.

"She knows a good deal about Greek constellations." Beatrice furrowed her brow. "Which did you say was your favorite myth, Abby?"

Abigail gave her head a slight shake.

Beatrice's eyes lit, and she jabbed her finger in the air. "Ah, yes. The story of Dionysus.

Geoffrey stiffened. *Dionysus.*

"Do you know it, my lord?" Beatrice went on.

Abigail touched her hand to Beatrice's. "I'm sure His Lordship doesn't want to hear about silly Greek myths."

Geoffrey shook his head. "No, no. You're quite wrong, Miss Stone. I'm intrigued." He returned his attention to Beatrice. "You must remind me, my lady, about the story of *Dionysus*. I must admit it has been quite a while since I've studied the Greek classics."

Abigail surged to her feet. "Er, if you'll excuse me, I should leave you and Lord Redbrooke to your visit."

Lady Beatrice sat forward in her chair. She reached for Abigail's hand. "No you mustn't!" Her blue eyes glittered with a faintly pleading expression. Then, with an unladylike show of force, Beatrice yanked Abigail back down into the seat she'd just vacated.

Geoffrey supposed he should be insulted. And he suspected he would have...if he wasn't having such fun teasing Miss Stone.

Beatrice went on. "Placed in a labyrinth as food for a monster, Theseus convinced the King of Minos' daughter, er..."

"Ariadne," Abigail supplied weakly. Her fingers plucked at the fabric of her skirts.

"To take her with him if she helped him escape. Ariadne helped free him but he journeyed with her to an island."

"The isle of Naxos," Abigail added quietly.

Beatrice nodded. "But the fiend took her and left her alone." A frown formed on her lips. "Everyone deserted her. Until Dionysus came to rescue Ariadne."

Geoffrey sat frozen.

Lady Beatrice seemed to note that she had a captivated audience and continued. "Dionysus rescued her from abject loneliness and despair, and as a sign of his love, gave her a crown of seven diamonds."

"Did he?" Geoffrey drawled. He glanced over at Abigail, who now trained her stare upon the mural painted at the central part of the ceiling. He wondered whether Abigail identified with Ariadne's sense of loneliness and sadness. His amusement died a swift death.

A knock sounded at the door.

The butler entered with a calling card upon his silver tray. "The Earl of Sinclair to see Miss Stone."

Geoffrey narrowed his eyes on the smiling, too damned affable Lord Sinclair, who filled the entrance.

Sinclair bowed low at the waist. "Miss Stone, my lady, how do you do?" He looked at Geoffrey. "Redbrooke."

Geoffrey's gut clenched as that unwanted emotion that felt remarkably like jealousy coursed through his veins with a life-like force.

Bloody hell.

Abigail and Beatrice rose simultaneously and curtsied.

Sinclair focused his attention on Abigail.

Geoffrey's jaw tightened at the roguish gleam in the other man's far too appreciative gaze. A gentleman didn't ogle a young lady in such a manner. He…well, hell…he just didn't.

Abigail and Beatrice sat.

Sinclair slid into the small, mahogany shell-back chair closest to Abigail. With its thin spindle legs, the seat was entirely too small for one of Sinclair's size…and what's more, too close.

Why when Sinclair sat in the blasted seat, Abigail's leg all but brushed his thigh in a most inappropriate manner. God how he hated the other man for that subtle touch of her body.

Geoffrey was filled with an unholy desire to see that fragile piece of furniture shatter under the weight of Sinclair's imposing frame.

Except, Abigail's placid expression, indicated she was a good deal less impressed with Sinclair's effortless charm than most other young ladies.

Ever the hostess, Lady Beatrice, engaged Sinclair in discourse. "We were just discussing the ancient classics before you'd arrived, my lord."

"Specifically matters of astrology and astronomy, it would seem," Geoffrey drawled, enjoying the heightened color that ran from the top of Abigail's head, down her neck, and he wondered just how much lower…

"My cousin is rather well-versed in the topic," Beatrice said.

Abigail dropped her gaze to her lap. "Beatrice is merely being polite."

Beatrice shook her head emphatically. "Oh, no. Not at all. Er, that isn't to say I'm not being polite. I am. But I'm also being truthful. Abigail knows nearly everything on the topic."

Sinclair's eyes lit with interest. He raised a brow. "Is that so?" He directed his question to Lady Beatrice. At his attention, color filled her cheeks and she dropped her gaze to the floor, clearly not immune to Sinclair's charm the way Abigail had been.

Geoffrey frowned. He suspected he should feel a hard resentment, even a stony annoyance at Sinclair's effect on Lady Beatrice, and yet...

His eyes went to Abigail.

She smiled at Geoffrey, clearly having noted her cousin's reaction to the roguish Sinclair.

"We were just discussing the tale of Dionysus and Ariadne," Beatrice said.

"Ahh, yes. The tale of Theseus' desperate attempt at survival."

Geoffrey gritted his teeth. Of course, the bloody perfect Sinclair would be so versed in the classics to remember the details of the myth.

"Is it really a tale of desperation?" Abigail asked. "I consider it a story of Dionysus' great love for Ariadne."

"You are a romantic, Miss Stone," Geoffrey bit out.

Three pairs of eyes swiveled his way. He stiffened under their intense scrutiny.

"Are you a cynic, then, my lord?" Abigail quietly asked. A sound, very nearly a groan, escaped Lady Beatrice, who dropped her head and shook it back and forth.

Geoffrey ignored her. His jaw tightened. "I am a man of logic. I'd not be so desperate as to pledge my love to a woman merely to escape Minos' labyrinth."

Abigail moved to the edge of her seat, her back stiffly held in a way that Lord Wellington himself would have applauded. "Then you, my lord, must have never known desperation."

Geoffrey moved to the edge of the seat. "Then you, Miss Stone, would be wrong."

Silence met his pronouncement. The steady tick-tock, tick-tock of the ormolu clock, blended with the rapid breathing of Miss Stones' heaving chest, filled the quiet.

Geoffrey balled his hands into tight fists, shamed by his unwitting revelation. He'd lived the past five years of his life guarded, protecting himself from outside notice and censure. In the span of a moment this woman had made him reveal a hint about the dark past he kept buried. He stood hastily. "Lady Beatrice, I shall leave you and Miss Stone to your visit with Lord Sinclair. Good day." Geoffrey sketched a quick bow.

As he took his hurried leave, he felt Abigail's eyes boring into the fabric of his garment.

With her romantic views and bluestocking tendencies, Abigail posed a threat to his well-ordered world.

Yet, for the first time in nearly five years, he craved the opportunity to live and laugh with the same reckless abandon the lady herself seemed to exhibit.

Geoffrey ran hands that shook through his hair.

God help him. It would appear he'd not changed at all.

ELEVEN

A gentleman must keep a private box at the theatre. He is not, however, to take part in the public display of gossip that occurs at that particular venue.
4ᵗʰ Viscount Redbrooke

S candalously loud whispers and too-polite laughter filled the auditorium of the Theatre Royal on Drury Lane. The candles from the chandeliers set the theatre aglow in a flickering light, throwing shadows upon the theatre boxes. In the dim light, Abigail scanned the crush of satin clad bodies.

"It hardly seems like people come for the sake of the show," Abigail said under her breath at the conclusion of Act I of Shakespeare's Othello.

Beatrice grinned. "Don't you know? The only reason Society attends the theatre is to gossip and gawk at one another."

Abigail's lips pulled in a frown. "That is a shame. Perhaps they'll be quieter for the second half."

Her cousin Robert snorted. He tipped back on the legs of his chair. "Hardly. Just the opposite."

"Hmph." Abigail's gaze moved with methodical precision through the crowd, taking the opportunity to study the people in attendance.

Beatrice cocked her head. "Are you looking for anyone in particular?"

Abigail started, and gave thanks for the darkness that concealed the rush of heat that flooded her cheeks. "No." She prided herself on the nonchalant delivery of that single word utterance.

Beatrice frowned, and leaned closer. She ran her pretty blue-eyed gaze over Abigail's face.

Abigail pressed her back against the red velvet cushions of her seat.

Robert winked at her. "Beatrice's trying to verify whether you are being truthful." He directed his attention out on the crowd below.

"Oh," Abigail said, lamely.

Her cousins studied her with such intentness that Abigail squirmed under their scrutiny. Still, she had one determined sister, and two, very obstinate brothers, three if one considered her youngest brother, back at home, and Abigail had long ago learned how to close her lips and aggravate them with her silence.

Knowing Beatrice studied her, Abigail quelled the urge to look for Geoffrey. It was utter madness, this desire to see him. Except…she touched the special pocket sewn into the front of her gown where she carried the frayed and battered scrap of Italian lace Geoffrey had twice rescued for her. She suspected there was more to him than the rigidity he presented to his glittering world: a man unafraid to intervene with the use of force if it meant the protection of a woman's honor, someone who would set aside propriety to wade into a lake to retrieve a memento to stave off a woman's sadness. He didn't mock her interest in the stars as Alexander had, but seemed to appreciate that she cared to speak on topics different than those expected of a lady.

And he belonged to her cousin.

"Ahh, there is, Lord Redbrooke," Beatrice said, seeming more to herself.

Abigail followed her cousin's gaze and knew the moment Geoffrey registered Beatrice's focus.

Geoffrey and Beatrice shared a smile. There, for all of Polite Society, to see. From the stoic lord, it may as well have constituted a formal offer of marriage.

Abigail curled her toes in a desperate bid to halt the urge to flee. All his heroic efforts on Abigail's behalf had merely been the actions of a gentleman. Here Abigail sat, making more of his rescue when in actuality, Geoffrey would have done the same for Beatrice—any lady, for that matter.

The curtain drew back.

"It is starting," Beatrice whispered, clapping her hands together with more enthusiasm than Abigail ever had seen demonstrated by her otherwise, reserved cousin.

The actors launched into Act II. Familiar with the tale of a love destroyed and betrayal, Abigail again sought out Geoffrey. Their gazes collided. She offered him a smile.

Unlike the polite smile he'd shared with Beatrice not very long ago, his lips flattened into a hard line, and he returned his focus to the stage below.

Abigail bit the inside of her cheek. Yesterday afternoon, Geoffrey had been stiff, proper, unrelenting...the kind of gentleman she'd never wanted in her life. His harsh revelation yesterday, and then his swift departure, had indicated that Geoffrey, too, carried secrets. She remembered the flash of pain in his eyes, the muscle that had throbbed at the corner of his mouth.

Her cousin, Robert had indicated Geoffrey had not always been the aloof figure who now courted her cousin. And not for the first time since he'd swept onto Lord and Lady Hughes's terrace and rescued her from Lord Carmichael, she wondered what had happened to Geoffrey, a man who so desperately needed life teased back into him.

She glanced over at Beatrice, thoroughly engrossed in the performance below. Abigail's heart tightened with unwanted feelings of regret and...envy. Geoffrey had been abundantly clear that he wanted Beatrice to be that young lady.

After all, gentlemen such as Geoffrey Winters, Viscount Redbrooke, did not wed ruined young ladies careless enough as to toss their virtue away. Regret tasted like the bitterest of fruits and it threatened to choke her as she recalled that night she and Alexander had been discovered in one another's arms, her gown in dishabille...

Abigail swallowed hard. All the humiliation and despair she'd carried crested like a wave at sea and nearly engulfed her, threatening to pull her under.

Abigail stumbled to her feet, nearly upending her chair.

"Abigail?" Robert looked at her questioningly.

"I-ah-I require a moment," she said. And before he or Beatrice should think to follow, Abigail fled. She registered the moment her maid Sally started after her, and picked up her pace, down the long hall, down a flight of stairs. She wanted to leave.

"Sally," she said, her voice raspy to her own ears. "Please have the coach summoned, and then return and tell the marquess I have a megrim."

Concern filled Sally's kindly eyes. "Are you certain I should leave you alone, Miss Stone? Perhaps I should return for the marquess."

"No!" Abigail said. "Please, just have the coach summoned."

Sally hesitated, and then hurried ahead, leaving Abigail at the main stairway of the theater.

Abigail froze, the tip of her slipper at the top step that represented the path to her freedom from the theatre.

Geoffrey stood at the base of the long, wide staircase. One hand rested casually upon the rail. He looked up at her.

Tears filled her eyes.

She blinked, but the blasted drops she'd been unable to shed since her voyage to London, refused to fall; instead the salty pools blurred her vision.

The unshed mementos of despair still could not mask the concern that blazed to life in the green-blue irises of Geoffrey's normally hard, impenetrable stare.

Abigail dimly registered his long, powerful legs striding up the stairs with marked elegance and determination.

Drat. Must he be so perfect as to even race up the stairs in a regal manner?

He stopped at the step below her, his gaze working a path over her person. "Abigail? Have you been hurt?"

The moment Geoffrey had seen Abigail surge to her feet and flee the duke's theatre box, he'd set out in pursuit. Even with the distance between them, and the dimly lit auditorium, he'd detected the panicky glitter in her eyes.

Geoffrey cursed, and glanced around but with the second act having just begun, the hall remained eerily quiet. "Abigail, what is it?"

She gave her head a shake. "I-I'm fine. Really. You shouldn't be here. It's not p-proper." Her chest heaved up and down, as she drew in gasping, ragged breaths.

To hell with propriety. Geoffrey took her by the hand and ushered her over to a nearby alcove. He shielded her body with his, in the event someone should come upon them. He studied her with a quiet intensity.

She implored him with her eyes. "You must go. If you're discovered..."

"I don't care about discovery," he said, sharply.

His body stiffened as he realized with a staggering shock, in that moment he didn't care about his image amongst the *ton*, or scandal, or the threat of impropriety, or his mother's expectations. He didn't even care about the crimes of his youth and Emma's betrayal. Or his courtship of Lady Beatrice. There would be time enough for logic and reason later. Just then, nothing seemed of greater import than driving back the raw pain reflected in Abigail's eyes.

The distant echo of Othello's words reached through the theatre into their sanctuary.

If it were now to die, 'twere now to be most happy; for I fear my soul hath her content so absolute that not another comfort like to this succeeds in unknown fate.

Othello's words swirled around them, and mocked Geoffrey with their eerie accuracy.

"Why are you troubled, Abigail?" Geoffrey pressed. By god, if one of those callow youths from White's had dared put their hands upon her person, he would destroy them.

She shook her head. "It's..." Abigail looked up at him. "It's..." The hint of unspoken words seemed to dangle upon her lips. Real, and tangible between them.

She bit her lower lip and her gaze skirted his, so uncharacteristic of the woman who brazenly met his stare. "It is nothing," she finished lamely. "I merely miss my family."

He narrowed his eyes. Did she expect he could not perceive the lie in her stormy-gray eyes? "Has someone hurt you?"

A bitter little laugh spilled past her bow-shaped, red lips, and she shook her head too—emphatically, confirming his earlier supposition.

Odd, in a mere handful of days he'd come to know her enough to read even the most subtle nuances of her movements. "Who?" The word emerged as a silken whisper. He'd kill the bastard who'd reduced her to this downtrodden figure before him.

"No one. Truly," she said at last. Her gaze locked with his. "You shouldn't be here, Geoffrey. We shouldn't."

Ahh, so she'd be rid of him?

"No," he agreed. But he remained.

And so did she.

When had propriety ceased to matter?

Geoffrey dropped his brow atop hers, inhaling the sweet fragrant lilacs that kissed her skin and tantalized his senses. "What have you done to me, Abby?" he whispered. She'd made him forget a pledge he'd taken nearly five years ago. She made him yearn for all manner of things he should no longer desire.

Geoffrey groaned.

I am lost.

His mouth closed over hers.

Abigail leaned up on tip toe and pressed her lean, lush body to his. The generous expanse of her breasts flattened against the wall of his chest.

His hands of their own volition went to her waist. He should set her away. He should turn on his heel and leave the bold young lady who made him forget.

He should do all manner of things proper.

Instead, he tugged her closer, and moved his hands along the curve of her hips, the base of her buttocks, until a little moan escaped her. Geoffrey parted her lips and swallowed that breathy sound of desire, his shaft hardening against her belly.

"Geoffrey," she whispered into his mouth.

His tongue danced an age old rhythm with hers. Parry and thrust. Thrust and parry. Her head fell back, and his lips left hers.

"No," she protested, tugging on the strands of his hair.

Geoffrey ignored her urging and used his lips to trail a hot path along the sensitive spot behind her ear, down to the rapidly fluttering pulse in her neck, and ever lower, to the exposed satiny flesh of her décolletage.

Abigail moaned.

"Now, by heaven, my blood begins my safer guides to rule, and passion, having my best judgment collied, assays to lead the way."

Othello's mocking words infiltrated the haze of passion. Geoffrey wrenched his head back. He released Abigail with such alacrity, she stumbled against him. He eyed her there with something akin to horror creeping around his mind with tentacle-like fingers.

Abigail looked at him. "Geoffrey," she whispered.

He shook his head hard enough to yank the muscles in his neck. He welcomed the stiff pain, embraced it for penance. Geoffrey spun on his heel, presenting Abigail with his back. All the while, he struggled to draw in steady, even breaths.

Christ. After Emma's betrayal and his father's death, he'd believed himself free of irrational, impassioned responses. And yet, here he stood, a stone's throw from Polite Society, lusting after Lady Beatrice's cousin. His eyes slid closed on a wave of guilt.

He'd failed in his responsibilities now, just as he had five years ago.

"Geoffrey," Abigail repeated softly.

He gave his head a curt shake and when he trusted himself not to cross over to Abigail and take her into his arms yet again, he turned to face her. "Go, Miss Stone." *Or I will not be responsible for what I do next.* "Go!" he repeated, his tone harsh and cold.

A flash of hurt filled her eyes.

Abigail stepped behind him and fled.

TWELVE

A gentleman recognizes the value in rising early
as beneficial to a healthy constitution.
4ᵗʰ Viscount Redbrooke

G eoffrey guided Decorum through the empty grounds of Hyde Park, giving the mount free rein to stretch his legs. Even as he galloped along the empty riding path, he longed for the open expanse of land in his country seat. Only there could he be free of Society's focus.

He hadn't always desired solitude.

At one time, he'd loathed the country and craved the balls and soirees of the Season. It seemed a lifetime since he'd been that man; a lifetime since Miss Emma Marsh.

He tugged on the reins of his horse, and brought it to a trot. He prided himself on the orderly manner in which he'd lived his life these past years. He'd reformed himself from careless rogue into sensible, responsible lord. No living soul; not his mother, nor Sophie, knew of the secret shame and guilt he carried. They didn't know that there had been a time when Geoffrey had placed his own selfish desires before everything that truly mattered; family, responsibility, his title as viscount—and that decision had proven a costly one.

Last night, he'd exhibited a shocking lack of honor in kissing Abigail.

Geoffrey swiped his hand over his face. Abigail had wrought havoc upon the carefully crafted life he'd built for himself after his father's tragic death.

Perhaps on this, his thirtieth birthday he was reminded that he still remained unwed and heir-less. Or perhaps the unconventional, bold-spirited Abigail Stone had woven a sorceress' spell upon him. But, the dream of her had kicked down the wall he'd carefully constructed around his heart.

"Whoa," he said to Decorum. He brought the mare to a halt at the edge of the Serpentine, and stared out at the impressive, man-made lake. He remembered back to the day he'd waded in to rescue Abigail's bit of lace. Those actions had belonged to the man he'd been, not the man he'd become.

Except, Geoffrey found the sanguine gentleman of his youth still lived inside him.

He continued to study the pristine, untouched surface of the lake.

His visit here, not mere happenstance.

It reminded him of her…

"Hullo."

Geoffrey jerked, and his knees bit unexpectedly into Decorum's flanks. In a desperate attempt to keep the horse from bolting, Geoffrey yanked hard on the reins. The suddenness of his movements startled the mare. Decorum reared on its legs, pawing at the air. Dust and gravel clouded around him.

"Bloody hell," Geoffrey muttered, as Decorum tossed him side-ways. He braced for the moment his body connected with the Earth, but couldn't prepare for the jolting, jarring pain as his side collided with the ground. He rolled out of the way to keep from being trampled by Decorum's hooves. All the air left his lungs.

Decorum bolted ahead several feet.

"Oh my goodness!" Abigail cried and raced the remaining distance until she reached his side. Her skirts whipped wildly about her legs, as she skidded to a stop in front of him. She sank to her knees. "Are you hurt?" Her worried gaze ran up and down his prone form.

"I'm…" *Sore and embarrassed.*

Abigail ran her hands over his person. Her fingers traveled down his forearms and along his back and over his side as she searched him for injury.

The gods surely tested him. Geoffrey groaned.

"Oh goodness, you're hurt." Abigail paused. "I'm so sorry." She momentarily raised her eyes to meet his. "I...I'm so sorry," she repeated. She resumed her tender ministrations.

Her fingers graced his hip.

Geoffrey's body hardened as she came entirely too close to that part of him that longed to lay her down, pull the pins free of her serviceable chignon, and allow her black curls to fall about them in a silken cascade. "Madam," he bit out. His gaze searched the surrounding area and then settled upon Abigail's pink cheeks. "Where is your maid?"

Abigail's eyes went wide as she seemed to realize all at once the impropriety of her actions. "I-ah...forgive me." She struggled to her feet, her gaze skirting his. She glanced down at her toes and scuffed the tip of her slipper along the pebbled path. "I left Sally some time to herself in the gardens."

He dropped his voice. "You ventured through Hyde Park, alone, madam? Even knowing the perils of being unchaperoned?" There were all manners of cowardly bastards like Lord Carmichael who would gladly shred the young lady's reputation without a by your leave.

She waved her hand. "What harm could come to me?"

Geoffrey closed his eyes briefly and prayed for patience. When he opened them, he found her studying him, head tilted at an endearing little angle. "I believe you've already learned the dangers to be found, even amidst fashionable Society."

The color drained from her cheeks at his unspoken reminder of Lord Carmichael's attack. Most women would have dropped their modest gazes to the ground. Abigail Stone, however, was no conventional young lady. Her eyes blazed with emotion. "I merely sought to help, my lord. I've helped my brothers and sister after many mishaps."

He stiffened at her innocent comparison. Even as he sat there lusting after her like an untried youth, Abigail looked to him the way she might one of her siblings. Geoffrey stood slowly.

She must have seen something dark and menacing in his eyes for her hand flew to her breast, and she took, one step, then another, and another, backward.

"Do you believe I'd hurt you?" he snapped.

His words brought her up short. Her chin went up a notch, as he continued to advance.

Geoffrey stopped so close that his boots kissed the tips of her ivory, satin slippers. He looked down at her; his eyes fixed on the tempting red, flesh of her full lips. His breath grew ragged. If he dipped his head down, even just a bit, their lips would brush.

"No."

God help him, he wanted her.

"What?" That single-word question ripped harshly from his throat.

Abigail reached for his hand. "I do not believe you'd hurt me. I do not believe you're capable of hurting anyone."

He remembered back to his father's broken body, and swallowed. Abigail could not be more mistaken.

"Oh, dear. You are hurt," Abigail said, mistaking whatever emotion she saw in his ravaged eyes for a physical pain.

She took his hand and turned it over, studying it for a moment. The distant cry of a kestrel, echoed overhead, and blended with the heavy beat of his heart. With the tip of her index finger, she dusted bits of gravel and rock from his palm. "You're bleeding," she murmured.

She released him and reached into the front of her pocket.

He said nothing as she removed that familiar scrap of lace and touched it to his hand. "No," he protested, too late. The thin thread of blood that ran a crimson path from the intersecting lines of his palm to his wrist soaked into the stark white fabric of her lace. "Abigail," he said, hoarsely.

"It is fine." She did not pick her head up from tending his person. "It does not mean more to me than your injury."

His heart tugged at those words. The lace had been a gift she carried with her always, a reminder of her home and family, and, Abigail had forever stained it with his blood.

"There." She tied the fabric about his hand. A smile played across her lips. "You look lovely in lace, my lord."

People didn't tease him. They hadn't in very many years. "Geoffrey," he corrected.

She blinked, and looked back up at him.

"I imagine when a young lady has come to the rescue of a gentleman then it is only appropriate she should refer to him by his Christian name," he said, turning her words back to her. "It is my birthday."

She blinked several times.

Geoffrey felt the sting of embarrassment at his hastily spoken words. He suspected he wanted to share that bit of information with someone considering no one, not even his own mother remembered that on this day, thirty years past, he'd entered into the world. "Forgive me. I don't know why I..."

"Well, Happy Birthday, Geoffrey. Now, you must certainly keep the scrap of lace from Lizzie."

"Lizzie?"

"My sister," she clarified.

Geoffrey struggled to swallow past a swell of emotion. She would give up the fragile reminder from home, for him.

How little he knew about this woman, and yet, he felt a connection to her that defied logic and terrified him all as one.

"You have a sister?"

Abigail nodded. "And three brothers. It is a full household."

"If it is anything like my household over the years with my sister Sophie, then I imagine there is a good deal of excitement there." How many days of his life had he spent lamenting that very fact? What a stodgy bastard he'd been.

"Oh, certainly. We were always coming into all kinds of trouble, much to Mama's chagrin." Her gaze took on a faraway, wistfulness.

"You must miss them."

A gentle breeze freed a strand of hair from her neat chignon. She tucked it back behind her ear. "Every day."

And if she did not make a match, then she would surely return to her home. The breath left him on a swift exhale as, for the first time, he considered that reality. This was not Abigail's home. Inevitably she'd either wed an English gentleman or board a ship back to America. A vise-like pressure tightened about his heart at both prospects.

He wanted Abigail to say more of her family, but she remained uncharacteristically silent. Geoffrey opened his mouth to ask her further questions, but something in the look she gave him begged him to let those questions die.

"Are you close with your sister, Geoffrey?"

Her question gave him pause. He'd been sternly disapproving of his sister these past years. With her tendency to land herself into scrape after scrape, she had represented chaos in his world. It hadn't been until she'd wed that he'd come to appreciate how Sophie had filled his household with some modicum of happiness, and how much darker it had become after she'd left. "I suppose more now, than in the past. Sophie possesses a bold spirit. I...I believe you'd get along famously."

Geoffrey shook his head, dislodging an image of Abigail as his wife; she and Sophie, fast-friends.

"I owe you an apology," he said.

She angled her head. The sudden movement displaced one of those midnight tresses, and Geoffrey caught it between his fingers, and studied it.

He continued before she could speak. "I kissed you last evening."

Abigail trailed the tip of her tongue along the seam of her lips and he followed that innocently seductive movement. God help him for being an utter bastard. For even now, with an apology upon his lips, alongside the Serpentine, he longed to take her into his arms yet again, and lay her down and make love to more than just her mouth.

"You needn't apologize."

With his uninjured hand, he claimed her fingers in his. "I do. My actions were unpardonable. You are an innocent. And a lady. God help me, I do not know what you've done to me, Abigail. I resolved to wed your cousin and honor my familial obligations to the Redbrooke line. And yet, in this short time, you've thoroughly bewitched me."

❧

You've bewitched me.

Something wicked dwelled inside her. Something wrong and wicked and vile. The kind of wicked that got ladies sent away to abbey's and shut away from Polite Society but she reveled in his words…

Abigail hugged her arms to herself. The memory of Geoffrey's lips upon her skin and on her lips still burned hotter than the July sun. It had the power to melt her inside and out, liquefying every single coherent thought.

Something stirred to life inside her breast. Her eyes ran a path over the angular planes of Geoffrey's chiseled face, his aquiline nose, the serious set to his mouth drawn by the harsh beauty of a man who so valued honor.

Her throat worked up and down, as she acknowledged the truth— a man such as him would never, could never find her an acceptable match.

Filled with a desperate need to put distance between them, Abigail took a step away from him. She wandered to the side of the lake and stared out as the morning sun peeked over the horizon. "Do you know why I like to come here?" She cast a glance back at him and smiled. "No, you wouldn't know that. I come here because it is quiet and I manage to forget that I'm an ocean away from home." *And here, I'm free of censure.*

Gravel crunched beneath Geoffrey's boot, indicating he'd strode over toward the edge of the lake. "Do you find American Society very different than English Society?"

A bitter laugh bubbled up her throat, and she hugged her arms close to her chest. Regardless, of American Society or English Society, all respectable people would find her lacking. Instead, she said, "No."

"Do you," he paused, "long to return?"

Abigail tilted her head and studied a graceful white swan as it dunked its long neck beneath the surface and come up a moment later, empty.

She yearned for the life she'd known before she'd given up her good name. "I…" in returning to America, however, she would only be returning to scorn and ridicule, forced to live with the constant reminder of her mistake.

Geoffrey's fingers brushed the side of her cheek, and gently turned her head to face him. "Is it a very complicated question?"

For all the pain of Alexander's betrayal, Abigail had never grieved the loss of what her foolish decision had cost her—a respectable husband who loved her—until now. Now, the most she could aspire to was an advantageous match with a gentleman willing to forgive her past transgression.

Geoffrey ran his knuckles along her cheek. "Abigail?" he prodded.

For the first time since she'd boarded her father's ship, she longed to share the great burden she carried. Of course, she could never tell this proud, proper English nobleman, even if he had saved her from Lord Carmichael.

No, Geoffrey could not save her in all the ways she desperately needed saving.

"I miss my family," she said after a pregnant stretch of silence. She gestured to the lake. "I miss the pure, clean sea air. Do you know they say there are so many trees across the whole of North America that a single squirrel could cross the entire continent upon the tops of the trees?"

His face may have been carved from stone as hard and unyielding was his expression. Geoffrey's green-blue eyes bore into her, and she wondered that he couldn't read every deepest, darkest secret she kept from him. "But do you long to return?"

Staring up at him, Abigail came to a staggering realization. "No, I do not," she whispered. She ached for the loss of her family but beyond that, there was nothing left for her there but shame, regret, and broken promises.

Her eyes slid closed.

God help her.

She longed for him.

Abigail took a staggering step away from him. She stepped so close to the lake, her pale yellow skirts brushed the mouth of the water. Geoffrey may as well be as unattainable as one of the stars in the sky.

She drew in a shuddery breath.

Geoffrey reached for her, and pulled her back from the water's edge. He dropped his brow to hers. "If you are seen here like this, alone with me, there will be a scandal."

Her eyes slid closed. The scandal of being alone with him would be tantamount to ruination. She knew that. He knew that.

It appeared she'd not learned the folly of her past. Her lids fluttered closed, as she prepared for his kiss.

That didn't come.

Abigail opened her eyes to find him watching her, with emotionless eyes.

"Abigail, I took a vow upon my father's death to honor my title and all the responsibilities that go with that."

An odd little pit formed in her stomach. Those words were enough. She silently begged him to cease talking, enumerating all the reasons she would never be a suitable bride.

Alas, he appeared immune to the stinging lash each word of his left upon her heart.

"If I were free to choose, I would—" He glanced off to a distant point over her shoulder. "That is neither here nor there. I'm not free to choose. There was one time when I would have, one time I did, set aside my personal obligations and responsibilities for my selfish desires. I cannot do that again."

The pit grew, to the size of a boulder and she pressed her palms along the front of her skirts to smooth that pain. Her efforts proved futile.

"I'm wholly unsuitable as a wife." Her words sounded flat to her own ears.

Geoffrey raked a hand through his hair. "No. Abigail you are…"

She held her hand up to silence him. Abigail didn't need him to wax on with false praise. Not when she knew the truth, and not when he, even if he were unwilling to acknowledge it, also knew that truth. "Don't. Please, don't." She squared her shoulders and dug deep for the pride that had allowed her to walk out of Mr. and Mrs. Van Buren's home with her head held high, even after being discovered en dishabille by all the leading members of society. "I see my maid, Sally. She is waiting for me." She dipped a curtsy. "If you'll excuse me."

A muscle throbbed in the corner of Geoffrey's eye. He gave a curt nod, and stepped aside so she could pass.

Abigail hesitated. "And Geoffrey," she said, softly. "Beatrice will make you a good wife."

Geoffrey tugged free the Italian lace wrapped around his hand, now stained with blood, and held it out to her.

She shook her head. "No. Please. Consider it a birthday gift."

Before he could say another word, she turned on her heel and fled.

THIRTEEN

It's both gauche and unwise for a gentleman to consume spirits before twelve o'clock in the afternoon.
4ᵗʰ Viscount Redbrooke

Geoffrey sailed through the front doors of his townhouse, and froze at the sight of his mother.

She stood in the foyer, arms akimbo. "I've been waiting to speak with you since last evening, Geoffrey."

He silently cursed. Following his meeting with Abigail, all he wanted was to nurse his regret with too much brandy in the confines of his office. "Mother," he greeted. He glanced pointedly at Ralston, who was good enough to keep his eyes averted from the private exchange.

His mother ignored his attempt at discretion. "What are you thinking, dear boy?"

He'd always detested when she called him dear boy, as though he were some kind of recalcitrant child…and she tended to use it when she was most disappointed. "This is neither the time nor the place."

She opened her mouth as if to protest. Then closed it. "Very well. Then I'd like to speak with you in your office." With a final glower, she stomped off.

Geoffrey followed after her. He hadn't even closed the door when his mother, who stood at the center of the room, threw her arms wide. "Whatever are you thinking, Geoffrey?"

He hesitated. His mother was a notorious gossip, but surely she'd not learned of his chance meeting with Abigail that morning. Not for the first time, Geoffrey began to feel a greater connection to his sister, Sophie, who'd had to endure untold scrutiny and gossip.

Geoffrey strolled over to the tray of crystal decanters. He poured himself a brandy.

His mother's eyes widened. "Brandy? Geoffrey, it is not even eight o'clock in the morning."

Which begged the question of why the viscountess was up at such an uncharacteristic hour and interrupting one of his stolen moments of quiet. He knew better than to ask as much. Geoffrey took a sip. "There's little harm in a brandy to celebrate my thirtieth year."

She blinked. "Is it...?"

"Yes."

Hi mother wrinkled her brow. "Hmph. Happy Birthday," And then..."You are causing a scandal with that American..."

"Abigail Stone."

"Woman."

"I observed you at the theater last evening, Geoffrey. You did not take your eyes off one another once."

"Mother—"

She jabbed a finger in his direction. "You made a promise after your father's death."

Guilt ripped through him. "And I intend to honor those promises." He downed the brandy. He reached for the bottle and poured another, to the rim. He had every intention of getting fully soused.

His mother took a deep breath. She held her hands up. "Geoffrey, I do want you to be happy."

Geoffrey looked down into the amber contents of his glass. He'd forfeited all right to happiness when he'd chosen Emma over his father and family. He took a long swallow, and set the glass down hard on the mahogany table. Liquid sloshed over the rim. "I have already stated my intentions, Mother. I've chosen Lady Beatrice as my future wife." *If she'll have me.*

His mother studied him intently as if to determine the veracity of his words. She seemed to find truth in his promise for she nodded.

"Forgive me, Geoffrey. After that *situation* with Miss Marsh, I sometimes still fear you'll be driven by your passions."

And here he'd believed he'd done a masterful job of handling himself with a suitable level of decorum the past four, nearly five years. It appeared his mother awaited the moment he would make his next, great misstep. Geoffrey looped his hands behind his back and walked over to the floor-length windows that overlooked the quiet street below. "This topic grows tedious, Mother."

From the smooth, clear surface of the windowpane his mother's reflection stared back at him. She rang her fingers together. "I've seen the way you look at that w…Miss Stone," she corrected. "No good can come of it, Geoffrey."

"I understand that."

But why can't it, a voice niggled somewhere deep inside. Abigail was the granddaughter of one of the oldest and most respected titles in the realm. Her father, though a former servant, had amassed a small fortune and established a flourishing shipping enterprise.

Abigail was not Emma. Abigail was incapable of the deceit and trickery that had filled Emma Marsh's black heart.

His mother touched his shoulder.

He stiffened.

"Geoffrey, I know you think me cold and unfeeling, but aside from the death of your father, nothing has caused me greater pain than seeing how Emma Marsh hurt you."

The agony of guilt robbed him of breath. For years he'd withheld the details of that night from his mother, knowing the truth would destroy her. Or mayhap he was merely a coward. In sharing the truth, he would always be the recipient of his mother and sister's deserved scorn.

"We've been invited to attend a dinner party at the Duke of Somerset's. I suspect he's gathered the nature of your intentions, Geoffrey. You are so very close to securing one of the most coveted matches of the Season."

He nodded.

His mother removed her hand from his shoulder. "Happy Birthday, Geoffrey."

Geoffrey touched a hand to the front of his jacket, where Abigail's stained lace rested against his heart. "Mother," he said, his voice tried to his own ears. "I've letters to see to."

She took her leave with a stony silence. As the door closed with a decisive click, he fetched his partially drunk glass of brandy and the crystal decanter, and carried them over to his desk. Geoffrey settled into the comfortable leather folds of his winged back chair, and sloshed the liquid into his glass. He set the bottle down.

This had been the exact spot Father had sat the moment Geoffrey had confessed his intentions to wed Emma Marsh.

His fingers tightened reflexively about the glass. Diminutive and possessed of hazel eyes and hair like spun gold, she could not be more different in appearance than Abigail. A bright-eyed, teasing flirt, Emma had been the youngest daughter to an impoverished baronet and with her tinkling laugh, she had captivated Geoffrey the moment he'd first seen her at Almack's.

She had led him a merry little chase, vowing not to settle for a match less than a marquess.

Geoffrey stared into the amber depths of his glass. When she'd suddenly shifted her attentions and affections wholeheartedly to him, he'd naively believed she'd loved him, besotted fool that he was.

He finished his brandy in one gulp, welcoming the fiery trail it blazed down his throat.

His mother constantly likened Abigail to Emma...but nothing could be further from the truth. Abigail did not crave and require pretty compliments and the undivided attention as Emma had. In fact, he could count on just one hand the number of sets Abigail had danced. Instead, she seemed to prefer keeping company of the partner-less young ladies, and skirted the edges of Society's periphery.

Geoffrey poured himself another brandy, well onto his way to getting thoroughly foxed.

He'd defied his family's wishes only once before. The outcome had proven disastrous. The consequence one he would never be fully absolved of.

But bastard that he was, Geoffrey still yearned to make a match not dictated by stiff propriety and decorum.

Tonight he would take dinner with the Duke of Somerset and see to his responsibilities...just as he had done for five years.

Geoffrey hadn't wanted for more...

Until now.

FOURTEEN

While attending dinner parties, a gentleman should give his
undivided attention to the persons seated next to him.
4ᵗʰ Viscount Redbrooke

*O*ne head of hare.
One serpent.

Abigail's gaze moved beyond Lord Lewlick's shoulder and focused on the window. The curtains were drawn back just enough to allow the moon to filter its white light through the brocaded fabric, and reveal a smattering of stars.

She craned her neck. Was there really just one serpent? She'd imagine with the powerful Medusa, the Greeks would have had more...

"I do so hope that frown has nothing to do with my company?" A deep baritone drawled close to her ear.

Abigail jerked her attention back to Lord Sinclair, the dark devil who'd been assigned the seat beside her during her uncle's dinner party.

She picked up her spoon and toyed with the pistachios and pomegranate garnish in her bowl of white soup. "Forgive me," she said, offering him a smile. "I was considering the stars," she confessed.

Sinclair sat back in his seat. "I was considering the stars as well," he confessed.

Abigail scrambled forward in her seat. "Truly?"

He leaned close, so close she detected the hint of red wine upon his breath. "I was thinking how the brightest star couldn't compare to your beauty, Miss Stone."

Abigail sat back in her chair, her jerky movements caused her elbow to knock the table. Soup spilled over the side of her bowl and smattered the ivory lace tablecloth. "Oh," she said, blinking down at it.

A servant rushed over and she used the diversionary opportunity to look away from Lord Sinclair's intense scrutiny.

She knew she should be appreciative, and honored by his effusive compliments and high-praise, and yet…she sighed, battling down disappointment.

"Do you know, Miss Stone," Lord Sinclair began when the servant slipped away, "you seem less than thrilled by my compliment."

She shook her head. "Oh, no. Not at all. It is just…" She cleared her throat. "That is to say…"

He rested his hands upon the arms of his chair, looking for all the world like a man who owned the dining room and was not a mere guest of the Duke of Somerset's dinner party.

Abigail glanced down the long dining table. Her stare landed on Beatrice, now conversing with Lord Sedgwick, who occupied the seat on her right.

To her left, sat the Viscount Redbrooke.

Abigail sucked in a breath. Instead of looking at Beatrice, Geoffrey's raw, heated stare was fixed upon Abigail.

"I've never known Lord Redbrooke to do anything so bold as to stare in public."

She jumped at Lord Sinclair's statement.

Even with the great space separating them, Abigail detected the four creases that furrowed Geoffrey's brow, and the subtle muscle that twitched in the corner of his lip.

"It appears you've captivated the viscount," Sinclair said, his tone peculiar.

Abigail shook her head. "No. He is courting my cousin…"

"He might be courting your cousin, Miss Stone, but he's not removed his eyes from you since the moment we were seated."

Abigail stared into the contents of her porcelain bowl, unwilling to meet Lord Sinclair's knowing expression. She picked up her spoon and tapped it distractedly along the side of her place setting.

When the silence between them stretched onward, she stopped, and set her spoon down, looking up at him.

A half-grin turned the corners of his lips. "And other than the stars, and now your bowl of soup, you've not removed your eyes from him."

Panic built in her breast. She shook her head emphatically, appalled that she'd been so very transparent. "No, you're mistaken." Because if Lord Sinclair had detected how thoroughly bewitched, how hopelessly besotted she was with Geoffrey, then surely others had as well. She folded her palms on her lap to hide their tremble. "You are mistaken," she repeated, this time more firmly.

His eyes lingered upon her face. "I wish that I was," he said, his words a near whisper. "You intrigue me, Miss Stone. And I'm not one intrigued by marriageable misses."

She managed a weak smile. "That is kind of you." Only, there could be no young lady further from appropriate marriageable material, than herself.

"I didn't say it to be kind. I said it to be truthful. If my mother insists I wed, I'd rather find an unconventional lady such as you."

A startled laugh burst from her lips, attracting the notice of those seated around the table. She buried her amusement behind her hand. From the opposite end of the table, Geoffrey glowered at her and Lord Sinclair.

Lord Sinclair leaned so close, his breath fanned her cheek. "I do believe he's jealous, Miss Stone."

She pointed her eyes to the ceiling. "You're wrong," she insisted. "You mistake his disapproval for interest."

"Come, Miss Stone. You are too intelligent to believe that." He winked at her. "He was not always serious, you know. Ahh, I see I have your attention now."

"Have you known Lord Redbrooke very long?" She strove for nonchalance.

Lord Sinclair picked up his wine glass and took a sip. "I say, it's rather humbling."

She blinked. "My lord?"

"I've sat next to you for more than a half-hour or so. I've attempted to charm you and capture your attention, but this is the first real interest you've paid me this evening."

Abigail's feet curled in her slippers. Mama would be shamed at the deplorable effort she'd put into securing a match. Lord Sinclair was everything a young lady should desire; wickedly handsome, abundantly clever, and quite complimentary. He should be everything she needed to make her forget Alexander's betrayal.

So why was she sitting here, ruminating like a silly miss about Geoffrey, seated alongside her cousin, holding a glass of wine with such graceful elegance.

After a long stretch of silence, Lord Sinclair sighed. "Yes. I've known Redbrooke for a number of years. At one time, we moved in the same social circles. He was always ready with a smile, and quite sought after by the...er...sought after," he finished lamely.

The ladies.

Abigail studied Geoffrey a moment. With his broad, powerful shoulders, and muscles that fairly strained the fabric of his garment, she imagined women would be mad not to desire the viscount, regardless of his seriousness—seriousness that she found she rather preferred.

"What happened to him?" Abigail asked, unable to call the question back.

Lord Sinclair frowned. "There was a scandal. I'm not certain anyone knows all the details, but it involved a young lady, a baronet's daughter, I believe. The details of what happened to the lady are not known, but after she disappeared from Polite Society, well, he was never the same." He followed her gaze to Geoffrey. "I've said enough," he murmured.

As if sensing he were the source of discussion between Abigail and Lord Sinclair, Geoffrey glowered at the both of them.

Lord Sinclair's next words interrupted her musings. "If I cannot steal your attentions from the very proper Lord Redbrooke, well then I'm going to enjoy making him writhe in his seat with envy."

"He is not writhing with envy." Abigail stole a glimpse of Geoffrey. And looked back to Lord Sinclair. "He's merely shifting in his seat."

"With envy," he added.

She smiled, shaking her head at him. "You are incorrigible, my lord."

A servant appeared, clearing their bowls of soup away and setting out the next course; loin of veal in a béchamel sauce.

"And I'm envious," he said. Something in his tone, an unexpected seriousness from the normally affable rogue, gave her pause.

Lord Braincourt, seated on the opposite side of Lord Sinclair said something that required his attention, for which Abigail was grateful. She picked up her fork and knife and delicately sliced the veal on her plate. She raised a bite to her mouth and considered Lord Sinclair's revelation about Geoffrey.

A pang of ugly, very real envy slashed through her.

There had been a young lady—a lady who'd surely made him smile, and considering his stern countenance, had forever changed him into the gentleman Polite Society now saw.

Abigail, however, had seen more. She'd seen a man who'd shed his boots in front of all to see just to rescue her token from Lizzie. She'd witnessed the fury he'd unleashed on Lord Carmichael to protect and defend her. She stared down contemplatively at the plate in front of her, wondering at the lady foolish enough to relinquish Geoffrey.

Having been shamed and humiliated by Alexander, Abigail had an even greater appreciation for a gentleman of integrity, capable of genuine love and devotion.

Her family spoke of Abigail making a match, and yet, for the first time since she'd learned the extent of Alexander's deceit, she began to believe that maybe, just maybe, she could love again.

Geoffrey could name all manner of things he'd rather to do than sit at the Duke of Somerset's long dining hall table, as Abigail conversed with Lord Sinclair.

Why, he'd rather be forced to sit through Mama's lecture about his duties as viscount.

Which was saying a good deal. Because he loathed the nuisance his mother so often made of herself as much as he detested being the subject of public scrutiny.

Geoffrey punished himself instead with the sight of Abigail seated beside Sinclair. It didn't escape his notice the number of furtive glances she stole in Geoffrey's direction. It didn't escape his notice, because he studied her with the same dogged intensity.

He growled. If Sinclair didn't remove his gaze from the generous swell of her décolletage, by God he'd drag the blighter across the table, and...

"You seem preoccupied, my lord," Lady Beatrice murmured.

Geoffrey blamed his distractedness on too much drink earlier that day. He shook his head, returning his attention to Lady Beatrice. "Forgive me," he murmured, and reached for his glass of wine. He took a sip, and then sat the glass back down.

"It is Abigail," Lady Beatrice interjected, her words nothing more than the faintest whisper.

Geoffrey choked on his red wine.

"Come, my lord. I see the way you study her."

He cleared his throat, mind curiously blank.

Lady Beatrice leaned closer and said quietly, "You do not want to court me, my lord."

"Of course, I want to court you," he said with a steely edge to his words.

Her lips twitched. "I'm almost flattered, my lord," she teased. "But your heart would never belong to me."

"Hearts needn't be engaged in a marriage," he said, his response automatic. "I would protect you. You'd never want for anything."

She gave him a sad little smile. "Anything except love." Lady Beatrice leaned back in her chair. "I mention love, and you look at me with such shocked horror, I wonder if I've merely imagined the way you study my cousin."

Unbidden, his gaze flitted to Abigail, and then back to Beatrice.

A smile played about her lips. "No. I do not think I'm wrong. I suspect, however, that even if you don't yourself realize it, you care for her. With no malice or regret, I encourage your courtship of Abby." With that dismissal, she turned her attention to Lord Sedgwick.

The logical portion of Geoffrey's brain urged him to protest, to maintain his devotion to courting her.

The words wouldn't come.

Lady Beatrice had rejected him. Quite simply and with a directness he'd not expected of the demure, gentle young lady. As Geoffrey sat there, he expected he should feel some regret or disappointment at Lady Beatrice's rejection. Since he'd inherited the Redbrooke title, he'd become accustomed to acquiring everything and anything he desired. He'd employed a ruthless determination to business ventures, and matters of politics. Even his familial obligations where his sister Sophie's future was concerned had been conducted with a needlelike precision and steely logic.

In a matter of days his world had been tossed upside down.

Instead of panic or regrets, Lady Beatrice had somehow freed him. He stared down at his plate of nearly untouched veal.

His mother, Lady Beatrice, they both spoke of his desire for Abigail.

He'd resolved to never give himself over to those fickle, unreliable sentiments. With Abigail's outlandish interests, and her birthright as a servant's daughter, she would never be considered a suitable bride.

Furthermore, ladies did not study matters of astronomy and astrology.

And young ladies in the market for a husband most certainly didn't publicly denigrate their own dancing skills. His lips twitched. Even if one happened to be a more than poor study.

And yet...

This lady did.

"My lord?"

Geoffrey started, and looked to Lady Beatrice. "Yes, my lady?"

"The meal has concluded."

Geoffrey blinked, and looked around. His cravat tightened with sudden embarrassment at the lords and ladies present who eyed him sitting there, staring at his plate like a moonstruck calf.

"Ahh, yes. Forgive me," he said quickly, and rose, grateful when the gentlemen withdrew to partake in brandy.

He required distance from Abigail Stone. With space between them, it would be easier to forget the glimmer in her gray-blue eyes, or the way her bow-shaped lips curved up in a smile, or her endearing tendency to trod upon her dance partners' toes, or...

He was a bloody liar.

He would never be able to forget the lovely Abigail Stone.

FIFTEEN

Following a formal supper, a gentlemen needs to strictly observe the after-dinner customs of withdrawing for port with his fellow gentlemen.
4ᵗʰ Viscount Redbrooke

bigail ignored the inane conversations about fripperies and soirées and everything else the young ladies and their mothers present happened to be discussing throughout the Duke of Somerset's parlor. She wandered to the edge of the room, tugged the curtain back and gazed out at the night sky.

From the corner of the room, Beatrice sat conversing with several young ladies. They broke off into a fit of giggles. Abigail marveled that she'd ever been so very innocent. How greatly her life had changed in the span of a few months. She'd gone from blushing, innocent debutante to scandalized woman forced to flee the shame she'd wrought upon her family's name.

Using the distractedness of those present, Abigail took the opportunity to skirt the edge of the room, and slip out the door into the silent hall. She closed her eyes, welcoming the bliss of privacy, and then wandered the length of the hall. She weaved her way toward the parlor that opened out onto her uncle's meticulously maintained gardens.

As a relative of the host, her presence could easily be explained away. Her lips twisted. And if not, well, there were far greater scandals than excusing herself from company to steal a silent moment in the moonlight.

Abigail slipped inside the Chintz Parlor, resplendent in floral décor. From the rose-patterned curtains to the Aubusson carpet stitched with lilacs and lilies, it inspired a desire for a different setting than the dirt-laden streets of London.

She closed the door behind her and turned around.

"Abigail," a deep voice murmured.

A startled gasp escaped her. She slapped a hand to her breast, and her eyes searched for his now familiar figure in the room lit only by the glow of the moonlight. "Geoffrey," she greeted, as her eyes adjusted to the dark room. Abigail located him over by the doors leading onto the terrace.

His gaze remained focused out the window, on the grounds below. She chewed her lip, looking from Geoffrey back to the door behind her. If they were discovered, she'd cause a scandal to nearly match the one she'd fled back home.

Reason told her to turn around.

Reason told her to flee.

She took one step forward.

"Lady Beatrice has rejected my suit."

Abigail froze, the tip of her slipper hovered a hairsbreadth above the floor. She completed her step. "I'm sorry, Geoffrey." And oddly, she found even with the envy she'd felt over his honorable intentions for Beatrice, she meant it. She didn't want to see him hurt.

Her words were met with silence.

Abigail took another step.

"I don't like seeing you with Sinclair."

She cocked her head. "I beg your pardon?" she asked quietly.

"That bastard Sinclair. I don't like the way he looks at you."

"Oh." Abigail blinked, stunned by his harsh pronouncement.

Geoffrey still remained stock still, his broad, muscular back presented to her. "I cannot explain my reaction. It shouldn't matter who courts you."

Her heart stilled.

"Yet it does, Abby. It matters for reasons I don't understand…and for reasons that terrify me," he said hoarsely.

She took a step toward him, and another, and another, until she hovered at the point just beyond his shoulder. He tensed, but she reached past him and pressed the handle of the door. Unseasonably warm spring air spilled into the room, and surrounded them with the sweet fragrant scent of roses and crocuses.

Abigail took him by the hand. "Come with me," she said.

Geoffrey hesitated a moment, and she waited for him to do the proper thing and take his leave. Except, he continued to defy every preconceived notion she carried of him as a stiffly formal nobleman. He allowed her to pull him along to the armillary at the center of the garden.

"What...?"

"Shh," she said, placing one finger against her lips, and then pointed her finger skyward. "That is Lyra." Geoffrey's indecipherable stare followed her finger, upward. Abigail studied the lute-shaped formation in the sky. "Orpheus was given the harp by Apollo. He would use the harp to play for his bride, Eurydice. Some say her playing was so beautiful, that when man or animal heard the sound of it, they would stop what they were doing and just listen." Geoffrey remained silent. "Eurydice died suddenly and Orpheus was left broken-hearted. So he journeyed into the underworld, begging Hades to return her to him." At one time she'd believed the stuff of legends, had believed that a man was courageous enough to fight to claim her as his, at all costs.

"What happened to her?"

Abigail dropped her hand to her side but continued to study the pattern of stars. Until that moment she'd believed his silence indicated he found her recounting silly. How very different he was from Alexander, who had found her fascination with the stars tedious, and encouraged her to pursue more ladylike interests.

"Hades allowed Orpheus to take her back, under the condition that he'd trust Hades and not look back over his shoulder at her."

"And he of course, failed to abide by Hades orders." There was something bitter and cynical in that succinct utterance.

"He did," she confirmed. "And so Hades swept Eurydice back to the underworld. The stars were put there by Zeus to honor the love Orpheus had for Eurydice."

From the corner of her eye, she noted the way Geoffrey's firm, square jaw hardened. "Or it served to remind man of the dangers in not honoring ones word."

A smile teased the corner of her lips. "Perhaps, that, too." And Abigail expected that Alexander's betrayal should have disabused her of any further dreams of love. Her gaze locked with Geoffrey's. "But I prefer the romanticism of the first one, Geoffrey."

She expected him to smile, or chuckle. Except, having come to know him these past days, Abigail should have known he'd not be given to expressions of mirth. Instead, a frown darkened the hard, angular planes of his chiseled face. "You desire love."

She'd thought she'd had love with Alexander. Only just recently had Abigail realized she'd carried nothing more than a girlish infatuation for him. She'd worshipped him the way one might have honored the Greek gods. He'd cared for her, made her laugh, but he'd not truly embraced Abigail's true interests. With a woman's eyes, she could appreciate the level of foolhardiness on her part that she'd ever done something so rash as to give him her virtue.

"You are quiet, Abby. And you didn't answer my question."

Abigail lifted one shoulder in a slight shrug. "I didn't believe it was a question." And because she was suddenly too very uncomfortable with his precise questioning, she turned his question back on him. "And what of you, Geoffrey. Have you ever been in love?"

A cold, stony glint reflected in the moss green irises of his eyes, something dangerous, and pained. She took a step away from him.

"Yes."

Her eyes widened, and she suspected she must appear like a lack wit with her mouth open.

Geoffrey directed his attention to Lyra in the stars.

Abigail's mind suddenly spun under the flood of questions that opened up inside her mind. *Who was she? What had happened to her? Did he still love her?* A vise-like pain squeezed her heart.

"Her name was…is…Emma. She…" A hard smile formed on his lips. "She betrayed me. And taught me the perils of turning oneself over to that empty emotion called love."

Emma. Without him even needing to speak another word, Abigail hated the other woman. Hated her because she'd earned Geoffrey's love, and had been so callous as to throw aside his affection. Unlike Abigail who'd had the misfortune of trusting her heart to a gentleman who'd wanted nothing more than the pleasure of her body.

And because Abigail knew the pain of a broken heart and the bitter agony of betrayal, all she said was, "I'm sorry."

He waved his hand. "It was a long time ago."

"I don't imagine that lessens the pain. What…happened?" she asked hesitantly.

Geoffrey clasped his hands behind his back, and walked ahead several paces. "My father warned me her interest stemmed from my family's vast wealth and power."

She made a sound, and he stiffened, seeming to mistake the expression for pity. Abigail wandered over to him, encouraging him with her silence to continue his recounting.

His mouth hardened. "I didn't heed my father's sage advice." Those perfect, sculpted lips twisted into a macabre rendition of a smile. "Instead, I made arrangements to elope to Greta Greene. It was a miserable night. Cold. Sheets of rain and bolts of lightning." He jerked his chin up toward the sky. "Perhaps those mythical gods trying to warn me against my folly."

He fell silent.

Abigail touched her hand to his shoulder. The muscles bunched beneath her fingers, but he didn't pull away.

After Alexander's betrayal, Abigail had yearned for someone to take her in their arms and hold her close, assuring her that everything would be all right. No one had. Perhaps because they'd known it would not be all right, that her life had been irrevocably changed by her impulsive actions. She sought to give Geoffrey that which she'd so craved.

"Why did you not marry her?" she asked gently, prodding him to continue.

Abigail's question emerged hesitant, and gentle.

Geoffrey closed his eyes a moment, unable to fight the bitter chuckle from escaping. He pressed his fingertips alongside his temple in a bid to drive out the memory of his father's broken body, his mother's agonized cries as she learned of her husband's death. Geoffrey had never before shared the shame he'd carried these nearly five years.

He gave his head a firm shake. "I shouldn't be talking about this." Not to her. A respectable young lady.

"I'd wager, Geoffrey, you should have spoken of it long ago."

He closed his eyes finding her willingness to listen, oddly freeing.

When he opened his eyes he found her studying him with a gentle patience in the elegant lines of her face. In that, he found the courage to continue. "In the middle of the night, in that raging storm, my father set out after us. He was determined to prevent me from making a mistake I didn't realize I was making. My carriage could not navigate through the muddied roads." He remembered Emma's insistence that they continue on regardless of the dangerous conditions. At the time, he hadn't understood her desperation.

What a bloody fool he'd been.

"We were forced to stop at an inn. My father located us there. He leveled some very harsh charges against Emma. But I was," his lip curled back, "in love. I insisted he leave. I was determined to wed her. I said some truly reprehensible things to my father."

Words he could not call back. Words that, until Geoffrey drew his last breath, would forever haunt him.

Abigail took one of his hands and gave it a faint squeeze; her silent support far greater than any spoken words she might utter.

"In spite of the harsh words I hurled at him, in spite of the fact that I rejected his plea to not wed Emma, he still would not disinherit me." That had been the loving, dedicated father that the Viscount Redbrooke was. "Instead, he left me to my own mistakes. He turned around and rode off. His horse stepped in a hole on the muddied road. It shattered its leg and threw my father. His body was found by several villagers on their way to the inn."

The fall had broken his father's neck.

"Oh, Geoffrey," Abigail said ever so softly. She wrapped her arms about his waist and held him.

He stiffened at the feel of her in his arms, but then the lavender and lilac scent that clung to her, blended with the fragrant aroma of the buds in bloom all around them, moved him, far headier than any spirit. His arms came up around her and he accepted her silent support. Geoffrey rested his chin atop the satiny crown of her midnight black tresses.

He didn't care they were a stones-throw away from being discovered, alone, unchaperoned in the Duke of Somerset's formal gardens. He craved an absolution he'd thought impossible to achieve—until he'd taken her in his arms.

"All my plans of elopement," he said, forcing himself to tell the rest of the whole sordid story, "were of course quashed. Emma, begged me to continue on to Gretna Greene. The schemer believed I'd wed her even in the immediate aftermath of my father's death. I, of course, refused. At which point, she revealed the truth." A harsh, humorless laugh spilled out of his lips.

"The truth?"

"She was carrying someone else's child." Time hadn't lessened the shock of that revelation. His father had been correct; Geoffrey's judgment had been flawed, and his father had paid the ultimate price. "It didn't even matter the identity of her nameless lover. My father was dead and I may as well have killed him by my own hand. And all because I foolishly believed I loved her."

"Whatever happened to her?"

Geoffrey shrugged a shoulder. "Her father sent her off to his country seat in the far flung corners of Northumberland." Geoffrey had never seen her again, nor had he ever wanted to set sight upon the woman who'd deceived him.

"Oh, Geoffrey," she whispered.

He shrugged.

Abigail leaned back and her eyes roved a path over his face. "It is not your fault."

Geoffrey stiffened, and set her away from him. "Of course it is my fault," he said, his tone harsher than intended. "If I'd honored my obligations and responsibilities, my father would be alive."

"But you loved her."

He held her gaze, and she must have seen something dark and primitive in his eyes for she looked away. "I did not love her. I loved the illusion she presented. My responsibility was always to find and wed a proper, respectable demure English miss."

She froze, and it occurred to him he'd inadvertently offended her. "And that is why…"

"You want to wed Beatrice," she finished for him.

He nodded. Or, rather, that had been true at one point. He owed it as a kind of penance for his past transgressions, and yet, he was still a helpless sinner for he no longer could commit himself to wedding the young woman—even if it was to honor his father's expectations of him.

"Because she is a proper, respectable, demure English miss," Abigail said, her voice peculiarly hollow.

"Yes."

Her hands came up and she folded them about herself, as if warding off a chill. She looked up toward the night sky, inhaling deep.

His eyes, of their own volition went to the rapid fall and rise of her chest. The generous swell of her breasts tempted, beckoned him to partake in the visual feast she represented. With her lush feminity, she was more captivating than Michelangelo's rendering of the temptress Eve.

And he was the serpent at her feet, sinful, and wicked.

"Giving up your happiness will not rid you of the guilt you carry. Only you can find forgiveness in yourself, Geoffrey."

He jerked at the unexpectedness of her words. His desire died a swift death.

"And you presume to know what would make me happy?" he asked, coldly. In that moment, he resented Abigail Stone for having turned him into the same, weak man he'd been once before.

She looked away from the night sky and met his gaze with a bold intensity. "I know it isn't Beatrice."

Geoffrey closed the distance between them in two long strides. "What kind of spell have you woven over me?" he asked, the words harsh and desperate to his own ears.

Abigail leaned up and kissed him.

His body stiffened at the brazenness of her touch, and then, God help him, he was as lost as Adam had been when he'd been offered that damning piece of fruit. Geoffrey took her in his arms and slanted his mouth over hers again and again. Punishing and pleading all as one.

She moaned, and he slipped his tongue inside to reacquaint himself with the moist cavern. She kissed him back with a wanton eagerness that set his body aflame. His flesh sprang hard against her belly, and he moved his hands over the exposed skin of her arms, lower, down the curve of her hip, until he cupped her buttocks in his hands. Geoffrey groaned, and urged her closer.

Abigail's head fell back on a moan steeped in desperation. "Please, Geoffrey," she pleaded.

He nipped at the skin of her neck and she cried out. "Yes!"

That word echoed around his mind like the blare of a pistol's report. He jerked upright and set her away from him.

She swayed on her feet; her thick, sooty black lashes drifted open. "Geoffrey?"

His name served as a reminder. His obligation. His sins. His failings.

She stepped so close her body's heat warmed him. "You came out here for a reason, Geoffrey. You set aside propriety and the threat of discovery for a reason."

For her.

Instead, he said, "I was taking my leave for the evening."

She touched the tip of her fingers to his lips. "But you didn't leave. You stole away into my uncle's parlor, and allowed me to lead you outside. Do you know why that is?"

Because he'd gone mad. There was no other answer that made rationale sense.

Abigail continued. "Because you are not this cold, commanding figure you present to Society." A gentle breeze ruffled his hair, and a strand fell across his brow. She reached up and brushed it back. "You can't punish yourself the rest of your life. I, of course, never knew your father, but I do not believe he would want that of you."

Her words swirled about him. All the muscles in his body tightened, until he feared the slightest night breeze would shatter him. He took a step away from Abigail, and closed his eyes. For nearly five years, he'd believed he'd known exactly what his father had wanted of him. And yet…Father had merely wanted to spare him the pain of wedding a pernicious woman. His father had set out on horseback that long ago, thunderous night to save his son, not to punish him.

It had been Geoffrey who'd felt the need to flagellate himself over the loss of his father. Geoffrey opened his eyes and stared up at the twinkling starlight above. Abigail's words, they were the benediction he'd needed for so very long. Geoffrey's throat worked up and down reflexively. "Thank you, Abby."

Her brow wrinkled. "I've not done anything, Geoffrey."

This woman, who'd been a mere stranger a short while ago, seemed to somehow know him better than anyone else. She'd allowed him to look inside himself and confront all the ugliest darkest things he'd done in life.

"Abigail! Whatever are you doing?"

Abigail dropped her hand like she'd been burned, and spun to face Lady Beatrice who stood at the gaping parlor doors.

All the color leeched from Abigail's cheeks. He settled a hand on hers, a paltry attempt at calming the panicked glint in her wide eyes. "I…"

Lady Beatrice looked disapprovingly at Geoffrey a moment, and then returned her attention to Abigail. She held out a hand. "Come along. Father is looking for you. I insisted you were abovestairs, but we must return at once, lest you're discovered out here. Alone. With Lord Redbrooke," she said, with a pointed frown for Geoffrey.

Abigail nodded, and with a final glance in Geoffrey's direction, hurried off with Lady Beatrice.

Geoffrey stood stock still for so long, the muscles in his neck and back began to ache.

In the moment they'd been discovered, he should have been beset with guilt and regret that Lady Beatrice had discovered him and Abigail together. Except, all he'd felt was the searing loss of Abigail's departure. For in the too brief time they'd stolen in the garden, gazing up at the stars, his entire world had been upended with the staggering realization—he wanted her. In spite of his duties and obligations and the promises he'd made after his father's death, he wanted Abigail with an intensity that frightened him. He'd prided himself on having become a resilient, unrelenting gentleman; one who wouldn't repeat the mistakes of his youth.

But he was powerless to resist it any longer.

He expected he should feel some sense of panic at throwing over the oath he'd taken five years ago, but with Abigail's spirit and her beauty and her boldness, his world had been toppled like Boney's troops on their winter march through Russia.

His gaze climbed up to the sky as he studied the glimmering stars of Lyra. Orpheus had braved the underworld to reclaim his Eurydice. Geoffrey's lips twitched with mirth.

He supposed he could brave his mother's disapproval when he shared his intentions to court and wed the American, Abigail Stone.

SIXTEEN

A gentleman should speak in calming, modulated
tones when dealing with a distressed female.
4ᵗʰ Viscount Redbrooke

"**A**re you mad? Utterly mad? The kind of mad to rival King George himself?"

Mother's high-pitched screech pierced Geoffrey's ears and he shifted in his seat. Leaning back, he studied her as she frantically paced the Aubusson carpet at the center of his office. She occasionally paused, glanced up, and then shook her head, as she continued her pacing.

"You are handling this remarkably well," he said dryly.

She glowered at him. "You dare to make a jest of this? You, Geoffrey? You do not make jests."

He had at one time.

He attempted to placate her. "Mother," he began.

She held a hand up. "Not a word," she muttered, more to herself. "Marriage to that, to that…*American.* Your sister, why she scandalized Society with…with…" She colored. "I needn't repeat what happened. But she had the decency to capture the Earl of Waxham. This…" she slashed the air with her hand, "why, this is unpardonable. You'd wed that…that…"

"American," he supplied sardonically.

"Exactly!" she agreed, and punched the air with her fist. Apparently her fury over Geoffrey's aims to wed Abigail Stone prevented her from detecting his intended sarcasm.

Geoffrey sat back in his chair, and folded his arms across his chest. "That American as you refer to her, is in fact the Duke of Somerset's niece."

"The Duke of Somerset's niece," she muttered under her breath, shaking her head. She stopped in front of him and threw her arms open wide. "You had assured me of your intentions to court Lady Beatrice Dennington."

Yes, he'd intended to wed the demure and perfectly proper Lady Beatrice. He'd believed she'd suited him.

Until Abigail.

"Things have changed, Mother," he said patiently, as though speaking to a skittish colt.

"Things have changed? Things have changed, Geoffrey?" Her voice steadily increased in volume and pitch. "Days change, Geoffrey. Minutes on the clock change. One does not simply *change* ones selection for a marital partner."

Geoffrey steepled his fingers and rested his chin upon them. "It was never my intention to…to…come to care for Abigail."

She resumed her frantic pacing, muttering under her breath in a most undignified manner. "She is wholly inappropriate."

"Her father is a wealthy shipping magnate in America."

She cringed. "Her father is nothing more than a servant." His mother's scathing tone cut into his defense. "Come Geoffrey, the scandal which precipitated her mother and father's rapid departure to America is not an old one, and it is well-known." Mother stopped pacing. Her rapid breathing indicated the thin level of control the normally composed viscountess had on her emotions.

It occurred to him that he'd been just as pompous as Mother in his viewpoints. He shook his head. What a bloody ass he'd been.

"You've so admirably maintained a cool, reserved manner these past years. I had imagined," she shook her head sadly, "or *hoped*, rather, after that scandalous woman, you'd put such heady passions aside."

His mouth went dry as she dredged Emma's betrayal to the surface. He looked away from her accusatory stare, too much a coward to confront the disapproval teeming in her gaze. "Abigail is not Emma," he said the words for himself, just as much as for her benefit. In the years since his father's death, Geoffrey had vastly more experience from the callow youth he'd been; he'd come to have a greater grasp on both his self-control and his ability to evaluate the character and worth of a person.

His mother stomped over in a most unladylike manner and stopped in front of his desk. She arched a brow. "Do we even know that for certain? After all, her mother was responsible for a great scandal. Is it unlikely that the daughter would be just as disreputable?"

Odd, he didn't know the details surrounding Abigail's mother's flight from England. It had never seemed to matter.

Geoffrey frowned. His mother's revelation mattered naught. He had little intention of altering his plans to wed Abigail.

He shoved back his chair and climbed to his feet, tired of his mother's unfounded charges against Abigail's reputation. "In the months she's resided in London, Abigail's done nothing Polite Society can find fault with."

Mother folded her arms across her chest. "She cannot dance. Why, she trods all over her dance partners' feet."

His lips tightened. "I'd not be so trite as to not court a woman because she's not skilled upon the dance floor."

"Hmph. Very well, then, there was the matter of her speaking to you without introduction." He started. "Oh, come, Geoffrey. Did you truly believe I wouldn't have paid attention to you and that scandalous creature's first meeting?"

Fury fell like a curtain across his eyes, and he blinked it back. His mother continued, either unknowing or uncaring of the volatile emotions thrumming through him. "And rumor would have it, that the Duke of Somerset allowed that American woman into his home because she is escaping some kind of scandal." She dropped her voice to a low whisper as though she were imparting some great secret that would forever destroy the Redbrooke reputation. "We do not even know the details of her being here!"

Geoffrey folded his arms across his chest. "I believed it safe to assume the lady was in fact here for a London Season."

If looks could burn, then Geoffrey would be reduced to a pile of ash at the viscountess' feet. "This is no game, Geoffrey. This. Is. The. Redbrooke. Line." She dropped her voice to a hushed whisper. "I also heard rumors of a most improper meeting between the young lady and Lord Carmichael…"

A loud humming filled Geoffrey's ears. His mother's mouth was moving, but he'd ceased to process words. Fury; potent and all-consuming spread to every corner of his body until he wanted to turn his desk upside down and storm from the room, hunting down that bloody bastard. By god, he would beat the old letch down all over again.

When he again trusted himself to speak, Geoffrey said, "Carmichael is a loathsome, reprehensible cad. It would do to not to listen to rumors from his lying lips."

His mother cocked her head. "You considered wedding Sophie to him."

He closed his eyes a moment, and then opened them. "I was merely trying to guide Sophie to making a match." Then, it occurred to him. "You didn't truly believe I would have seen Sophie wed Carmichael?"

Her silence served as the answer to his question.

Were his mother and sister's opinion of him so low that they truly believed he'd ever accept the suit of that foul fiend?

His mother made an impatient sound. "Regardless, Sophie is now wed to Waxham. It is your marital circumstances I wish to discuss. I do not want you to wed that American woman."

"Abigail," he corrected automatically.

"Bah," she cried. "What manner of name is Abigail? Even her name is wholly inappropriate for the next Viscountess Redbrooke."

He'd had enough. Geoffrey clenched his jaw and squeezed his next words out past tight lips. "Mother, I intend to wed Abigail. There are no great scandals…"

"How can you be sure?" his mother cried.

He continued, ignoring her interruption. "She has noble blood-lines and her family is well-connected." Those things mattered to his mother…and just a short while ago had mattered very much to

Geoffrey. Until Abigail. "And she makes me happy," he added, not expecting those last words to hold any real weight with his mother.

Her next words proved him correct. "Then take a mistress, Geoffrey. But please, I implore you, do not dilute your noble bloodlines with that American woman and her common family." Tears filled his mother's eyes.

Guilt twisted around his stomach. He had no intentions of deviating in his plans to wed Abigail, but that didn't lessen the guilt of causing his mother pain. Not, when he'd already caused her the greatest agony with his father's death. "I'm sorry, Mother," he said quietly. The least of what he was sorry for, however, was Abigail Stone.

She held her palms outward, in supplication. "Please, Geoffrey. You know so very little about the lady and yet you'd offer her your name and all that goes with the distinguished Redbrooke title."

He frowned. Odd, how in so short a time Abigail had tossed his life into such an upheaval he'd brave Mother's disapproval for the opportunity to again laugh and smile. It was, as mother said, sheer madness to forget himself for the sake of a woman. However, Abigail was a siren, and Geoffrey had been lured by her effervescent spirit; a spirit that had only served to remind him that he himself was very much alive.

Mother studied him. She seemed to use the time to compose herself, for when she spoke, her tone was more steady, the look in her eyes less desperate. "Very well, Geoffrey. If you intend to wed this…"

"Abigail," he interjected, sternly. The sooner she accepted his intentions to wed Abigail, and acknowledged that Abigail would be the future Viscountess Redbrooke, then the easier it would be.

"If you insist on wedding *Abigail*," she amended. "Then I would put a favor to you."

He eyed her warily. "What is it?"

"I would ask you to act with more prudence than you did with Miss Emma Marsh. Court her. But there is no reason to move hastily in this regard."

Geoffrey reclaimed his seat. He drummed his fingertips along the arm of his chair. His mother was indeed correct. His urgency stemmed from nothing more than a desire to make Abigail Stone his. He remembered Sinclair, last evening. The bold, bastard's roguish stare fixed upon Abigail. The other man had barely uttered a word to the guests around him, his focus reserved solely for Abigail. Geoffrey knew as much. Because he'd studied Abigail and Sinclair's every interaction. Sinclair's head bent close to her ear, the teasing grin on the other man's lips, the delicate pink of Abigail's blush.

He shook his head forcefully. "No. I'll not wait to make her my wife."

"Geoffrey!" his mother cried out. "Have you not learned from your mistakes? Your father…"

She must have seen something horrible written on Geoffrey's face, because her words died.

Geoffrey gripped the wood arms of his chair so tight, his nails left indents into the hard surface. He studied the opened ledgers upon his mahogany desk, the same desk his father had used to see to his business affairs.

"A fortnight," he said at last.

"And the three consecutive Sundays for the banns," his mother insisted, a determined edge had replaced the plaintive tone she'd employed for their discourse, up to that point.

Geoffrey inclined his head. "I'll not request a special license from the archbishop." The scandal created by his sister and brother-in-law, the Earl of Waxham had necessitated a special license. In Geoffrey's case, there was no scandal, merely impatience on his part.

He did not allow himself to consider the possibility Abigail might reject his suit. Any marriage between them would require she forsake all she'd known and begin a new life, in a new country.

Geoffrey shoved the thought aside. Abigail would say yes. The alternative…he shook his head. There really was no alternative.

His mother clasped her hands in front of her. "Are you certain there is nothing I can say that will make you see reason?"

"There is not."

She said nothing for a long moment. Then, nodded slowly. "Very well, then, Geoffrey. I hope you will not be hurt."

Again.

He set his jaw at a stony angle. "I don't intend to be, Mother."

She shook her head with infinite slowness. "Mark my words, Geoffrey. You are acting rashly. Now, if you'll excuse me. I've a visit with Lady Davenport." Mother gave a flounce of her hair, and spun on her heel.

"Mother," he called, when she reached the door.

She paused with her hand on the handle but didn't turn to face him.

"She is a good woman."

"Well, I imagine time will reveal whether or not *that* is accurate," she said frostily.

With that, she opened the door, and closed it behind her.

SEVENTEEN

When courting a young lady, a gentleman would be wise to pro-
vide the young lady with flowers from the hothouse.
4ᵗʰ Viscount Redbrooke

Seated at the small rose-inlaid mahogany writing desk, Abigail
stared at the blank parchment in front of her. She'd intended to
draft a note for her brothers and sister. Instead, she sat, considering
last evening's exchange with Geoffrey. She trailed the tip of her pen in
a circle upon the parchment. Then, sighed, and tossed the pen down.
There was no hope for it; Abigail could not concentrate. She glanced
to the full floor-length terrace door that overlooked her uncle's gardens, remembering back to her meeting with Geoffrey.

Her heart bled for the pain he'd been dealt by that viperous creature and for the guilt Geoffrey still carried. Abigail knew those sentiments all too-well, for she woke up with it every morning—the constant
reminder of the disappointment she'd been to her family.

"Are you all right? You, seem distracted."

Abigail started and looked at Beatrice, seated upon the sofa with
her embroidery frame in her hands.

"I'm all right."

Beatrice lowered her frame. "Are you certain?"

"I'm certain. Please, do not let me distract you from your efforts."

Beatrice set the floral stitched cloth aside, a hurt expression on her
lovely face. "You are no bother, Abby."

Abigail stood and walked over to her cousin. She slid into the seat
alongside Beatrice, and studied the purple, blue, and green threads

that made up the immaculate piece. How very gifted her cousin was; gifted in all the ways young ladies were intended to be.

Gentlemen desired flawless ladies, such as Beatrice. No gentleman sought a blue-stocking with an inordinate amount of interest in Greek mythology and constellations.

Her heart twisted. Though in the end, it hadn't been Abigail's lack of ladylike talents that had destroyed all possible marital prospects.

Geoffrey's visage flashed to her mind. The way he'd been two nights ago; raw pain, etched in the angular lines of his noble cheeks, the brittle twist of his hard lips.

Or mayhap it had been that her wounded soul had recognized a kindred spirit in him?

"You seem distracted again, Abby."

She jumped. "I am," she admitted, hearing the sheepish tone to her confession.

"Is it Lord Redbrooke?"

Abigail blinked. Surely she'd misheard her. "I…uh…" Oh, goodness. "Are you certain you don't have feelings for the viscount, Beatrice? Because if you do, I swear I'll never think of his name again." It was a lie. For the remainder of her life, she'd remember the solemn gentleman who'd made her again dream of love.

Beatrice snorted. "Surely I've been rather clear in my feelings for Lord Redbrooke. Oh, he seems like a nice enough gentleman," Beatrice hurried to assure her. Abigail released a breath she'd not even realized she'd been holding. "He is far too serious, Abby." She wrinkled her nose. "I do not want a too-serious gentleman."

Abigail did. That seriousness is what had first drawn her to Geoffrey—his sober, stoic honesty.

Her stomach tightened at the irony. She craved honesty even as she carried a secret shame. Those muscles in her belly contracted, and she had to fold her arms across her waist to drive back the pain of it.

"I was going to visit the shops today for some ribbon. Will you join me?" her cousin invited, seeming unaware of the tumultuous thoughts raging through Abigail.

Abigail managed a wan smile and waved her hand. "I wanted to finish writing a letter to my family."

Beatrice stood in a flounce of skirts. "Letter writing?" She wrinkled her nose as though Abigail had stated her intentions to pay a visit to Newgate Prison. "Are you certain?"

"I am."

Beatrice sighed. "Very well, then."

Abigail stared after her cousin's retreating figure. When the door closed, Abigail stood, and wandered over to the terrace windows. The gray sky, filled with large, dark, black clouds perfectly matched her mood. As if Zeus, Lord of the Sky, God of the Rain had taken offense at her promise to Geoffrey, a drop of rain fell upon the window pane. Then another. And another. Until a torrent opened, and water fell from the sky in great, streaming rivulets. Abigail studied two beads of rain and followed their downward race upon the windowpane, until they disappeared.

Anything to keep from thinking about Geoffrey's confession. Her efforts proved futile. Not unlike her, Geoffrey had given his heart to an undeserving person. In Abigail's case, however, she carried the shame of having given up her virtue. She closed her eyes. Geoffrey would think her no different than the deceitful Emma.

A man such as he, who'd come to value respectability above all else, could never take to wife a woman who by her actions, had demonstrated herself to be less than a lady. She managed a wry smile. Not that Geoffrey had any intentions, honorable or dishonorable, toward her.

Abigail opened her eyes and stared out at the grounds where they had stood two evenings ago.

Except…

If that were true…

Why had he shared the pained remembrance of his past; truths, that by his own admission, he'd not shared with any other?

Abigail shook her head back and forth against the smooth surface of the cool windowpane. Why, hadn't she merely confessed to him the reason for her journey to London? It had been a night of shared truths…and yet, she'd withheld the shameful pieces of her past. The truth was, she was a coward.

Geoffrey's sole mistake had been in loving a woman, a woman who'd wronged him.

In Abigail's case, her mistake had been loving a man, and acting on that love. She would forever remember her mother's bitter, agonized tears of despair, her shouted protestations that Abigail did not know what she'd done.

And until she'd come to know and care for Geoffrey, Abigail hadn't truly grasped the extent of her actions.

"Fool, fool, fool."

"If you're counting fools, you will never run shy of names in London."

Abigail screeched, at the unexpected intrusion, and spun around.

Her cousin Robert sat upon the yellow sofa, eyeing her with an inscrutable expression, and a gentle smile on his lips.

Her skin warmed, not realizing she'd spoken aloud. "I did not hear you enter. Forgive me," she said, lamely, wondering how long he'd been there, privy to her silent humiliation. She dropped her gaze to the floor.

"You're not a fool, Abby," he said quietly.

Abigail wrenched her gaze back to his. Apparently he'd been present even longer than she'd hoped.

"You're not a fool," he repeated.

"I…" She folded her hands in front of her, clasping them tightly.

"I know why you came to London, Abby, and if there wasn't an ocean between me and that bastard, I swear on God himself, I would gladly put a bullet through the blackguard's heart."

Her throat bobbed up and down. She hadn't realized Robert had known about the reason for her visit. Of course, it was foolish to imagine the duke hadn't shared the details with his only son and heir.

"And I don't believe Redbrooke is worthy of you, either."

She jerked her head up so quickly, the muscles in her neck wrenched painfully. Abigail ignored the ache. "Beatrice told you."

Robert hooked his ankle across his knee. "Come, do you believe I'd be so blind as to fail to note your notice of Redbrooke?" He arched a brow, and then grinned sheepishly. "And yes, Bea might have mentioned it."

Abigail managed a laugh. She walked over, and took the seat alongside him on the yellow-velvet sofa. "He's very proper."

"And quite stodgy," Robert added.

She frowned at Robert's words so very similar to Beatrice's...and not at all flattering. He's not stodgy." She felt the need to defend.

He scratched his head. "You do know I'm speaking of Redbrooke. Not Sinclair?"

"I do."

Robert swiped a hand across his eyes and shook his head.

"What?" Abigail said, shifting in her seat.

"You've gone and fallen for him." A protest sprung to her lips, but Robert continued. "My father said Lord Sinclair was interested in a match."

Abigail fisted the fabric of her skirts.

"Sinclair smiles a good deal more than Redbrooke," Robert said.

Abigail remembered Alexander's quick smile. Yes, grinning gentlemen were not to be trusted. "He does."

"He'd make you a better husband than Redbrooke."

Perhaps. But not in the ways that mattered. "On what do you base your opinion?"

Robert draped his arms along the back of the chair, a contemplative gleam in his sapphire blue eyes. "Well," he began at last, "Sinclair will make you laugh." Alexander had used to make her laugh. "And Sinclair is an earl."

An earl, a viscount, a bread-maker. It was all the same to Abigail. Robert must have seen as much in her expression for he said, "And Sinclair will likely care a deal less about the fact that you're not," he colored. "That you're not..." A virgin. He tugged at his cravat. "English by birth," he finished lamely.

"My mother is English," she said.

"Uh, yes, that's right..."

She took pity on him, returning the conversation he'd begun. "I'm sure Lord Sinclair will make some young lady a very nice husband."

"But you don't want to wed him," Robert interjected.

She nodded. "But I don't want to wed him."

"And you do want to wed Redbrooke?"

She jerked at his words, taken aback. She blinked several times. Did she want to wed Geoffrey? She cared for him. Admired him. Understood the pain he'd known, and respected the convictions he carried after the hurts life had dealt him.

But did she want to wed him?

"I shall take your silence as confirmation," Robert drawled.

"No. No," she said a touch too hurriedly. She took a slow breath. "No, I don't want to wed him."

"Because he's stodgy?"

Robert didn't know the great heartache Geoffrey lived with. Geoffrey had done a masterful job in presenting himself as an aloof, unfeeling lord. Her cousins, just like the rest of the world, saw the hard-edged, always-proper figure Geoffrey presented to Polite Society. No. No one delved deeper to see the man he truly was; a man so honorable and good and loyal. "He's not stodgy."

Robert sighed. "You care for him, then?"

Abigail studied the folds of her emerald green skirts. "I do," she uttered quietly, the words oddly freeing. She cared about Geoffrey. This man who'd rescued her from the unwanted advances of a lecherous old nobleman, and saved her scrap of lace from Lizzie. He'd not looked down upon her fascination of the Greek constellations as Alexander and her brothers had been wont to do. And he'd confided in her, as if seeking an absolution of sorts, from her—regular, Abigail Stone from America.

Robert said nothing for a long moment. When at last he spoke, all traces of humor were gone from his expression and words. "Redbrooke values propriety above all else. All of Society knows that."

In other words, she, Abigail Stone, scandalous miss from America was no match for Lord Redbrooke.

"Perhaps no one will ever learn of what I've done," she murmured, hating the desperate hopefulness threading her words. She continued to pluck at the fabric of her skirts.

Robert placed his hand on hers, staying her movements. "Look at me, Abby."

She raised her gaze to his.

"It will matter to Redbrooke. Do you understand what I'm saying?"

Geoffrey would care that she'd thrown her virginity away as though it were nothing more than a smattered piece of parchment paper.

"It might not," Abigail insisted. Even as she spoke, she doubted the veracity of her own words.

Still, Geoffrey had made mistakes in matters of the heart. Surely he would understand that Abigail had done the same.

"You're wrong, Abby. I wish you weren't. But for some men, well, these things matter. And I strongly suspect Redbrooke will be one of those for whom it matters."

A knock sounded at the door and they looked up in unison.

The butler cleared his throat. He bore a silver tray with a card upon it. "The Viscount Redbrooke."

Abigail's heart lifted in her chest, buoyed with a lightness that sent her rising to her feet with embarrassing speed.

Geoffrey's tall, powerful frame filled the doorway.

"Lord Redbrooke," Robert drawled.

"Westfield," Geoffrey returned, never taking his gaze from Abigail. She felt herself coloring under the heated intensity of his scrutiny.

"Well," Robert cleared his throat. "Allow me to leave you two to your visit."

Geoffrey entered the room, thus allowing Robert to take his leave.

Abigail and Geoffrey stood there with only the echo of rain hitting the windowpanes to fill the quiet. "Geoffrey," she said.

"Abby."

Her heart warmed at her name as it tumbled so intimately and effortlessly off his lips. He advanced deeper into the parlor; a predator stalking its prey, and by god she wished to lay herself at his feet in supplication.

Abigail swallowed, her eyes going to the bouquet of striking violet buds interspersed with sprigs of ivy. Geoffrey appeared dogged in his intentions to court and wed Beatrice. For even after Beatrice had rejected his suit, he should continue to visit with such a beautiful offering. Abigail eyed the unfamiliar flowers that in their vibrancy put her in mind of the purpling sunset across the wide-expanse of ocean in her Connecticut home.

A hideous yearning crept around her heart like the relentless ivy growing along the duke's garden walls. The model of ladylike perfection, Beatrice would surely know the genus of each flower, and master the art of floral arrangements with the same excellence she showed for dancing and embroidering. "Allow me to get Beatrice." Then, Abigail could make her escape and spare herself the pain of Geoffrey's determined courtship of her more deserving cousin.

Abigail took a step toward him, and he held his hand up.

She stopped.

He said nothing, and the moment of silence lengthened.

Geoffrey beat his open-palm over the side of his leg in a distracted manner.

"Excuse me," Abigail said, and made to step around him.

He stepped into her path, yet again.

"They are for you," he blurted.

Her gaze fell to the flowers he held in his free hand. Abigail glanced around for her cousin Beatrice.

Geoffrey's fingers grazed her chin, and he gently turned her face toward his. "They are for *you*, Abby."

He held them out.

Her fingers closed around the bouquet wrapped in a violet-satin ribbon and hers and Geoffrey's fingers brushed. She closed her eyes remembering back to the feel of his hands upon her person. Oh god, he'd brought her flowers. "I…" *Do not know what to make of this gesture.* Abigail raised them to her nose and inhaled the sweet, delicate fragrance. "Thank you. They are beautiful." Why? Why would he do something like this? Why would he come calling with the stunning arrangement and wreak havoc upon her heart in this manner?

Geoffrey clasped his hands behind his back and looked toward the small crackling fire within the hearth. Abigail followed his gaze, unable to read the unfathomable expression in his eyes; the blue-green hue reminiscent of the Caribbean waters she'd sailed upon with Papa and Mama long, long ago. "My lord?"

"Geoffrey," he corrected. He wandered over to the terrace doors, and with hands still clasped behind his back, stared outside. "Do you know they say Theseus once travelled to Athens to present himself to his long lost father, King Aegeas." Geoffrey at last turned to face her. "The king's wife, Medea tried to give Theseus a glass of wine poisoned with the aconite flower." He motioned to the flowers in her hands.

Abigail followed his gesture, and realized he referenced the unfamiliar bloom in her hands. "Oh," she said. Her lips twitched. Not the most romantic of tales, still Geoffrey's gesture remained a beautiful one.

He nodded at the bouquet yet again. "The ivy I'm told was a symbol of immortality associated with Dionysus."

Abigail cocked her head.

Geoffrey cleared his throat. "It seemed fitting that the green of Dionysus be placed amidst the flower of Theseus as a reminder of his folly in giving up Ariadne." He took a step toward her. "I'll not be Theseus. Do you understand what I'm saying, Abby."

She bit the inside of her cheek, because well, she really didn't know what he was saying. Abigail only knew what she wanted those words to mean.

Geoffrey strode over to her with a power and strength the God Kratos would admire. He stopped in front of her. He brushed his knuckle along her cheek. "I don't want to lose you." He spoke with the bold, assurance of a man who knew what he wanted. "The day I nearly toppled you over, you tossed my world into utter chaos."

She leaned into his touch. "I'm sorry," she said softly. Sorry for so very much. For transgressions she was too much a coward to put into words.

He smiled, and opened his fingers to cradle her cheek as though she was more precious than Blackbeard's treasure. Gone was the trace of bitter cynicism which usually accompanied his grin. "Abby, until you, I'd thought myself incapable of ever smiling again. You made me yearn for things I'd kept buried for so long, I'd thought they'd died inside me." Geoffrey glanced away a moment. "I do not expect you to understand those sentiments," he murmured. "You are innocent. Untouched of the ugly things I've borne witness to in my life."

Her heart went careening, crashing back down to the reality of her foibles. She stiffened. Geoffrey had constructed an image of her as one who was without flaws, when in reality, there surely was not a more perfect, imperfect individual.

"Geoffrey," she said quietly. She touched her palm to his hand, staying his movement. "I fear you carry an undeserving opinion of me."

He turned his lips into her palm, caressing her skin with the gentlest contact. "You're wrong," he insisted.

Abigail could not think. She needed distance between them. Abigail disentangled herself from his touch and stepped away.

Bile burned like acid at the back of her throat, and she wished it would singe the words she'd rather never have to speak. She knew the moment she confessed the truth, all the warmth in his eyes would die faster than a shooting star that blazed a path across the sky. She could not, however allow him to maintain this paragon-like vision he'd associated with her.

"Geoffrey—"

"I want to court you, Abby," he interjected. He reached for her hand, but she gripped the sides of her skirts to keep from reaching out and grasping the dream he dangled before her. "I want to marry you."

Oh, God. She closed her eyes, and shook her head back and forth. "You don't truly know me, Geoffrey." *If you did, then you'd not look at me with such warmth.*

A roguish half-grin tipped the right corner of his mouth, so very different than the stranger she'd first met at Lady Hughes's who'd looked upon her with stern disapproval. "I want to know everything about you, Abby."

A hysterical giggle worked its way up her throat, and spilled past her lips. No, he'd assuredly not want to know everything about her—certainly not the great shame she concealed. The proper, and propriety-driven viscount did not want to know the sordid details that had precipitated her voyage to London.

Geoffrey's brow furrowed, and his smile dipped. The regal, austere viscount was back in place. "What is it?"

Abigail opened her mouth and closed it, several times. She could not wed Geoffrey. Not without him knowing all the details, and yet... hope, stirred in her breast. Perhaps her secret would not matter to him. He had known the agony of betrayal, and regrets for past mistakes. A man of his reason and logic would surely recognize that they were not unlike one another.

So, why didn't she fully trust that?

"It is nothing." The denial emerged as a halting whisper.

"You don't want me to court you," he stated, his voice, curiously flat.

Her head jerked up. "No, no. Never that. Not that at all," she rushed to assure him.

Geoffrey nodded. "Then it is settled. I will court you."

Abigail closed her eyes. So it was settled.

She was nothing more than a coward.

EIGHTEEN

A gentleman should rely on a well-written list to maintain a well-ordered life.
4th Viscount Redbrooke

The next morning, Abigail entered the breakfast room. Her uncle glanced out from behind the paper in his hands. "Abigail," he murmured.

She smiled. "Uncle."

Beatrice's eyes lit upon seeing Abigail. She paused in spreading butter onto a flaky piece of white bread. "Abby! There you are. Why, you've slept quite long this morning."

Abigail's skin warmed under their scrutiny. She rushed over to the sideboard and placed several strips of bacon, a baked egg, and a piece of bread onto her plate. With her gaze trained upon her fare, she walked over to the table.

A footman rushed to pull out her chair, and Abigail slid into it. "Thank you," she murmured.

Abigail picked up the still warm piece of bread and broke it in half. Crumbs fell onto her chintz plate, and she studied those small bits, content to bury focus into the dish until the conclusion of the meal.

She nibbled at the corner of her bread, and feeling eyes upon her, looked up.

The duke and Beatrice studied her in silence.

Abigail choked, and dropped the bread in her hands. She reached for the glass of water and took a tentative sip, and then another.

"I understand Lord Redbrooke brought flowers," her uncle said at last.

Abigail set her glass down and folded her hands upon her lip, hiding them from sight. "He did," she said. She returned her gaze to her nearly untouched plate.

Beatrice giggled.

Abigail's gaze flew up.

Her cousin picked up a delicate tea cup and took a sip. "Never tell me you'd encourage Lord Redbrooke's suit?"

"Beatrice," her father chided. He folded his paper and set it down on the empty place beside him.

Beatrice ignored his unspoken admonition. "If he makes you happy, Abby, then there is nothing more I would want than for you to accept his suit."

For one, too brief moment, her cousin's blessing seemed the only boundary that prevented Abigail from grasping onto to the dream of Geoffrey as a serious suitor. Then, reality came crashing, careening down upon her. She reached for her bread, and chewed it; but it turned to dust inside her mouth.

"Lord Redbrooke is an honorable gentleman," her uncle said, his tone quiet.

She nodded woodenly. How could an honorable gentleman ever take to wife such a dishonorable woman? She picked up her fork and shoved the baked egg around her plate.

"Abigail?" The duke's sternly worded question, her name, brought her head up.

"He would make you an excellent match."

Abigail's gaze flitted off to the footmen stationed over by the sideboard. This place, she looked over to Beatrice, and with her innocent cousin here, was not the place in which to discuss an unlikely match between Abigail and Geoffrey.

The butler appeared and Abigail was saved from responding. "Lord Redbrooke to see Miss Stone. I've taken the liberty of showing the gentleman to the Chintz Parlor."

Abigail's fork clattered noisily upon her china flatware. "Forgive me," she said hastily.

Beatrice's smile grew. "Go, Abby," she said gently.

Abigail rose so quickly her legs knocked the back of the chair, and it scraped noisily along the wood flooring. She began to pace beside the dining room table.

Geoffrey had called yesterday and stated his intentions to court her. At the time, she'd been besieged by a heady sense of joy. It had clouded her logic and the calm rationality she'd sworn to maintain after Alexander's betrayal. For an all too brief moment she'd allowed herself to operate under the illusion of 'what-ifs': what if her lack of virtue didn't matter to Geoffrey? What if word of her scandalous past never crossed the ocean? What if...what if...what if...?

Now, in the light of a new day, she could not deny the insurmountable boundaries that made a match between them—impossible.

"Abigail," her uncle said quietly.

She jumped, and spun to face him.

"I believe Lord Redbrooke to be a fair man. He..." His gaze shifted momentarily to Beatrice, and then back to Abigail. "He is not one of clouded judgment. I'm certain of it."

Abigail's throat worked up and down.

"Go, Abby," her cousin urged.

Abigail swallowed past the swell of emotion and managed a nod. "If you'll excuse me?" She dipped a curtsy and hurried from the breakfast room.

As she made the long march to the Chintz Parlor she rehearsed everything she would say to Geoffrey. He was as her uncle said, a man of integrity and honor. As such, he deserved to know the truth...and he deserved to hear it from her. With each step, her resolve to confess the all, strengthened...

Abigail paused outside the parlor and smoothed her hands over the front of her day dress. She straightened her back and, taking a deep breath, entered the room.

Geoffrey stood with his back to her, one hand upon the fireplace mantle, his gaze fixed on the empty grate. Her eyes slid closed. He stood there six feet of towering masculine perfection, his muscle-hewn frame carved in a stone, giving him a look of the ancient Gods whose stories filled the skies. The breath left her on a whispery sigh. "Geoffrey."

He spun around. His gaze, hotter than a physical touch, moved over her face. "Abigail."

That was it. Abigail. Her name, and yet from that one utterance he conveyed masculine approval, possessiveness, desire.

God help her.

She'd imagined crossing the ocean and leaving behind her family the greatest trial she'd ever endured.

Looking at Geoffrey, wanting him as she did, she now knew there could be no greater trial than the one she now confronted.

He bowed. "Forgive me."

Her eyes slid away from him. This is the kind of proper man he was. He begged pardon for failing to bow. She shook her head. "Geoffrey, I…"

He stalked across the room. "I've brought this."

Abigail blinked down at the scrap of parchment he held out, and hesitated a moment. She took it in her fingers.

Ices at Gunter's.
A walk in Hyde Park.
Several waltzes.
A trip to the theatre…

Abigail glanced from the list, up at Geoffrey. He stood with his hands clasped behind his back, eying her expectantly.

She smoothed her fingers along the thick, ivory velum. "Uh…"

"It is a list," Geoffrey interrupted.

Abigail looked down blankly at the parchment again. "Yes. Yes it is." Geoffrey held out his hand.

Wordlessly, she turned it over and contemplated him. A small frown tilted the corners of his lips downward as he examined the meticulously written scrawl.

Geoffrey cleared his throat. "I created this list of proper events and activities for a gentleman courting a suitable young lady."

Her mouth went dry. There it was again—a *suitable* young lady.

He continued, seeming oblivious to her inner turmoil. "We've walked in Hyde Park. Granted it was before I'd settled on you as a match."

A desperate laugh bubbled up in her throat. Oh, Geoffrey. Sweet, wonderful Geoffrey. How carefully he plotted out every aspect of his life. Her nervous amusement died as she wondered how much of his devotion to order stemmed from the pain of Emma Marsh's betrayal. "It is…very romantic."

He held the paper up and closed it in his fist; the crackle of the wrinkled parchment filled the space like a dry log of wood being tossed into a fiery hearth. "You're right. It seems I'm rubbish at this." He took a step away from her.

Abigail rushed over to him, realizing he'd interpreted her words as mocking. "Oh, no. You aren't rubbish at all." *You're good, and kind, and valiant.*

A half grin formed on his lips. "I'd written this list before you. I had every detail for the rest of my life carefully plotted and planned, Abby."

That sounded remarkably like the proper man she'd first come to know with his somber frown, and his seeming difficulty in managing a smile. Such a man would do something as practical as create a list to help secure a match in a most expeditious manner.

Geoffrey claimed her hand. "Will you accompany me?"

She studied their interlocked fingers. *Anywhere.* "Where?" she murmured. "I've not been to Gunter's. Lord Sinclair mentioned it and it sounds divine."

Geoffrey growled and lowered his head so his brow nearly rested upon hers. "I don't want to hear you mention Lord Sinclair's name."

At the possessive note in that strongly uttered demand, warmth fanned out and filled Abigail. "To Hyde Park?"

Geoffrey flicked her nose with the tip of his finger, and grinned. "We've already been to Hyde Park. Twice."

"Well, you must cross that off the list, then," she said with a smile.

He took her by the hand and led her to the terrace doors. "Come," he murmured, and pushed the doors open, he led her outside.

Abigail's skin burned from the feel of his hand, strong, and hard in her own delicate palm.

"I was an absolute wretch to you, Abby."

She blinked and looked up at him. A cloud shifted above the sun and cast half of his angular face in shadows. Then the cloud passed, and bathed him in sunlight. "When?" she blurted.

A wry half-grin turned the right corner of his lips. "I rather think on a number of occasions." He settled his hand upon her waist, and pulled her close.

Abigail's breath caught in her chest, and she tipped her chin up. *He is going to kiss me, here amidst the fragrant blooms and sun-filled sky, and, I am shameful and improper because I want that so very desperately.*

"The evening I first danced with you," he continued, seeming unaware of the heady effect his presence had upon her.

She blinked back the thick haze of desire.

"I was a boorish lout. I was rude and condescending, and arrogant. Until you, Abby, I hadn't realized what life had turned me into. You've reminded me how to laugh."

Unable to bear the heated intensity radiating from his eyes, Abigail dropped her gaze to the immaculate lines of his white cravat. *Tell him.* She could not allow him to harbor these false views about the kind of woman she was.

She wet her lips.

He guided her hand upon his shoulder.

"What...?"

"I'm dancing with you. Again. I want to start anew with you, Abby."

And then he proceeded to waltz her through the clusters of roses and crocuses up from the ground. He hummed a discordant tune.

Her body stiffened. "Oh, Geoffrey, I'm truly a dreadful dancer." She stepped upon his foot, her graceless body seemed desperate to confirm the truth of her words. "I'm forever falling all over myself."

He dropped his brow to hers, and tightened his hold about her. "Well, then. It seems I must be there to catch you should you fall."

Amidst the sun-filled garden, with the chirping coy and Geoffrey's humming as their symphony, Abigail fell in love.

Abigail had given her girlish heart to the handsome Alexander Powers. But there, in the duke's parlor, Abigail fell in love with a woman's heart.

Panic warred with joy, two very competing emotions within her breast. She could not love him. It was not to be countenanced. After Alexander's betrayal she'd thought herself incapable of ever again trusting the fickle emotion called love. But God help her—she loved Geoffrey.

Tell him the truth. Tell him everything, you selfish, cowardly creature.

Later.

For now, Abigail intended to steal this final, beautiful moment before the truth killed all the warmth in Geoffrey's eyes.

NINETEEN

A gentleman should take care to avoid public displays of emotion.
4ᵗʰ Viscount Redbrooke

From his spot behind the white, marble pillar, Geoffrey surveyed Lord and Lady Ainsworth's ballroom. He peered over the rim of his champagne glass, in search of Abigail.

An ominous rumble of thunder sounded in the distance, and an icy chill stole through him. Since the tragic night of his father's death, rain and thunder transported him back to the moment he'd come upon his father's broken body, eyes opened, staring lifelessly up at the storm-ravaged sky.

"I believe it is going to rain."

Geoffrey froze, and turned to greet his sister, Sophie. She smiled up at him, her arm looped through her husband's.

Waxham inclined his head in greeting.

"My that is a dark look," she said. A clap of thunder punctuated her words.

"Sophie, Waxham," Geoffrey greeted.

Waxham gave a slight bow.

"You scoundrel," Sophie whispered. She crossed her arms over her middle. "You had me so thoroughly convinced of your intentions for one lady, and then I must find out from the scandal sheets that you've in fact been courting another?"

Geoffrey took another sip of champagne. "It appears you've done an even poorer job in reigning in my sister's cheekiness," he said to his brother-in-law.

"I wouldn't even begin to dare try," Waxham drawled and waved over a passing servant. He accepted a glass of champagne and returned his attention to Geoffrey. "My efforts would prove futile, especially after you've indulged her hoydenish behavior through the years."

Sophie swatted her husband on the arm. "Oh, do behave. The both of you." She arched a brow. "And do not think to shift the topic, dear brother. Are the reports correct? Am I to acquire a sister-in-law?" Enthusiasm underlined her conspiratorial whisper.

Geoffrey choked around the mouthful of champagne.

His sister's eyes lit up like a child's who'd tasted her first ice at Gunter's. "I am! You needn't deny it. Your reaction quite confirmed your intentions."

He frowned, glancing around to determine whether anyone happened to overhear Sophie's pronouncement. Lords and ladies throughout the room eyed him with a rabid curiosity that made him grit his teeth. If it weren't for the desire to see Abigail, he'd have taken leave of the evening's festivities a long while ago. "Do you have no control over your wife?" he said from the corner of his mouth.

His brother-in-law snorted. "If you must ask such a question, it would seem you know your sister a good deal less than I'd originally believed."

Sophie went on as though they hadn't spoken. "I can hardly imagine that my very proper, very dull brother has gone and won the affections of an American woman." At Sophie's pronouncement, a bolt of lightning lit the ballroom.

Geoffrey's body jerked. The jagged light lit up the sky and spilled through the floor-length windows and into the room.

Sophie blinked. "Never tell me you're afraid of a little lightening, brother?" He was spared from answering as she returned to the matter that had driven her over to his private corner of the ballroom. "By mother's clear displeasure I take it that the rumors are in fact correct."

Geoffrey's gaze sought and found his mother. She stood conversing with their gaunt, heavily wrinkled hostess, Lady Ainsworth. A black scowl marred his mother's face. She held herself with such a stiff rigidity it was a wonder the wind that whipped against the windows didn't topple her right there.

"The rumors are correct." His tone sounded weary to his own ears. He'd not have expected the sharp stab of guilt would sting this much. His mother had barely uttered a word to him since he'd very clearly stated his intentions to wed Abigail.

Sophie's smile dipped.

Waxham cleared his throat. "It is never easy to deviate from the desires and wills of one's parent," he said. The gravity of his tone spoke of a man who could identify with Geoffrey's secret shame. Waxham's gaze settled momentarily upon his wife's head. "But, matters of the heart should not be decided by logic and order."

Just then, at the entrance of the ballroom, Abigail appeared upon the arm of her cousin, Lord Westfield. Geoffrey's breath hitched in his chest.

Abigail's violet satin skirts shimmered in the glow of the candlelit ballroom. An intricate floral design threaded with glimmering diamonds had been stitched upon the bodice of her gown. It drew his attention to the generous swell of her bosom and his mouth went dry. She had the look of Eve in the garden of sin, and how he longed to throw aside all that was proper and join her there.

She scanned the ballroom, as though searching for someone, and then their gazes met and held.

Abigail smiled, dipping her head in a subtle greeting.

Geoffrey imagined he was grinning like a love-struck simpleton. But god help him, he wanted her.

"Oh dear," his sister said, shattering the pull. "You've fallen quite hard."

Waxham pat him in a commiserative gesture upon his shoulder.

Geoffrey shook his head, and started toward Abigail. Yes. He'd fallen quite hard.

For the better part of the day, Abigail had wrested an impending sense of disaster. She'd credited the thundering skies for the odd apprehension that caused gooseflesh to dot her skin. The storm was the kind of storm that had shattered too many great ships at sea.

The carriage bearing the duke, Robert, Beatrice, and Abigail had arrived a short while ago at Lord and Lady Ainsworth's ball. The torrents of streaming rain and the deep puddles through-out the London streets had made their carriage ride a long one. Then they'd had to wait in an endless row of carriages until they'd reached the entrance of the townhouse, as everyone made a desper-ate attempt to shorten the distance between their carriages and the front door.

Abigail's gaze landed upon several ladies. They snapped their fans open, and over the rim of the satin accessories ran their eyes over Abigail. Then, they averted their stares with a pointed flourish.

Her stomach roiled at the cut direct that had been so very familiar at home. The ugly reminder of her past only intensified her earlier misgivings.

"Oh, my. I believe I was wrong," her cousin murmured.

Abigail forced aside the portentous musings. "Hmm?"

"About Lord Redbrooke," Beatrice clarified. "I never believed that particular gentleman capable of anything beyond stiff politeness." Beatrice sighed. "I would trade my little finger to have a man look at me the way Lord Redbrooke is looking at you."

Abigail's heart tripped at a funny little pace as Geoffrey's long-legged stride closed the space between them. He stood taller than most gentlemen in the ballroom, making it easy for Abigail to follow his path. He navigated through the throng of guests with a masculine grace.

In all the time Alexander Powers had courted her, he'd never looked at her in the hot, penetrating manner that Geoffrey now did. Geoffrey's was the primeval gleam of a man who wanted to lay claim to her.

And all her earlier reservations, her unfounded fears lifted as he stopped in front of her. She tilted her head back and her breath caught. Geoffrey studied her through thick, lowered lashes. She curt-sied. "My lord." *Did that breathless greeting belong to her?*

He took her hand in his and raised it to his lips. Even through the thin fabric of her glove, Geoffrey's touch heated her skin, and sent warmth radiating out through her body.

Just then, a harsh, bold laugh cut into the charged exchange, and she froze. Pinpricks of unease ran along her spine. Her gaze collided with a gentleman who stood just beyond Geoffrey's shoulder. The foppish dandy, garishly dressed in violet, satin breeches had his lascivious stare trained upon her bosom. Abigail's apprehension grew.

"Miss Stone, may I have this dance?" Geoffrey's request jolted her back to the moment.

"I..."

A shocked gasp cut into her reply, and yanked Abigail's attention to a nearby stern-faced matron with a frown upon her fleshy cheeks. The woman raked a frigid gaze over Abigail's person.

"Abigail?" Geoffrey's question reached her, muffled and vague the way she'd used to hear her mother and father's calls from when she'd been submerged beneath the ocean's surface.

Oh, God. Abigail sent a prayer skyward.

"Abby?" Beatrice's voice laced with concern blended with Geoffrey's.

The pointed stares, and too-loud whispers carried her back to a different night, to the time she'd been discovered in Alexander's arms, when her world had crumpled down around her. She shook her head.

"I'm all right." Her protest sounded halfhearted to her own ears.

Of course no one knew. No one could know. This was not her shoreline home. This was a country of different people, an ocean apart from the shame of her past.

Then her gaze tripped upon her uncle and cousin Robert as they cut a determined swath through the crowd of people who peered down long, noble noses at Abigail. Purpose drove the steps of both the duke and his son.

Her eyes slid closed.

Not now. Not here.

She recognized their matched, hardened expressions.

Geoffrey frowned. "Abigail?"

Abigail opened her eyes and looked up at him. "Forgive me, Geoffrey," she whispered.

He lowered his brows. "For…?"

Her uncle and cousin reached her side.

Geoffrey turned to greet the duke. He bowed. "Your Grace. I'd like to request an audience with you tomorrow morning."

The duke's lips flattened into a hard line. "Redbrooke."

What matter of business could Geoffrey have with the duke? Then Geoffrey looked at her, his eyes warm, and gentle upon her face…and she knew. He intended to offer for her. She folded her hands around her waist and looked around, confronting the expressions of the *ton* who were taking great relish in her public fall. Agony formed like tight knots in her stomach until she wanted to twist and writhe to escape it.

Abigail took first one steadying breath. Then another. And another. Perhaps it was merely her own insecurities and memories of the past that drove cloying fear up her throat, and threatened to choke her.

Then she spied Lord Carmichael, the old bastard who'd put his hands all over her person; his fleshy lips were pulled back in a victorious smile. Her heart froze, and she knew. Oh God, how she knew. Somehow the old letch had discovered her scandalous past.

Robert took her gently but firmly by the arm. "We need to leave, Abby."

No! Not again.

She managed a jerky nod and tugged her arm free of Robert's hold; her toes flexed within the soles of her slippers, as she was filled with a restive need to run and keep running until she'd escaped the all too familiar disdain.

Beatrice's brow furrowed. "Leave? Why we've only just—"

"Beatrice," the duke's single, harshly uttered word silenced Beatrice. He looked to Geoffrey. "Tomorrow, then."

Her uncle was mad. Tears flooded her eyes, and Geoffrey's face blurred before her. With his value for propriety and honor, Geoffrey would sooner send her to the devil than see her to the altar. She swayed on her feet, the room dipped and spun like her youngest brother's wood whip top that he'd played with over and over.

Geoffrey cursed and reached for her. He caught her against him, even as outraged gasps escaped the lords and ladies around the ballroom.

She tilted her head back, and gazed at him through the blasted moisture that filled her eyes. "Please, don't." *Because if you continue to hold me, I'll dissolve into a puddle of shame and despair at your feet.*

His square jaw tensed as he scraped a frantic gaze over her person, tightening his hold upon her. "Abigail, what is it?" The faint thread of panic that underlined his words sent guilt spiraling, until it filled every corner of her body. In mere moments, the look of gentle concern and caring would die to be replaced with revulsion. She'd braved the scorn of her American compatriots, and been mocked and ridiculed as an American interloper in British Society...she could not stand to bear witness to the moment all affection went out of his eyes.

"I...I..." She shook her head...

"We have to leave. Now." The duke bit out.

Robert disentangled Abigail's forearm from Geoffrey's grip and with determined steps, guided her through the sea of taunting sneers, and leering gentlemen. Bile climbed up her throat, and she fought the urge to keep from casting the accounts of her stomach upon the ballroom floor.

She shot one last parting glance over her shoulder.

Geoffrey remained where she'd left him, legs planted wide, his focus trained on her.

Abigail jerked her attention forward, thinking how so very close she'd been to being happy. Her lips twisted into a bitter smile. What a fool she'd been.

Again.

TWENTY

A gentleman should not allow himself to be bated by a dishonorable gentleman.
4ᵗʰ Viscount Redbrooke

Geoffrey stared after Abigail. A bolt of lightning broke the night sky, and splashed bluish light across the ballroom floor; it cast sinister shadows about the room that danced along the walls and vibrant fabrics of the waltzing ladies. The distant rumble of thunder shook the panes of the floor-length windows. As he stared at Abigail's swiftly retreating figure, ominous darkness that accompanied a turbulent rainstorm filled him.

Then she looked back at him.

His breath froze at the agonized despair that bled from her eyes.

A viselike pressure squeezed his heart. Christ. What had happened to wreak such a transformation about the smiling, spirited beauty who'd captured his heart?

Geoffrey blinked. The chatter of Lord and Lady Ainsworth's guests blended with the outside rain, in a loud hum, that slowed his thoughts.

He loved her.

A jolt when through him. He, who'd sworn to never turn himself over to the uncertain, volatile emotion which had destroyed his family, had gone and fallen in love with Abigail. The staggering realization threatened to bring him to his knees.

His body remained immobile. With her keen wit, and ability to laugh, she'd entered his life and upended his well-ordered world. She made him yearn for a life filled with laughter…and he wanted that life with her.

He grinned, knowing he must look like a lack-wit to Society's leading peers who studied him as though he were a Drury Lane Theatre act. At one time he'd been the same manner of snide, pompous bastards who'd found fault in her merely for the origins of her birth. It had taken Abigail to show him the kind of man he'd been, and made him aspire to more.

He'd not make apologies for having fallen in love with Abigail Stone.

"I hope you are happy with what you've done," his mother hissed.

Geoffrey started. "Mother…"

"Wipe that foolish smile off your face," she snapped. "We have to leave. Immediately."

Another rumble of thunder shook the room.

There it was again, the looming sense of calamity that flared and pulsed with a life energy. He remembered Abigail's hasty departure, the panic in her eyes, his mother's enraged eyes…"What is it?" he asked, quietly.

"Not here. Waxham has already had the carriage summoned for us," she said from the corner of her mouth.

A sniggering laugh caught Geoffrey's attention, and his frown deepened.

"Now, Geoffrey." His mother barked the command like a colonel giving orders to his troops.

Only, Lord Carmichael stepped into Geoffrey's path.

Carmichael's wide smile revealed an uneven row of rotten, yellow-stained teeth. The overwhelming scent of garlic threatened to bowl Geoffrey over. Then his eyes fell to Lord Carmichael's hands clasped in front of his cumbersome belly. A thin haze of red rage clouded his vision as he remembered the moment he'd come upon Abigail with this fiend's gnarled hands pawing at her person.

"Step aside, Carmichael," he seethed.

A loud chortling laugh escaped Carmichael, but broke off into a fit of choking. "Redbrooke," he said when he'd again managed to breathe.

His mother placed her fingertips along his coat sleeve, and she gave a faint squeeze. "Geoffrey," she said quietly.

"Rushing off, eh, Redbrooke?" He waggled his overgrown, bushy white eyebrows. "Can't run from a scandal, really, though can you? Why, not even an ocean away is enough, sometimes." He dissolved into another round of laughter as though he'd delivered the wittiest of jests.

Geoffrey peered down his nose at Lord Carmichael. "What are you on about?" he said brusquely.

Carmichael's eyes went wide in his fleshy face. He slapped a hand to his chest, and looked around in feigned disbelief.

"Geoffrey," his mother said again, the thin thread of desperation there sent off the first warning bells within his mind.

"Never tell me, you've not heard," Carmichael said in a loud whisper.

Geoffrey should continue onward and leave the old bastard prattling on like the bloody fool he was, but something compelled him to feed that question. "Heard?"

The old lord shook his head, the swift movement displaced a strand of white hair, and it fell over his eye, displaying his carefully covered balled pate. "Why, that scandalous bit of goods. Your Miss Stone. Tsk. Tsk."

Geoffrey's mouth went dry, and his hands balled into tight fists at his side. He clenched and unclenched them, until he realized what he was doing. Again, Abigail's tormented visage flashed behind his eyes: her hasty flight from the ball, the bleeding anguish in her eyes.

Forgive me.

"Geoffrey, please," his mother said again. The uncharacteristic desperate plea in that utterance should have propelled him forward.

"What are you talking about?" Geoffrey could no sooner call the words back than he could cut off his right limb.

Lord Carmichael's eyebrows shot to the middle of his brow, and he slapped a hand to his chest. "Why, never tell me you don't know?" he said with feigned shock. He shook his head back and forth pityingly.

"What?" Geoffrey's voice sounded flat to his own ears.

"Well, about that American miss." He leaned so close, his stale breath slapped Geoffrey's face, but Geoffrey's struggle to breathe had nothing to do with the fetid odor. "Apparently there was a scandal. But then, I'm sure you knew that. All the gossip says you planned to wed the creature. You'd not do something as foolish as that. After all, you're a proper and honorable sort of fellow. Surely you'd not taint the Redbrooke line with…" He must have seen something written in Geoffrey's face, for his eyes widened. "Oh, you *haven't* heard." He dropped his voice to a conspiratorial whisper.

"Heard?" Geoffrey asked his voice wooden.

Carmichael waved his hand in a flourish. "About the whole incident of her being discovered with her lover." A chortling laugh burst from his thick chest. "Her family hastily packed her up and sent her off to the Duke of Somerset, apparently trying to marry the girl off to some unsuspecting gentleman." He gave Geoffrey a pointed look. "Then, her father is nothing more than a servant, so one shouldn't be too shocked by it."

Geoffrey's heartbeat slowed, slowed, faltered, and then paused for an infinitesimal moment. Carmichael's words blurred and blended together until Geoffrey blinked, trying to make sense of them.

Abigail…Lover…Scandal.

"No," he whispered. His Abigail was not capable of treachery or deceit. "You're wrong," Geoffrey said when he trusted himself to speak through the rage thrumming through his body. He'd face the bloody bastard at dawn for daring to impugn her honor.

Carmichael waggled his brows, and then shook his head. The subtle movement displaced another stringy white strand of hair. "I don't think I am," he said with clear relish. "I've contacts in America who happened to mention the scandal in a recent correspondence." He cast a glance over at the viscountess. "Why, all the details about Miss Stone aren't appropriate for a lady's ears." He bowed with a flourish. "If you'll excuse me, Redbrooke?" With a snorting laugh, the corpulent lord took his leave.

Geoffrey stared blankly after Carmichael's retreating figure.

Abigail had not have taken a lover. She could not have.

Lover. His gut clenched as that scandalous, horrific word twisted about his brain like an insidious poison seeping into every corner of his mind and body.

He thought of her hasty retreat, the panic in her eyes...she had borne the look of a woman hunted. He clenched his fists so tightly, he raised blood on his palms.

Geoffrey suddenly became aware of the crowd's gaze riveted upon him. She'd been a woman hunted by English Society.

"Let us go, Geoffrey," his mother said quietly.

Wordlessly, Geoffrey fell into step beside his mother. Lord and Lady Ainsworth's guests parted, allowing him to make his exit; all the while they studied him with a gleeful fascination.

He swallowed hard, but kept his stony gaze directed forward, and silently counted steps.

One. Two. Three.

She'd had a lover.

Four.

She'd deceived him.

Five. Six.

All with intentions of trapping him into marriage.

Seven.

Like Emma.

Oh god, he was going to be ill.

He and his mother made their way outside into the violent storm. A servant rushed to help the viscountess into the carriage. Geoffrey paused, outside, and sucked in deep, gasping breaths of air. He embraced the torrents of rain that poured upon him, the wind that whipped strands of hair into his eyes.

"Geoffrey, come in here now," his mother called from within the dry, confines of the conveyance.

Geoffrey waved aside the servant and climbed inside. He stared blankly out the window as the door closed behind them.

The carriage rocked into motion, and Geoffrey continued to say nothing on it. His mother remained uncharacteristically silent; no vitriolic words, no shrieking recriminations, and somehow it made his transgression all the worse.

"I'm sorry, Geoffrey," his mother said at long last. "I know you cared for her."

I didn't care for her.

I loved her.

TWENTY-ONE

A gentleman should not bother with Society's gossip.
4th Viscount Redbrooke

A *certain American relative of the Duke of S was forced from her country in disgrace after...*

Geoffrey tossed the copy of The Times onto his desk, and pinched the bridge of his nose.

Since the paper had arrived earlier that morning, he'd read those same seventeen words over and over and over. Each time, he'd willed there to be another Duke of S with a scandalous American relative.

His heart tightened.

He had been a bloody fool where Abigail Stone was concerned, but he was no idiot.

There was only one American relative of the Duke of S who'd been forced from her country in disgrace for lying with a gentleman outside the bonds of marriage.

Geoffrey surged to his feet. The leather of his seat crackled in protest of the abrupt movement. He picked up the copy of The Times and strode over to the fire raging inside the hearth.

Geoffrey tossed the paper into the flames, and stared on with blank eyes as black singed the corners of the parchment. The ends curled, and then a reddish-orange flame swallowed it in a small fiery-red conflagration until it was no more. He didn't need to punish himself with the sordid details of her past; the hell of his private imaginings was quite enough.

Geoffrey braced his hands upon the mantle, and took a steadying breath. If only it were as simple to rid himself of the truth that had been contained within those pages.

Thunder rumbled in the distance. The Gods laughing at him for having given his heart to another woman who'd only intended to deceive him.

A knock sounded at the door.

He ignored it.

It opened, and then the soft thread of footsteps registered. "You must not closet yourself away like this, Geoffrey."

He stiffened at his mother's censorious tone.

God she was tenacious.

"People are talking. Please. Visit your clubs or accept an invitation to some event this evening. It doesn't do for it to appear you felt any real feelings for that woman."

"Abigail," he said tiredly. He scrubbed the back of his hand over his face. "Her name is Abigail." He sucked in a slow breath.

I know we've not been properly introduced but after your timely intervention, I imagine we've moved beyond rigid politeness. My name is Abigail. Abigail Stone.

"Surely there is a mistake," he said, aloud those flat, deadened words spoken to himself, came as if they belonged to a stranger.

His mother reached over and placed her hand upon his other hand, until he forced his fingers to lessen the unholy grip he had upon the mantle. "I don't think so."

And neither did he.

He'd seen the horrified shame and guilt that had radiated from the depths of her storm-gray eyes. *Forgive me,* she'd whispered.

No, there was no mistake. No lie told by anyone but Abigail.

An icy cold filled him, a chill that had nothing to do with his rain-sopped garments. His heart hardened, the organ froze inside him and cracked.

What a fool he'd been.

Again.

"Geoffrey…"

He glanced over his shoulder at his mother disinterestedly. "Mother, I have business matters to attend to. If you'll excuse me."

"But…" she must have seen something in his eyes that indicated his total lack of desire to discuss Miss Abigail Stone or his plans for the afternoon or anything else. Her lips pursed and she gave a curt nod. After the door closed behind her, Geoffrey returned his attention to the fire.

Against all his better judgment, against his highly-valued logic, he'd been unable to resist Abigail's allure. He'd become hopelessly and helplessly besotted by her.

Geoffrey grimaced. He'd vowed to never again give himself over to the heady emotions of love, and instead establish an advantageous match based on nothing more than wealth and status.

And with just one snag of her too-long hem, he'd tossed aside everything that mattered.

His stomach tightened as he at last allowed each bit of Abigail's betrayal to seep into his agonized musings.

She'd forced him to feel again. Made him yearn for the impractical. He slashed his hand through his hair. Christ, he'd shared the most personal details of Emma Marsh and more, the death of his father— words he'd never before uttered to another soul.

He'd been honest with her in every regard, and how had she repaid that honesty? With lies.

And with her betrayal, he, who valued his privacy, had been opened up to Society's scorn and ridicule.

Geoffrey shook his head. He wished he'd never scratched Lady Beatrice Dennington's name upon his bloody list, because then he wouldn't know there was a winsome American named Miss Abigail Stone with a fulsome laugh and a penchant for studying the stars.

He bowed his head, and embraced the soothing hiss and snap of the flames.

Damn you, Abigail.

TWENTY-TWO

A gentleman must maintain a calm, collected
demeanor...even when under duress.
4th Viscount Redbrooke

For two days, it rained.

Abigail stood in the corner of her chambers. She tugged back the sapphire blue silk curtains and peered out into the ravaging storm. A bolt of lightning lit the sky. She touched the windowpane, and with the tip of her finger, followed the swift path of a raindrop down the side of the glass.

The sky had not lessened the torrential wrath it had unleashed upon the earth, since her hasty flight from Lady Ainsworth's ballroom last evening.

She closed her eyes.

Like a coward, she'd once again fled.

Only this time, she'd fled and left Geoffrey to discover the truth there in front of all polite English Society.

Her stomach churned.

By now, Geoffrey, like all of the *ton*, would know the truth of her—she had left America in shame.

By now he would know she didn't carry the most important commodity required of a lady upon the marriage mart—her virginity.

And he would know she was nothing more than...than...

A fallen woman.

A harlot.

A whore.

How many times had those vile words been hurled at her? Only Geoffrey had been different. Not once had he looked at her with condescension and ridicule.

When she'd been discovered in Alexander's arms, she'd imagined there could be no greater pain than what she'd felt upon seeing the shocked hurt reflected in her parents' eyes. In the days that followed, when it had become clear Alexander had little intention of offering for her, pain had blossomed into an aching despair.

She dropped the curtain and gripped the edge of the window sill so tight her nails left crescent indents upon the wood.

She'd been wrong on both scores. Her heart spasmed. The inevitable loss of Geoffrey would destroy her. Tears, blasted tears, filled her eyes, but the salty mementos would not fall. She blinked them back. She'd come to London, convinced there could be no future for her in the foreign land. She'd resolved never to trust again.

Geoffrey had shaken the walls she'd constructed around her broken heart; he'd unknowingly mended the wounded organ, and breathed life into her, so that it beat at last with a love for him. Foolishly she'd dared to hold onto the dream he represented; of a family, of a gentleman who'd love and protect and cherish her. She hugged her arms tight to herself.

The door opened and the soft thread of slippers upon the hard wood of the floor echoed in the quiet. "Abby, we missed you at supper."

Abigail's stomach roiled at the mere mention of food.

"You've not left your rooms since last evening. You cannot remain in here forever." Her cousin's hesitant words slashed into Abigail's private agony.

Thunder rumbled in the distance. The gods angry at her silent deception, mocked her.

"Oh, Abby," Beatrice whispered. She settled her hands upon Abigail's shoulders, and rested her cheek against her shoulder. "Lord Redbrooke loves you. I'm certain of it."

The words twisted the knife inside her breast. "He doesn't, Beatrice." Her voice broke.

He'd loved his Emma Marsh. Abigail, why she'd never been anything more than an impudent American who'd teased her way into his affection. He cared for her, but love? No, he had not loved her before, and most certainly not after, this.

"He does." Beatrice's tone shook with earnest insistence. She forced Abigail around. "I've seen the way he looks at you, Abby. He's always been a stodgy, pompous bore. Now, he smiles. That is because of you."

Abigail stared blankly at a point beyond Beatrice's shoulder. If Geoffrey had loved her, that had been before he'd known he was carrying on with a fallen woman. The proper gentleman she'd first known would never have sullied his presence with her wicked self.

She swallowed. "A man such as Lord Redbrooke can never wed me. I…" Her words died on her lips. Beatrice was innocent, unsullied, and Abigail could not share the shame of what she'd done.

"You need to speak to him."

Abigail again folded her arms to her chest. "I can't," she said brokenly. She squeezed herself tight. "I can't bear to witness his derision."

Beatrice slashed the air with her hand. "Bahh, you are no coward, Abby. He loves you. And you love him. And if you do not speak to him, you'll forever regret your cowardice."

Her cousin's words penetrated the thick fog of despair that shrouded her thoughts. What if Beatrice were right? What if none of it mattered to Geoffrey? Perhaps he cared for her more than he cared about the gossip that clung to her name.

She shoved aside the misgivings that swiftly followed that hopeful thought. "I need to see him."

A smile wreathed her cousin's cheeks. "Yes, you do."

"Now."

Beatrice's smile dipped. "Now?" She looked to the window. Another rumble of thunder shook the foundations of the house. "You can't."

Abigail glanced over to the pellets of rain that lashed against the window. It would be the height of foolishness to venture out in such a volatile storm. Only a woman with little regard for her reputation or the threat of scandal would risk being seen visiting the viscount's residence.

Then, Abigail had thrown away her reputation long ago. "I must." She grasped Beatrice's hands, and with her eyes, silently beseeched her cousin for assistance.

"Oh, Abby," She caught her lower lip between her teeth. "Think of the scandal."

A sound half-sob, half-snort wrenched from Abigail. "There can be no greater scandal than the one of my past. No one will be out on this night. I'll go by hackney. Please, Beatrice. Please," she implored, squeezing Beatrice's hands.

Beatrice's concerned blue eyes ran over Abigail's face, and Abigail knew the moment her cousin capitulated. "Oh, dear."

Abigail flung her arms around her cousin. "Thank you."

Her cousin continued to trouble her lip. "You'll need to go through the kitchens. I'll have one of the footman hail a hackney."

Abigail nodded, for the first time since last evening, humiliation buoyed with a budding sense of hope. She would speak to Geoffrey. He would understand. She would make him. "Go," she urged, lest her cousin change her mind.

Beatrice hesitated, and with a curt nod, fled.

Abigail hurried over to the rose-inlaid armoire at the center of the room, and threw the doors open. She reached inside and shoved aside gowns, pushing them out of the way. She grasped her black, muslin cloak and pulled it out.

She remembered the moment Geoffrey had tossed aside propriety to wade into the lake at Hyde Park and rescue her lace. Hope grew and blossomed within her chest. If he loved her as Beatrice said, then perhaps he'd wade deeper into the quagmire of scandal that was her life.

Abigail draped the cloak over her shoulders, and clasped the fish hooks at her throat. She took a deep breath, and pulled the hood overhead. Her uncle and cousin had been good enough to not speak to her of their hasty flight from Lady Ainsworth's; they would surely desire an audience with her sometime, in order to address her fate. Abigail suspected they would pack her up with the same swiftness as her parents had. As it was, she'd already greatly compromised Beatrice's ability to make a match.

Abigail opened the door, and peeked first left and then right. When she'd ascertained the hall was empty, she slipped outside and made her way swiftly down the long corridor. The muslin fabric rustled in the quiet like the shot of a cannon and with bated breath, she expected discovery to come at any moment.

But it didn't, and Abigail continued forward, taking the servant's passageways lower into the house, and into the now silent kitchen. The fires in the kitchen had long since gone cold. Abigail's eyes struggled to adjust to the dim light.

A flash of lightening lit the sky and spilled light into the room.

She gasped, and slapped a hand to her breast as the bluish-white light bathed Beatrice in an eerie glow.

Beatrice held her finger to her lips. "Shh," her cousin mouthed. She motioned Abigail forward.

Abigail raced into the kitchen and wrapped her arms about Beatrice.

"You must return quickly," Beatrice whispered against her ear, the words muffled by the muslin fabric. "Father mustn't discover you gone. The hackney is waiting at the end of the street." She touched her hand to Abigail's cheek. "It is horrid weather, but I can think of no other way to make sure you remain unseen. One of the servants will follow you for protection, Abby."

Abigail nodded. Tears of gratification clogged her throat.

Her cousin offered a tremulous smile. "I know," she whispered. "There is no need to thank me. The driver has your destination." She gripped her forearms and gave a slight squeeze. "Now, go!"

Abigail fled through the opened door. A blast of wind sucked the breath from her lungs. It whipped the fabric of her cloak and skirts wildly against her ankles. She raced down the pavement; her slippers sank into ice-cold puddles. A gasp escaped her as she stumbled. Abigail quickly righted herself and peered into the sheets of rain, sending a silent thanks to the heavens when she spied the hackney.

She raced the remaining distance and skidded to a stop in front of the conveyance. The driver tossed the door open, and quickly handed her inside.

He closed the door, and a moment later, the carriage rocked forward.

Abigail huddled against the side of the carriage, seeking warmth and finding none in the hard, wooden seats of the hack. She resisted the urge to glance out the curtained window, into the empty streets.

Her reputation could hardly be shredded any more than it had this evening, but she still needed to protect her uncle and his family from further shame.

As the carriage wheels rolled through the muddied puddles of the London streets, her mind turned over what she would say to Geoffrey.

She smoothed her palms over the front of her cloak. She'd tell him all...as she should have, when he'd made his honorable intentions toward her clear. She would tell him of Alexander's betrayal, the shame of what she'd done...and he would understand. She would make him. Because the alternative was not to be countenanced.

The carriage rocked and swayed. Abigail gasped as her hip bit painfully into the side of the carriage.

"Whoa," the driver shouted against the roaring wind.

The carriage righted itself and a sigh of relief escaped her as it continued down the streets, until it came to an abrupt stop directly in front of a white stucco townhouse.

Abigail gripped the side of the seat to keep from careening forward.

Suddenly the brashness of her actions just now, the boldness in coming here, and worse the fear of Geoffrey's response, turned her to stone.

The driver pulled open the door, and there was no turning back. Rain poured inside the carriage as he extended his arm to help hand her down.

Abigail pulled her cloak close, and sucked in a breath, accepting the driver's assistance. The pads of her slippers sank into a cold puddle upon the cobbled road, and she trembled from the chill of it.

The driver nodded up at the only townhouse with candlelight blazing in the windows.

She raced the short distance to Geoffrey's home; her feet splashed and sprayed water as she ran.

Abigail came to a jerky halt at the front door. She raised her hand and knocked just as a bolt of lightning crashed around her, drowning her efforts. Abigail pounded again.

The fury of the storm was her only response.

She turned out and peered through the torrents of rain at the hackney that had driven a short way up the street.

The door opened, and she spun around to face an older gentleman. The servant's gaze took in her thoroughly rumpled cloak and his eyebrows shot up to his hairline.

She tipped her chin up a notch. "I must see Lord Redbrooke."

The servant's nostrils flared in surprise. He hesitated and for a long moment she thought he might turn her away like some street urchin who'd tried to infringe upon the viscount's palatial townhouse. But then, he nodded and held the door open.

Abigail swept inside.

From where he sat in his library, a half-drunk decanter of brandy at his feet, Geoffrey stared blankly down at the box in his hands. His jacket lay in an untidy heap alongside the bottle.

With one hand, Geoffrey reached for the bottle and took a swig. He'd ceased to feel the burn of the alcohol long ago. Vision blurred from too-much drink, Geoffrey set his drink down on the table next to him and passed the small package back and forth between his hands. He absently studied it, and then set it down.

Geoffrey's gaze fell on the leather book of Greek mythology that sat beside him. He picked it up and fanned the pages. He'd foolishly invested time in reacquainting himself with all those puerile stories of Dionysus, Ariadne, and Theseus. What an imprudent fool he'd been. And for what purpose?

For her.

It had been for her.

All of it.

Geoffrey stood and hurled the volume across the room. It hit the solid plaster hard, and then landed with a quiet thump upon the floor.

An ugly laugh built in his chest, half-demonic to his own ears. The close rumble of thunder, followed by the crack of lightning fueled his pained fury.

Since he'd learned the truth of Abigail's deception last evening, he'd expected he should feel a sense of relief at being spared her scheming machinations. Yet, the jagged agony and humiliated hurt of her betrayal had not lessened. He suspected it never would.

Rather, it had seemed to intensify with the raging storm outside.

His butler Ralston's cry of shock from somewhere within the house, penetrated Geoffrey's stupor, and he furrowed his brow.

What the hell had ruffled his normally unflappable butler? Geoffrey yanked the door open hard enough it threatened the hinges, and strode from the room.

As he stormed down the hall toward the foyer, Ralston's insistent tone grew increasingly in volume.

"What the hell is the meaning of this?" Geoffrey bellowed from the top of the stairs. If it was his bloody brother-in-law again, by God he would toss him out into the street.

"If you'll wait here. I'll see if His Lordship is receiving callers," Ralston said in a stiffly disapproving tone.

"Ralston…" He staggered to a halt. The air left Geoffrey on a hiss.

Abigail shoved back the hood of her black muslin cloak. She glanced up the long, winding marble staircase and held her palms up as if in supplication. "Geoffrey." Even with the space between them, her whisper reached him.

And for the tortured pain she'd brought him, Geoffrey ached to close the distance between them and take her into his arms and make her forget there was ever another man who'd known her body and held her heart.

His bleary gaze fixed on those outstretched hands and he tortured himself with the insidious thoughts of her with another, and all warmth died inside him.

Geoffrey gripped the rail and stood there, unable to move. All the while, Abigail studied him with wide, wounded eyes.

A growl worked its way up his throat. *As though you have a right to be wounded, Abigail.*

Geoffrey folded his arms across his chest. "Well, madam? What is the meaning of this improper visit?"

TWENTY-THREE

A gentleman should be sensible, and avoid impassioned decisions.
4ᵗʰ Viscount Redbrooke

Abigail's heart thumped to a stop inside her breast.

Geoffrey stood at the top of the stairs, but he may as well have stood on the opposite side of the world. The white cambric shirt, opened at the collar, revealed the stiff tension within his muscle-hewn frame. He remained frozen, as though he'd been turned to stone by the serpent-headed Medusa.

A wet strand of hair fell across her eye and she brushed it back.

Geoffrey ran a dark, cursory stare of that single lock. Her toes curled within her wet slippers as she considered how she must appear to him, with her hair hanging limply, shamefully down her back.

She cringed as Geoffrey's gaze, teeming with hot loathing, scraped over her face.

"Geoffrey," she said, hating the way her voice cracked.

The servant gasped, and a mortified heat rushed her cheeks at having been discovered calling upon a gentleman and using his Christian name.

"That will be all," Geoffrey called, almost bored, from where he stood, hand resting casually, elegantly upon the rail. He made his way swiftly down the stairs, and all the hope, all the dreams she'd carried in her heart since Beatrice had made her mad prediction about the viscount's feelings for her, died as he stopped before her.

He raked his cold stare over her trembling frame, and she tugged her muslin cloak closer. "Madam, I do not know the meaning of your visit."

"I needed to speak to you Geoffrey. Please," she implored him, holding her palms up.

He folded his arms across his broad chest, and arched a single, chestnut brow. He, in his dry, immaculate fawn-colored breeches and white cambric shirt, looked so coolly perfect and elegant. His perfection only served to highlight the fact that she now stood before him, a bedraggled mess amidst a puddle formed by the water that clung to her ruined skirts and soaking slippers. "Well, madam."

Madam. He uttered that word as though it were a vile epithet.

"Please, Geoffrey…"

"Madam, it is late. I am tired. And you…" he peered down his aquiline nose at her. "And you are making quite a mess of my marble foyer."

She flinched, his words hurt like he'd physically struck her. *How can you be so coldly unforgiving? How when I love you as I do?*

He took a step around her, and Abigail dimly registered that he'd reached for the door handle. "No." Abigail held a hand up, begging him with that staying motion to please hear her out.

Geoffrey stopped, his hand remained on the door, as though one wrong word on her part, and he'd throw the door open and toss her onto the steps like yesterday's refuse.

"Say what it is you've come to say and be done with it?"

Abigail's throat burned with the realization that he'd not grant her a private audience. He'd make her spill her shame here upon his foyer. Her back went up. Well, that was fine. She'd braved a far greater humiliation than this.

"There was a man," she blurted.

His body went taut. The well-chorded muscles of his chest strained against his white cambric shirt, the only telltale indication that he'd heard her words.

Abigail took a deep breath, and searched for the resolve to tell the story. "I loved him." She grimaced. "Or I believed I did." She hadn't truly known love. Not until Geoffrey. She knew that now.

He remained silent, but he did not open that door and so she had to believe that meant something. She sucked in a breath. "He was my brother's dearest friend." Her gaze slipped away from Geoffrey. "I believe he saw me as nothing more than an inconvenience. He began to visit my brother more and more. Only I soon realized, it was too see me. He brought me flowers, and told me wicked, little jests, and teased me quite mercilessly." Abigail's gaze skittered off to the wood panel of the door just beyond Geoffrey's shoulder. She focused on the white polish of the wood door to spare herself the wintry disdain she saw etched upon the sharp planes of Geoffrey's cheeks. Odd, she'd expected the recounting of events to hurt greater than this. "Papa and Mama didn't approve of him," she said at last.

An odd, garbled kind of laugh seemed to work its way up Geoffrey's throat and lodge there. She jerked her gaze up and found that mocking sneer on his lips. "Oh?"

Just that one derisive utterance; a clear indication that nothing she said next would matter, but still, she'd not leave until she'd said it all.

Abigail thought to the great many arguments that had ensued over the suitability of Alexander as a match. "He was the illegitimate son of a powerful and wealthy barrister from Connecticut. It didn't matter," Abigail said quietly. It had never mattered. Oh, it had to Mama and Papa but not to her. "My parents claimed he merely sought the wealth that marriage to me would bring." All the burning resentment she'd carried for so long had gone, instead replaced by recognition with the decisions she'd made. "It turned out my mother and father were indeed, correct. Alexander had planned it all. We were attending a soiree at one of the homes of a leading member of society. Alexander lured me to the host's library and fool that I was, I went."

She could and would forever regret her personal folly, but she now accepted her own culpability in that one, great mistake. As a woman, she'd made the choice to follow Alexander. "We were…" She felt herself coloring. "Discovered," she finished lamely.

Geoffrey's already taut body, stiffened. A muscle ticked at the corner of his eye.

She rushed to have the whole of the story told. "My father threatened to cut me off without a penny. I didn't care. But Alexander did." Even now she wondered if the threat leveled by her father had been real. As a child, and until she'd been discovered in Alexander's arms she had thought her father loved her with an unconditional love… after that moment, she'd begun to doubt the depth of that love.

Abigail took a step toward Geoffrey. She held her palms up. "I thought my heart died that night, Geoffrey. I hated my parents for forcing me to give up my family, forcing me across the sea." She managed a tremulous smile and took another step until only the space of a palm separated them. "But then I met you, Geoffrey. And it all became clear. If there had been no Alexander and no scandal and no rejection by my parents," she lifted her eyes to his. "There would be no us." She raised her hand to his cheek. "And that would be the greatest tragedy. I love you."

Geoffrey stiffened at the feel of Abigail's satiny smooth palm upon his cheek. His eyes closed.

He didn't want her story to matter. He didn't want to care that there had been another man who'd teased her, and showered her with pretty compliments and bouquets of flowers. He didn't want to care that she'd lain with that nameless man, and given him the gift all ladies were supposed to cherish.

Except the nameless man now had a name.

Alexander Powers.

Geoffrey didn't want to care.

But he did…and he hated himself for it.

I love you.

He stared unblinking, gaze fixed upon her long, elegant fingers. Then, found the strength to close his fingers around her wrist and remove her hand from his person. From the moment he'd met Abigail, she had lied to him. He'd laid himself bare before her and shared every, agonizing bit of Emma's betrayal, his father's death, and yet deceived him with her silence, not sharing the guarded secrets she carried. She'd made him care for her…he winced, no, *love her*, and how had she repaid that love?

By opening him up to Society's censure. What a bloody fool he must seem? He'd courted her with the most honorable of intentions.

He did so against his own better judgment, against his own mother's adamant protestations. Once again, he'd allowed his selfish desires to supersede responsibility.

Geoffrey released her.

"Tell me, madam," he said, arching a brow. "Did you have any intentions of telling me of your," he ran his eyes over her person, "lack of virtue." She jerked as though he'd physically struck her. Guilt stabbed at him, but he shoved it aside, embracing instead the pain of her betrayal.

Her regret merely stemmed from the fact that he'd discovered her duplicity. "Come, no answer, Miss Stone? Would you have waited until our wedding night for me to discover your secret?"

Her eyes flared wide. She held her hand extended up, toward him. "Wedding?"

A sharp, ugly chuckle escaped him. "What intentions did you expect of a gentleman courting the Duke of Somerset's niece?"

She wet her lips, and lifted one shoulder in a little shrug. "I did not allow myself to dare dream of marriage to you, Geoffrey." Her eyes bled agony.

For all that had transpired last evening at Lady Ainsworth's soiree, the sight of Abigail's suffering threatened to shatter him. He stretched a hand out, and then remembered himself. With a ragged sigh, Geoffrey stepped away from her. He swiped the back of his hand across his eyes. God help him for being the same, weak, reckless fool he'd always been.

Abigail's face shifted, and in his mind became another. A long-buried memory resurfaced; Emma's harsh laugh as she'd at last confessed the truth to him. Geoffrey hadn't mattered to her. He'd merely been a wealthy, titled gentleman who could give her unborn babe a name. He blinked back the remembrance and steeled his heart. He'd not be fooled. Not again.

He clapped his hands, slowly, and rhythmically. "Brava, madam, your false innocence could rival the greatest Covent Garden actresses."

Her midnight black brows stitched into a single, mutinous line. "I've not lied to you."

"A lie by omission is still a lie."

She snapped her mouth closed, and glanced to a point beyond his shoulder. "There is nothing I can say," she said softly, as though she were speaking more to herself. Then she squared her shoulders, and tossed her chin up; even with her hair hanging in long, limp strands about her person, she had the regal elegance to rival a queen. "Tell me what I can say to make you understand. Tell me what you'd have me do?"

She stood there, chest heaving up and down, her eyes imploring. Ahh god, even with her betrayal, the sight of her suffering hit him like the edge of a steely dagger being plunged into his gut.

He spun around, and stared at the wood panels of the door, unable to confront the sight of her. Because he was so very close to capitulating, and saying to hell with all her treachery.

He could not do that. Not again.

Thunder rumbled in the night sky, and shook the door…a reminder of the sins of his past, of the selfish man he'd been who'd put a woman before his father. The muscles in Geoffrey's stomach tensed. His father had paid the ultimate price for Geoffrey's desires.

"Madam, there is nothing you can say." Nothing that would take away the dull ache that throbbed inside his heart.

And before he did something foolish like take her in his arms and throw aside his pride and honor, Geoffrey jerked the door open.

Sheets of rain slanted down sideways and pounded upon the marble floor.

"Geoffrey, please," she begged.

He gritted his teeth so hard, pain radiated along his jawline. "I am the Viscount Redbrooke and you no longer have leave to use my Christian name."

A spasm of grief contorted Abigail's face, and he gripped the sides of the door, embracing the bite of the rain upon his cheeks. He silently cursed himself a thousand times a bastard. Even now, he couldn't bear the sight of her anguish…and that it was at his hand…

She gave a jerky nod, and walked the remaining distance to the front door, with the kind of regal carriage that could rival a queen.

"I've reconciled the shame and sins of my past. You're no different than everyone who has judged me and found me wanting, Geoff… my lord." She stopped so that her slippers touched the tips of his toes. She leaned up close, and her breath fanned his cheeks, the warmth of her mint-scented breath drove back the chill inside him. "But I'm not unlike you. I loved and trusted…and was deceived."

Geoffrey's lips pulled back in a sneer. "We are nothing alike, madam. I am a respectable proper lord, and you…you are a fallen woman." He motioned to the entrance of the doorway.

Abigail recoiled like he'd struck her across the face. "Very well," she whispered, her voice hollow. "I needed to come, and now I-I k-know." Her voice broke and he momentarily closed his eyes, and searched for the resolve to not capitulate and take her in his arms, but they were standing in the entrance of his home, and faced the threat of discovery.

He peered out into the raging storm. "Where is your carriage, Ab…Miss Stone?" She would always be Abigail.

Her lips twisted in a macabre rendition of a smile and she pulled the hood of her cloak back into place, obscuring the precious lines of her face. "You needn't concern yourself with me, my lord."

His jaw tightened. "Regardless, I'd see you to your arrangements home, madam." She stiffened as he took her by the hand and guided her outside. The wind and rain whipped her thoroughly sopping cloak about his legs. Rain soaked his hair, and beads of water ran in steady rivulets down his forehead, into his eyes. Geoffrey and Abigail stopped in front of her hired hackney.

The misgivings of handing her up into the waiting carriage reared in his mind. "You've taken a hackney?" he shouted into the storm.

The driver pulled the door open.

"I could hardly take the duke's carriage to your home," she spat into the rain.

The driver made to hand her up, but Geoffrey tightened his grip about her wrist, keeping her at his side. "It is not safe for you." Not on this night. Alone, with this driver. She'd deceived him, shattered his heart, but he'd not have any harm befall her.

Just then, a young servant scrambled down from the top of the carriage, a cap pulled low over his eyes. The young man's livery revealed him to be of the duke's staff. Lightning illuminated the sky; the flash of light displayed the protective fury in the servant's eyes.

Abigail took advantage of Geoffrey's distractedness. She tugged her hand free with such force she went reeling toward the street. Geoffrey's heart lurched as she stumbled sideways, and tipped over the side of curb. Geoffrey reached out to steady her but the fabric of her muslin cloak slipped through his fingers. "Abby," he shouted even as the driver reached out righted Abigail before she could fall.

She nodded her thanks, and allowed the man to hand her up into the carriage. Her eyes caught and held Geoffrey's. "Rest assured, I'll never again burden you with my presence. Good bye, my lord."

Good bye, so much more permanent and all the more aching for its finality than good night. He took a step forward, but the driver closed the door.

From perched atop his seat alongside the driver, the young servant scrambled back up into his seat. He glared down at Geoffrey as though he were the dirt upon his heels. Geoffrey's throat worked up and down. Just then he found, he rather agreed with the young man... he didn't much like himself.

Geoffrey stood there staring, long after the carriage disappeared from sight. The finality of Abigail's departure from his life threatened to cleave him in two. He sucked in an agonized breath.

"Geoffrey, come inside!" His mother called from the gaping front door. "Geoffrey!" she called again. "Think of the scandal."

He gave his head a shake, and numbly moved through the rain, strode up the stairs, and into the now soaking wet foyer. Geoffrey stared blankly down at the puddle Abigail had left upon his marble floor. The servants would come, they would dry away all remnants of rain and with it they would wipe away the remaining trace of her from his life.

"I am proud of you, Geoffrey," his mother said quietly and then picked her way carefully around the wet floor and made her way back abovestairs.

Geoffrey stared down into that wet puddle. A boulder-like pressure weighted upon the spot where his heart had once beat.

At least one of them could be proud of his shameful behavior that evening.

TWENTY-FOUR

A gentleman should make decisions that are clear, well-thought out, and not driven by emotion.
4th Viscount Redbrooke

Abigail stared blankly out into the passing London streets. The grind of the carriage wheels against the pavement was swallowed by the pounding stream of rain, and the nearby rumble of thunder.

She tried to drag up the deserved indignation at Geoffrey's self-righteous outrage but found herself wholly numbed. Abigail could not fault Geoffrey his feelings. Since their first meeting, she'd known him to be a man who valued propriety and honor above all else. Such a gentleman could never forgive her indiscretion.

And yet, knowing that, and accepting it did nothing to lessen the agonizing pain that ripped at her insides.

Abigail pressed her forehead against the carriage window, and closed her eyes. Because in her heart, she'd held onto the fragile thread of hope that mayhap she mattered more to him than even his sense of propriety. She had allowed herself to believe he would recognize she, like him, had been betrayed.

In the end, he'd likened her to the heartless woman who'd attempted to trap him into marriage.

She dropped the curtain and settled back into her seat, acknowledging the hideous, horrid truth—with her silence, she'd not been different than his Emma Marsh. Abigail had allowed Geoffrey to court her with the most honorable of intentions all the while, knowing, she could never be an acceptable match.

A bead of rain trickled down her cheek. Followed by another. She wiped it away but another drop swiftly replaced it. Then another. And another.

She started, realizing they were in fact tears.

Abigail sank the back of her head onto the hard squabs of the rented hack. Sharp laughter worked its way up her throat. After Alexander's betrayal, she'd thought herself incapable of ever shedding another of the salty droplets. It turned out she'd been wrong.

Lightning lit a crisscross pattern across the sky, followed by a sharp crash.

She gasped as the carriage jolted sideways. It tipped on its side. The loud, frantic whinny of the horses broke through the fury of the storm.

She closed her eyes on a silent prayer as the conveyance seemed to right itself.

Crack.

Abigail's stomach lurched; she gripped the sides of the seat, and pressed tight against the corner. She braced herself as the carriage tipped, and swayed, and her heart froze inside her chest. A scream worked its way out of her throat, as the conveyance bobbed and swayed like a ship at sea. It tossed Abigail against the opposite seat.

"Oomph!" Her shoulder struck the side of the carriage, and the window exploded into a shower of glass. She screamed, as the carriage jolted to a slow, sideways halt. The velocity of the movement whipped her neck back. She struck her head, even as the wood splintered and shards of glass sprayed the inside of the hackney.

From where she lay amidst glass and broken wood, Abigail stared sightless at the now opened roof over head. Her shoulders and back throbbed from where she'd been flung. She blinked seeing bright light dot the sky ahead. It couldn't be stars. Not on this cold, vile night.

She touched her hand to the rain that streamed a salty path into her eyes, her breathing came in slow, shallow spurts. She raised trembling fingers and stared at her crimson stained fingers, and then slipped into the blessed painlessness of unconsciousness.

TWENTY-FIVE

A gentleman should be able to name one or two gentle-
men as close friends and confidantes.
4ᵗʰ Viscount Redbrooke

In the light of a new day, with the rains passed, and nothing but his own mournful thoughts and pained regrets, Geoffrey Winters, 5ᵗʰ Viscount Redbrooke, came to a staggering, if humbling revelation—he didn't have a friend in the world.

The harsh truth of it flashed never more clear than now, as he sat alone with his misery at White's. After an infernally long night, he'd resolved to confront the shame and pained humiliation of the scandal boldly, with his head held high.

Except as he sat at his private table, he felt no calming peace. He felt…oddly…empty.

Geoffrey stared down at the scrap of blood-stained lace in his hands, passing it back and forth between his fingers. He should burn the blasted piece of fabric, a memento that should mean nothing to him. *Well, Happy Birthday, Geoffrey. Now, you must certainly keep the scrap of lace from Lizzie*

After Abigail had left last evening…His heart convulsed—no, after he'd sent her away, sleep had proven a fickle friend, indeed. He'd stared blankly out the window at the torrents of rain that fell from the sky until it faded to a slow stream, and then a steady trickle—until it stopped altogether.

Since he'd arrived at White's nearly an hour past, he'd resolved to get himself well and thoroughly foxed.

Only, alcohol had little effect in helping him to forget Abigail.

With a curse, Geoffrey stuffed the lace back into the front pocket of his coat, and reached for his brandy.

Sunshine spilled through the front windows of White's, and Geoffrey squinted at the nauseating brightness. He glared into the amber contents of the glass, silently cursing the sunlight that seemed to mock his foul temper and dark thoughts.

But then, following two days of violent storms, there couldn't possibly be another drop of rain left in the sky.

He made the mistake of glancing up, and noted the cluster of dandies eyeing him with morbid fascination. Geoffrey growled, and they hastily averted their gazes. He downed the contents of his glass and reached for the crystal decanter. To those dandified fops, and all of the *ton*, Geoffrey happened to be nothing more than a juicy morsel of gossip passed about parlors, and bandied about through the pages of gossip columns.

But this was his life, and his pain.

And it was the kind of pain that haunted men until they lay, feeble and old at the end of their days.

Geoffrey took a small sip, and grimaced at the fiery, but welcome path the brandy trailed down his throat. He embraced even the small sting, and looked forward to getting himself completely and thoroughly soused. Only then could he drive back the memory of the pain that bled through the storm-gray of Abigail's eyes as he'd escorted her from his home like a thief from Newgate.

"May I join you?" A deep voice murmured, interrupting his despondent musings.

Geoffrey continued to stare at the surface of his table, even as Lord Sinclair slid into the seat across from him. Geoffrey finished his brandy. No, he had no friends.

"May I?" Sinclair asked.

Wordlessly, Geoffrey poured himself another, and then shoved the bottle toward Sinclair.

Sinclair accepted a glass from a servant, and then waved the liveried waiter off and proceeded to pour his own glass. "You look like hell," he said without preamble.

Geoffrey took another long swallow and grimaced around the burn of the liquor. "Go to hell, Sinclair."

Sinclair sat back in his chair and stretched out his legs in front of him. He hooked one of his ankles over the other. "It looks like you yourself have already been there," he drawled.

Geoffrey tossed back another brandy. He set the glass down hard upon the table. All Sinclair's presence served to do was remind him of Abigail. Abigail as she'd waltzed with the too-affable gentleman. Abigail as she'd spoken candidly with Sinclair about her dreadful dancing skills. Would Sinclair have turned her away in shame as Geoffrey had done? No, he rather suspected the charming, roguish gentleman would have told the all of Society to go to hell with a wave and a smile, and done right by Abigail.

Not like Geoffrey. Selfish, cowardly bastard who couldn't sort out which was of greater importance—his heart's desire for Abigail Stone or his familial obligations. "What do you want?" he asked tersely.

The hard planes of Sinclair's face settled into an uncharacteristically serious mask. "I thought you might need a friend."

Geoffrey chuckled, the sound harsh and raw to his own ears. "And is that what you are? A friend?"

"Yes."

That simple confirmation struck Geoffrey. "I don't have any friends."

An inelegant snort escaped Sinclair. "Probably because you're such a pompous prig."

Geoffrey managed his first half-grin since Lord and Lady Ainsworth's ball two days past. Odd, he'd imagined he'd never be able to muster a hint of a smile again after Abigail had walked out of his life. The grin died on his lips. Geoffrey reached for the bottle and sloshed several fingerfuls into his glass.

He took a long swallow, no longer feeling the sharp burn of the brew.

"You loved her."

Geoffrey's fingers tightened hard about his glass at Sinclair's statement. The faint tremor in his hands sent liquid drops spraying onto the table. He wanted to snap and snarl like a caged beast. How dare Sinclair come and force him to speak of her, in White's, with his ragged spirit bared for all to see?

Geoffrey swirled his brandy. "I did." The whisper tore from deep inside him. *I do.*

Sinclair raised his glass to his lips. He studied Geoffrey over the rim, took a sip, and then tugged his chair closer to the table. "Do you think any of this matters, Redbrooke?" He waved his hand, gesturing to the club. "Do you believe these heartless bastards were more important than your own happiness?"

Geoffrey's throat worked up and down. "It is not that simple," Geoffrey said hoarsely. "She lied. She deliberately deceived me." He cleared his throat, squaring his jaw. "And, in her actions the lady had sneered in the face of propriety and I cannot in good conscience wed such a woman."

"Surely you're not so foolish as to believe those words." He dropped his voice to a harsh whisper. "What would you have had the lady do? Bandy her shame about the *ton*? Would you have had her share the fact that she'd been forced across the ocean because she'd been discovered with her lover?"

Oh, God. Geoffrey gripped the edge of the table, his nails bit hard into the hardwood surface. Sinclair's words ate at him like poison that destroyed.

Sinclair sat his glass down with a loud thunk. He planted his elbows upon the table. "This isn't about your title or propriety. This is about nothing more than your own jealousy, Redbrooke."

Geoffrey froze, allowing that volatile charge to seep into his brandy-laden brain. He shook his head. "No."

"Yes. I'm telling you this because I'm your friend."

"I don't have any friends," Geoffrey said blankly.

"No, you don't. With the exception of me, of course." Sinclair took a sip of his drink. "Have you attempted to speak to the duke?"

Geoffrey shook his head jerkily. He'd intended to. At Lady Ainsworth's he'd made plans to call on the duke and request Abigail's hand in marriage. Had it been only two days since his world had fallen apart.

"I haven't." Nor would he. There was nothing left to say. He'd said everything and then some, on that thunderous night when he'd shoved Abigail into a hired hackney

Sinclair shook his head. "I never took you for a coward, Redbrooke."

His life had been coldly empty and meaningless until her. She'd taught him to again laugh, had forced him to confront the feelings of guilt and shame he carried over his role in Father's death. Could Geoffrey trade all that he valued, his mother's stringent expectations, his own self-pride, for her?

I'm not unlike you. I loved and trusted...and was deceived.

And how had he repaid her love? He'd turned his back on her, treating her as nothing more than a common strumpet in the street.

Oh, god, what have I done?

Geoffrey's shoulders stiffened, as a steely resolve filled him. "I love her," he said into the quiet. He shoved his chair back. "I need to see her."

Sinclair's eyes went wide. All the color drained from his olive-hued cheeks. "Christ," he hissed. He reached for the decanter and poured a glass full of brandy. He proceeded to down the contents in a long, steady swallow.

Something in the man's horrified expression, the blend of shock and pity in his blue eyes gave Geoffrey pause. His heart thudded in his breast.

"What is it?" he asked, his voice hoarse.

Sinclair set his glass down hard, and shoved it away. He leaned across the table; his eyes seemed to search Geoffrey's face. "You do not know," he said, the spoken words a statement, not a question, said more to himself.

The odd thumping of his heart increased its rhythm, pounding hard, and painful, threatening to shatter his chest. "Know what?" He reached across the table and gripped Sinclair by the lapels of his double-breasted jacket.

Shocked gasps and loud whispers filled White's. Geoffrey ignored them. "Know what?" he asked, giving a shake.

Sinclair turned his palms up. "There was an accident."

And Geoffrey's world stopped.

Geoffrey rode at a maddening speed through the streets of London. He kneed his horse Decorum onward toward the Duke of Somerset's townhouse.

The pounding of Decorum's hooves echoed around his mind.

There was an accident.

There was an accident.

Oh, Christ.

A carriage accident. Head injuries. Injured arm. Possibly broken. Unlikely she'll survive.

Bile burned like acid at the back of his throat, and his stomach churned until he nearly cast the contents of his stomach onto the muddied London streets.

As he came to the duke's townhouse, Geoffrey jerked on Decorum's reins with such force, the horse reared and pawed the air with its front legs. Geoffrey leapt down, and tossed the reins over to a nearby street urchin. He tossed the boy a sovereign. "Wait for me. There will be more," he said, his words harsh and hard.

He raced up the steps, and pounded upon the front of the door.

I sent her away.

I put her in that carriage and sent her off.

The butler pulled the door open and Geoffrey shoved past the butler.

"My lord, the family is not receiving callers," the servant said, his flinty eyes as hard as the edge to his words.

Geoffrey swept a circle about the foyer. He scraped a hand through his hair, and glanced up the stairway. He considered storming the bloody townhouse until he located her. "Abigail," he forced out. And then remembered himself, "Miss Stone. I'm here to see Miss Stone."

Mayhap Sinclair had been mistaken. Mayhap a gossipy *ton* had merely circulated a story fashioned on hideous rumors.

Something flashed in the other man's eyes and Geoffrey knew with all the intuitiveness of a man who'd suffered great loss, that the rumors were indeed true. "Miss Stone is indisposed." The butler motioned to the door. "Now if you will, my lord."

Geoffrey stepped around the butler and made for the stairs.

The butler gasped. "My lord," he planted himself in front of Geoffrey halting his advance.

"Get the hell out of my way," he seethed. He knew how he must look; like a madman escaped Bedlam and for the first time in his life, he didn't give a damn for propriety.

"What is the meaning of this?" A sharp voice barked from the top of the stairs.

Geoffrey looked up as the Marquess Westfield stomped down the stairs.

"You?" Westfield growled. His lip pulled back in a sneer.

Geoffrey didn't anticipate the other man's right handed jab to his cheek.

The air left Geoffrey as the force of Westfield's unexpected blow knocked him to his knees.

"You bloody bastard," Westfield seethed. Westfield dragged him up by the front of his jacket, and gave him a solid shake. "You dare come here?"

Geoffrey staggered to his feet. He pressed the back of his coat sleeve to staunch his bleeding nose. He winced, certain Westfield had broken it which was no less than Geoffrey deserved. "I…Abigail…I heard…Is it true…?"

Westfield's eyes narrowed to impenetrable slits. "What do you want?" he finally said. "It is my understanding that you were very clear in your feelings for Abigail."

His mind raced. "She told you." *That I sent her away. That I handed her up into the carriage. That I said she was unworthy of me.* When in actuality, Geoffrey had never deserved her. Abigail had always been entirely too good for him.

Westfield's eyes blazed with fury. "The bloody servant who escorted her to your townhouse was very informative." He stuck his finger out, pointing to the door. "Now get the hell out." He clasped Geoffrey by the forearm.

Geoffrey jerked his arm free. He pulled a kerchief from his jacket and held it to his nose. "I'm not leaving, Westfield."

"By god, I'll summon a team of servants to have you removed from this foyer if you do not leave immediately." As if he'd been waiting in the wings for his master's orders, the butler reappeared.

Geoffrey ignored the stocky servant. "Abigail…"

"Is dead," Westfield spat, and with a curt nod to the butler, spun on his heel and marched purposefully back up the stairs.

Geoffrey stared up after him, unblinking. His heart thudded to a slow halt.

Dead.

Dead.

He took his head in his hands, and shook it wildly back and forth. Surely he'd heard Westfield wrong. Surely he'd know if Abigail had died because his heart would have known, and would have ceased to beat. Geoffrey dug his fingers into his temples and searched the foyer.

"Oh, God," the agonized entreaty tore from deep inside him. The crimson stained handkerchief fell to the floor.

Geoffrey searched for purchase, and found none as the life drained from his legs. He collapsed to his knees. He dimly registered the butler speaking to someone, but the voices came as if down a long hall. Geoffrey sucked in deep, gasping breaths as his past and present blurred together with a dreadfully remarkable likeness.

Someone touched a hand to Geoffrey's shoulder, and he snarled feeling like a caged beast set free.

"Lord Redbrooke?" The delicate, gentle female tone broke through the cloud of madness that gripped him.

He blinked. "Lady Beatrice," he said, his voice hoarse.

Lady Beatrice glanced around, and said something to the butler. The servant nodded and with a bow took his leave. "I overheard your conversation with my brother. I do not approve of your treatment of Abby last evening, but my brother's actions were unforgiveable."

Geoffrey struggled to put her words into some semblance of order that made sense.

"Abigail is not dead," she said.

Geoffrey's eyes slid closed, as a prayer slipped from his lips. He grabbed Lady Beatrice's hands in his. "Thank you."

Lady Beatrice tugged him to his feet. "Hurry. My brother and father mustn't find out. Come, I'll take you to her."

Energy filled his strides. "How is she?" he rasped.

Lady Beatrice shot a pointed look over her shoulder, and touched a finger to her lips. "Hush." She guided him abovestairs and down the hall, past several wide-eyed servants. She stopped in front of a door, and looked up at him. "Abigail injured her arm. She suffered a head injury, and has not awakened since the accident. Now, you must be quick, my lord." She reached for the door handle, and then hesitated. "She is...not well, my lord."

Geoffrey reached past her, and pressed the handle. He entered the room.

Beatrice closed the door behind him.

His eyes struggled to adjust to Abigail's dark chambers. He took a tentative step toward the massive, feather-down four poster bed at the center of the room.

"Abby," he called quietly.

The popping of the embers within the fireplace hearth made the only sound in the ominously quiet chambers.

Geoffrey took several tentative steps toward the bed, and stopped when his knees knocked the white coverlet. He sucked in an anguished breath, and sank onto the stark white coverlet. "Abby," he breathed.

Her face looked an artist's palate of green, purple, and blue hues. A large, ugly, distended knot marred the center of her forehead. "Oh, Abby," he whispered. He reached for her hand, and froze at the sight of a sling that had been fashioned to stabilize her arm. He wanted to toss his head back and hurl vile epithets at the heavens. And yet, he had no one to blame except himself. He'd done this. Just as he'd sent his father away, he'd sent Abby fleeing. An odd gurgling rumbled deep in his chest. Geoffrey's vision blurred, as he realized the great, gasping sobs came from him. "What have I done?" he rasped.

The cruel emptiness of silence, his only answer.

Through tear-filled eyes, he studied Abigail's injured arm and his stomach churned as he imagined the pain she'd suffered when the dislocated limb had been popped back into place.

Geoffrey reached for her other, uninjured hand. He picked up her delicate palm and turned it over in his hand, studying her long, elegant fingers.

His mind tripped back to the night she'd interlocked their hands and held them up to the star-studded skies.

That is Lyra.

He raised her hand to his mouth, and brushed his lips along the inner portion of her wrist. "Oh, Abby, I love you." He studied her blackened eyes for any sign of awareness but she remained in the thick haze of slumber that had stolen her from the now, and kept her in the darkened world at the edge of death. "I have loved you since the moment I knocked over Lord and Lady Hughes's servant's tray of champagne and nearly toppled you to the floor." He dropped to his knees beside her bed. "I am nothing without you." His words broke. "Do you know Abby, I thought the greatest crime I'd committed against my father lie in failing to honor my responsibilities. Only now," *too late,* "do I realize, how very wrong I've been. My greatest offence lies in not listening to him, and now...you. Forgive me."

The door opened and closed.

Geoffrey didn't take blurry gaze from Abigail's swollen, bruised eyes.

"Lord Redbrooke. You must go," Lady Beatrice whispered.

He managed a jerky nod. Except, he could not make his legs move. "I can't leave her."

The soft pad of her slippered feet upon the hardwood floor filled the quiet. She stopped next to Abigail's bed. "You must, my lord. I promise I'll send word."

"Why would you help me in this way?" *Why, when I am the contemptible bastard who treated Abigail like the refuse upon my boots?*

"Because you love her. And she loves you."

Or she had. His eyes fixed on her too-still form. She had to get well. Because the alternative would break him down until he was nothing more than an empty shell of a human-being. There was no life worth living if she were not part of it and when she opened her eyes, he would spend the rest of his days proving himself worthy of her, proving himself different than the bastard who'd stolen her innocence and viciously betrayed her. And she would open her eyes. He willed the words to truth.

Geoffrey stood on shaky legs. "Thank you, my lady."

She nodded. "Now, follow me." Lady Beatrice started for the door.

"And you'll send word?" Geoffrey asked, as he walked beside her.

"Every day," she promised.

As Geoffrey slipped from the duke's townhouse like a silent thief absconding with the Crown's jewels, Geoffrey resolved to become the man Abigail deserved.

And propriety and respectability could both go to the devil.

TWENTY-SIX

A gentleman should recognize when he errs, and is
not too proud to then make his apologies.
4ᵗʰ Viscount Redbrooke

A bigail lived in a world where reality blended with dream; where pain blended with terror. She thrashed upon her pillow as fingers poked at her person. A cry gurgled up her throat and spilled past her lips as large, sure hands prodded at her shoulder.

She registered the Duke of Somerset conversing with another man. The tormentor; the prodder whose excruciating touch filled her with agony, murmured something to the duke.

Head injury.

Accident.

Dire.

Unlikely she'll live.

Who did they speak of? Pity filled her for the poor, unfortunate soul who fought for her life. Abigail struggled to open her eyes and form words…as with a mounting horror, hideous memories crept in.

Geoffrey.

The numbing throb behind her eyes, intensified until nausea boiled in her stomach and she remembered.

Geoffrey's derision.

His rejection.

The accident.

Oh, God. The poor soul they spoke of…

It is me.

I hear you. I can't die. But the fingers of unconsciousness tugged her back into its inky black folds, and this time she gladly sank into the slumberous state.

She wavered in and out of a murky consciousness, filled with a desperation to see her family and assure them she would survive. In the deepest yearnings of her suffering, Geoffrey came to her, knelt at her side, pleaded forgiveness. And then, the soft, loving gentleman would transform into a derisive, sneering figure she didn't recognize. Through it all, Abigail remained trapped in the silent state.

Until at last, she blinked her eyes open.

A guttural groan wrenched from deep inside and increased the throbbing pressure behind her eyes. She turned her head slightly, taking in the darkness of the still room.

Abigail closed her eyes again in attempt to rid herself of the piercing pain that pounded at her skull.

Someone gasped.

Abigail tried to look toward the frantic patter of footsteps. The click of the door echoed around her aching head, and she forced back nausea. Abigail rested her head upon the pillow and stared up at the cherubs dancing on the mural above her bed.

Then…the door opened again.

"Abigail."

She sorted through muddied thoughts as she tried to place the voice. Then, taking a slow breath she turned her head on the pillow.

Her uncle strode over to the bed and sat in the empty chair beside her, his somber gaze moving over her. "Thank God, Abigail. We had feared you would not recover."

The memory of that thunderous night went ripping through her thoughts, and she gasped as she recalled the horror of Geoffrey's rejection, the mind-numbing terror of the carriage accident, then the unbearable soreness of her head and body.

She wet her lips.

"Would you care for water?" He reached for a pitcher that sat beside her bed.

Her stomach churned at the thought of filling her belly with anything. "No," she said, that one word hoarse, and near unrecognizable as belonging to her.

He froze, and sat back in his seat.

"How long have I been asleep?" she whispered.

"Nearly three days, Abigail." He folded his arms across his chest. "Do you recall what happened that evening?"

God, she wished with the pain the accident had brought her, it could have managed to somehow shake loose the all too familiar sting of Society's rejection, and worse, Geoffrey's disdain.

For the remainder of her days she would recall the precise moment when the warm, caring look in Geoffrey's eyes had been replaced with the cool, flinty ice of a man who'd found her actions unforgiveable. Her heart twisted with a bitter resentment. "I remember." Until she drew her last breath she would love him, but she would not, could not forget how easily he had turned her out.

"You injured your arm quite badly."

She touched her fingers to the sling over her left shoulder that restricted her use of the limb. The screams of horror as the arm had been tended to by some faceless doctor filtered through her remembrance.

"You suffered a very serious injury to your head. The doctor feared you'd not recover." He leaned over and touched the fingers of her uninjured hand. "You have too much of your mother's strength and courage to die that way," he said, his words gruff.

If she were truly strong and courageous she would have never humbled herself at Geoffrey's feet on that stormy night.

A sudden onset of guilt besieged her as she silently confronted the shame of all the turmoil she'd visited upon her uncle and his family, and for what? A man who didn't love her? A gentleman who had treated her like the refuse upon his boots?

The duke had taken her in, treated her as another daughter, and she'd repaid that kindness with the scandal of her past and the recklessness in going to Geoffrey.

Abigail embraced her burning resentment because it kept her from weeping useless little tears for a man not deserving of those salty droplets.

"Would you care to speak of him?" the duke said quietly. The hiss and pop of the embers within the hearth filled the quiet.

Not of the stormy night, but rather, him.

Geoffrey.

No. She'd rather bury the memory of Geoffrey with all the other painful, shameful sins of her past. Instead she said, "There is nothing to speak about."

"It is my understanding he turned you away."

Her uncle would not let the matter rest. Abigail turned her head, and looked toward the heavily curtained windows. "Yes, he did." Geoffrey had more than turned her away; with his vitriol he'd reduced her to the broken and shamed creature she'd resolved never to be again after Alexander's betrayal. She cringed in shamed remembrance.

"If Redbrooke hadn't sent you away…"

"But he did," she said with a steely rage she'd not felt even after Alexander's betrayal. She didn't want to speak of Geoffrey. *I can't.*

She wanted to begin throwing bits of dirt upon the memory of him until he was nothing more than a dream of what-ifs.

Her uncle leaned over and touched her hand. "I believe he does care for you, Abigail."

Abigail looked away a moment. She winced as pain radiated out from her forehead and raced down the side of her cheek, and along her jawline. *I should not have gone to him.*

She wondered if in the light of a new day, if he'd had time to reflect, would Geoffrey have been more forgiving?

The memory of him as he'd been—hard, unyielding, with, his stiffly held shoulders and a flinty expression in his blue-green eyes confirmed the emptiness of that possibility. No, she thought with more hurt than he deserved. His reaction would not have been different.

Abigail took a deep breath. "I should never have gone to him." For so many reasons. "I just…"

"You just love him, Abigail."

She closed her eyes again. "I am so very sorry," she whispered. For too many things to put to words. "I repaid your kindness with this great scandal." She seemed incapable of bringing anything but shame to those she loved.

"Abigail, I'm a duke. My family is capable of weathering far greater scandals than this." Ducal arrogance leant credibility to his words.

Her throat worked under a swell of emotion. Her uncle's leniency did little to assuage the guilt of her past and present wrongs. In her need to see Geoffrey, she'd set out without a thought to the consequences of being discovered...consequences which would only hurt Beatrice.

He said nothing for a long while, and then he let out a long sigh. "Your mother has proven there is no logic when it comes to matters of the heart."

Mama, who had braved her family's scorn, the stinging censure of her social peers, and began a life anew, in a new country, all for the love of a man. Except, Mama's world had unfolded like the sweetest bloom in spring; bright and vibrant and joyous.

Her lips twisted.

Love hadn't been as kind to Abigail.

"I do believe, Abigail," her uncle began quietly. "That he did, perhaps still does love you."

No, Geoffrey had never loved her. He'd never given her those three beautiful words...and it had not mattered. All that had mattered is that he'd been willing to trust again, and laugh again after his own heart had been shattered.

"Perhaps," she said, flatly. She thought of Alexander's desire for her wealth, which had mattered so much more than a life with her. Gentlemen were inconstant. Alexander, now Geoffrey had proven as much.

Her uncle opened his mouth to say something, and then closed it. He rose. "I will send for the doctor, Abigail. And your cousins have been riddled with worry. May I send them in?"

"Of course," she murmured.

As he took his leave, Abigail stared at the closed door, foolishly wishing love had been enough, this time.

TWENTY-SEVEN

A gentleman should not conduct himself in a way
that earns Polite Society's censure.
4th Viscount Redbrooke

With his free hand, Geoffrey pounded on the front door of the Duke of Somerset's townhouse. The nobles passing by in their fashionable phaetons and upon horseback, halted, mouths agape, as Geoffrey darkened the duke's doorstep for the seventh day in a row.

The butler pulled the door open and wordlessly, Geoffrey held his card out.

The servant looked down his nose at the card, but made no attempt to take it. "Miss Stone is not receiving guests." He started to close the door.

Geoffrey stuck his booted foot inside the door-jamb, halting the man's efforts. He squared his jaw. "I'd like to see the Duke of Somerset."

"His Grace is not receiving guests, either," the butler said through the small opening.

Geoffrey wedged his hip inside the door, and he'd wager his family seat in Kent that the usually stoic servant cursed. "Will you tell him I'm not leaving? I've every intention of remaining right on the steps of his townhouse until he grants me an audience."

The butler sighed. "I will again remind His Grace. Good day, my lord." He shoved his hip into the door.

Geoffrey stumbled backwards. With a black curse, he took his all too familiar seat upon the top step and set down the bouquet in his hands. His lower back ached from sitting on the hard stone but the discomfort seemed so very insignificant when compared to the bruises and injuries Abigail had sustained.

His stomach clenched in a familiar knot, as he once again imagined Abigail's terror the night of the accident. He tortured himself with image of her lifeless body being flung about the hired hack.

Geoffrey glanced up at the thick blanket of gray and black clouds that rolled over the sky. A single raindrop landed on of the bridge of his nose.

Then the skies opened up.

Bloody *wonderful.*

From where she stood in the drawing room, Abigail parted the thick curtains just enough to peer down into the streets below. A steady stream of rain pounded the pavement. Geoffrey stood, and drops of water sprayed from the fabric of his cloak as it swirled about his feet. Moisture ran in rivulets down his collar and soaked the finely tailored russet garment.

He awkwardly brushed an elbow across his brow but the movement upset his equally drenched beaver hat. A chestnut lock tumbled over his eye and oh, how she longed to brush it back.

She was a fool.

He banged the door.

Her love for him should have died a swift death on that dark, threatening night.

He banged again.

His rejection would forever haunt her.

And again.

But she loved him; hopelessly and helplessly, in a manner that defied all sensible logic.

His pounding increased.

She closed her eyes.

Why would he not go away?

He'd been very clear when he'd turned her away that he found her unworthy, and yet, he now created no small scandal by visiting the duke's townhouse, seeming to enact a kind of penance.

Surely, nothing more than a sense of misguided guilt drove Geoffrey's impulsive actions.

The moment she'd awakened from her unconscious state, she'd embraced the animosity and fury she felt over Geoffrey's treatment. It had served as a kind of protection against further sorrow. But with each knock of that blasted door, he rattled her carefully crafted defenses.

Abigail dropped the curtain back into place and leaned into the wall. She groaned as her injured shoulder collided with the hard surface.

"Abigail, you must sit," the duke called from the King Louis chair he occupied. He folded his arms across his chest. A scowl formed on his austere cheeks. "If I'd imagined you would be up as you are, I'd have never agreed to you being down here. The doctor said—"

"I cannot lay in bed any longer, Uncle." She would go mad with nothing but her pained regrets to keep her company.

"Do you suppose he'll go away soon?" Beatrice asked. She set aside her embroidery frame. He's been out there for nearly an hour." Her eyes took on a faraway expression, and a sigh escaped her. "I think it is so very romantic."

Robert came up beside Abigail and pulled the curtains back enough to look outside into the growing rainstorm, and down at Geoffrey. He growled. "I think it is bloody foolish." A rumble of thunder punctuated his words.

A tremor went through Abigail's body, and she closed her eyes in a desperate bid to fight back this new, irrational fear she had of storms. Memory of that night, the sting of the rain, the bite of the wind, the shattering carriage, haunted her.

Abigail swayed on her feet.

Robert cursed and carefully caught her against him.

"Abby!" Beatrice cried out, and jumped to her feet.

"I'm all right," Abigail whispered. Except she didn't think she would ever be all right, again. The ache of Geoffrey's abandonment, the cold, icy disdain that had fairly dripped from his hardened eyes, all of it so at odds with this resolute gentleman who continued to request an audience.

"He's bloody mad," Robert bit out as the steady rain picked up in intensity.

Beatrice wandered over to the window and peeked outside. "He's brought flowers." Her brow wrinkled. "That poor bouquet is nearly ruined." She leaned closer to the window.

"Beatrice," the duke called pointedly from across the room. "Come away from the window."

She waved her father off. Her brow screwed up. "Whatever kind of flowers are they? I do say they are lovely. But they are not at all familiar."

"Ivy and aconite," Abigail whispered. She remembered back to the flowers he'd brought before he'd discovered the truth about her, before her world had crashed down upon her.

"Aconite? I've never heard of it. What an odd flower to pick out. One would think he'd select roses, or lavender…" Her cousin continued to prattle on, as Abigail sank into a nearby sofa.

"I'll have one of the servants remove him," the duke muttered.

"No!"

Three pairs of eyes swiveled to Abigail.

She swallowed, feeling the hot flood of color rush her cheeks. "I…" She glanced down at the floor. It shouldn't matter and yet she couldn't bear the sight of proud, proper Geoffrey humbling himself outside the duke's townhouse for all to see.

"Absolutely not," Robert barked. "That blackguard isn't to set foot in this house." He waved a hand at Abigail. "It is Redbrooke's fault you're in this condition."

With his gruff, commanding presence, he reminded her so much of her brothers.

"No," she said quietly. Upon first awakening, she'd been filled with acrimonious rage over Geoffrey's treatment. She would forever regret Geoffrey's inconstancy, his unwillingness to see her as a woman who'd made a mistake with her heart…just as he'd done with Emma Marsh.

But, as much as she longed to hate him, and blame him for the injuries she'd suffered, she could not fault him for putting her in the carriage that stormy night.

With the experience of life, she could regret decisions she'd made but she now knew she must accept the consequences of those decisions. Abigail could not fault Geoffrey or Alexander or anyone else for the mistakes she made.

And it had been a mistake to go to Geoffrey's residence.

"Uncle," Abigail began, turning to the duke. "I need to see him." Unless she spoke to him, she would never be free to move forward. "He'll not go unless I speak to him."

He held her gaze, and then after a long while, a sigh escaped him. "Robert, have him shown in."

Robert cursed. He held his father's stare, but then gave a slight nod.

Abigail directed her attention to the window yet again.

"Beatrice, I require a word with Abigail," the duke said to his daughter.

Beatrice hesitated, and then touched Abigail's right hand. "He loves you, Abby," she whispered for Abigail's ears alone.

Abigail bit the inside of her cheek to keep from tossing out a denial. Geoffrey didn't love her. He may have cared for her—at one time. But never love. His heart had been dead and buried with Miss Emma Marsh's betrayal and his father's death.

"He does," Beatrice insisted. "I saw him, Abby and I've never witnessed greater despair than Lord Redbrooke the moment he saw you."

"Beatrice," the duke called.

She nodded. "He made a mistake, Abigail. But I believe, in my heart that he loves you." Beatrice ran her gaze over Abigail's face, and then hurried from the room.

Abigail stared after her, contemplating her cousin's words. Geoffrey's actions since the accident were surely motivated by nothing more than guilt.

The duke stood, and strode over to her. "You need to sit."

"I do not—"

"Sit." The stern ducal command brooked obedience.

Abigail sat.

"What would you like me to do?"

She blinked.

He spoke without preamble. "Do you want to wed him?"

Wed him? At one time she had. Once upon a time ago when she'd believed him to be a man of courage and strength who would brave scandal just to be with her. She shook her head. "He does not want to wed me."

"If he offers for you—"

"He won't," she interrupted. The duke didn't know the vile, hateful words Geoffrey had hurled at her in the foyer of his townhouse.

"If he does," the duke continued. "I'd encourage you to consider his suit. I believe Beatrice is correct when she says the viscount does indeed care for you."

She said nothing, grateful when he took his leave, closing the door behind him with a quiet click.

Abigail sat there, waiting for Geoffrey.

She would listen to him, and then she could begin to move on from the pained reminder of all she'd lost.

TWENTY-EIGHT

A gentleman should be committed to goals that he sets for himself.
4th Viscount Redbrooke

Rain poured from Geoffrey's hat, and filled his eyes. He dashed the back of his hand over his face, blinking back the moisture. He tucked the small box he'd arrived with under his arm, and with bouquet in hand, pounded on the duke's door.

It opened.

He stared wide-eyed, stunned by the unexpected admittance.

Fearing whoever had permitted him entry might change their mind, Geoffrey swiftly entered. With his free hand, he pulled off his drenched beaver hat and handed it over to the servant, who helped him from his cloak. Water sprayed the duke's Italian marble floor.

Then Geoffrey froze. The Marquess Westfield stood at the base of the staircase, arms folded across his chest.

"Must you persist?" he snapped. "You're a soaking mess *and* you're making a bloody fool of yourself."

Geoffrey's mouth tightened. He'd not explain himself to Westfield. The words in his heart were reserved for Abigail. "I'd like to see Abigail."

Westfield's scowl deepened. "She doesn't want to see you, Redbrooke. I've notified her each day since you've been here and every day she instructs me to send you on your way. Today is no exception."

Geoffrey's throat worked reflexively, and he dropped his gaze to the wet bouquet in his hands. How could he blame Abigail? He deserved her scorn and loathing. And yet...he needed to see her.

He glanced up, past Westfield's shoulder to the staircase that led to Abigail's chambers. Geoffrey trusted he could just slip past the other man. It remained questionable how far he could advance before...

"Don't even think of it, Redbrooke," Westfield snapped.

"Robert, that is enough."

Geoffrey froze at the sudden, unexpected appearance of the duke. The man peered down at him from his long, noble nose.

Westfield's glare darkened, but he nodded curtly and took his leave.

Geoffrey bowed, and sent drops of rain flying onto the duke's immaculate black boots.

"You are rather determined, Redbrooke," the duke said in a flat, unreadable tone.

"Your Grace."

"Abigail requires her rest but has asked to see you." He jerked his chin, and began walking, clearly expecting Geoffrey to follow.

Geoffrey hastened his stride, and fell into step beside the duke. She asked to see him. Hope flared in his chest.

"You have fifteen minutes, and after that you are to leave, Redbrooke. My niece will determine whether she again sees you. If she asks to never see you again, then you are to leave my doorstep and not return. Is that clear?"

Fifteen minutes. He had but fifteen minutes to plead forgiveness for being a pompous, self-important ass. He had fifteen minutes to declare his love, and convince Abigail to allow him to spend the remainder of his days trying to be worthy of her. It wasn't enough time.

"It is clear, Your Grace," he murmured.

They stopped beside a closed door. The duke pressed the handle, and motioned for Geoffrey to enter. "Fifteen minutes," he repeated quietly.

Fifteen minutes.

It would have to be enough.

Geoffrey stepped inside. His gaze swept the impressive parlor until he found her. He placed the awkward box shouldered under his arm down upon a nearby rose-inlaid table and set the bouquet of flowers atop it.

His stomach tightened like he'd been kicked in the gut by Decorum's back hooves. The air left him on a whoosh as he saw her. "Oh, God." Vibrant greenish blue bruises stood bright and angry upon her lovely face. His eyes slid closed. He forced them open. He'd been coward enough.

Abigail's lips tipped up in a sad little rendition of a smile. "That bad?"

He swallowed painfully and crossed over to her. He dropped to a knee beside the floral upholstered sofa. "That bad," he said, gruffly.

Something sparked in her eyes; a glimmer that bore traces of the merriment she'd always carried. "You always were rather candid, weren't you?" A hint of wistfulness threaded those words together.

Geoffrey reached for her hand, and froze at the sight of her left arm kept tight to her chest. When he'd been a boy, there had been a small wren that had shattered its wing. The bird had hopped about his mother's garden with that broken wing. With her fragility, Abigail put him in mind of that injured creature.

Geoffrey's gut clenched. "This is my fault."

She touched her fingers to his head. "It is not."

He didn't deserve her absolution. "It is. I should have never allowed you to leave. I should have seen you home myself." He should have been there to protect her, and support her, and sneer in the face of a cruel Society. Instead, like the worst kind of bastard, he'd put her into that hackney and sent her off alone.

"Geoffrey," she touched her hand to his cheek. "I am a woman. The mistakes I've made, they are my own."

She referred to Alexander Powers...and now him. God, with every fiber of his filthy being, he loathed the category he now kept with that faceless coward.

"Is that why you have come?" she asked. "Out of a sense of guilt? That isn't necessary. I should have never gone to you that evening. It wasn't proper." A macabre rendition of a smile turned her full-red lips.

He glanced away unable to look at the transformation his betrayal had wrought on his tender-hearted, hopeful Abigail.

He remembered back to their first meeting.

Miss, we've not been properly introduced; therefore, all manner of discourse between us is improper.

Geoffrey no longer recognized the man he'd been.

"Oh, Abby," he whispered. He covered her uninjured hand with his. "I've been such a bloody ass." Sinclair had been correct. "I couldn't see past my own jealousy." In the days since he'd learned of her accident, Geoffrey had managed to reconcile that Alexander Powers represented a part of her past. Just as Emma Marsh would forever be part of his dark, shameful youth. Both of those relationships had shaped each of them into the people they had become. "You were right, Abigail."

She pulled her hand back, and tucked it in her lap. "Oh?"

He stared, unblinking down at her long fingers. He no longer had a right to touch her. He'd turned her out, and now must forsake the privilege she'd granted him with her love.

"We were not dissimilar. We were both hurt by love." *Only, you never hurt me, Abby. I betrayed you.* "But I will never hurt you again. If you'll allow me, I will spend the rest of my days endeavoring to deserve you. I love you, Abby."

I love you, Abby.

Abigail's heart flipped inside her breast, and she blinked back the tears that clouded her vision.

Before Geoffrey had entered the parlor she'd resolved to make peace with their past. She would hear his words. And then send him on his way to live his entirely proper, staid life, and she would carry on just as she'd done since she'd been forced from America.

That had been before he'd come to her with more unrestrained emotion than she'd ever seen from him. Now, he'd thrown her earlier resolve into upheaval.

Abigail sucked in a breath. She could not trust him. Not again. She shook her head sadly. "Geoffrey, you can never forgive me for the mistakes I made," she said at last. As much as her heart ached for a future with him, she knew he would never be able to truly forgive her lack of virtue.

He leapt to his feet. "I love you, Abby," he said again, his tone harsh. Her eyes went to his tan skin breeches as he paced in front of her. "I understand I'm no longer deserving of your trust, Abby, but I do not care about the gossip."

In that moment, with his emotion-laden eyes, and the hard, determined set of his mouth, she almost believed him. She smiled woefully up at him. "That might be true now. But that won't always be the case. You'll tire of the gossip and unkind gentlemen snickering about you."

Geoffrey jerked to a stop. "I'll not allow anyone to shame you."

Abigail came unsteadily to her feet. With her uninjured hand, she reached for the back of the sofa, and found support there. "If you wed me, you'd spend the rest of your days trying to defend my honor...and when you realized you could not, you would grow to hate me." And that she could not bear.

Geoffrey closed the distance between them. He dropped his brow close to hers. "Oh, sweet Abby, how can I make you see? I do not care." He slashed the air with his hand. "About any of it, Abby. I am nothing without you. Nothing," His imploring tone shook her already weakened resolve.

"Please, Geoffrey," she whispered. "Do not."

A commotion outside the door cut into Geoffrey's response.

She looked over just as the door opened. Her uncle entered, followed by a too-familiar, commanding figure.

It took a moment for her muddled mind to work through that which her eyes saw but which her mind could not process.

"Nathaniel?" she whispered. Her brother couldn't be here. He was in America. Surely her imaginings were a product of the injury she'd sustained to her head.

His eyes did a quick search of her face. "Abby, we've come to bring you home."

We've come to bring you home?

Then Nathaniel shifted. A loud humming filled her ears. She blinked, trying to make sense of it.

The familiar, blonde-haired devil she'd hoped to never see again took a step closer. His eyes shifted momentarily from Geoffrey, then back to her. His square jaw hardened. "Abby."

She blinked. "Alexander?"

Nathaniel looked momentarily over at Geoffrey, who still held her hand and Geoffrey released her. "A great crime was committed against you and Alexander," her brother said. Again, he glanced over at Geoffrey as if trying to determine the identity of this interloper in their private exchange. Nathaniel dismissed him with a single look, and turned back to Abigail.

Her heart stopped.

She shook her head trying to make sense of Nathaniel's utterance.

Alexander's steely gaze burned through her. "I did not betray you, Abby."

And Abigail fainted.

TWENTY-NINE

A gentleman should know when to pardon himself from private exchanges.
4th Viscount Redbrooke

Abigail blinked back the fog of unconsciousness and tried to sort through a jumbled dream in which Geoffrey and Alexander both were guests of the Duke of Somerset. There'd been an accident. And pain.

But no pain greater than the defection of Geoffrey's regard for her.

She winced at the dull, throbbing ache at her temples.

She touched her fingers gently to her forehead, and paused at the thick knob at the center of her head.

Abigail's eyes slid closed. It had been no dream.

She recalled the carriage careening wildly out of control, the cry of the horses, and then pain.

And Alexander.

Alexander?

Her eyes flew open and she flinched at the suddenness of her movements. Her body jerked upright, and she registered at once the familiar sandalwood scent that clung to her brother's shirt.

"Nathaniel," she whispered. She wrapped her arms around him much the way she had as a child when she'd fallen and scraped the skin from her knees. Bitter, hurt tears blazed a trail down her cheek. She'd not expected to ever see her family again. She had imagined with the space that separated them, and her father and brother's business ventures, that they'd have no time to ever again see the daughter and sister who'd visited such shame upon the family.

228

"Shh," Nathaniel whispered. He rubbed soothing circles over her back just as he'd done when she'd been a small hurt girl.

When her sobs became a shuddery little hiccough, Nathaniel helped her down into the sofa.

"What are you doing here?" she blurted. Her gaze shot over to Alexander who stood facing the blazing fire within the hearth, his hands clasped behind his back.

"His Grace spoke of an accident. He mentioned you'd been out, unchaperoned during a storm. He suggested I speak to you for further details. What happened to you, Abby?"

I fell in love. My heart was broken. I was turned away...in shame...again.

"I'm well," she hurried to assure him, even as her dislocated arm throbbed in protest to the lie she told.

He folded his arms over his chest. "What happened, Abby?" he pressed.

She swallowed, and looked past him to where Alexander stood, unyielding and silent like the dead. How could she speak of Geoffrey here to either of these men? Abigail couldn't lay herself bare in front of them; not like this when the pain of Geoffrey's rejection was still raw. "Please don't make me speak of it?"

Nathaniel's eyes narrowed, and he looked prepared to press the point, but then the fight seemed to leave him. "You look like hell," he said bluntly, his gaze fixed on her bruised face.

Her lips tipped up at the corner; she winced at the subtle movement.

"Why have you come, Nathaniel?" She repeated her earlier question. Her eyes flitted once again over to Alexander's broad back. He stiffened, but remained otherwise stock-still.

Abigail jumped as Nathaniel took her hand. He turned her palm over. His familiar hazel eyes earnest and angry all at once. "You and Alexander were wronged."

Her heart flipped over as she tried to sort through that statement.

"I love you, Abby," Alexander said, from across the room, his tone flat and emotionless.

She shook her head. "I don't understand." After they'd been discovered, Alexander had spoken to Papa. Papa had vowed Alexander would never see a penny of her dowry, and Alexander had left—her money had been the only thing that mattered to him. Father had told her.

"He lied, Abby," Nathaniel said softly.

She froze. "No," she whispered. Her father loved her.

Her brother gently nudged her chin, and forced her eyes back to his. "Yes."

Abigail scrambled to her feet so quickly, the room spun. She gripped the edge of the sofa, her nails pressed into the upholstered fabric. "Why would he do that? Why?" Her voice steadily increased in volume. "Why?" she cried.

Alexander at last turned around, a sad, bitter smile on his lips. "Come now. You know your parents never approved of me." He glanced away, and then back to her. "Your father believed I cared more about your dowry than your heart, and set out to prove as such." His face contorted as if in pain. "And how easily you believed his lies."

Bile burned like fire in her throat. "He wouldn't do that." Mama and Papa's had been a love match. They defied the late Duke of Somerset, been forced to start anew in a new country. Her father would not be so cruel as to prove Alexander's unsuitability by orchestrating the events that followed her ruin.

The note.

Her heart shuddered to a slow halt.

As much as we'd wished for you to have a marriage based off love, we realize your comfort and happiness requires you to find a suitable gentleman who will properly care for you.

Her stomach turned over as the sudden depth of her father's betrayal sank into her mind. "I'm going to be ill," she whispered.

Nathaniel touched her shoulder, and she shrugged his hand off. "Did you know? Did you know he planned to separate Alexander and I?" she asked, her words harsh to her own ears.

"Of course not, Abby."

Then there was Alexander, who, through all this, remained stoically silent. She looked to him. How many days and weeks and months had she spent hating him for his betrayal? Resenting him for not loving her enough?

When ultimately, she had been the fickle one for doubting his love.

Nathaniel cleared his throat. "I'll allow you and Alexander an opportunity to speak."

She dimly registered the soft tread of his booted footsteps along the floor, the opening and closing of the door, and then silence.

Abigail and Alexander continued to study one another. Odd, how she'd given so much to this man, had known him nearly all her life, but in that moment, with the veneer of ice that fairly seeped from his tautly held body, he might as well have been a stranger.

"Alexander...I..."

Her words died as he arched an icy brow.

"I didn't know," she implored him to understand.

Another sad smile formed on his lips. "I believe that is what hurt the most, Abby. Your willingness to have believed the absolute worst of me." He averted his gaze. "But then, I'm the blackguard who took your virtue outside the confines of marriage."

And in doing so, he'd cost Abigail her good name. She, however, had been complicit in that act.

Her throat bobbed up and down, as she continued to stand there looking at him. And perhaps she was nothing more than a feckless, faithless woman, for in that moment, with her past and present now converged, she accepted that she'd never truly loved Alexander. The pain of that realization gripped her; it sucked the life from her legs. She sank into a puddle of satin skirts on the nearby sofa. She'd been so besotted by him, this, her brother's friend, a dashing gentleman she'd known and admired as a child.

But she'd not loved him with a woman's heart.

And she hated herself for it. Because he deserved far more than her.

"You deserve someone better than me, Alexander," she said softly.

Alexander shook his head; a golden lock fell across his brow. He strode across the room and stopped at her feet. "Don't you do that," he bit out. "Don't you dare, Abby." His chest rose and fell with the force of his emotion. "I love you."

Oh, God. For the wrong she'd inadvertently done him, he still would love her.

She closed her eyes.

"But you don't love me." That broken and pained whisper cut across the quiet. "The gentleman who left…" he said, those five words flat.

Geoffrey.

Her heart sped up. He'd been here in the room with Alexander, and had taken his leave. Surely with his great sense of propriety he would applaud her marriage to Alexander. Alexander's presence had in a way, freed Geoffrey of any obligation he might feel toward her. "I…" She studied the tips of her slippers. She loved Geoffrey. Even with all that had come to pass between them.

"He doesn't deserve you, Abby."

A humorless laugh escaped her. "How can you believe that when I've betrayed you as I did?" Her duplicity, though unintentional, had hurt him, and for that, Abigail could never forgive herself.

He touched his hand to her bruised and swollen cheek. "Because I love you, Abby. And that is what you do when you love someone. You forgive them. Love is not logical."

No. For if it were, she'd return to America under the mantle of Alexander's affection and live out a comfortable life in the land that had been her only home, surrounded by her siblings. But Alexander deserved far more than that. "You are going to find a woman—"

He spoke, his words a hoarse please. "Don't, Abby."

"Who deserves you," she continued. "And the time will come when you realize that she holds your love, and I'll be nothing more than a dream of something that once was."

Alexander's throat moved up and down. "There will only be you."

Abigail did not labor the point with him because not long ago, she'd been like him. She had believed herself shattered by his perfidy.

It had taken Geoffrey to show her the truth…that her heart hadn't fully lived—until Geoffrey had entered her life.

Alexander raised her hand to his lips, and placed a kiss upon her knuckles. Then, with a long, elegant bow, he took his leave.

Abigail stood there long after he made his solemn exit. The fire crackled in the hearth; the embers popping and hissing loudly. In the span of mere hours, the entire foundation of her world had been shaken by the truth of her parent's deceit, Geoffrey's profession of love, Alexander's reappearance in her life.

Her gaze snagged upon the forgotten items Geoffrey had brought with him.

Abigail angled her head, and studied the blooms of aconite and ivy. She wandered over and picked up the rain-dampened bouquet, and raised it to her nose, inhaling the sweet scent of the red bloom. She'd believed guilt had driven his offer of marriage. And yet...

She touched the tip of her finger to the spriggy, harsh ivy leaf. Were these romantic gestures of a gentleman motivated by a sense of guilt and rightness?

Abigail set the bouquet down, and reached for the oddly shaped box no larger than the span of her hands together. She turned it over, and then set it aside.

She loved him.

Loved him with a depth of emotion that defied humility and pride.

For the first time since the carriage accident a week ago, Abigail smiled. She embraced the liberation of acknowledging her love of him.

She would wed him.

Just as soon as he returned to her.

THIRTY

When consuming spirits, a gentleman should demonstrate restraint.
The 4ᵗʰ Viscount Redbrooke

From the alcohol-induced stupor Geoffrey had dwelt within for twenty-six hours, eighteen minutes, and…he glanced bleary-eyed up toward the ormolu clock…the blasted numbers were too small.

He tugged out his watch fob and tried to bring the numbers into focus. Hell, he'd lost count. Twenty-six hours, now nineteen minutes, and…he picked up his half-drunk brandy and tossed it back. It didn't matter.

Time had ceased to matter.

None of it mattered.

"You must speak to him. I'm ever so worried." From outside his office door, his mother's murmured words cut across the numbed haze that gripped him.

The wood panel of the door drowned out his brother-in-law, Waxham's response.

Geoffrey reached for the nearly empty bottle of brandy, and poured himself a tall glass. They could all go to hell.

Because now, Alexander Powers, once a faceless bastard who'd broken Abigail's heart was real. A vise-like pain gripped his heart. The other man had stood there looking like one of Michelangelo's damned sculptures, a golden foil to Abigail's dark beauty.

No amount of alcohol could drive back his remembrance of the masculine possessiveness and love in Powers' eyes.

I love you, Abby.

234

Geoffrey clenched his eyes tight but could not, would never be able to escape the dagger-like pain cloying at his insides. Until he died, he would forever remember the moment of Alexander Powers' return... because it had been the moment when all Geoffrey's hopes of earning her love had died a swift, and agonizing death.

Geoffrey had caught her as she'd fainted and he would cherish every last one of the thirty-seconds or so when he'd cradled her close.

He'd handed her off to her brother, and fled faster than Abby's fabled Hermes.

Ever since, Geoffrey had been foxed.

"Please, speak to him. It is that..." *woman.*

"Abigail," Geoffrey whispered. "Her name is Abigail."

Waxham spoke. "I..." But his words were muted.

The door opened.

Geoffrey swiped the back of his hand across bloodshot eyes. "Get the hell out, Waxham. I'm not accepting company."

The door closed. "I should hope not. You smell horrid."

Geoffrey's eyes shot open. His sister stood near the door, gazing at him with far more concern than he deserved. He'd been a bastard to her.

"Mother asked Christopher try to reason with you. I assured her I would speak to you, Geoffrey." Her lips twitched. "I don't believe she found any comfort in that." Sophie wandered over to the full floor-length windows, and threw the curtains wide. "Mustn't have you sitting here alone in the dark."

He flinched at the sharp burst of sunlight that streamed through the windowpanes.

Whatever words she cared to utter about Abigail would be a futile waste of her energies. The devil with his silver tongue couldn't convince Geoffrey that Abigail had been anything but the most perfect thing to have ever happened to him. For a brief moment, the gods had seemed to think him worthy of happiness, and sent Abigail into his life.

And he'd spit in the face of his fate.

Sophie advanced further into the room and claimed the leather winged back chair at the foot of his desk. "I told her I'd speak to you about Miss Stone."

"And?" Geoffrey slurred. He reached for the decanter of brandy, but Sophie leaned over with far more speed than he imagined her capable of, and yanked the bottle off his desk.

She set it down on the floor beside her. "And, as a young lady, I have it on good authority that other ladies do not admire a gentleman who wallows in self-pity."

He growled. "I'm not wallowing." Pause. "Perhaps I am," he conceded. "May I have my bottle?"

Sophie wagged a finger at him. "No more of that," she murmured. "You will not win back your Miss Stone if you're..." she wrinkled her nose, "smelling like a hot pig in a summer sun?"

There would be no winning Abigail back. He'd lost her before he'd ever had her.

He sat back in his chair and swiped his arm across his eyes. "Please, leave," he said.

Sophie drummed her fingertips along the arms of her leather seat; the grating sound echoed around his mind. "You know, I don't think I will. You need a friend."

A harsh chuckle escaped him, and his arm fell back to his side. It appeared Sophie and Sinclair were of like opinions. "I don't need a friend."

I need Abigail.

His sister went on as though he hadn't spoken. "For years, Geoffrey, I've believed you to be a pompous ass."

At one time Sophie's vulgar language would have appalled him more than the charge she now leveled at him. It had been Abigail who'd forced Geoffrey to confront the weaker aspects of his character and aspire to be a better, more honorable person.

"That is because I am a pompous ass."

Sophie smiled. "Yes. There is truth there. But you weren't always that way." She scooted to the edge of her seat.

No. His life had been irrevocably changed when he'd come upon his father's body that stormy night five years ago. Geoffrey appeared to be the same cowardly bastard he'd always been, because even after all this time, he couldn't find the courage to tell Sophie of the events that had precipitated their father's death.

Sophie continued on, seeming unaware of the inner turmoil roiling through him. "And you haven't been that way since you met your Miss Stone."

"She isn't my Miss Stone," he said, tiredly.

For a mere flicker in time, Geoffrey had been fortunate to have her in his life but she had always belonged to Powers.

Sophie's smile dipped. "Oh, dear."

He glanced past her shoulder, toward the gold brocade curtains.

She sighed. "You are supposed to ask, 'what, Sophie?'"

"What is it, Sophie?" He wanted nothing more than his half-drunk bottle of brandy.

"You love her rather desperately, don't you?"

The vise about his heart tightened, and he rubbed his chest, to dull the steady, throbbing ache, to no effect. "I do," he breathed the word into existence. And he'd uttered them, too late. In the end, she'd not believed him.

Alexander Powers' tall, powerful visage flashed to mind and Geoffrey buried his head into his hands. He pressed the heels of his palms against his eyes in a desperate attempt to rid himself of the image of Abigail and Alexander together. She would leave. She would board a ship with the man who had in fact been faithful to her...and exist as nothing more than a memory in Geoffrey's heart.

The crackle of leather, followed by the flutter of muslin fabric registered.

Sophie knelt down at his feet and took one of his hands between her own. "Geoffrey, she is not lost to you." She gave a faint squeeze.

"She is," he said, his voice hollow.

"You must go to her."

Geoffrey pulled his hand free, and climbed to his feet. "I did go to her, Sophie." He dragged a hand through his mussed hair, and proceeded to pace a small path in front of his desk.

"And?" she prodded.

"And the gentleman she loved," *Loves*. "Has come for her. It would seem some kind of misunderstanding occurred." He grimaced.

Misunderstanding. One seemingly innocuous word. Yet, it represented the death of Geoffrey's dreams.

Sophie wrinkled her nose as though she'd taken in a distinctly unpleasant odor. "A misunderstanding?"

After Geoffrey had handed Abigail over to her brother's arms, he'd fled but not before he deduced that some manner of lie had been told to separate Abigail and Powers. Odd to think if that one untruth hadn't been perpetuated, then Abigail would have never come to London and Geoffrey would have never lost his heart to her generous, spirited hands.

Even suffering as he was, he could not bring himself to regret having met her.

Instead, Geoffrey would have to find solace in knowing Abigail was once again happy—even if that joy came in the arms of another man.

His heart lurched.

Oh god, this would destroy him.

His sister sat back on her heels. "Hmph." She tapped her finger alongside her jaw. "Well, there is nothing for it. You must fight for her."

Geoffrey froze mid-movement. Could he fight for her? At one time, Geoffrey had believed nothing mattered more than his pride and honor. What Sophie proposed would require him to set aside all those aspects of his character, and humble himself in the vain hope that Abigail would forget her love for Powers, and...

His breath died on a long sigh. "No, Sophie."

Her cornflower blue eyes went wide in her face. "But..."

"No," he said, this time more adamantly. He'd caused Abigail enough pain. She'd been bruised and battered and nearly killed because of Geoffrey's faithlessness. He remembered back to that miserable night when she'd stood before him, pleadingly in his foyer. A good deal of her suffering had transcended physical wounds. "I cannot."

Sophie stood, with fire snapping in her eyes. "Then you do not truly love her." With a flounce of her curls she turned around and stormed toward the door.

Denial tore from him, harsh and guttural. "Don't." He could imagine how someone such as Sophie believed him incapable of that emotion. Geoffrey had been an utter bastard to Sophie over the years. "I cannot cause her more pain," he said at last.

Sophie spun to face him. Her gaze moved over his face. "Oh, Geoffrey," she whispered.

He looked away, hating that he'd become an object of his sister's pity.

"Please, let me help you."

Unless she could convince Abigail differently of the feelings she carried in her heart, then nothing could be done. His throat moved up and down. "I do not deserve your kindness, Sophie." Not after the great hurt he'd done his family all those years ago on a different road, on a different thunderous night.

"You are my brother," she said simply. "I love you. Now, we must devise a plan."

"No," he said.

Her widened eyes indicated she heard the finality in that succinct utterance.

She folded her arms across her chest, a determined glint in her eyes. Then, she nodded once. "Very well, Geoffrey. But this is not done."

He stared at her as she took her leave.

It was done.

It had been done the moment Alexander Powers entered the Duke of Somerset's parlor.

THIRTY-ONE

A gentleman should always be punctual.
4ᵗʰ Viscount Redbrooke

Abigail stared down at her packed trunks and valises. They rested in an orderly heap at the foot of her bed. Her maid, Sally, continued to pull garment after garment from the armoire, and lay them upon the coverlet of Abigail's four-poster bed.

He'd not come.

He'd not returned for her.

Pain twisted Abigail's heart, and she drew in a deep, shuddery breath.

Odd, how very similar this moment was to another. Abigail stood, numb while Sally moved to place the remaining gowns inside the trunks.

Abigail folded her arms across her middle. Only this time, she'd not been forced away in shame. She'd chosen to leave.

Nothing remained for her here. There was no life in England without Geoffrey. His world had very clearly resumed its proper, practical course—a course that did not include the shameful, American Abigail Stone.

The door opened.

Abigail glanced over distractedly. Her cousin stood at the front of the room. Her wide, blue eyes filled with sadness tugged at Abigail's already broken heart.

"Oh, Abby, you mustn't leave," Beatrice said softly.

Abigail picked up her silver comb and brush. She turned the delicate pieces over to Sally who accepted them, and rushed over to another trunk and began to pack Abigail's accessories.

"I must," Abigail murmured.

Beatrice walked over to Abigail. She stopped several feet away, and ran her gaze over Abigail's face. "Is it because you love Mr. Powers?" She caught her lower lip between her teeth. "Because I did believe that perhaps you loved Lord Redbrooke."

Abigail shook her head. "I…" She took a deep breath. "No. It is not because of Alexander."

Beatrice picked up one of Abigail's butterfly jewel-encrusted combs and moved it back and forth between her two hands. She wandered over to Abigail's bed littered with gowns, and sat upon the only empty corner. "I did believe you would wed Lord Redbrooke." She glanced up from the combs in her hand. "Did you not want to wed him?"

Abigail swallowed. Her gaze slipped over to the now wilted bouquet in the large porcelain vase upon her mantle. "I did want to wed him. He…"

Does not love me.

Never came back for me.

Was merely motivated by a gentlemanly sense of honor and guilt.

"He…" Her words ended on a sigh. "It's not to be, Beatrice."

Beatrice settled back in her seat, hopelessly wrinkling the golden satin gown beside her. "I do not like this forlorn side of you."

Sally reached for the unopened box Geoffrey had left behind at his last visit. Her maid placed the oddly shaped package into a trunk. "No!" Abigail exclaimed. She felt herself coloring. "Uh…that is just, thank you," she said, and rushed over to remove the small item from the trunk.

Beatrice cocked her head and studied the box. "What is it?"

Abigail shrugged. "I don't know. Lord Redbrooke brought it the day he called, and…"

"You never opened it?" Beatrice snorted. "I believe you are the only woman in all the kingdom who'd fail to open a gift."

Abigail looked down at the package. It's not that she didn't *want* to open it, per se. She did. Rather desperately. It wouldn't, however, in light of Geoffrey's rejection, be proper to retain the unopened gift. She'd been meaning to have it delivered to his townhouse with a very informal, polite letter. But she'd never gotten herself round to doing it.

Perhaps because the minute the flowers wilted and the box was gone, it would be the end of something that almost was.

She sighed and set the box down on her vanity. "Will you see that it is delivered to him, Beatrice?"

Beatrice rushed to her feet. "You'd merely return it?"

Abigail nodded. "It is the right thing to do." After all, it would be the height of impropriety to accept a gift from a gentleman.

Beatrice propped her hands on her hips and tapped her foot on the floor. "Bahh, love is wasted on you and Lord Redbrooke! The two of you are a perfect match." She threw her hands up in an air of resignation and marched over to the door.

Beatrice yanked it open with great force and stumbled into Nathaniel.

Abigail's brother stood poised, hand raised as if he'd intended to rap on the wood panel.

"Forgive me," Beatrice muttered, and slipped by him.

Nathaniel gave his head a bemused shake. "What was that about, poppet?"

She shook her head. "I'm a bit old to be called poppet."

He crossed over and tweaked her nose. "You'll always be poppet."

It appeared her brother still viewed her as the same young girl she'd been; the one who'd chased after him, and put spiders in his boots, and ink in his tea. He somehow had seemed able to look past the scandal and simply see his sister—Abby Stone.

Nathaniel surveyed the room, and seemed to do a kind of inventory of the stacked trunks and valises. "It appears you're nearly packed."

She attempted to swallow, with little success. Instead, she nodded.

Nathaniel motioned for her to sit.

He clasped his hands behind his back. "When I journeyed here, Abby, I did so with the intention of reuniting you and Alexander. I expected you'd reconcile, and we would return. The three of us. It isn't that simple, is it?"

It hadn't been that simple in very many years. "No," she whispered.

"You love him?"

She didn't pretend to misunderstand. "I do."

"If you wed him, then you'll have to remain here, and there is nothing more I would hate in the world than to board my ship and sail away knowing that this is where you'll spend the rest of your days."

"Well, you needn't worry, because he has no intentions of wedding me." If Geoffrey's offer that day had been a serious one, he would have returned for her. Now, it appeared his proposal had been driven out of his misplaced sense of guilt, and when Alexander had returned, Geoffrey had been relieved of that responsibility.

"The duke informed me that Redbrooke made you an offer."

Her mind raced. Geoffrey had spoken to the duke?

"Apparently a well-placed servant happened to overhear your conversation, before mine and Alexander's arrival."

She blinked. "Oh." Her fingers plucked at the smooth fabric of the coverlet.

Silence fell, punctuated by Sally's determined feet, as she padded across the floor packing up Abigail's trunks.

"Abby?" Her brother said at last.

She looked up at him.

"Would you be willing to give up your family? Mama and Papa, and your brothers and sister all for Redbrooke?"

When Abigail had first journeyed to England, she'd believed there could be no greater pain than the loss of her family's presence in her life.

Having grown to love Geoffrey, she'd found her love for him had filled the empty loneliness she'd felt for her family.

Her brother asked if Abigail could give up her family for Geoffrey.

For Geoffrey, she'd be willing to give up the country she'd been born to, even her family—if he'd have her. "I would, Nathaniel." *I would give up everything for him.*

Nathaniel tapped his hand along the side of his thigh, his expression contemplative. "You have the courage to brave a sea voyage alone, and begin a life anew without the presence of your family…and yet, where Redbrooke is concerned, you are coward?" He shook his head. "Abby?"

"Yes?"

"You aren't a coward."

His words seeped into the haze of misery that had gripped her since the stormy night when Geoffrey had turned her out of his house. Abby stilled. As her brother had said, she'd braved the scorn and censure of her American compatriots, an ocean voyage alone to an unfamiliar country, a carriage accident…she was no coward.

Nathaniel winked. "That is better."

Geoffrey might very well have regretted his decision to ask for her hand. It may have been nothing more than a hasty, obligatory offer. But it also might not have been. And she could not make a journey home unless she knew for certain.

Seated behind the desk in his office, Geoffrey stared blankly down at the opened ledgers in front of him. He gave his head a clearing shake and then, dipped his pen in ink. He made a mark in the column.

After living in a week long inebriated state, Geoffrey had drank his last brandy. His responsibilities were many. His obligations great.

His role as viscount required him to forget that his heart had been shattered, and focus on those who still relied upon him.

A knock interrupted his silent musings.

"Enter."

The door opened.

His mother swept inside. She hovered a moment at the threshold of the room.

He tossed his pen down and motioned her forward. "Mother."

She inclined her head. "Geoffrey." She steepled her fingers and held her hands in front of her skirts. "You're sober."

It had taken him the better part of four days to realize no amount of spirits would ever lessen the blow he'd been dealt in losing Abigail. "I've been sober for three days now."

"Have you?" she asked, a distracted air about her.

"I have."

Silence.

Geoffrey picked his pen up and dipped it into the crystal inkwell.

"I never approved of your Miss Stone."

He froze. Ink splattered the parchment in front of him. He resumed writing. "I know that."

"Just as I'd never approved of your Miss Marsh."

Abigail could not have been more different than Emma Marsh. He knew that, even if his mother didn't. His mother didn't know or appreciate Abigail's great intelligence, or the courage she'd shown in crossing an ocean and beginning anew after a great scandal.

Geoffrey again dropped his pen. He pinched the bridge of his nose. "Is there something you wish to say, Mother?"

"You love her," she said baldly.

"I do."

She dropped her arms by her side and drummed her fingertips together. "I still do not approve of her. Love is not an agreeable emotion for you, Geoffrey."

In his mind's eye, he saw his father's broken body. Geoffrey rested his elbows on the arms of his chair. He could no sooner stop loving Abigail than he could stop his own heart from beating.

"Geoffrey, there are many respectable, properly bred English ladies. Please remember your responsibilities as viscount. Why, the scandal that surrounds her," she shook her head. "It would forever taint your good reputation."

One's good reputation made for very lonely company. "She is a far better person than I am, Mother. She is too good for me."

Mother gasped. "You're speaking madness, Geoffrey."

A commotion sounded in the hall. Ralston's murmured words were lost to the thick solid structures of the corridor walls. The door flew open with such velocity it bounced back and nearly slammed into Sophie. She put her hand out to prevent it from hitting her in the face. Then with grace and aplomb, she closed the door with a decisive click.

"Enough, Mother," Sophie ordered.

Mother glowered at her. "This is not your affair, Sophie."

Sophie jabbed her finger at the air. "Stuff it, Mother." She swept into the room with all the bravado of a commanding officer and pointed at Geoffrey. "Your Miss Stone is leaving."

His sister might as well have delivered a solid punch to his midsection. All the air left him on a swift exhale. Geoffrey's closed his eyes. Ahh, god, he couldn't bear this. It would destroy him.

"Her ship leaves tomorrow morning, Geoffrey." Sophie planted her arms akimbo. "What do you plan to do about it, brother?"

"I…"

Another knock sounded on the office door.

Geoffrey sent a prayer skyward for patience. "Who is next? The bloody prince regent?" he muttered under his breath. "Enter!"

Ralston cleared his throat. "A Mr. Nathaniel Stone, my lord."

Abigail's brother entered the room. The tall, serious looking gentleman eyed him as though he were trying to ascertain Geoffrey's worth. Geoffrey could have spared him the effort and told Abigail's brother that he was a worthless blighter.

Nathaniel Stone glanced momentarily at Mother and Sophie. He returned his attention to Geoffrey. "May I request a word with you, Redbrooke?"

Geoffrey's heart thudded wildly in his chest. "Out," he said to his Mother and Sophie.

THIRTY-TWO

A gentleman should never be too proud.
4ᵗʰ Viscount Redbrooke

Abigail sat within the confines of the Duke of Somerset's carriage. She reached for the red velvet curtains, and then pulled her hand back. She folded her hands on her lap and resisted the urge to look out at Geoffrey's townhouse.

Nathaniel must have been in Geoffrey's home nearly thirty minutes, now. Whatever could they be discussing?

Abigail reached for the fabric of the curtain again, and gave her head a shake.

"Twelve Titans," she muttered into the quiet.

Hyperion—Titan of Light, Lapetus—Titan of Morality, Coeus—Titan of Intelligence, oh, and then Cronus, leader of the Titans.

It occurred to her then, that she'd not counted the mythical Greek figures in a very long time.

It also occurred to her, that she didn't give a bloody blast about the Twelve Titans.

The door opened.

Abigail scrambled forward in her seat. "Whatever took you so long? You were…oh…" Her words died on her lips. "You."

Geoffrey peered up at her from outside the carriage. "Yes, me." His emotionless tone gave little indication as to his thoughts. And then he hefted himself in. He pulled the door shut behind him and took the seat opposite her.

Geoffrey's tall, muscular frame managed to make the wide expanse of the carriage seem small.

Abigail studied his strong, powerful hands as he set down a very familiar looking package. Her heart thumped wildly. She wet her lips. "You," she whispered again.

He continued to eye her with that inscrutable expression. "Still me."

"Oh." She ran her eyes over him. She'd feared she would leave and never again see him, that her last memory of Geoffrey Winters, Viscount Redbrooke would be the moment he'd walked out of the duke's parlor, and out of her life.

Geoffrey adjusted his gloves.

How can he be so coolly unaffected by me? How can he not realize that my heart died the moment he left?

Then, as though he spoke to himself, he said, "Do you know, Abigail, I do not know what to make of that 'oh'? Does that 'oh' mean you want to leave and never see me again? Does it mean you still foolishly, somehow still care for me? Is it mere surprise?"

"No," she said quickly. She shook her head. "It is none of those things."

He caught his chin between his thumb and forefinger. "So then I'm forced to wonder if you merely had your brother escort you here to return my gift, a gift you've still not opened."

"I cannot accept a gift from you," she said automatically. "It wouldn't be proper."

The ghost of a smile played about his lips. "No, that is what your brother explained."

He folded his arm across his broad chest. "I once asked if you found fault in a gentleman who valued respectability."

Abigail sat forward, and ran her eyes over the angular planes of his cheeks. "How could I ever find fault with such a gentleman?" she whispered.

Geoffrey leaned across the carriage. "Oh, Abby." He cupped her cheek in the palm of his hand.

She leaned still closer, until their breaths mingled; her heart feeling complete for the first time since her world had crumbled down around her scandalous ears. "I wonder as to the meaning of that 'oh', Geoffrey? Does it mean you'd like to be rid of me? Does it mean you're eager to return to whatever important business it is viscounts tend to? Does it mean you pity me?"

He placed a feathery kiss upon her closed lids. "No. It is none of those things."

His lips moved a delicate trail down her cheek, his butterfly gentle kiss still so tender upon the nearly healed bruises. "That 'oh' means I love you. It means I am nothing without you. It means the day Alexander Powers re-entered your life, my world ceased to mean anything." Geoffrey trailed his finger along the curve of her cheek, to her chin, then to her nose, as if he were attempting to commit her every feature to memory. "It means, if you'll still have me, I'd make you my wife."

Abigail tilted her head back and received his kiss. Geoffrey's lips moved over hers with a gentle searching that brought tears to her eyes.

She pulled back, and a groan escaped him. "You do not have to marry me, Geoffrey. I understand you value propriety and respectability and by nature of my scandal, I am neither proper nor respectable."

Geoffrey's jaw hardened and his furious eyes bore into her. "You are worth far more than every lady in all the British Empire." And when he said it with such fiery conviction, she found she could believe those words. Geoffrey reached into the front pocket of his coat and pulled out a folded parchment. "Here."

Abigail stared at the ivory velum, with its unfamiliar black seal.

Geoffrey pressed it into her hand and jerked his chin at it. "Open it."

She hesitated, and then worked her nail under the seal. She unfolded the parchment.

Abigail read the first two sentences and stopped. Her gaze flew to his.

He squared his jaw. "It is a special license from the archbishop to wed."

"Ah, I, uh, see that." She wet her lips. He'd wanted to wed her enough that he'd gone and requested special permission to do so. "You want to marry me?"

He blinked. "Bloody hell, I'm making a muck of this, Abby." Geoffrey's olive-hued cheeks went red, and she never loved him more than she did just then.

"Yes," she blurted.

He slashed the air with his hand. "There is any number of gentlemen more worthy of you than my miserable self. I know I've wronged you, but…"

Abigail touched her fingertips to his lips. "I. Said. Yes."

Geoffrey's brow furrowed. "You said yes?"

"I did."

A devilish grin formed on his firm lips. "Well, then." He made to kiss Abigail, but then pulled away. "I've treated you poorly, but in this, I would honor your wishes. If you'd rather us wait to have the banns read, or…"

She kissed him into silence. Geoffrey's body went taut. The muscles within the elegant lines of his double-breasted black coat stiffened under her touch.

He pulled her onto his lap, and ran his hands over the curve of her hip, the swell of her buttocks, as if reacquainting himself with the feel of her beneath his fingers. She gasped as he cupped her breast. Her lids fluttered and she angled away from him, peering into his hooded eyes. "You do know this isn't proper?" she whispered against his lips.

Geoffrey curled his hand around the nape of her neck and angled her head. "Being proper is too highly lauded," he whispered, and then his mouth closed over hers.

A knock sounded on the carriage door and they jerked apart. Their chests rose and fell in fast, matching rhythms.

Abigail looked around frantically, even as Geoffrey shifted her back onto the opposite seat. He tucked two loose strands of hair that had fallen across her shoulder, back behind her ears.

Another knock.

"What is it?" Geoffrey called in the same, cool, composed tones of the gentleman she'd first met at Lord and Lady Hughes's ball.

Nathaniel opened the door. He looked back and forth, between them, and Abigail felt her skin heat. "Well?" he demanded.

Abigail shifted under his intense scrutiny.

Her brother's angry stare swung back toward Geoffrey. "When is the wedding to take place?"

The wedding between Abigail Stone and Geoffrey Winters, the 5th Viscount Redbrooke would take place at the Earl of Sinclair's townhouse in the Grosvenor Square section of the London district. Or rather, that was the plan...

If Sinclair's butler bothered to open the front door.

Geoffrey pounded again.

"Perhaps we might find another, er location to perform the...er ceremony, my lord?" The lips of the same, dour-faced vicar, who'd performed the ceremony between his sister, Sophie, to the Earl of Waxham, tipped downward, in apparent disapproval. He pushed his spectacles up on the bridge of his nose.

Geoffrey ignored him, and continued knocking, mindful of the stares from passing lords and ladies. Still uneasy with undue attention from the *ton*, Geoffrey pounded the door harder.

"Perhaps," the vicar began again. He fell silent when Geoffrey leveled a glare upon him.

Where the hell is he?

He glanced over his shoulder at the carriage where Abigail and her brother remained. Sinclair's front door opened, and Geoffrey spun back around. The butler, a short, stout fellow with wizened cheeks and small brown eyes squinted up at him. The older servant, more than a foot smaller than Geoffrey's own six-foot frame leaned out the doorway. He trained his glassy-eyed gaze first upon Geoffrey, then, the vicar. "How can I help you?"

Geoffrey flinched as the older man's booming voice, carried down the street. Christ, so much for privacy. "I'd like to speak to Lord Sinclair."

The butler cupped his hand around his ear. "You'd like to have a chair?" he shouted.

Geoffrey closed his eyes and prayed for patience. "Sinclair."

"Yes?"

Saints be praised. Geoffrey looked over the butler's shoulder at Sinclair. The earl stood in the foyer, studying the meeting on the front steps of his home with no small amount of humor. If he weren't here begging a favor of the man who'd proclaimed to be his friend, then he would have told him to go to the devil.

"You said you were a friend."

Sinclair angled his head.

"I need a favor," Geoffrey continued.

Sinclair's eyes widened with interest. "Oh?"

So it was, one hour, seven minutes, and a handful of seconds later, with Nathaniel and Sinclair as their only witnesses, Abigail and Geoffrey were wed in the Earl of Sinclair's office.

Geoffrey glanced around the sparsely furnished office. With the exception of the earl's desk, a rose-inlaid table, and a handful of chairs, the room appeared largely unused. There were no well-wishers and bountiful flowers. There was no bridal trousseau as Abigail had deserved. And it struck him—he'd failed her again.

Geoffrey lowered his brow to Abigail's. "Forgive me," he whispered.

Her brow wrinkled. "For what?"

He traced his finger along the side of her cheek. "You deserved so much more than this, Abby. You deserved a proper courtship and a gown designed specifically for you and…and…everything else young ladies might dream of."

Abigail pointed her eyes to the ceiling. "Geoffrey, none of that matters."

Sinclair strode over and slapped Geoffrey upon the back. "Allow me to have my cook prepare dinner."

"No," Geoffrey said. He'd been parted too long from Abigail and would not take the time for social niceties…even if that were the proper thing to do. He took Abigail by the hand, and pulled her along to the front of the earl's office.

She squeezed his hand hard. "Be polite." She silently mouthed.

Geoffrey's mouth tightened. He sighed and looked back at Sinclair. "No, thank you."

Abigail tugged her fingers free of his grasp and turned to Sinclair. "My lord, thank you so much for everything you've done this day."

Sinclair reached for her hand, and bowed over it. "It was an honor, my lady."

Geoffrey's frown deepened and he reached between them, disentangling their hands. Though appreciative of Sinclair's efforts on his and Abigail's behalf, Geoffrey did *not* appreciate reminders of how bloody engaging and charming the Earl of Sinclair happened to be. Geoffrey gritted his teeth. "Very well, thank you again, then."

Abigail's brother stepped forward. He slapped Geoffrey on the back with a hard thwack, the casual gesture belied by the hard glint in the other man's eyes. "Hurt her, and I'll kill you, Redbrooke."

"I promise to care for her," Geoffrey vowed." He'd make it his life vow to fill her every day with the joy she deserved.

Nathaniel placed his hands on Abigail's shoulders, and gave a gentle squeeze.

She nodded. "I know, Nathaniel." She leaned up and placed a kiss on her brother's cheek, and just like that, she became Geoffrey's to care for and love for the remainder of their days.

THIRTY-THREE

In matters of the heart, a gentleman should honor the emotion called love.
4ᵗʰ Viscount Redbrooke

The fingers of dusk edged out the day sky, and met in a vibrant explosion of violet and crimson hues that filled the night's horizon.

Abigail's stomach lurched as the Duke of Somerset's barouche rocked to a halt in front of Geoffrey's townhouse. She released the curtain and it fluttered back into place.

"Are you ready to go in, love?" he whispered against her ear.

She jerked her gaze over toward Geoffrey.

Her mouth went dry under the sudden realization that she'd need to face Geoffrey's mother. The proper lady had never looked at Abigail with any hint of warmth or kindness. "Your mother will be displeased," she murmured, wishing she could remain unaffected by the older woman's disdain. Except this was Geoffrey's mother, and the woman's opinion mattered because of it.

Geoffrey brushed back several loose strands of hair that had fallen around Abigail's shoulder. He placed his lips to her wildly fluttering pulse. "Mother is never pleased," he whispered.

She slapped at his arm. "You are incorrigible. Your mother—"

"Will be attending one event or another this evening."

A cowardly sigh of relief escaped Abigail. No matter how small, Abigail welcomed the reprieve.

The driver opened the door and a soothing, spring breeze caressed her face.

Geoffrey leapt down, and tucked that small, unopened package under his arm. Next, he turned and helped Abigail from the carriage.

Once on the pavement, Abigail tilted her head to the right and shifted her lower back in attempt to stretch the cramped muscles. Then, she placed her fingers on Geoffrey's coat sleeve and followed him up the steps of the impressive townhouse.

She looked at the familiar stone steps and the white stucco façade, remembering back to a vastly different night, and a chill stole through her.

Geoffrey touched a hand to the small of her back. He whispered close to her ear. "Don't. Please, do not let that be what you think of whenever you are here. It would break me, Abigail."

The front door opened.

Geoffrey guided her inside where they were greeted by the severe looking butler who'd bore witness to Abigail's humiliation a fortnight ago.

"Ralston, may I introduce you to the Viscountess Redbrooke."

Ralston's eyebrows shot to his hairline. He swiftly remembered himself and bowed. "May I wish you felicitations on your nuptials, my lord?"

"Nuptials?"

As one, Abigail and Geoffrey's gaze swung upward to the top of the long staircase to where the viscountess stood in a burgundy satin evening gown.

Abigail swallowed. It would appear her reprieve was to be far shorter lived than she'd either anticipated or hoped.

The viscountess swept down the stairs. Her skirts snapped and swirled angrily about her ankles. "Nuptials?" she hissed. "Nuptials?"

Abigail curtsied. "My lady."

Geoffrey's mother looked through Abigail like she was nothing more than an apparition haunting the townhouse. The regal viscountess' attention fixed on Geoffrey.

Geoffrey caught Abigail's hand and gave a faint squeeze in unspoken support. "Mother, remember yourself," he bit out.

Her mouth opened and closed in way that reminded Abigail of a bass fish she'd once caught. The fish had flipped and twisted upon the ground, before she'd taken mercy upon the creature and tossed him back into the sea.

Abigail held her palms up. "I know you do not approve of me, for very many reasons," she began. She took a deep breath. "But I love Geoffrey, my lady. And you are most assuredly right, in that I'm improper, and inadequate in many ways. And yet, I cannot help but love him."

Some emotion filled the viscountess' eyes. She snapped her skirts aside, and marched down the hall without a backwards glance for Abigail or Geoffrey.

Regret slammed into her, as she and Geoffrey continued onward toward her chambers. What had she expected? That Geoffrey's mother would graciously welcome Abigail into the family's fold?

Geoffrey winked down at Abigail. "Well, I do say she handled that remarkably well."

She tried to muster a smile, and he must have seen something somber in her expression for he cursed. "I am sorry, Abigail. You don't deserve such a cold welcome. I've not prepared the staff. I hadn't really considered anything beyond making you my wife."

They stopped beside a closed door. She reached up and caressed his cheek. Gone was the well-ordered gentleman with too many lists. "And I haven't considered anything beyond how much I love being your wife."

He shoved the door open, and Abigail entered. Her eyes went to the wide four-poster bed at the center of the room. The Staff not having expected guests had left the hearth cold. She turned about the pale green and golden gilded room.

Geoffrey bowed. "I will send someone to assist you, my lady."

Before she could protest, Geoffrey took his leave.

The door closed on a soft click.

"Hmph," she muttered. She circled the room, trailing her fingers along the rose-inlaid table that rested alongside the bed, and moved over to the shepherdess figurine atop the fireplace mantle. Abigail picked it up and turned it over distractedly.

The day had moved in such a speedy blur, she'd not considered her fears of that night—until now.

The figurine trembled in her fingers and she set it down quickly lest it tumble to the floor. Abigail sucked in a deep breath. She came to Geoffrey without her virginity. She'd given that gift to another, and yet, she remained largely untried in matters of lovemaking. The night she'd been discovered in Alexander's arms, had been quick, and painful.

To give her hands something to do, Abigail again picked up the expensive porcelain trinket. She caught sight of her reflection in the full-length bevel mirror across the room. Bright red color splotched her cheeks. Her toes curled in the soles of her slipper as she cringed at the idea of doing... *that*, with Geoffrey.

The door opened, and she turned to greet the maid Geoffrey had sent. "Thank you for..." Her words faded. "Oh." The shepherdess tumbled to the hard wood floor and fell with a loud thump.

The head popped off one of the sheep at the shepherdess' feet. Abigail blinked down at it, and then forced herself to look at her husband.

Geoffrey stood at the closed door with his arms folded across his broad chest. He leaned his hip against the wall. He appeared so blasted comfortable and unaffected and sophisticated while Abigail stood like a bumbling fool with a shattered porcelain shepherdess at her feet. A *broken* shepherdess.

He grinned, displaying two perfect rows of pearl white teeth. "Oh."

"You aren't a maid." She clasped her hands in front of her.

"Good of you to note," he said dryly.

The color in her cheeks heightened. She stooped down to pick up the broken figurine. A gasp slipped from her lips when she stood up, and the poor figurine tumbled to the floor. This cost the shepherdess with golden ringlets her head. Geoffrey stood a hairsbreadth away. Abigail slapped a hand to her chest. "Goodness, you mustn't sneak up on a person like that."

He frowned. "Viscounts do not sneak."

"You do." She glanced at the shattered glass. "The figurine..."

"I don't give a jot about the figurine."

Oh dear, she fanned herself. "It is warm in here? Isn't it? Yes, a bit warm," she said, not allowing him an opportunity to respond. "Which is odd because when I first entered the room, I was chilled, but no longer. Now I seem..."

"Warm?" he supplied with wry amusement in that one word response.

She nodded her head emphatically. "Yes, very. Warm that is." Abigail clamped her lips closed. *You are rambling, Abigail.*

Geoffrey reached for her, but Abigail danced out of his reach. She craved Geoffrey's kiss, desired his touch, but loathed the idea of ruining the beauty of this moment with the harsh, pained swiftness of their coupling.

"I-ah...I should turn the bedcovers down." She turned hopefully to Geoffrey. "Perhaps it is best if we call for someone to turn down the..." Geoffrey crossed over to the bed, and folded the coverlet down.

"There."

Abigail chewed the inside of her cheek. "Perhaps dinner?"

He arched a chestnut brown eyebrow. "Are you hungry?"

"No," she answered without thinking. "Er..." She fanned her cheeks again. "I thought you might care for supper," she finished weakly.

Geoffrey touched a hand to her shoulder and she jumped. The backs of her knees bumped against the mattress, and she sank into the hastily turned down bedding.

"Abigail, are you nervous?"

"No," she squeaked. Abigail grasped the Jacquard patterned coverlet and fisted it in her hands. The truth of it was in spite of her scandalous past, she remained largely inexperienced in the matters of lovemaking.

Geoffrey stared at her with a warm, gentle patience.

She sighed. "Very well, *yes,* I am nervous." Her gaze fixed on the fabric of his white cambric shirt and she lifted her shoulder in a shrug. "You must consider me er, proficient because, because..." Her voice cracked and she stood quickly, and slipped past him. "*Because.*" She wet her lips. "I'm not, however. Experienced that is." Abigail furrowed her brow. "Well, in the strictest meaning of the word I suppose one could argue I am in fact. Experienced, that is." She studied the tuft of brown hair that peeked from the opening in his shirt and then forced herself to look at him. "But I find I don't like *it*, Geoffrey. I'm afraid you are to be disappointed."

Geoffrey bit back a grin at the dejected slump of his wife's shoulders.

Abigail may have lain with another, but she remained innocent in nearly every sense of the word. She belonged to him, and nothing that had happened before this moment mattered. None of it. This marked the beginning of their forever.

She narrowed her eyes. "Are you laughing at me?"

Geoffrey coughed into his hand. "I wouldn't dream of it."

Abigail's glower deepened, indicating his paltry efforts were futile.

"Well, not at you, sweet, Abby. I could never laugh at you. Come to me."

"I'm already right next to…Oh!" Her eyes rounded, giving her the look of an owl as he pulled her close.

Geoffrey released the magnificent combs that held her midnight black tresses in place, and tossed them to the floor. Her hair tumbled like a silken smooth waterfall about them. "Oh," he whispered against her cheek.

Geoffrey turned her around, and began to unfasten the buttons that lined the back of her pale yellow gown, one at a time. He placed his lips along each piece of magnificently smooth, flesh, until only her thin shift shielded the graceful curve of her back from his eyes. The gown fell in a fluttery heap at their feet.

Then, in short order, he proceeded to divest her of her shift and stays, placing his mouth to each sacred part of her body. "I must. Admit." He spoke between kisses.

Her legs wavered beneath her, and Geoffrey caught her in his arms, and carried her the remaining way to the bed. He lowered her down upon the turned down sheets.

"Admit?" she moaned, arching her neck.

"As to the meaning. Of. That. Oh." He cupped the generous swell of her pale white breasts. The pink peaks that crested her stunning flesh pebbled under his scrutiny. Geoffrey's gaze moved over her. In her stunningly lithe, curved naked glory, Abigail rivaled the goddess Athena in beauty. He closed his mouth around the tip of her right breast. He drew the bud deep, and gently sucked the tender flesh.

Abigail's hips arched. "Oh! You...mustn't," she gasped, even as her hands came up to clasp his head close to her. "It isn't at all. Proper, that is." Her words ended on a keening cry.

Geoffrey pulled away, and she reached for him. He tugged his shirt overhead and tossed it to the floor, where it landed atop her discarded gown and stays. He bent down to remove his breeches just as Abigail jerked her legs up. His eyes widened as she caught him in the groin. Geoffrey hissed.

He collapsed atop the bed, his breath coming fast.

"Oh, dear!" Abigail cried. She scrambled to her knees alongside him and began to run her hands down his person. "I told you, I'm rather awful at all this. I'm sorry." She reached out and her fingers brushed his manhood. "Geoffrey! Are you all right?"

"Fine," he said between clenched teeth. If she touched him again in that seductively innocent way, he'd lose control.

"Are you certain? Because you groaned rather loudly...oh."

Geoffrey removed his breeches and threw them over the side of the bed.

Abigail peeked down at his manhood, and her cheeks flamed the red of a ripe summer berry. She fanned herself again. "Oh, dear."

He grinned, and reached between them. His fingers found the hot, moist nub of her center.

Her moan blended with his shallow breathing in an erotic symphony. Beads of moisture dotted his brow, and trickled down into his eyes. He ignored the sting and continued to work her. His fingers explored. Teased. Tempted. Until Abigail writhed with a wild abandon under his ministrations.

"Geoffrey," she cried. "Please!"

Geoffrey nudged her thighs apart and settled himself between her legs. He paused with his hard, aching shaft at the threshold of her womanhood, and then on a swift plunge entered her.

Abigail cried out. "Oh, my. Oh, dear." She panted heavily. "That didn't." He began to move inside her in slow, rhythmic strokes, easing her to the feel of him sheathed within her center.

Abigail reached up and brushed the sweat back from his brow. "Hurt."

His body stiffened, and he went immobile as he hovered on the cusp of shattering in her arms. "I've hurt you." He made to pull out but Abigail frantically shook her hand and wrapped her legs about him, firmly anchoring him close.

"No! It didn't hurt. It felt...feels, rather delicious," she gasped as he began to move inside her again. And again.

Geoffrey increased his rhythm, driving into the hot, molten warmth of her, and Abigail met his wild thrusts.

"Geoffrey!" she cried. "I believe...that is...I think...something... oh my....!" A soft scream burst from her lips as she came undone in his arms, bucking wildly, and then Geoffrey joined her, falling over the precipice of desire. He turned his body over to that which he had craved since the moment he'd stepped upon her hem. He spilled his seed deep inside. His harsh, guttural groans blended with her high, breathy moans.

Geoffrey collapsed. He rolled off Abigail, and pulled her close to his side, unable to open his eyes, unable to think, or move, or....

"Geoffrey?" Abigail whispered. She turned on her side to face him, and tapped him on the chin. "Are you sleeping?"

"I'm not," he said. His body stirred again, filled with desire for her.

"Was I, that is," she cleared her throat. "Was it acceptable?"

A languid smile formed on his lips. He reached for her.

"Again?" she squeaked.

He caressed the generous curve of her buttocks.

Her eyes widened as he stirred against her.

"Again," he whispered. "What do you have to say to that, wife?"

She smiled, and brushed a strand of hair from his forehead. He parted her thighs and reentered her. Her mouth fell open. "Oh."

"Oh, indeed."

Then, he proceeded to show her the true meaning of that single utterance.

Abigail woke a short while later. Geoffrey stroked his hand up and down the curve of her hip, and she leaned into his touch. "Have I told you I loved you?" His lips caressed the sensitive flesh where her neck met her ear, and she giggled as his breath tickled her skin.

"You have," she assured him. In fact…"Eight times."

Geoffrey rolled onto his back and pulled her against him. "You've counted?"

She nodded against his chest, a delicious shiver ran down her languid frame as he turned his attention to the swell of her breasts.

"Is that all?"

Abigail fought through the thick fog of desire that clouded her senses, confused his words. "I-I'm c-certain of it," she managed on a gasping breath as he moved his tender ministrations higher, to the nape of her neck.

He pulled back and flicked his finger along the tip of her nose. "Well, that will never do. I love you." He kissed her lips. "I love you." He kissed her again. "I love you."

She leaned up, and rested her arms upon his muscled chest, liberally sprinkled with springy brown hair. "Can one die of happiness?"

He snorted, and rubbed smooth circles over her back. "I certainly hope not."

A smile played about her lips.

"You do know you've still not opened your gift," he said casually.

She blinked. Her gaze flitted over to the now thoroughly rumpled looking package. The top of the box had been crushed on top. Abigail scrambled up onto her knees.

Geoffrey reached for her, but she swatted him away. "Behave." She opened the box, and the air left her on a whoosh.

Geoffrey cleared his throat. "Do you like it? If you do not I'm certain I can have something different commissioned."

Wordlessly, Abigail withdrew the golden crown, encrusted with seven, large oval-shaped diamonds. Her eyes flew to his. The piece must have cost a small fortune.

"You once told me of the story of the Corona Borealis. The fool, Theseus abandoned the beautiful Ariadne, deserting her. Then there was her…

"Dionysus," she whispered.

He nodded. "Who loved her the way she deserved to be loved." Geoffrey reached for the crown and gently took it from between her fingers. "I do not want to be your Theseus, Abigail." He carefully placed the jeweled piece atop her head. "I want to be your Dionysus."

Tears filled her eyes. "Oh, Geoffrey," she whispered. "You foolish man. I do not need a mythical god. I have something so much more than that."

Geoffrey cupped her cheek in the palm of his hand. "What is that, sweet?"

She leaned into his touch, a smile upon her lips. "Why, I have a very proper lord."

EPILOGUE

*A gentleman recognizes the importance of being truth-
ful and forthright in all matters.*
Geoffrey Winters, 5ᵗʰ Viscount Redbrooke

Arms clasped behind his back, Geoffrey stared out his office window, down into the bustling street below.

Abigail touched her hands to his shoulder, and turned her cheek
against his back. "Are you all right, husband?"

Husband. They'd been wed now these two months, and this had
served as the happiest, most uncomplicated aspect of his thirty years.
Abigail filled him with joy and hope...and made him forget for an
infinitesimal moment the purpose of his mother and sister's impending visit.

Geoffrey turned around and began to pace. "I've matters of business to attend, Abby. I have the ledgers...and then there is also the
shipping venture your brother would like to speak with me on...
and..." His gaze moved away from the gentle understanding he saw
reflected in the deep gray-blue irises of her eyes.

And...

He remained the same bloody coward he'd always been.

"You are strong and courageous," Abigail said softly. She took his
hands in hers, and held up their interlocked digits. "I admire your
strength, Geoffrey."

He didn't deserve her high-praise, not when he wanted to turn and
flee.

A knock sounded.

Geoffrey swallowed.

Abigail gave his hands a squeeze.

The door opened.

Abigail turned and greeted Mother and Sophie with a generous smile. She extended her arms and reached for his mother's hands. His mother blinked. She still seemed shocked by Abigail's outward displays of affection; affection that hadn't erased Mother's displeasure, but had seemed to lessen it.

Sophie, on the other hand…

She threw her arms around Abigail. "Oh, Abby! It is so very good to see you."

Geoffrey nearly choked on the ball of guilt that clogged his throat. His sister would not feel such unabashed kindness when she learned the reason she'd been summoned here.

With the grace and poise of the most accomplished matrons, Abigail gestured to the seats. Abigail proceeded to pour tea as Mother and Sophie sat.

Sophie reached for a pastry on the tray of refreshments Cook had provided. Her hand hovered over Cook's confectionaries, before she settled on a cherry tart. She took a bite. "Will you not sit, Geoffrey?" she asked after she'd swallowed.

"I…" He looked toward the door. He'd rather flee through the streets of London like a madman loose from Bedlam than have this discussion.

Abigail reached for his hand. Her delicate grip infused strength into his trembling frame and fueled his resolve.

"I need to speak to you," he said quietly.

His mother sipped from her teacup, and from over the rim of the glass, looked at him curiously. "What is it, Geoffrey?"

"You are very serious," his sister said, and set her pastry down upon a porcelain china plate. "Is everything all right, Geoffrey?"

"It is about Father." He took a deep breath, and before his courage deserted him, told his mother and sister of the great shame he carried.

He spoke of the sordid, ugliness of Emma's betrayal, his father's desperate pleading, and ultimately...Father's death on that dark, lonely road.

When Geoffrey finished, he realized he gripped Abigail's hand so tightly, her skin had turned white. He lightened his hold, and braced for the disgust, the hatred, the loathing upon his mother and sister's face as they came to terms with the great crime Geoffrey had committed.

The tick-tock, tick-tock of the clock punctuated the silence, somehow more deafening than the blare of a pistol.

Sophie and his mother sat, unmoving, expressionless. His mother folded her hands upon her lap, and studied the interlocked digits for a long while.

What he expected? That they should so readily forgive him for the selfish act that had robbed Father of his life?

Sophie spoke first. "It is not your fault, Geoffrey," she said quietly.

He closed his eyes. "It is." Pained regret made his voice hoarse.

Mother drew in a jerky breath, and released it on a slow exhale. The teacup in her fingers rattled, and sloshed bits of tea over the side. She set it down quickly. "There never lived a more deceitful, horrid woman than Miss Marsh. And if you'd not defied your father's wishes, then yes, he would surely be alive." Her voice broke.

Guilt twisted inside him at the raw pain in his usual stoic mother's eyes. He opened his mouth, but there were no words. He could never find any sufficient words to absolve him of his complicity or ease her suffering.

"Mother," Sophie said sharply. She glowered at their mother and then turned her attention to Geoffrey. "It is certainly not your fault. You did not make that viper deceive you, and I know you believe yourself powerful but you cannot control the rain. Nor did you make Father ride out in that storm." She offered him a sad, little smile. "I am so very sorry that...that woman broke your heart." Sophie glanced over at Abigail. Her smile widened. "But if she hadn't broken your heart then there would certainly be no Abigail, and that, well that would be sad, indeed."

His mother continued to sit there, motionless. After a long while, she smoothed her palms along the front of her burgundy silk skirts. "I am incapable of lying to you, Geoffrey. I have missed your father every day since the moment h-he..." Her voice broke, and she coughed into her hand, in an apparent attempt to conceal any display of emotion. "Since the moment I learned of his accident," she amended. "And I do wish you had made far different decisions so he'd not been on that road that miserable night." Her gaze slid momentarily over to Abigail, then back to Geoffrey. "And loving Abigail as you do, I imagine if you lost her, then you would give anything to alter the events that led to her death. Do you understand what I am saying?"

Abigail gave his hand a firm squeeze, and he swallowed hard, borrowing strength from his wife. He well understood. His had been an empty, meaningless existence until Abigail. If someone's carelessness caused Abigail her life, Geoffrey would never be able to find any hint of forgiveness within his heart—not even if it was an, as of yet, unborn child, responsible for taking her from him.

"I am not fool enough to believe I can be forgiven this irrevocable wrong, but you and Sophie were...are deserving of the truth."

Mother shook her head. An uncharacteristic gentleness settled around the lines of her mouth. "Oh Geoffrey, I can and will always regret all that came to pass, but I cannot hold you solely to blame for your father's death."

He drew in a shaky breath. "But..."

"I begged your father to set out after you, Geoffrey," she said, her words so quiet he had to strain to hear them. "He disapproved of Emma Marsh, but I demanded he put a stop to your elopement." She looked to a point just beyond his shoulder. "And for *that*, well, I can never forgive myself." For a moment, a sheen of tears glazed her eyes, but then, she blinked several times, and they were gone, so Geoffrey wondered if he'd imagined them.

Mother reached for her teacup, raised it to her lips, and took a slow sip.

In a silent show of comfort, Sophie touched Mother's knee, giving it a faint squeeze. The satin fabric rustled beneath Sophie's subtle gesture.

Abigail looked at Geoffrey.

Geoffrey cleared his throat. "Mother, Sophie, there was, *is*, an additional reason I've asked you to visit this morning."

His mother paused, glass mid-way to her mouth.

"I wanted to, *we* wanted to inform you, that Abigail is recently with child."

Sophie's eyes went wide; a smile wreathed her cheeks. "Oh, Geoffrey, how very exciting!" She clasped her hands together in front of her.

Geoffrey looked to his mother. She said nothing for a long, long moment. And then, a slow, wide smile turned her lips upward. "Well, this is wonderful news, Geoffrey." She reached for a pastry and took a bite of the flaky confectionary.

Geoffrey's gaze fell to his wife. She looked up at him and smiled.

He imagined a little girl with sparkling gray-blue eyes and dark black tresses, and grinned.

Yes. It most certainly is, wonderful.

The End

*The Sinful Brides features ravishing tales of London's
gaming hell rogues—and the women who love them.*

THE ROGUE'S WAGER

London, 1821

Lord Robert Dennington, the Marquess of Westfield, has long reveled in the freedom afforded him as the ducal heir. He knows he must someday do right by the Somerset line, but he's in no hurry to give up his carefree existence.

Helena Banbury is a bookkeeper in a gentleman's gambling club, adept at analyzing numbers and accounts but helpless for lack of influence. She's never belonged among the nobility on the gaming hell floors, but neither does she feel completely herself among the men who run the Hell and Sin Club, despite the fact that they are family. The once-illiterate girl from the streets wants more than the gilded walls her protective cage can offer.

When Robert mistakenly enters her chambers one night, Helena is forced out of her predictable life and thrust into the glittering world of Society. Will the charms of the marquess prove more perilous than any danger she ever knew on the streets?

OTHER BOOKS BY
CHRISTI CALDWELL

"To Woo a Widow"
Book 10 in the "Heart of a Duke" Series by Christi Caldwell

They see a brokenhearted widow.

She's far from shattered.

Lady Philippa Winston is never marrying again. After her late husband's cruelty that she kept so well hidden, she has no desire to search
for love.

Years ago, Miles Brookfield, the Marquess of Guilford, made a friv-
olous vow he never thought would come to fruition—he promised to
marry his mother's goddaughter if he was unwed by the age of thirty.
Now, to his dismay, he's faced with honoring that pledge. But when he
encounters the beautiful and intriguing Lady Philippa, Miles knows
his true path in life. It's up to him to break down every belief Philippa
carries about gentlemen, proving that not only is love real, but that he
is the man deserving of her sheltered heart.

Will Philippa let down her guard and allow Miles to woo a widow
in desperate need of his love?

"The Lure of a Rake"
Book 9 in the "Heart of a Duke" Series by Christi Caldwell

A Lady Dreaming of Love

Lady Genevieve Farendale has a scandalous past. Jilted at the altar years earlier and exiled by her family, she's now returned to London to prove she can be a proper lady. Even though she's not given up on the hope of marrying for love, she's wary of trusting again. Then she meets Cedric Falcot, the Marquess of St. Albans whose seductive ways set her heart aflutter. But with her sordid history, Genevieve knows a rake can also easily destroy her.

An Unlikely Pairing

What begins as a chance encounter between Cedric and Genevieve becomes something more. As they continue to meet, passions stir. But with Genevieve's hope for true love, she fears Cedric will be unable to give up his wayward lifestyle. After all, Cedric has spent years protecting his heart, and keeping everyone out. Slowly, she chips away at all the walls he's built, but when he falters, Genevieve can't offer him redemption. Now, it's up to Cedric to prove to Genevieve that the love of a man is far more powerful than the lure of a rake.

"To Trust a Rogue"
Book 8 in the "Heart of a Duke" Series by Christi Caldwell

A rogue

Marcus, the Viscount Wessex has carefully crafted the image of rogue and charmer for polite Society. Under that façade, however, dwells a man whose dreams were shattered almost eight years earlier by a young lady who captured his heart, pledged her love, and then left him, with nothing more than a curt note.

A widow

Eight years earlier, faced with no other choice, Mrs. Eleanor Collins, fled London and the only man she ever loved, Marcus, Viscount Wessex. She has now returned to serve as a companion for her elderly aunt with a daughter in tow. Even though they're next door neighbors, there is little reason for her to move in the same circles as Marcus, just in case, she vows to avoid him, for he reminds her of all she lost when she left.

Reunited

As their paths continue to cross, Marcus finds his desire for Eleanor just as strong, but he learned long ago she's not to be trusted. He will offer her a place in his bed, but not anything more. Only, Eleanor has no interest in this new, roguish man. The more time they spend together, the protective wall they've constructed to keep the other out, begin to break. With all the betrayals and secrets between them, Marcus has to open his heart again. And Eleanor must decide if it's ever safe to trust a rogue.

"To Wed His Christmas Lady"
Book 7 in the "Heart of a Duke" Series by Christi Caldwell

She's longing to be loved:

Lady Cara Falcot has only served one purpose to her loathsome father—to increase his power through a marriage to the future Duke of Billingsley. As such, she's built protective walls about her heart, and presents an icy facade to the world around her. Journeying home from her finishing school for the Christmas holidays, Cara's carriage is stranded during a winter storm. She's forced to tarry at a ramshackle inn, where she immediately antagonizes another patron—William.

He's avoiding his duty in favor of one last adventure:
William Hargrove, the Marquess of Grafton has wanted only one thing in life—to avoid the future match his parents would have him make to a cold, duke's daughter. He's returning home from a blissful eight years of traveling the world to see to his responsibilities. But when a winter storm interrupts his trip and lands him at a falling-down inn, he's forced to share company with a commanding Lady Cara who initially reminds him exactly of the woman he so desperately wants to avoid.

A Christmas snowstorm ushers in the spirit of the season:
At the holiday time, these two people who despise each other due to first perceptions are offered renewed beginnings and fresh starts. As this gruff stranger breaks down the walls she's built about herself, Cara has to determine whether she can truly open her heart to trusting that any man is capable of good and that she herself is capable of love. And William has to set aside all previous thoughts he's carried of the polished ladies like Cara, to be the man to show her that love.

"The Heart of a Scoundrel"
Book 6 in the "Heart of a Duke" Series by Christi Caldwell

Ruthless, wicked, and dark, the Marquess of Rutland rouses terror in the breast of ladies and nobleman alike. All Edmund wants in life is power. After he was publically humiliated by his one love Lady Margaret, he vowed vengeance, using Margaret's niece, as his pawn. Except, he's thwarted by another, more enticing target—Miss Phoebe Barrett.

Miss Phoebe Barrett knows precisely the shame she's been born to. Because her father is a shocking letch she's learned to form her own opinions on a person's worth. After a chance meeting with the Marquess of Rutland, she is captivated by the mysterious man. He, too, is a victim of society's scorn, but the more encounters she has with

Edmund, the more she knows there is powerful depth and emotion to the jaded marquess.

The lady wreaks havoc on Edmund's plans for revenge and he finds he wants Phoebe, at all costs. As she's drawn into the darkness of his world, Phoebe risks being destroyed by Edmund's ruthlessness. And Phoebe who desires love at all costs, has to determine if she can ever truly trust the heart of a scoundrel.

"To Love a Lord"
Book 5 in the "Heart of a Duke" Series by Christi Caldwell

All she wants is security:
The last place finishing school instructor Mrs. Jane Munroe belongs, is in polite Society. Vowing to never wed, she's been scuttled around from post to post. Now she finds herself in the Marquess of Waverly's household. She's never met a nobleman she liked, and when she meets the pompous, arrogant marquess, she remembers why. But soon, she discovers Gabriel is unlike any gentleman she's ever known.

All he wants is a companion for his sister:
What Gabriel finds himself with instead, is a fiery spirited, bespectacled woman who entices him at every corner and challenges his age-old vow to never trust his heart to a woman. But...there is something suspicious about his sister's companion. And he is determined to find out just what it is.

All they need is each other:
As Gabriel and Jane confront the truth of their feelings, the lies and secrets between them begin to unravel. And Jane is left to decide whether or not it is ever truly safe to love a lord.

"Loved By a Duke"
Book 4 in the "Heart of a Duke" Series by Christi Caldwell

For ten years, Lady Daisy Meadows has been in love with Auric, the Duke of Crawford. Ever since his gallant rescue years earlier, Daisy knew she was destined to be his Duchess. Unfortunately, Auric sees her as his best friend's sister and nothing more. But perhaps, if she can manage to find the fabled heart of a duke pendant, she will win over the heart of her duke.

Auric, the Duke of Crawford enjoys Daisy's company. The last thing he is interested in however, is pursuing a romance with a woman he's known since she was in leading strings. This season, Daisy is turning up in the oddest places and he cannot help but notice that she is no longer a girl. But Auric wouldn't do something as foolhardy as to fall in love with Daisy. He couldn't. Not with the guilt he carries over his past sins…Not when he has no right to her heart…But perhaps, just perhaps, she can forgive the past and trust that he'd forever cherish her heart—but will she let him?

"The Love of a Rogue"
Book 3 in the "Heart of a Duke" Series by Christi Caldwell

Lady Imogen Moore hasn't had an easy time of it since she made her Come Out. With her betrothed, a powerful duke breaking it off to wed her sister, she's become the *tons* favorite piece of gossip. Never again wanting to experience the pain of a broken heart, she's resolved to make a match with a polite, respectable gentleman. The last thing she wants is another reckless rogue.

Lord Alex Edgerton has a problem. His brother, tired of Alex's carousing has charged him with chaperoning their remaining, unwed sister about *ton* events. Shopping? No, thank you. Attending the theatre? He'd rather be at Forbidden Pleasures with a scantily clad beauty upon his lap. The task of *chaperone* becomes even more of a bother when his sister drags along her dearest friend, Lady Imogen to social functions. The last thing he wants in his life is a young, innocent English miss.

Except, as Alex and Imogen are thrown together, passions flare and Alex comes to find he not only wants Imogen in his bed, but also in his heart. Yet now he must convince Imogen to risk all, on the heart of a rogue.

✍

"More Than a Duke"
Book 2 in the "Heart of a Duke" Series by Christi Caldwell

Polite Society doesn't take Lady Anne Adamson seriously. However, Anne isn't just another pretty young miss. When she discovers her father betrayed her mother's love and her family descended into poverty, Anne comes up with a plan to marry a respectable, powerful, and honorable gentleman—a man nothing like her philandering father.

Armed with the heart of a duke pendant, fabled to land the wearer a duke's heart, she decides to enlist the aid of the notorious Harry, 6th Earl of Stanhope. A scoundrel with a scandalous past, he is the last gentleman she'd ever wed...however, his reputation marks him the perfect man to school her in the art of seduction so she might ensnare the illustrious Duke of Crawford.

Harry, the Earl of Stanhope is a jaded, cynical rogue who lives for his own pleasures. Having been thrown over by the only woman he ever loved so she could wed a duke, he's not at all surprised when Lady Anne approaches him with her scheme to capture another duke's affection. He's come to appreciate that all women are in fact greedy, title-grasping, self-indulgent creatures. And with Anne's history of grating on his every last nerve, she is the last woman he'd ever agree to school in the art of seduction. Only his friendship with the lady's sister compels him to help.

What begins as a pretend courtship, born of lessons on seduction, becomes something more leaving Anne to decide if she can give her

heart to a reckless rogue, and Harry must decide if he's willing to again
trust in a lady's love.

"For Love of the Duke"
First Full-Length Book in the "Heart of a
Duke" Series by Christi Caldwell

After the tragic death of his wife, Jasper, the 8th Duke of Bainbridge
buried himself away in the dark cold walls of his home, Castle
Blackwood. When he's coaxed out of his self-imposed exile to attend
the amusements of the Frost Fair, his life is irrevocably changed by his
fateful meeting with Lady Katherine Adamson.

With her tight brown ringlets and silly white-ruffled gowns, Lady
Katherine Adamson has found her dance card empty for two Seasons.
After her father's passing, Katherine learned the unreliability of men,
and is determined to depend on no one, except herself. Until she
meets Jasper...

In a desperate bid to avoid a match arranged by her family,
Katherine makes the Duke of Bainbridge a shocking proposition—
one that he accepts.

Only, as Katherine begins to love Jasper, she finds the arrangement
agreed upon is not enough. And Jasper is left to decide if protecting
his heart is more important than fighting for Katherine's love.

"In Need of a Duke"
A Prequel Novella to "The Heart of a
Duke" Series by Christi Caldwell

Author's Note: This is a prequel novella to "The Heart of a Duke"
series by Christi Caldwell. It was originally available in "The

Heart of a Duke" Collection and is now being published as an individual novella. It features a new prologue and epilogue.

Years earlier, a gypsy woman passed to Lady Aldora Adamson and her friends a heart pendant that promised them each the heart of a duke.

Now, a young lady, with her family facing ruin and scandal, Lady Aldora doesn't have time for mythical stories about cheap baubles. She needs to save her sisters and brother by marrying a titled gentleman with wealth and power to his name. She sets her bespectacled sights upon the Marquess of St. James.

Turned out by his father after a tragic scandal, Lord Michael Knightly has grown into a powerful, but self-made man. With the whispers and stares that still follow him, he would rather be anywhere but London…

Until he meets Lady Aldora, a young woman who mistakes him for his brother, the Marquess of St. James. The connection between Aldora and Michael is immediate and as they come to know one another, Aldora's feelings for Michael war with her sisterly responsibilities. With her family's dire situation, a man of Michael's scandalous past will never do.

Ultimately, Aldora must choose between her responsibilities as a sister and her love for Michael.

"Once a Wallflower, At Last His Love"
Book 6 in the Scandalous Seasons Series

Responsible, practical Miss Hermione Rogers, has been crafting stories as the notorious Mr. Michael Michaelmas and selling them for a meager wage to support her siblings. The only real way to ensure her family's ruinous debts are paid, however, is to marry. Tall, thin, and plain, she has no expectation of success. In London for her first Season she seizes the chance to write the tale of a brooding duke. In her research, she finds Sebastian Fitzhugh, the 5th Duke of Mallen, who unfortunately is perfectly affable, charming, and so nicely…configured…he takes her breath away. He lacks all the character traits she needs for her story, but alas, any duke will have to do.

Sebastian Fitzhugh, the 5th Duke of Mallen has been deceived so many times during the high-stakes game of courtship, he's lost faith in Society women. Yet, after a chance encounter with Hermione, he finds himself intrigued. Not a woman he'd normally consider beautiful, the young lady's practical bent, her forthright nature and her tendency to turn up in the oddest places has his interests…roused. He'd like to trust her, he'd like to do a whole lot more with her too, but should he?

"A Marquess For Christmas"
Book 5 in the Scandalous Seasons Series

Lady Patrina Tidemore gave up on the ridiculous notion of true love after having her heart shattered and her trust destroyed by a black-hearted cad. Used as a pawn in a game of revenge against her brother, Patrina returns to London from a failed elopement with a tattered reputation and little hope for a respectable match. The only peace she finds is in her solitude on the cold winter days at Hyde Park. And even that is yanked from her by two little hellions who just happen to have a devastatingly handsome, but coldly aloof father, the Marquess of Beaufort. Something about the lord stirs the dreams she'd once carried for an honorable gentleman's love.

Weston Aldridge, the 4th Marquess of Beaufort was deceived and betrayed by his late wife. In her faithlessness, he's come to view women as self-serving, indulgent creatures. Except, after a series of chance encounters with Patrina, he comes to appreciate how uniquely different she is than all women he's ever known.

At the Christmastide season, a time of hope and new beginnings, Patrina and Weston, unexpectedly learn true love in one another. However, as Patrina's scandalous past threatens their future and the happiness of his children, they are both left to determine if love is enough.

"Always a Rogue, Forever Her Love"
Book 4 in the Scandalous Seasons Series

Miss Juliet Marshville is spitting mad. With one guardian missing, and the other singularly uninterested in her fate, she is at the mercy of her wastrel brother who loses her beloved childhood home to a man known as Sin. Determined to reclaim control of Rosecliff Cottage and her own fate, Juliet arranges a meeting with the notorious rogue and demands the return of her property.

Jonathan Tidemore, 5th Earl of Sinclair, known to the *ton* as Sin, is exceptionally lucky in life and at the gaming tables. He has just one problem. Well…four, really. His incorrigible sisters have driven off yet another governess. This time, however, his mother demands he find an appropriate replacement.

When Miss Juliet Marshville boldly demands the return of her precious cottage, he takes advantage of his sudden good fortune and puts an offer to her; turn his sisters into proper English ladies, and he'll return Rosecliff Cottage to Juliet's possession.

Jonathan comes to appreciate Juliet's spirit, courage, and clever wit, and decides to claim the fiery beauty as his mistress. Juliet, however, will be mistress for no man. Nor could she ever love a man who callously stole her home in a game of cards. As Jonathan begins to see Juliet as more than a spirited beauty to warm his bed, he realizes she could be a lady he could love the rest of his life, if only he can convince the proud Juliet that he's worthy of her hand and heart.

"Always Proper, Suddenly Scandalous"
Book 3 in the Scandalous Seasons Series

Geoffrey Winters, Viscount Redbrooke was not always the hard, unrelenting lord driven by propriety. After a tragic mistake, he resolved to honor his responsibility to the Redbrooke line and live a life, free of scandal. Knowing his duty is to wed a proper, respectable English miss, he selects Lady Beatrice Dennington, daughter of the Duke of Somerset, the perfect woman for him. Until he meets Miss Abigail Stone...

To distance herself from a personal scandal, Abigail Stone flees America to visit her uncle, the Duke of Somerset. Determined to never trust a man again, she is helplessly intrigued by the hard, too-proper Geoffrey. With his strict appreciation for decorum and order, he is nothing like the man' she's always dreamed of.

Abigail is everything Geoffrey does not need. She upends his carefully ordered world at every encounter. As they begin to care for one another, Abigail carefully guards the secret that resulted in her journey to England.

Only, if Geoffrey learns the truth about Abigail, he must decide which he holds most dear: his place in Society or Abigail's place in his heart.

"Never Courted, Suddenly Wed"
Book 2 in the Scandalous Seasons Series

Christopher Ansley, Earl of Waxham, has constructed a perfect image for the *ton*–the ladies love him and his company is desired by all. Only two people know the truth about Waxham's secret. Unfortunately, one of them is Miss Sophie Winters.

Sophie Winters has known Christopher since she was in leading strings. As children, they delighted in tormenting each other. Now at two and twenty, she still has a tendency to find herself in scrapes, and her marital prospects are slim.

When his father threatens to expose his shame to the *ton*, unless he weds Sophie for her dowry, Christopher concocts a plan to remain a bachelor. What he didn't plan on was falling in love with the lively, impetuous Sophie. As secrets are exposed, will

Christopher's love be enough when she discovers his role in his father's scheme?

"Forever Betrothed, Never the Bride"
Book 1 in the Scandalous Seasons Series

Hopeless romantic Lady Emmaline Fitzhugh is tired of sitting with the wallflowers, waiting for her betrothed to come to his senses and marry her. When Emmaline reads one too many reports of his scandalous liaisons in the gossip rags, she takes matters into her own hands.

War-torn veteran Lord Drake devotes himself to forgetting his days on the Peninsula through an endless round of meaningless associations. He no longer wants to feel anything, but Lady Emmaline is making it hard to maintain a state of numbness. With her zest for life, she awakens his passion and desire for love.

The one woman Drake has spent the better part of his life avoiding is now the only woman he needs, but he is no longer a man worthy of his Emmaline. It is up to her to show him the healing power of love.

Non-Fiction Works by Christi Caldwell
Uninterrupted Joy: Memoir:
My Journey through Infertility,
Pregnancy, and Special Needs

The following journey was never intended for publication. It was written from a mother, to her unborn child. The words detailed her struggle through infertility and the joy of finally being pregnant. A stunning revelation at her son's birth opened a world of both fear and discovery. This is the story of one mother's love and hope and...her quest for uninterrupted joy.

AUTHOR BIOGRAPHY

Christi Caldwell is the bestselling author of historical romance novels set in the Regency era. Christi blames Judith McNaught's "Whitney, My Love," for luring her into the world of historical romance. While sitting in her graduate school apartment at the University of Connecticut, Christi decided to set aside her notes and try her hand at writing romance. She believes the most perfect heroes and heroines have imperfections and rather enjoys tormenting them before crafting a well-deserved happily ever after!

When Christi isn't writing the stories of flawed heroes and heroines, she can be found in her Southern Connecticut home chasing around her feisty five-year-old son, and caring for twin princesses-in-training!

Visit www.christicaldwellauthor.com to learn more about what Christi is working on, or join her on Facebook at https://www.facebook.com/christicaldwellauthor and Twitter @ChristiCaldwell

For first glimpse at covers, excerpts, and free bonus material, be sure to sign up for my monthly newsletter at http://bit.ly/1Ngqcfj! Each month one subscriber will win a $35 Amazon Gift Card!

Made in the USA
Middletown, DE
03 December 2022

16910324R00163